The
Distaff
Side

The Distaff Side

Elizabeth Palmer

Thomas Dunne Books ✦ St. Martin's Press
New York

THOMAS DUNNE BOOKS.
An imprint of St. Martin's Press.

www.stmartins.com

Design by Irene Vallye

ISBN 0-312-32539-8
EAN 978-0312-32539-8

First Edition: December 2004

10 9 8 7 6 5 4 3 2 1

For David

Whilst Adam slept, Eve from his side arose:
Strange his first sleep should be his last repose. . .

—THE CONSEQUENCE

PART ONE

Striking Out

France

Paris, November 1917

Chapter One

It was extraordinary that something as humble as a clutch of eggs could generate such a surge of excitement.

Wonderingly, Vera picked one of them up. Between finger and thumb, she held it up to the light. Though not the same, she had seen something like it once before. In the Yusupov palace, if she remembered rightly. This egg was made of some sort of dark green stone flecked with red and was the size of her palm. Round its smooth ellipse slid a gold snake whose back was studded with rose-cut diamonds. An impressive ruby formed the flat head. Hands trembling, she lifted aside the crimson shawl within whose folds the other eggs lay. They were equally opulent. Her avaricious eye dwelt upon lapis and jade, cabochon moonstones and sapphires and more diamonds. Resisting the impulse to examine and revel in her loot, she returned the egg she held to its cashmere nest.

Act now, gloat later.

For after all, there might be more where these came from.

Eyed by the stricken woman who lay on the bed, Vera rose from the table at which she had been sitting, glided across the room, and methodically began to search it. With silent, chilly precision she went through cupboards, pulled out and sifted through drawers, and even examined the pockets of the shabby clothes in the wardrobe. Nothing. Finally, she turned her attention to the bed and, as though there was nobody in it, coolly investigated that.

And (possibly) found what she sought.

It seemed she had. The face of the other, who could not speak and barely move, contorted with a frantic mixture of impotence, rage, and hatred. Predominant was hatred. Agitated ringed fingers feebly plucked at the edge of the blanket. Oblivious to this distress, Vera went in search of something with which to cut the string binding the package and finally found a small knife in the kitchen. Like a child at Christmas, before setting about it she tried to guess what was in it. Not eggs this time, that was for sure, it was too flat. Breaking into an edgy, hysterical laugh, she lost patience and savagely ripped the parcel open, after which she tipped the contents onto the bed. Revealed were three exquisite cigarette cases, one in solid gold and very heavy (plenty of *zolotniks* there), an enamel and jasper match case with a tassel, and, quaintly, a caviar spoon. There was also a jewellery roll. Homing in on this and temporarily setting the rest to one side, she undid the tie.

Ah!

The sigh was so soft as to be almost soundless.

She stared in silence at what slid out of the velvet. A rope of peerless pearls. And emeralds! Emeralds the size of quails' eggs set in diamonds. Mesmerised, she ran her fingers over their cold magnificence. A choker and a matching pair of earrings, stones fit for a nabob. Or a tsar . . .

Or *me!*

Vera licked her lips. The look on her face was concupiscent, as though just handling the gems had given her a sexual charge.

Concentrate.

Pulling herself together with an effort, she became aware that the light in the apartment had dimmed and got up to trim the wick. There was a chill in the air too, so she tipped the last of the coal onto the embers. The sudden flare of the fire as she did this lit up her pointed, vulpine face, throwing into relief sharp cheekbones and aquiline nose.

The thoughts of the other, who never shifted her gaze from Vera, were venomous. *Bitch! Wicked, scheming, grasping bitch! She looks like the devil incarnate leaning over that fire. I never should have trusted her. . . . I've been such a fool. . . . Such a fool . . . Too late now . . . Oh, too late now . . .*

Impervious to this corrosive mental beam, Vera drew her thin pelisse around her and then made another tour of the room, replacing what had been moved, closing doors and drawers and generally eradicating all signs of her visit and, more important0, her search. In one of the closets she found a carpet bag into which she shovelled the jewelled haul and prepared to leave. On her way to the door, pulling on her gloves as she went, she noticed a rather fine fur and appropriated that too, together with its muff.

Pulling on her gloves—she's going . . .

The look on the face of the woman on the bed changed from one of hatred to one of alarm.

Surely even she wouldn't leave me alone in this state after all I've done for her. No one knows I'm here. That would be murder! Don't leave me to die. Please don't leave me here to die! A tear slid down the rouged cheek. Again she struggled to speak and could not.

As if telepathically sensitive to this supplication, the marauder unexpectedly changed tack and once again approached the bed. Any burgeoning hope of a reprieve was doomed to be transient. Vera lifted her compatriot's head off the pillow and slipped a gold chain over it, thereby removing a long-coveted, finely enamelled cross set with a spectacular pearl, which she dropped into the carpet bag where it joined the rest of the booty. Then, without a backward glance she left, closing the door behind her as quietly as a cat. Noiselessly she picked her way down what had once been a grand staircase and now was uncarpeted and stank, opened the front door and stepped past its peeling brown paint into the street. Outside, the pewter light of a late winter afternoon was darkening. The cold was intense, though nothing like the subzero temperatures of those long, savage Russian winters that Vera remembered all too well. Cabs passed her in the dusk as she made her way carefully along the cobbles. Unwilling to draw attention to herself, she did not take one until she was well clear of the seventeenth arrondissement. Finally, as her feet in the worn-out little ankle boots began to ache, she hailed a cab. Once inside it, she drew the fur around her, settled the carpet bag with its precious cargo on her lap and, with a thrill of anticipation, contemplated the future.

The following day was Sunday. As was her habit, more to stave off boredom than anything else, Vera took herself to the St. Alexandre Nevsky Cathedral in the Rue Daru. Discretion dictated that she did not wear the fur since there were those who might have recognised it. Too early for the service, on arrival, she briefly sat down in the courtyard. Others had done the same. The sweet, aromatic smell of crushed lavender where it had grown over the wall on which she sat was all around. She looked up at the cathedral. Built by Alexander II, it was, as it had been intended to be, a familiar thing in an alien land. Its onion-shaped golden cupolas and golden mosaic of a severe Christ resonated with memories of Russia, though a Russia that had gone, probably for ever. Even for Vera, whose talent was for looking forward rather than backward, it was still a potent sight. When the doors opened, she let everyone else go in before her and then followed in their wake up the steps.

Under a huge gilded dome surrounded by mosaics of the saints, the interior of the cathedral was murkily claustrophobic, lit only by huge chandeliers boosted by the flickering light from large, brass torchères that stood beside the most precious icons. On each of these, the main church flame was surrounded by clusters of thin coffee-coloured votive candles. Vera purchased one of these and carried it forward, weaving through the crowd and making for her favourite icon. This depicted an angel. Vera did not like children or other women very much and the fact that angels were neither male nor female, and therefore sufficient to themselves in their sexlessness, appealed to her. Once before it, she lit her candle from one of the others, then by the same means melted the wax at its base and pushed it into one of the spare receptacles on the torchère.

Then, shamelessly: *I light this candle for me.*

Almond-eyed and oddly remote, glimmering in the fitful shooting flares of a clutch of other tallow hopes and prayers, the icon looked dispassionately back at Vera as she leant forward to kiss it, before crossing herself and then stooping low to touch the floor. She straightened. The church had filled up. Vera threaded her way to the back where, hooded and cloaked, she stood watching tendrils of incense winding serpentine through the air and upwards towards the golden cupola where they began to mass in a dense, fragrant cloud. Gold was everywhere, its richness counterpointed by the black garb of the nuns and the long-haired, bearded priests. This was the nearest Vera got these days to Petrograd. Maybe it was the nearest she would ever get again. In those days she used intermittently to attend the Cathedral of St. Nicholas, which was close to the Mariinskiy, where she danced as a member of the corps de ballet. Though even then she had regarded dialogue with the Almighty as a potential personal leg up rather than as a selfless spiritual experience. Despite her religious family, Vera, who was a great believer in luck and seizing opportunities when they presented themselves, had always been superstitious rather than devout. Here as there, all around her throaty, melancholy voices rose and fell, chanting, voices of other émigrés presumably praying for Mother Russia and for family left behind who might by now be dead, wiped out in the bloody aftermath of revolution.

Bowing her head, Vera, who also had left family behind, though not in Petrograd, prayed too.

But not for them.

For I couldn't care less if I never saw my family ever again.

No.

Rather: *Holy Father, I never want to be poor ever again. Make me rich!* Without a scintilla of embarrassment Vera fervently prayed on: *Make me very, very rich. Give me wealth and position and I promise I'll deserve it. You'll see.*

She did not, the Holy Father might have noticed, elaborate on how she would deserve it.

Following the delivery of this self-serving request, she stared intently forward to where she could just discern her candle, standing among the rest in front of the enigmatic angel. Lost in her own thoughts and aspirations, Vera stood where she was for a very long time, in the service but not of it. When she finally roused herself from her private trance, it was to find the crowd was moving forward in an orderly queue for communion. Vera joined it and, when she finally reached the front, waited while the priest gave her a spoonful of wine out of the chalice. At the end of the ritual, she kissed its silver base.

Very, very rich, Vera mentally reminded the Almighty at this point, before dropping back. As she did so she reflected that, as a matter of fact, she had got a substantial part of the way already without any help from the Holy Father and his angels whatsoever.

All the same, it was politic to exploit every avenue.

England

West Sussex, July 1917

Chapter Two

If they wish to go on wielding power, celebrated beauties past their prime have to acquire other skills. Augusta Langham was one such. Now in her sixties, having achieved a brilliant marriage and produced the required heir, Augusta ruled her household with the proverbial rod of iron and a glacial disregard for other people's sensitivities. These days, steely regality had replaced steely vivacity, thereby making Mrs. Langham an even more formidable adversary than in her disdainful heyday. Height, presence, and chiselled cheekbones still as sharp as razor blades all combined to intimidate so that even her son trod warily in her drawing room. Where her husband, Henry, was concerned, Augusta was more judicious. Though these were the days after the Married Woman's Property Act and despite the fact that, in her opinion, Henry was very stupid, it would not have done to alienate Henry. Status was all. She was aware, of course, that her husband had a mistress, more than one for all she knew, just as she herself had had lovers down the years. All of this paled into insignificance when considered beside the social edifice that they had built up between them in the course of an otherwise indifferent marriage. Nothing should be allowed to destroy that. So Augusta apparently deferred to her husband, every so often deigning to flirt with him and carefully concealing from everyone what a fool she really thought him. Augusta risked no confidantes. Henry might have been just a cipher, but he was crucial to her survival. All in all, according to her own lights and the perceived aspirations for women born into upper class Victorian England, Augusta, who was, in fact, a highly intelligent woman, was generally agreed to have made the most of what was open to her. The fact that her brain was mostly underemployed probably explained her extreme aggression.

Today, luncheon being over, she was sitting in the shade of a very old plane tree. Warm July sunshine and the summer hum of a sprawling English garden soothed and enervated. The Hall, built by William Talman in 1690, stood some four miles north of Chichester and was both handsome and imposing. Mainly brick with stone dressings, its front was decorated by an elaborately carved pediment and an elegant set of steps which led up to a door flanked by Corinthian columns and surmounted by more carving. Beyond the park the Sussex Downs undulated into the distance. Despite a slight feeling of drowsiness, aided by a combination of discipline and whalebone, Augusta did not allow herself to relax physically. Parasol propped against her seat, she sat ramrod straight surveying the grounds, skirts in a graceful sweep, complexion (alas, no longer what it had been) safeguarded by a large hat swathed in tulle. Behind her, hybrid musk roses massed, their clustering scented blooms painterly daubs of cream and apricot. If she closed her eyes, she could almost imagine herself to be young again and surrounded by beaux. *Champagne and candlelight and white dresses,* remembered Augusta. In those days she never sat alone like this. Age, it appeared, caused invisibility.

A sudden murmur of voices caused her to turn her head. Through the open terrace doors, as though a Sargent painting had come to life, passed a group of tall young women all carrying croquet mallets, sashed dresses billowing. Mai, her daughter-in-law to be, was one of them, walking arm in arm with her cousin Maude. Despite the sombre backdrop of world war, when the wedding took place it would be, as they say, the match (or catch, depending on how one looked at it) of the season. Chattering and laughing, the girls moved across a sun-dappled lawn. The men must be playing billiards. *In my heyday, nobody wanted to play billiards when I was present.* Watching them go, and Mai especially, Augusta was reminded of slender, white irises, spiked with green, the sort which did not do well in vases. Mai was the daughter of neighbours who lived near Lavant and had known Bertie since childhood. Once Bertie married her, he would move outside his mother's sphere of influence. Loathe as she was to give up control of anything, she also realised that, insofar as such a thing existed, Mai

Binnington was the perfect daughter-in-law. Beautiful, biddable, and rich. *On the other hand, if I am clever about it,* thought Augusta, *maybe there will be no need for my son to pass beyond my reach.*

Two months later, while being driven in a hackney carriage back to her London house following a visit to her couturier for a fitting, Augusta noticed a large meeting of some sort. This appeared to be composed mainly of women, some of whom were wearing placards, though at this distance she could not see what these were advertising. Suddenly curious, she tapped to attract the attention of the driver of the hansom.

"What is happening here?"

"Suffragettes, madam," was the laconic, noncommittal reply.

Suffragettes?

"Stop! I wish to walk for a while," commanded Augusta. "You may follow me at a distance."

Carefully, she alighted and began to follow those drifting along the street with a view to tacking themselves on to the back of the gathering. Most of the placards, which she was now close enough to read, proclaimed: VOTES FOR WOMEN! Others bore the legend MRS. PANKHURST LEADER OF THE ENGLISH SUFFRAGETTES. Augusta, who had never needed a vote of any sort to get her own way, was contemptuous. She looked back to satisfy herself that her carriage was still idling along in the wake of the crowd as she had instructed it to do, and then moved forward. With the help of a pair of sharp elbows and her parasol, she began to make her way towards the front, where a young woman, who appeared to be standing on a soapbox, was making a speech. Halfway there, Augusta, whose eyesight was not what it had been, snapped open the gold lorgnette which hung on a black watered ribbon round her neck.

Exuding disapproval, lips pursed, she raised it.

And received a shock.

For the fashionably dressed young woman making a spectacle of herself addressing (*No, haranguing!! Like a fishwife!*) the audience through (*Ye gods!*) a *megaphone* was none other than the gently reared, biddable one, her future daughter-in-law, Mai Binnington.

Ha! We'll see about that!

With a face like thunder, Augusta strode back to the hackney. Noting her expression, the coachman assiduously helped her into the carriage.

"Drive on!" said Augusta.

The following evening, she summoned her son to her sitting room. Bertie was apprehensive. He had watched his mother throughout dinner dangerously glittery in aubergine, drumming her fingers on the table in between courses and clearly in a bate. It was the sort of performance she put on when somebody was for the high jump. Bertie hoped it wasn't himself.

"You may have a brandy, if you wish."

Normally Augusta did not approve of Bertie's drinking habits (most of the day, on and off) but tonight wanted cooperation and backbone, probably in that order. As usual when in the presence of her son she felt a twinge, no, more than a twinge, a rush of exasperation. There was a quality of obedience which grated. However, it had to be said that the opposite would have grated more where a controlling personality such as Augusta's was concerned.

Swirling his drink around in its balloon glass, Bertie waited.

Deliberating on how to begin, Augusta decided to initiate proceedings by discovering how much, if anything, her son knew about what had been happening.

"Tell me, do you have any idea where Mai was yesterday?"

Mai? Bertie was astonished. The wedding was months away. Until it took place he did not expect to know what his fiancée was doing every second of the day. He wondered where this was leading. No doubt she was about to tell him.

"Very well, since you appear to have no idea, I'll tell you where Mai was. Mai was standing on a soapbox in Trafalgar Square shouting through a megaphone about rights for women! *That's* where Mai was!"

Bertie gaped. Not for the first time Augusta wondered how she possibly could have produced a son for whom practically everything was a source of such bafflement.

Very tart. "Yes, you may shut your mouth now, Bertie."

"*Mai* is a suffragette? *Mai?*"

Augusta mentally cast her eyes to heaven. "*Yes!*"

"I say, you have to admire it, don't you? Of course Mai's always been her own woman . . ."

Choosing to disregard the admiration *bêtise* for the moment, Augusta leant forward. "What do you mean?"

"Well, Mai's got very strong views on lots of things. . . ."

"None that she ever expressed to me!"

Well, she wouldn't, would she? thought Bertie. *You aren't exactly everyone's favourite confidante.*

Unaware of this unspoken insubordination, she said, "What sort of things?"

"Politics for a start . . . and social equality . . ."

Augusta was beginning to wonder if they were both talking about the same Mai.

". . . Mai's got far more gumption than I have, you know," continued Bertie.

Augusta forbore to observe, *So has just about everybody,* and said instead, "Are you telling me that if your *fiancée*" (she could not bring herself to utter the name) "had the vote, she would cast it against the Conservative Party?"

She got to her feet and with a swishing of stiff aubergine silk began to walk up and down the room. As a small boy, Bertie had once heard Mrs. Harkness, the cook, say about her difficult employer when she hadn't thought he was listening, "She's wearing her hat today, all right." Now as then. Logging the expression on his parent's face, Bertie decided to sidestep this one. With a view to regrouping, he took a nervous swig of his brandy.

Not at all certain, he said, "I'm sure Mai will settle down when we're married."

"Mai will only settle down after you are married if you tell her you expect it!"

It struck Bertie that this was rich coming from Mother, who had always done exactly as she pleased and who had never deferred to Father except on very anodyne matters which affected her own convenience not at all. But then, *Father's very like me,* recognised Bertie, *Father likes a quiet life.* With this in mind he decided to turn away wrath with a soft answer.

Intending to do no such thing, he said, "Very well, Mother, I will have a word with Mai." Speaking the words it occurred to him to wonder why Mai had not told him of her association with Mrs. Pankhurst. He could see why she hadn't told her prospective mother-in-law, but why not him?

One possible answer was that he might have let the cat out of the bag. No doubt *would* have let the cat out of the bag, Bertie admitted to himself.

Undeceived, "What are you going to say?" unwisely pressed his relentless parent. "Remember, you must be masterful, Bertie . . ."

The worm turned.

"Mother, you've asked me to do it, and I'll do it, but don't tell me *how* to do it. And now, bed for me."

Bertie tossed back the remainder of his drink at a swallow, kissed his mother and made for the door. Once outside it, he did not head for the staircase and his bedroom but set off instead for the smoking room where he intended to treat himself to another stiff tot.

Here he found another refugee. Father was sitting, peacefully wreathed in cigar smoke, in the wing armchair.

"Hallo, old boy. Made your escape, then. Good show. What did your mother want?"

Had Mother told Father about Mai's activities? If not, this was a hare Bertie did not particularly want to start. It was bad enough one of them telling him what to do, another deluge of good advice would have been intolerable. In the end, he fudged it.

"She wanted to talk about the wedding."

"Ah yes, the wedding. What about a whisky?"

"Mine's a brandy," said Bertie. "I'll get them."

As they sat companionably together, Henry Langham, who did not miss much, despite being docketed stupid by his own wife, suddenly opined apropos of nothing in particular, "You want to watch your step there, Bertie."

Bertie pondered this remark and got nowhere with it. Finally, still mystified, he said, "Watch my step where?"

"With the two ladies. They'll tear you in pieces, you know. Remember your classical education? Orpheus and the Thracian women? Like that."

Bertie who, all else apart, had a musical tin ear, had never seen himself as Orpheus. As to the others, Father must be talking about Mother and Mai Binnington. Whoever it was, as prophesies go it did not sound reassuring. It *was* Mother and Mai, for he went on to say, "Your mother's a fine woman, Bertie, a fine woman, but she takes no prisoners. . . ." At this point Henry saw in his mind's eye pretty, curvaceous, easygoing Daisy Mainwaring, wife of a neighbour, who was his current mistress. Daisy was such fun, whereas nobody could accuse Augusta of being fun. Although Augusta had the edge where running a very large house was concerned. Certainly this one ticked over like an impeccable military operation, he had to give her that.

"You were saying," prompted Bertie, who had been waiting patiently for his father's reverie to end.

Pulling reluctantly away from the memory of Daisy's breasts, Henry cleared his throat. "What was I saying?"

"Mother takes no prisoners."

"Ah, yes, that's right. Now, having spent years married to her, I can spot a strong-minded woman at a hundred paces and Miss Binnington's one. Wouldn't surprise me if she didn't believe in votes for women. That sort of thing."

Bertie blinked. Father must be clairvoyant.

Flushed out, he said, "As a matter of fact, she does!"

"Oh, does she! Aha!" Henry was immediately alerted, not to say triumphant. "Well, there you are then. Is your mother aware of this?"

"*She* told *me.*"

Henry was put in mind of the Eyes and Ears portrait of Elizabeth the First. Like that particular monarch, Augusta seemed to know everything.

"Well, I predict mayhem. Mayhem! When's the confrontation?"

Wincing at the prospect in the light of this discussion, Bertie said, "Well, no, she wants me to tackle Mai. . . ."

"And I'll bet you said you would and don't intend to do anything about it. You won't get away with that, you know. At any rate, best of luck, old boy. You'll need it."

"I think I need another brandy."

When he returned with it, Bertie said, "Perhaps you can explain something to me, Father. Mother is a formidable woman and an intelligent woman. So why is she so against the suffragette movement?"

"That's easy! Your mother has many qualities but philanthropy isn't one of them. She's always got exactly what she wanted all her life without the benefit of the vote and she's not prepared to help anyone else settle their problems on that score. Besides, it wasn't her idea."

Bertie felt glum. Marriage, which had seemed to offer a release, a chance to get out from under his controlling parent, now looked set to turn into a battlefield instead of a pleasurable event which was also a rite of passage to liberty. Not very highly sexed (though, of course, there had been no question of that with Mai before marriage) Bertie esteemed and was fond of his fiancée but was not in love with her. Like so many dynastic marriages, he rather hoped it would all fall into place afterwards and if it didn't, then they would just rub along. However, if Father was right, and it had to be said Father had a lifetime of research behind him on the subject of exacting women, frying pans and fires came to mind. It further occurred to Bertie that he and Mai had really hardly talked at all and that most of their meetings had been conducted in artificial, chaperoned surroundings. It also occurred to him that proposing to Mai Binnington had been Mother's idea: ("So *suitable*, Bertie!") But suitable for whom? Why, for Mother, or, rather, the furthering of Mother's social machinations. Now, by revealing herself to be someone who thought for herself and, worse, looked to become controversial courtesy of the militant Mrs. Pankhurst, Mai had rendered herself *un*suitable.

Something else struck Bertie. Why was Mai marrying *him*?

He voiced it.

"I'm stumped too," was his parent's unflattering rejoinder. He stared across at his son. Bertie was tall, easygoing to the point of inertia and not bad looking. Plus Bertie was eventually going to have a very great deal of money and social cachet. No young woman who married Bertie was going to want for much except, perhaps, stimulation. Maybe, on the other hand, Miss Binnington was marrying Bertie in a manifestation of what Henry thought of as the Augusta syndrome, i.e., because of all the drawbacks rather than in spite of them. With indolent Bertie at her side, and the social status of being a married woman, Mai could indulge herself in a more or less unfettered dash at life as she chose to live it. On one level all that was superfluous because whatever the reasons for the marriage, the problem was never going to be Bertie and Mai but Augusta and Mai.

Chapter Three

The following afternoon, as he sat opposite Mai in her mother and step-father's country house, Bertie wondered how to introduce the purpose of his visit. His fiancée was looking very pretty today, her dark blonde head bent over some needlepoint embroidery. Mai's hair was up, but at the nape of her neck clustered small, nascent curls too small to be gathered into the glorious mass on top. A cream, high-necked blouse with leg-of-mutton sleeves was tucked into an ankle-length narrow skirt of French blue whose broad belt emphasised a tiny waist. Charming!

Flirtatious and very feminine, she shot him a sly, sidelong glance. Bertie tried to imagine this demure paragon shouting through a megaphone at a horde of obstreperous suffragettes and could not. For one hopeful moment he entertained the idea that Mother had made a mistake. Fat chance! Mother and her lorgnette *never* made a mistake. Mai sat, needle poised, and waited for him to tell her what was on his mind, for plainly something was. Unsure how to proceed, Bertie dickered and then, feeling very unhappy, came straight out with it.

"Mai, dear, Mother tells me that she saw you addressing a suffragette rally in London. I told her she must have made a mistake, but she . . ."

"Bertie, why would you think she had made a mistake?" interrupted Mai.

"Well . . . Um . . . I . . . er . . . Well, I didn't think you did that sort of thing." Bertie was conscious of sounding lame.

Outside the open doors to the garden, Mai's mother, Juno Berensen, upper crust Bohemian in floating draperies, could be seen cutting long-stemmed roses and chaperoning after a fashion. In fact, she had probably forgotten all about them. Bertie wished his own tricky parent was more like her.

"*What* sort of thing, Bertie?"

Coupled with the threatening, emphatic use of his name, there was an edge to his fiancée's voice which he had never heard before.

Be masterful, his mother had said. *Don't stand any nonsense.* Bertie tried it.

"I'm afraid it won't do when we are married, Mai!" More to reassure himself than her, he added, "No, it won't do at all." He got up and walked across the room finally taking up a magisterial stance by the fireplace. "I'm sure you can see that, my love."

Mai smacked the embroidery frame down on the table beside her. She rose to her feet and faced him. She was plainly very cross.

"No, Bertie, I can't see that! Are you saying that the moment we are man and wife, my principles are supposed to fly out of the window? Are you? Because, if you are, then we shall never be married."

What? Bertie was aghast. How had they got to this in three sentences? This was where being masterful got you. In the garden there was no longer any sign of Mrs. Berensen, who must have tactfully wafted off at the first sound of a raised voice.

Mai was continuing. "I *never* concealed my views from you, *never!*"

Here Bertie might have pointed out that she hadn't gone out of her way to highlight the extent to which she was prepared to go to broadcast them either. In his opinion Mai had been less than frank, but saying so when she was in this mood was clearly inadvisable. All the same, considering the fact that other people must have known what Mai had been doing, it was astonishing none of it had got to Mother's ears. On the other hand, Mother seldom went to the capital these days and when she did it was to see her dressmaker rather than to socialise. Come to that, blissfully content as he was with his shooting and his fishing, neither did he. Also, presumably because she had never even entertained the idea that the gently reared Mai Binnington might have been a covert (in her vicinity, anyway) vote-mad termagant, for once Mother had neglected to do any research in that direction. The question as to why nobody had taken it upon themselves to tell her was probably a result of a long social history of killing the messenger. Nobody had dared. But never mind about all of that. What to do next was the question.

By now Mai was stamping up and down the Berensen drawing room in high dudgeon with a red spot on each cheek bone and her hair beginning to come adrift.

"It's her, isn't it, she's at the root of this! *Your mother, I mean!* Well, I intend to go and see her. I'm going to tell her that if I want to make a spectacle of myself on a platform with a megaphone in the middle of London then I'm going to do it. And I expect you to be there when I do, Bertie, supporting *not* undermining . . ."

Masterful appeared to pose no problems for Mai.

Soothingly, "Now, my love, I'm sure there won't be any need for that. . . ."

Catching up with her briefly, he put a tentative hand on her arm. It was summarily brushed off.

"There is no need for that. I had the misguided idea I was marrying you, not her. *You*, Bertie, may not mind, but I don't want to spend the next forty years being told what to do by her! Now I would prefer it if you left."

It seemed he had no choice. He went. With a war on, most of the grand houses had lost their able-bodied male staff to the army and as there was nobody to conduct him to the door, Bertie let himself out. Going towards the Lagonda, he spied Mrs. Berensen at the other side of the garden still with the flat basket of roses on her arm. She did not see him and appeared to be either singing or talking to herself and then broke into an Isadora Duncan–type dance.

Making himself scarce, Bertie reflected that if his prospective mother-in-law had not been a member of the aristocracy, she would probably have been diagnosed mad and locked up long ago. As it was, eccentric was the name of the game. There had been a scandal and social ostracism when she left Mai's father and went to live in the East End of London in an artists' colony where, rumour had it, she not only painted (rather badly) but, and probably more usefully, also posed in the nude. Seven years later, by which time the rigours of the Bohemian life had palled and Juno Binnington was ready to re-embrace privilege, social rehabilitation had come in the shape of a marriage to Jacob Berensen the banker. Edwardian society was sniffy about Jewishness, but not about wealth and on that level ambitious mothers were prepared to bite the bullet and Berensen, by then in his thirties, was considered a catch. So in the drawing rooms of houses where there were unmarried daughters, there were chagrin and noses very out of joint followed by a certain amount of ungenerous speculation as to how Juno Binnington and Berensen had met, for after all, Jewish or not, eminent bankers did not, on the whole, spend too much time in Whitechapel. Bertie knew the answer to this because Augusta had made it her business to find out. Berensen, who was an enthusiastic patron of the arts, had fallen in love with a painting and had bought it, after which he had made it *his* business to discover who the naked beauty was. Having found her, he married her. The painting had never been seen again. Presumably it hung in his dressing room. It was interesting, thought Bertie, who was under no illusions concerning his own parents' much more suitable but ultimately distant union, that from an unpromising beginning, Jacob and Juno appeared to have forged a love match. Moreover, it occurred to him that as another member of an embattled stratum of society, it was quite likely that Berensen approved of women's suffrage and had passed his own enthusiasm on to his stepdaughter. Whatever the reason for Mai's militancy, he, Bertie, who only wanted a peaceful life, now found himself between the hammer and the anvil.

On his return to The Hall, it was his intention to slip in quietly and secrete himself somewhere where Augusta could not find him. Anything to put off the inquisition. No such luck. She must have been looking out for him.

"Ah, Mr. Albert," said Stiggins the butler, opening the door for him. Stiggins was almost seventy and therefore not eligible for the war effort. "Mrs. Langham would like to see you in the drawing room." It appeared there was no getting out of it. Bertie went.

The drawing room would have been a pleasant room had it not been indelibly associated in his mind with the sort of social warfare which, when she was not intimidating bridge partners, was his mother's preferred diversion. Today Augusta was sitting in her favourite button-backed armchair by an open window. The smell of freshly mown grass and roses lingered, blown in on the lightest of light airs. Like his strong-minded fiancée, she was embroidering when he entered, a ladylike occupation he had hitherto associated with the weaker and, legend had it, gentler sex. Now Bertie was not so sure. This reminder of the previous encounter made him wince.

Augusta saw no point in beating about the bush.

"Well? Is it sorted?"

Given what had happened, Bertie saw no point in beating about the bush either and was uncharacteristically crisp.

"I suppose it depends what you call sorted, Mother."

He paused awhile to let her stew before resuming, "It is perfectly possible that in the light of what happened this morning, Mai is going to sack me."

With a last jab of the needle the embroidery was abruptly discarded.

"*Sack* you?"

For once it was gratifying to be the one patiently doing the explaining.

"Yes, sack me. You know, end our engagement . . ."

Speechless, Augusta stared at her elder son for a full minute. Then, rallying: "You must have made a complete mess of things, Bertie! What did you say to Mai to produce such a reaction?"

"I said to Mai exactly what you told me to say, Mother. . . ."

Another infuriating, even smug, pause.

". . . I was masterful!"

"*And . . . ?*"

"Mai wasn't impressed. . . ."

No, I don't suppose she was, was Augusta's exasperated reaction to this. *I might have known Bertie would get it all wrong. I should have conducted the interview myself.*

Aloud. "But she hasn't actually told you that she no longer wants to marry you?"

Uncomfortable silence.

"Or has she?"

"She said that if marrying me meant compromising her principles, then she thought marriage was out of the question."

Momentarily diverted by the quaint idea of principles getting in the way of anything, Augusta finally said, "Principles, fiddlesticks! *I'll* talk to Mai, Bertie. Woman to woman. That will do the trick."

Seared by his own experience, he privately doubted it, but let her find out for herself. The question now exercising Bertie's mind was whether or not *he* still wanted to marry *Mai*. Though given Mai's intransigence, it now seemed likely that, unintentionally, Mother was going to solve that one for him.

"When do you intend to have this heart to heart?"

Augusta had already thought this out. The following day was Sunday.

Aside from the cathedral, St. Mary's in East Lavant was the nearest church to both the Berensens and the Langhams and it was customary for both families to attend.

"Tomorrow morning. Maybe, after one of the vicar's improving sermons, Mai will be in a receptive mood and humility and common sense will win the day."

Hmm. Maybe.

They all briefly coincided under the horse chestnut trees at the church gate on their way in. Pleasantries were exchanged, during the course of which Mai studiously avoided Bertie's eye and Augusta took the opportunity of announcing that it was her intention to call on the Berensens and Mai in particular after the service and before luncheon.

"What I need to talk to Mai about will not take very long," stated Augusta.

She did not enquire if this was convenient. Irritated by the assumption that it was, Juno, her daughter by her side, took her seat in the Berensen pew. As usual they were there without Jacob. Jacob would not like the Sunday intrusion, although it sounded as though Augusta's business was with Mai rather than them. Henry Langham was also absent, she noticed, though without the religious excuse. Waiting for the service to begin, she looked around the church, parts of which dated from the twelfth century. It was one of the intimate country variety. There were stained glass windows, though not of the garish sort. Elsewhere plain glass prevailed and every so often the odd prettily tinted random pane stencilled its own subtle square of colour on the stone flags. Outside, the sun struck through the clouds causing the small, packed interior to flood with golden light. As this happened, the organ struck up not entirely tunefully, and they all launched into the first hymn. Juno stole a sidelong glance at her daughter. She was aware that there had been some sort of contretemps between Bertie and Mai and had noticed the *froideur* in the porch on their way in, but had no idea what it was about. On one level it was reassuring to know that Bertie, who reminded Juno of her first husband, *could* have a row with someone. Staring stonily ahead, Mai sang without animation. The tilt of her chin had a combative look.

The sermon was a tactless one, all about camels and eyes of needles and the difficulties facing the rich when it came to securing an entry to the Kingdom of Heaven. It was also very long. With interest Juno watched Augusta, who was sitting in the Langham pew right at the front, eyes boring into the man of God, give the face of her watch three loud staccato taps. The vicar reddened with annoyance, debated whether to admonish or not admonish and went on for another ten minutes as originally intended and then reluctantly prepared to wind up.

Outside in the church yard after a turgid and, in the opinion of some, inappropriate dissertation, all congratulated the priest. (*Why do we do it?* thought Juno. *No wonder they keep coming. Better if we all suggested that God deserves better, never mind his luckless parishioners.*) Standing admiring afresh the graceful lanterned arch above the gate, she noticed that today it was prettily decorated with silk bows. There must have been a wedding. Augusta, she observed out of the corner of her eye, did not waste time on the vicar but made straight for Bertie.

"You'll have to walk home, Bertie," said Augusta. "I intend to take the motor car to the Berensens'."

Bertie did not look very surprised by this edict. Presumably he knew what it was she was going there for. Soon they would all know.

Mai and Juno arrived before Augusta. Lavant Park, which had once belonged to Juno's parents, was a mildly eccentric gothic villa surrounded by a magnificent garden. During her entertaining (though not always comfortable) sojourn in Bohemian society, when the rigours became too much for her, Juno had gone home to her family home to regroup. Frequently, when she went back to London, she left her daughter behind, sometimes for weeks at a stretch, which was how Bertie and Mai had got to know each other as children. Finally, when her father had died and her mother had required somewhere smaller to live, Lavant Park had gone to Juno who, even now, always felt a lift of the heart as the horses turned through the gates and clattered up the wide arc of the drive, past box and yew.

I'm fortunate, was Juno's view, *I've had it all and now, just when I need my comforts, here is Jacob, wealthy enough to cock a snook at Society, to give them to me and moreover, we are in love. As the vicar himself might have said, God moves in mysterious ways. Very mysterious, since, if I'm honest, I don't deserve any of it.*

She sent another speculative sidelong glance in the direction of her daughter. And what about Mai, who still had the best years of her life ahead of her? It was Jacob's view that Bertie Langham was a dolt and this being the case, what was his darling Mai doing marrying him? Juno had tried to explain. Juno said, "Jacob, marriage can be just the vehicle, it is not necessarily the point. Mai is independently rich but Mai still needs someone and that someone might as well be Bertie. Bertie won't get in her way," adding vaguely, "They can go to parties together . . . you know, that sort of thing . . . and you have to admit Bertie is very handsome . . . but it isn't just that. Where we differ is that, unlike you, I *like* Bertie. It is my view that you have always underestimated him and I think he could make Mai happy, otherwise, bearing in mind my own chequered marital career, I wouldn't be encouraging the match."

"Juno, I hope you didn't marry me just so that we could go to parties together."

The memory of his alarm made her smile.

The carriage drew up and, as it did so, Augusta Langham's motor car, driven slowly and with trepidation by the ubiquitous Stiggins, swung around the corner and stopped beside it. Very queenly, Augusta alighted. Yet again they all greeted one another and then walked past the Berensen equivalent of Stiggins into the hall. Here Juno said tactfully, "Mai, dear, why don't you show Mrs. Langham into the drawing room while I go and find Jacob and tell him we're back."

Leading the way, Mai heard the receding rustle of her mother's dress as she climbed the stairs, calling her stepfather's name and then there was silence. In the drawing room the two women faced each other. Each, as Mrs. Harkness the cook would not have failed to notice, was still wearing her hat.

"Won't you sit down, Mrs. Langham?"

Mai gestured to the sofa.

"Thank you, no," was the answer to this polite invitation. "I should prefer to stand."

Easier to dominate.

"Well, now, Mai," continued Augusta, "I gather from Bertie that he spoke to you concerning a certain matter yesterday morning . . ." She did not elaborate.

Neither did Mai, who had decided to keep her powder dry for as long as possible. "Yes, we spoke yesterday morning."

"Am I to understand that the matter is resolved?"

"What matter is that, Mrs. Langham?"

Ha, so that is how it is to be! Augusta braced her back with a snap so that the feathers on her hat straightened up as well.

"The matter of your unseemly association with the suffragette movement!"

"That," replied Mai, "is my business, Mrs. Langham."

Getting frostier by the minute, Augusta said, "*Not* when you are about to marry my son, Mai!"

"It may, at that point, be Bertie's business, Mrs. Langham, but I really cannot see that it is yours." As Bertie had noticed, the batting backwards and forwards of names, while it should have been ultrapolite, in fact added an intimidatory dimension to the exchange.

The effrontery of it!

Augusta was aware that to lose her temper would also lose her the moral high ground. Better if Mai lost hers, the way she had with Bertie. With this aim in mind, Augusta decided to escalate the aggression with an acid tone rather than a raised voice.

"And, even more distasteful, beside brazenly, no! worse! *noisily* campaigning for the vote (and that is when they are not disrupting horse races. I refer, of course, to the Davison woman). I believe one of those Pankhursts to be *a pacifist!* Maybe they are *all* pacifists!" The moment had come for a patriotic thrust. "This, *this*, when the men of this country are risking their lives at the front! Disgraceful. *Disgraceful!* Are *we* a pacifist, Mai? Are we? I hope not!" The feathers on Augusta's hat trembled as if in anticipation of a disappointing answer. "I sincerely hope not!"

Mai, who now regretted flying into a rage with Bertie, had also worked out that whatever the provocation (and God knows there was plenty of it about today) it was imperative that she remain mistress of the situation by keeping calm. Deeply offended by the tasteless reference to the death of Emily Wilding Davison and inwardly seething, she could only trust herself to say shortly, "No, of course *we* aren't, Mrs. Langham. The idea is ridiculous."

Augusta did not appreciate being called ridiculous and was about to underline this fact, when, mindful of Bertie's minimal spell in the army at the end of which he had been temporarily invalided out with dysentery, Mai added, "The more so since Bertie will no doubt soon be recalled to the front to continue fighting for his country and I, because of my fervent conviction that this is a war that must be fought, shall encourage him to go."

This was an unwitting but nevertheless telling strike which gave Augusta a severe jolt. *Back to the front? Only son and heir?* Her lips became a thin line. *Never. Not if I can stop it. After all the tedium of making love to Henry in order to provide an heir in the shape of Bertie, I absolutely refuse to allow him to be slaughtered along with everyone else just when he is becoming useful.* Since Mai, along with Bertie himself (and Henry, come to that) was unaware of the fact that, courtesy of his mother's string pulling, Bertie had been shipped home when others had been expected to get on with it, the idea that he might be sent back again came as a very unwelcome surprise. Maybe Mai knew something she did not? Dismissing the matter for the present since there was nothing she could do about it right now, Augusta suddenly noticed the colours Mai was wearing. Green and white, the elegant ensemble topped off by a dashing purple hat trimmed with a green rosette. Weren't those the suffragette colours? If so, the defiance was breathtaking. Bile rose and by dint of a supreme effort of will was forced down again. The aim of the exercise, namely to bring Mai to heel and get the feeble Bertie back on track as master in his own house, was proving a signal failure. Faced with a rout, the question was what to do next. With a view to trying to regain the initiative, Augusta said, "Very well, since it seems I must, I shall underline my stance in this matter. It is my express desire that you do not persevere with this ill-advised cause."

With impressive composure Mai said, "There, Mrs. Langham, we differ. I do not see the cause as ill-advised and I have no intention of abandoning it. It is my opinion that we in the suffragette movement will succeed. However, you are, of course, perfectly entitled to your own opinion on the matter."

Which is more than she is prepared to allow me.

Like all bullies when confronted by someone who was neither cowed nor prepared to have a row, whether this was the likes of Mai (misguided stubbornness) or one of those she thought of as the servant classes (dumb insolence) Augusta was foxed and consequently neutralised. Frustrated and furious, in an attempt to move things on, and assuming that the Berensens had also been kept in the dark concerning what Mai had been up to, she decided to play the elders and betters blackmail card.

"I presume your family have no idea what has been going on. When I tell them, *if* I tell them, Mai, I am quite sure they will be mortified." And then, just to rub it in, "Mortified!"

And came unstuck.

With a faint smile, Mai said, "They do know. Mother isn't all that in-terested . . ." *No, she wouldn't be,* was Augusta's sour reaction to this. *When it comes to the social imperatives, Juno Berensen has always had only half a brain, if that.* ". . . but my stepfather is very supportive. After all, don't forget the Jewish race has also suffered its share of discrimination down the ages. . . ."

This was too much! Augusta did not feel like being lectured on the sensitivities of the Jewish race. It was bad enough in Augusta's view that one of them was about to become a member of her own family. How to extract with dignity in order to recover and come back to fight another day was the next hurdle. The answer to a prayer, a clock sweetly chimed the half hour. Twelve thirty. Luncheon at The Hall was always at one P.M. sharp.

"I should go," said Augusta, ostentatiously consulting her watch. "Nevertheless, we must discuss this further . . ."

Discuss?

"If there is anything to discuss, I will discuss it with Bertie, Mrs. Langham. Allow me to see you out," said Mai.

On the gravel Stiggins, jack of all trades, was standing to attention by the motor car and probably had been since his mistress entered the house. As he opened the door he noted her expression. Thunderous was the only word for it. Someone was for it. Mai handed her prospective mother-in-law, whose kid-gloved hand felt rigid and unforgiving, into the back of the car and then stepped back a pace where she stood silently, hands folded, feeling like some-one who has just laid a wreath on a cenotaph. Stiggins installed himself in the driver's seat and began unconfidently to fiddle about with the ignition. Finally, after two false starts, the Ford bumped off at a snail's pace. Augusta did not look back. Then the car turned the corner and vanished from sight.

Looking away from an upstairs window, Juno said to her husband, "She's gone!"

"Thank heavens for that!" Jacob had never liked Augusta Langham. "If Mai persists in this alliance, it's my belief that she's storing up a packet of trouble for herself."

Juno looked at her husband with affection. Jacob was what she thought of as the Disraeli type. In his youth a narrow, subtle face had been crowned by a shock of shiny black curls. These were now grey, and the face had filled out a little with age but his dress remained dandified to this day, flamboyant waistcoats being much in favour along with velvet jackets and exotic cravats. That, however, was as far as frivolity went. A combination of an acute business brain and impeccable timing had made Jacob a very rich man and afforded him his passport into society. *Ruthless* was a word commonly used behind his back along with *too clever by half*.

"For what it's worth, dear, it's *my* belief that Mai won't go ahead with it. I suspect that Augusta has overplayed her hand."

"Let's hope so!"

PART TWO

Vicissitudes
1919

Chapter Four

The collapse of the Binnington/Langham alliance was the talk of the drawing rooms for weeks. Because they moved in the same social circles, it was impossible for Bertie and Mai to avoid each other completely, much as each might have wished to do so. This evening, for instance, they were both guests at a large dinner given by a mutual friends who lived near Petworth, the climax of which was to be a bel canto recital by a well-known opera singer. Listening to Bellini, Bertie hungrily watched Mai, whose little gilt chair, courtesy of a vigilant hostess, had been placed as far away from his as it was possible to be.

> *. . . ed a lei che m'innamora*
> *conta i palpiti e i sospir . . .*

lamented the soprano. Bertie was not in the least musical, but even Bertie, who had retained a smattering of Italian following an improving sojourn in Florence, was moved by the haunting cadences of the music.

> *Dille pur che lontananza*
> *il mio duol non puo lenir,*
> *che se nutro una speranza,*
> *ella e sol nell'avvenir . . .*

At this moment it would be true to say that Bertie yearned for Mai. Unattainable in oyster silk with aigrette feathers in her hair, she looked proud and distant and did not once glance in his direction. Not for the first time Bertie wondered what would have happened if he had stood up to Mother and was forced to confront the fact that in all probability this would have been followed by a lifetime of standing up to the strong-minded Mai. So no change there then. Bertie gave up on it.

The Bellini drew to its plaintive close and, after a flurry of applause graciously acknowledged with a bow and a wave of a white glove, the singer launched into some altogether more bracing Rossini. This time the note was reproachful, accusatory even:

> *Crudell in te t'offesi?*
> *Farmi penar cosi,*
> *crudell in che t'offesi?*
> *Farmi penar perche?*

Unnoticed, Mai's fan slipped off her lap. Jealously Bertie watched Ned Fielding retrieve it and gallantly hand it back to her, receiving as his reward the coquettish flash of the eyes she used to reserve for him. He had occasionally seen the two of them out riding together on the Downs near Funtington accompanied by Ned's sister, Isabel. The Fielding property, or what was left of it, was situated at Woodend amid a confusion of tiny tunnelled lanes, darkly overhung by ragged trees struggling to survive the stranglehold of bindweed and ivy and reminded Bertie of the tangly Arthur Rackham illustrations in his childhood storybooks. The Fielding family history was equally complicated. Ned's father, Hubert, self-promoted as something of an aesthete, had been revealed, probably more accurately, as a compulsive gambler when he shot himself in a London hotel leaving a scandal and considerable debts behind. As a consequence, Ned had been brought up by his protective mother and a gaggle of sisters in comparatively straitened circumstances. Maybe that was why the Fieldings had been able to come to terms with women's suffrage in a way in which his own family had not. By now it was the end of 1919 and the war was over, just in time to prevent Bertie's second call to arms. Part of him regretted this. Despite the privations and the fear, Bertie had enjoyed the camaraderie of life at the front and had felt considerable embarrassment at being ordered back to England when others had been expected to get on with it. Fielding, on the other hand, hadn't gone at all, which fact had caused a great deal of gossip, finally quelled when the family let it discreetly be known that this was due to a medical condition, though what this was exactly was never made clear. Certainly to Bertie's disenchanted eye there didn't seem to be anything the matter with Ned now. One of the results of the dreadful carnage in the battlefields was a surfeit of eligible, unmarried girls but none of them touched his heart as his childhood friend Mai had done. And maybe, now he came to think of it, childhood had got in the way and familiarity had prevented him falling violently in love with her as he might have done had he met her as a young woman for the first time.

In the interim, women, or rather some women, had achieved the vote which, had it happened in time, just might have saved the engagement from foundering. Mai's behaviour scotched this, for Mai, it transpired, was neither satisfied with nor grateful for what she regarded as a mean concession and with the Pankhursts and other stalwarts she was bent on carrying the banner for universal female enfranchisement.

Following a lull in the music, during which Augusta had been mulling over all this anti–status quo behaviour, she voiced her displeasure. "If it goes on like this, housemaids will have the vote next!"

"You are right, my dear, I believe that is the aim," concurred her husband mildly, unable to resist it. "And why not?"

More Bellini coinciding with this inflammatory query saved the day. Electing to ignore his wife's incredulous stare, Henry sat back in his chair and let the music form its own natural barrier between himself and her. The room in which the concert was taking place was elegantly furnished. On that level, reflected Henry, it was as though there had never been a war. A large chandelier, all candles lit for the benefit of the pianist, dominated a ceiling charmingly painted with birds and butterflies, the lustres providing their own muted accompaniment as they briefly touched. At a lower level the tall, shooting flames of candelabra enhanced the dull sheen of silk and velvet and struck scintillating prismatic sparks of light from the jewellery of the ladies.

But there has been a war, thought Henry, *and, in my opinion, nothing will ever be quite the same again.*

Chapter Five

It was at one of Lady Londonderry's receptions that the princess first electrified London society.

The men were mesmerised, the women alerted. "Who is she?" was the question on all lips, followed by, "Where is she from?"

The cause of all this speculation did not walk like an ordinary mortal but appeared to levitate up the Londonderry House grand staircase. A complicated train of the type that was notoriously difficult to manage gracefully also appeared to float in the wake of a spectacular silver gown. At the head of the stairs, accompanied by the eccentric but impeccably connected Countess Olga Carstairs née Fedorovna with whom she appeared to have arrived, the princess was greeted by their hostess. Watching this taking place from a distance, hawklike, through her lorgnette, Augusta noted with a certain amount of satisfaction that beside the svelte newcomer and despite, or maybe because of, dripping with showy Londonderry diamonds, Edith looked like a Christmas tree. It grated that Edith, to the disapproval of not just Augusta but members of her own family as well, was an active suffragist. On the other hand, to refuse an invitation to one of Edith's glittering receptions, especially with the inert Bertie back on the marriage market, would have been unthinkable and Augusta had been forced to come to terms with the Londonderry activities in this direction. The year was now 1920 and, in the wake of the Mai Binnington debacle, the Langhams, mother and son, accompanied by a reluctant Henry, were spending time in London with a view to marrying Bertie off.

("And try to get it right *this time, Bertie!")*

The countess, who was in her seventies, with failing eyesight together with a hectoring manner and a pronounced foreign accent, could be tiresome. Because of this, though Augusta knew Olga, she usually tried to avoid her. Not this evening. It was maddening, therefore, not to be able to get anywhere near her or her charming charge. She did get close enough to see the emeralds, though. They were the largest emeralds Augusta had ever seen. *(And I've seen some in my time.)* Huge, flat stones whose simple cut allowed them to smoulder with sulky green fire and all set off with equally opulent diamonds also of unfussy cut, size and quality rendering further artifice unnecessary. Choker and earrings. The whole ensemble must have been worth a king's ransom. Or maybe a tsar's ransom. As they waited for Olga to turn in their direction, Augusta took the opportunity to appraise the Princess Zhenia. What she saw was a young woman of middle height with titian hair piled in a cloudy mass above a small, pointed face, whose high, Slavic cheekbones were perfectly counterpointed by a mobile, discreetly painted mouth. So slender was the princess it almost seemed to Augusta that if touched she might break, thereby briefly raising the practical, dynastic question as to whether she would be any good for breeding. *All in good time . . .*

At last Olga deigned to notice them. Augusta thought she detected a malicious gleam in the cataracted old eyes and correctly deduced that Olga had deliberately kept her waiting.

"Augusta!"

"Olga!"

"Bertie!"

"Countess!" He kissed her hand. Augusta looked around. Typically, when he was most needed Henry was nowhere to be seen.

"Allow me to present my great niece, Princess Zhenia Dashkova."

Much bowing.

Zhenia, Augusta noticed, also had a pronounced foreign accent but backed up as it was by the stupendous emerald set this did not get on her nerves as it otherwise might have done. Jewellery aside, the princess appeared to have pleasing manners of the demure, eyes cast down, speak-when-spoken-to variety. Although it had to be admitted that getting a word in when Olga was holding forth was not easy. She was presently answering the unspoken *Where is she from?* question.

"Zhenia left Russia when the revolution broke out. Luckily, she was in the country house when the worst excesses took place. The rest of the family were not so fortunate. They remained in Petrograd and were eventually murdered by the Bolsheviks. Thrown alive down a well, I believe."

Listening to this insensitive, not to say blunt account, Bertie sent the princess a commiserating look and was affected by the sight of a dainty gloved hand brushing away a tear.

"What rotten luck!" exclaimed Bertie, artlessly succeeding in stopping the countess's interesting flow, thereby irritating his inquisitive parent who had been poised to enquire about the fate of the family estates in the wake of this catastrophe. Too late. The countess had been diverted by another ambitious parent with a marriageable son in tow. Never mind. Augusta decided to call on Olga the following day. That way she would have her to herself and could set about a forensic extraction of the sort of information she needed to know about the princess.

As they moved away, she asked, "So, Bertie, what did you think?"

"Of . . . ?"

Ye gods!

"The princess, of course."

"Very fetching. Assume she must have jumped a ditch or two to get out of Russia in time."

"No doubt she did." Augusta was short. The resemblance to his phlegmatic father was depressing. She wondered what it would take to get Bertie moving. Sisyphus and his stone came to mind.

The following afternoon found the countess and Augusta Langham taking tea together in Olga's cluttered drawing room. Small tables and chairs, the former covered in Russian knickknacks, were everywhere. It was a miracle that her hostess with her atrocious eyesight did not trip over them. Maybe her maid steered her around. Elaborate velvet curtains were swagged, tailed, and fringed and the walls were decorated with Chinese silk which was almost rendered redundant by hordes of icons, paintings, and photographs of gloomy, whiskery Russians. The only thing missing was a samovar and she probably had one of those somewhere. Augusta tried to imagine Olga's English husband, long since dead, in the middle of this riot of ethnic memorabilia and could not. Maybe he died of overdecoration.

She leant forward and replaced her teacup in its saucer with a click.

"So tell me, Olga, all about your charming great niece. She was quite the most attractive girl in the room last night."

"And the most sought after!" responded Olga with satisfaction. "Never mind about Zhenia, it's a long time since I received so much attention. I have been literally deluged with cards. *Everybody* wants to call on me."

The inference of this was not lost on Augusta. For once she needed Olga more than Olga needed her and Olga was not above pointing this out. It was perhaps a pity that she had not been more diplomatic in the past, Augusta saw. Now there would be no special favours. She would have to move fast to keep ahead of the competition and no doubt she would also be forced to endure commiseration on the debacle of Bertie's engagement to Mai Binnington.

In the light of the last remark it seemed politic to concentrate on Olga before moving the conversation in the direction of Zhenia. It might even prove to be the fact that she would have to concentrate on Olga for the whole of this call just in order to atone for years of cavalier snubs. *If only I'd known then what I know now,* thought Augusta, gritting her teeth and preparing to get on with it.

Talking about Olga proved harder than one would have thought for it began to emerge that since her husband died and until her interesting relation had come on the scene, nothing much had happened to Olga apart from large, impersonal soirées such as the Londonderry reception. Though in the course of this groundwork Augusta did learn certain pertinent facts. She already knew that Olga had no children, but had not realised that, with the exception of the princess, she had no other close living family, either here or in Russia. Which, in turn, raised the question of what would happen to Olga's considerable fortune when she died.

"But I'm sure Princess Zhenia will be a great comfort to you," said Augusta. "Tell me, how did you find out that she had escaped the fate of the rest of her family?"

"She literally turned up on my doorstep!" said Olga. "I could hardly believe it."

No indeed.

Augusta stared at Olga.

"But when was this?"

"A month ago."

Olga fell silent, remembering the young woman who had materialised out of nowhere and her own immediate reservations concerning the new-comer.

A month ago!

"So when did she leave Petrograd?"

"In 1917. She tells me she spent two years in Paris living with other émigrés. It was, I believe, a hand-to-mouth existence."

"Then why not contact you immediately? If I understand the situation correctly, you are, after all, her only remaining family."

"Zhenia is proud and did not want to go cap in hand to beg help from someone she had never met. Don't forget it is a very long time since I myself last saw that side of the family. When I married I left Russia for good."

That's all very well, but she did go cap in hand, thought Augusta. "What about the emeralds?"

"They are family jewels. I remember my mother's sister wearing them. Zhenia had the presence of mind to sew them inside the bodice of her dress before making her escape. . . ."

"But if you have never met her before, how could you be sure that she is in fact your great niece?"

With a frown, the countess picked up a small enamelled Fabergé egg from a clutch on the table beside her and began rolling it around between the palms of her hands like a worry bead. The clouded eyes stared into the middle distance.

"Initially, I was sceptical. Of course I was. But she knew so much. She knew things about the family that only a bona fide member of it could have known. I could not fault her. And then there were other things, other items of jewellery. It's the knowledge that counts, though. . . . That is what persuaded me. . . ."

And also you are a lonely old woman who wanted to be persuaded, perhaps.

"Presumably there are family estates . . ."

"*Were*," corrected Olga. "I believe all such have been sequestered by the state and turned over to the peasants to be run as cooperatives. The aristocracy has been dispossessed and those who survived were lucky not to be murdered. Life as I knew it in Russia is over."

This was a blow, although one that Augusta might have foreseen. It sounded as though the princess had made her escape with the family jewels and the emeralds in particular plus a collection of the sort of unremarkable memorabilia to which the countess was so inordinately partial, and that was it.

Olga rang for some more tea. A huge cat of the longhaired variety rubbed against her chair and then jumped onto her lap. It sat facing Augusta. Its tiny, blue-eyed, snub-nosed face, surrounded by a flaring aureole of silky fur, stared her out.

"This is Ivan," stated the countess.

Augusta looked back at Ivan with distaste. *Never mind about Ivan. Where,* she wondered, *is the princess?*

Apparently able to read her thoughts, Olga said, "Zhenia is having a dress fitting this afternoon. It is important that she should be properly turned out. . . ."

Beginning to wonder if this hadn't all been a waste of time, along with a second cup of tea Augusta accepted an unprepossessing little dumpling, which had the look of a Russian speciality about it.

"Vareniki," said Olga. "Delicious! Have another! No?" She helped herself to two before continuing:

". . . for, after all, the next step must be a brilliant marriage. Which should not be too difficult to attain, since it is my intention to make Zhenia my heir . . ."

Ah! That put a different complexion on everything. Emeralds and a fortune. Not a wasted afternoon after all.

"Perhaps I *will* have another. . . ."

Olga proffered the plate.

". . . and, while we are on the subject of marriage, you must tell me what happened between Bertie and Miss Binnington. *What* a shame. Such an eligible, beautiful young woman. There was a great deal of speculation in the drawing rooms, I can tell you. We all felt so *sorry* for you. Bringing about that sort of union takes an inordinate amount of time and trouble, and then, to see it fall apart before your eyes . . ."

Chapter Six

Mai Binnington married Ned Fielding. This was generally regarded as one in the eye for Augusta Langham and a coup for the Fieldings. Jacob did not understand Mai's second choice any better than he had understood her first.

"None of these young men *do* anything," grumbled Jacob. "They are drones. Mai is a clever girl who deserves better."

Reflecting that however much she tried to explain them, Jacob would never understand the mating mores of the English, Juno said, "You just don't want to lose her."

"No, I don't," her husband frankly admitted. "But I'd mind a lot less if I thought he would make her happy. As it is, he might as well be Bertie Langham!"

"Ned has one inestimable advantage over Bertie Langham," Juno felt constrained to point out.

"Oh, really? And what is that?"

"He comes without Augusta."

She had him there.

"Besides, Ned does do things. I believe he's writing a book about butterflies. . . ."

"Butterflies! Huh!" Jacob was contemptuous. "Mai should be marrying a man of the world, not a lepidoptera-fixated youth. As it is, she has married just for the status without knowing anything very much about the outside world or herself. Just as you did, Juno. What happens when boredom sets in?"

Well, yes. Looking back at her own chequered past, Juno saw exactly what he meant. "Never forget dearest, that was how we met."

"Eventually, yes! But what about all those years in between?"

Ah, yes, the years in between . . .

Juno knew better than to go into that. Jacob was ambivalent about the years in between and by no means as broadminded about her rackety life before they met as some might have supposed. The nude painting he had found so seductive hung, as Bertie Langham had rightly surmised it would, in his dressing room. Other sketches and studies had been assiduously tracked down, bought up, and locked away. *It was odd*, reflected Juno, *because when one thinks about it, all of that made me the woman he fell in love with. Whatever he likes to think about it now, Jacob certainly wouldn't have been impressed by the niminy piminy miss I was before I married for the first time.* And in those days, the only passport to a more adventurous life was to be a married woman. After the children, or child in her case, sex came into its own as a delectable diversion to be discreetly enjoyed during the course of sybaritic country house weekends with no questions asked provided all observed the rules. All the same, boredom had set in, just as Jacob was predicting it would with Mai and Ned.

In the end Juno said, "I don't know why we're talking about it. After all, they're married now and there's nothing to be done. It's either going to work or it isn't. My own view is that it will."

Jacob was not so sure. Mai was headstrong, as had been demonstrated by the way she had seen off Augusta Langham, but where marriage was concerned displayed a conventional, even passive side, which he found hard to comprehend. On the other hand, maybe the way to look at it was that just as Mai had got married, she could get unmarried, though the social opprobrium this would occasion would be inconvenient to say the least. As Juno had found out.

"When are they back from the honeymoon?"

"Next weekend," said Juno, "though if I was in Venice, wild horses wouldn't drag me back sooner than I had to come."

"Darling Juno, I'll take you to Venice if that's where you'd like to go."

"Accepted! But not this week. We don't want to get in the way. And now I'd like you to come and see my rose garden."

———

Augusta Langham discussed her call on the countess with her husband.

"So you see," concluded Augusta, "although, sadly, the estates in Russia are all gone according to Olga, when, in the fullness of time, the princess inherits her fortune, she will be a very wealthy woman in her own right. And Olga can't go on forever, she must be seventy if she's a day."

Listening to this hard-headed assessment of the situation, Henry was of the opinion that there was many a slip between the intention to bequeath cup and lip.

"What if they fall out?"

"Why should they fall out? Owing to the presence of the princess in her house as her protegée, Olga is getting more attention than she's had for years. As for Zhenia, she would be a fool to alienate such a rich relation. No, no, it won't happen."

It struck Henry that, as usual, Augusta was applying her own rules of engagement to everyone else. Which was where she had come unstuck with Mai Binnington.

"And you want Bertie to pay court to this mysterious beauty! I use the word *mysterious* advisedly. We have no idea where the princess comes from. We know who she *says* she is, but that's a different matter. Why can't Bertie marry a nice, uncomplicated English girl? Someone from his own background who will understand him."

Extremely short: "Understanding Bertie isn't very difficult."

Despite the fact that Augusta had harboured exactly the same doubts concerning the provenance of the princess, since conveniently set aside in the interests of netting Olga's fortune, it was thoroughly irritating to have to listen to them being voiced all over again by Henry.

"Olga herself seems satisfied that Princess Zhenia is who she says she is."

"Olga's dotty, you've always said so. *And* blind. I'm by no means sure Olga has the required equipment to recognise anyone."

It was beginning to seem to Augusta as if Henry was determined to be obstructive. By now exasperated, she said, "What does any of that matter? The princess is graceful and presentable. If he marries her, Bertie will be allying himself with Zhenia's pedigree and Olga's fortune. Oh, and those emeralds. Who could object to that? Only you, it seems!"

Maybe because when he married her, Augusta had been relatively impecunious, she now appeared to be obsessed with money.

"We've got plenty of money. Why can't Bertie marry for love or at least inclination? And, by the way, have you spoken to *him* about this?"

"Not yet. I intend to make it my business to get to know the princess first. . . ." Then, mindful of the dark horse that had been the insubordinate Mai Binnington, she added, "Just to make sure . . ."

"Because," continued Henry, "I'm not sure Bertie would know what to do with such exotica. Bertie is a simple fellow who likes simple pleasures. . . ."

Here her candour was breathtaking.

"What has that got to do with marriage?"

It certainly hadn't had much to do with theirs. That was certain. Not for the first time, Henry wondered what he had thought he was doing when he proposed to Augusta Drummond. All the signs of what was to come had been in evidence then. He supposed he had done it because she had been generally acknowledged as the belle of the season. Looking back, even then his bride-to-be had been a crashing snob with an imperious manner. On the other hand, although deficient in the softer qualities more usually associated with the distaff side, Augusta had had style and, in those days, dash. The handsomest girl in the room, his own bossy mother had called her. By the time he found out about her profound indifference with regard to the sex act, or maybe her profound indifference to the sex act with regard to himself, it was too late, for they were married and that was that. Nothing left to do but make the best of it.

Luckier than most though, for at least I've got Daisy.

Yes. Daisy.

Henry cleared his throat.

"I've been meaning to tell you, I shall have to go to Sussex next week. One or two things require attention. . . ."

Augusta was put out. "But I need you here!"

And then suspicious. "What sort of things?"

Deliberately vague. "Oh, work on the estate. That sort of thing." Then with masterly understatement, he said, "After all, three thousand acres doesn't just run itself. . . ."

He had her there and both knew it.

Grudgingly, she asked, "Can't it wait?"

"Look," said Henry reasonably, "you don't need me to help you get to know the princess better. I'll only be away a couple of days."

"But this is the season. We have invitations *everywhere*. I need you to escort me."

"Bertie can escort you. He doesn't have anything else to do and presumably, since I see I can't dissuade you from this course of action, you'll need him to get to know the princess better in the fullness of time."

Augusta did not miss the flick of sarcasm here. Henry could be very stubborn. When he was in what Augusta called *one of those moods* there was no shifting him. And maybe, since in any case he seemed determined not to endorse her proposed matchmaking strategy, he was better out of the way rather than standing around making unhelpful observations.

"Well, I suppose if you must go, you must go. But could I ask you to do *one* thing for me, Henry?"

Put like that it sounded as if he never did *anything* for her.

"Of course, my love. What is that?"

"Please do not, I repeat, do *not*, pass on your reservations to Bertie."

Henry, who already had, promised he would not. Anything for a quiet life. He must remember to brief Bertie on the subject of what he had and hadn't told him.

Ned and Mai arrived back from Venice. Even Jacob had to admit that there was a bloom about his stepdaughter that had not been in evidence before. Fielding, it seemed, must be getting something right. He said as much to Juno.

"Well, there you are," said Juno, "and now they've come back from Venice, we can go there without being *de trop*."

In fact the marriage of Ned and Mai did not unravel in the way Jacob predicted. Initially it worked on several levels, one of which was sexual. A virgin on her wedding day, Mai had very little idea what to expect. Questioned on the subject before the event, Juno proved elusive not to say infuriatingly airy-fairy. It was odd, reflected Mai, that her mother should be so coy when one considered that before she met Jacob, she had been widely shunned by society as fast. Fast and loose. Now she was in love with and faithful to Jacob, she seemed disinclined to help anyone else on the road to sexual enlightenment, which proved that there was nothing like a convert to the straight and narrow.

On their wedding night Mai's ignorance was masked by an anticipatory thrill at the thought of what was going to happen next, together with a mysterious air of containment which charged Ned as nothing else could and, as he took his naked bride in his arms for the first time and kissed her, he thought himself a lucky man. By the end of their honeymoon, an awakened Mai discovered that not for nothing was she her mother's daughter. In the mornings she watched Ned with tenderness as he dressed and marvelled in her good fortune as they took their breakfast together looking out over the lagoon towards the city where clusters of leaning campaniles rose out of the translucent mist above a green sea. Delight in her marriage did not totally inhibit analysis, however. Reassessing her husband on the basis of living with him instead of seeing him in mainly artificial circumstances, it became apparent to Mai that temperamentally he was quite different from herself and that to a large degree he lacked her own uncomplicated joie de vivre. There was a fastidious languor about Ned and it almost seemed to Mai that here there was a shortfall and he *needed* her energy and zest for life to make him whole. It was not that there was a lack of masculinity about her new husband, but rather that, like a cat, every movement was a study in graceful economy. Cats could be cruel. Mai wondered whether Ned could be cruel.

On their arrival back in England, they moved into a pretty Georgian house on the outskirts of the village of East Dean which was their wedding present from Jacob and which Juno had prepared for them. Once they had settled in, Mai invited her parents to lunch. Over the pudding Juno said, "You missed the beginning of the newest Augusta Langham spectacle."

"Since I was a leading player in the last one, I don't think I mind too much about that," observed Mai.

"What's she done now?" asked Ned.

"It's not so much what she's *done* as what she's *about* to do."

"Which is . . . ?"

"Oh, *do* stop tantalising, Juno, or I'll tell the story," interjected Jacob.

"Well, along with a thousand of Edith Londonderry's other acquaintances, including the Langhams, we went to a reception at Londonderry House. Also there was Countess Olga Fedorovna . . ."

"Who is . . . ?" The speaker was Ned.

"You don't know her? Mai does and therefore you soon will! She's a well-heeled member of the now defunct Russian aristocracy who married an English stuffed shirt, and settled in London, where, since her husband's death, she still lives in some splendour. Anyway, with her this particular night was the *most* glamorous creature. *All* the men's eyes, including Jacob's I may say, were out on stalks! Yes they *were*, Jacob. Don't deny it!"

Mai was intrigued.

"Who is she? And how old?"

"We subsequently heard, though not from Olga—nobody could get anywhere near Olga—that her companion was her great niece Princess Zhenia Dashkova, whose family were eliminated in the Russian revolution. I should say she is about twenty-one or twenty-two, what do you think, Jacob? So: young. But my dears, what presence! That dress! Silver with one of those tricky trains. She seemed to float! But the emeralds! The largest *I've* ever seen. Necklace and earrings. The set must be worth a mint. And I don't believe it to be Olga's, if so I've never seen her wearing it. So presumably the princess must have brought her jewellery out of Russia when she took off. Next thing you know, Augusta has raised her lorgnette and we all know *that* look! Then, with Bertie in tow, she began to stalk Olga and finally, with considerable difficulty, succeeded in separating her from the rest of the herd whereupon a conversation took place and Bertie was introduced to the beauteous one. I may tell you, by the way, in the normal course of events, Augusta wouldn't give Olga the time of day. Since when, my spies inform me, she has called on the countess, not once but twice, though so far without Bertie. Reconnoitering presumably. I have no doubt that by now she knows the princess's prospects down to the last rouble."

"Poor old Bertie," said Ned, who was less interested in this turn of events than Mai. Then, turning to Jacob, he said, "Could I interest you in taking a look at my butterfly collection, sir?"

"Yes, you can." Normally Jacob could take butterflies or leave them but today was not sorry to get away from Juno's barbed remarks concerning his own initial reaction to the exquisite Princess Zhenia.

When the men had gone, Juno said to Mai, "Well? Did you have the most wonderful time?"

Blushing, Mai said, "Yes. Yes we did. Rome was divine and so was Florence but Venice! Venice was just out of this world!"

Fielding's butterfly room had an airless, stuffy atmosphere. Jacob watched in silence as his son-in-law pulled drawer after drawer out of the specimen cabinets. There they all were, row upon decorative row, a selection of fritil-laries, pearl-bordered, queen of spain, dark green, followed by graylings, painted ladies, orange-tips, peacocks, male and female, all carefully labelled and dated. On and on it went.

"But look at this."

They both bent over the relevant drawer.

"This," said Ned, "is a mazarine blue. Very, very rare!" He looked up and smiled at Jacob, his face irradiated with pleasure. For reasons he did not attempt to work out at that precise moment in time, Jacob found the sight of all this regimented transfixed beauty repellent. He tried to imagine the languid Fielding rushing around the countryside with a butterfly net and could not.

Without really wanting to know, he asked, "How do you go about mounting them?"

"First, I pin them," answered Ned, "and in doing that, it's very impor-tant that the pin passes through the centre of the thorax, if possible in a straight line. After that comes setting . . ."

"Setting?"

"Yes. Most lepidopterists in this country go for low setting, but I pre-fer the high setting continental style. Let me show you."

He picked up a board which had a cork-covered groove down the middle of it and sloping sides on either side.

"The key to this is to engineer the wings so that they settle flat. That is perfection. Here I should say that for this method I have to use a special type of foreign pin called a Carlsbad." Out of a bottle he selected a but-terfly. "Having pinned my delicate specimen . . ."—deftly he did it—". . . using these entomological forceps I place the body of the insect in the groove and then I sink the pin into the cork."

By now Fielding seemed almost to be talking to himself. Jacob found himself unable to take his eyes off the other's long thin fingers which, in the light of the conversation they were having, reminded him of nothing so much as antennae.

"Then, and here comes the precise part, a couple of strips of tracing cloth are needed which I carefully place on the wings, so! taking care to leave that part closest to the body exposed for it is here that I manipulate the wings into position with a needle ... like this ... forewing first, with a pin beneath it to keep it in place, hind wing second and again we use a pin. After that we position the antennae ... following which the specimen has to remain on the board for a fortnight or so while it sets, preferably in a drying house. Would you like to see the drying house?"

Surreptitiously Jacob looked at his watch.

"Fascinating, quite fascinating ... but the drying house is for another time. I think we should get back to the ladies, don't you?"

"The ladies?" Clearly Fielding had forgotten all about them. "Yes. Good Lord, is that the time?" Reluctantly, he said, "Yes, I suppose we should...."

Later that evening as they were dressing to go out to a dinner, Jacob said to Juno, "That man makes my flesh creep!"

Juno put down her hair brush in surprise. "*Ned?* Darling, I know you have never been that mad about him, but isn't that a *bit* extreme. Besides, he does seem to be making Mai very happy."

"Yes, at the moment he does."

"So what is the problem?"

"Do you realise he has a thing called a killing bottle! Cyanide! That's how he does them in...."

Juno was startled. "The butterflies, I hope you mean!"

"Well, of course I mean the butterflies. Despite the fact that I don't like Fielding very much, I'm not about to suggest that he's in the process of decimating the human population. Lepidoptera is another matter. All the same I wouldn't like to be a butterfly with Fielding and his net in the offing."

"You didn't like Bertie Langham either, don't forget."

"I prefer Bertie to this one. With Bertie what you see is what you get...."

Juno was not about to let Jacob get away with this.

"You always said that's what irritated you. Bertie is an open book with nothing in it, you used to say."

"I know, I may have said that and it still stands, by the way, but this one's in a different dimension."

"I expect you'll find all butterfly collectors have those dreadful little bottles," commented Juno vaguely, putting on her earrings. "I think my brother did when he was still at school. His passion in those days was moths. I have to say he doesn't seem to be very interested in them now. What do you think of these?"

Cursory glance: "Very nice. Look, Juno, promise me you will make it plain to Mai that if she ever needs sanctuary, she can always come back to us!"

As things stood, it appeared there was no need for this. The Fielding marriage showed every sign of being one of the more tranquil ones. Though as the novelty of being a married woman with her own establishment to be run began to wear off, Mai found herself with time to spare and a resurgent desire to do something for the greater good. In the light of what had gone before, she decided to resume her work with the suffragette movement with a view to joining in the push for universal female voting rights. For reasons she could not or, maybe, would not acknowledge to herself, she did not immediately inform Ned of her decision. Though Ned had always professed his support for her activities in this direction and she saw no reason for him to have changed his mind. But Ned, she had noticed lately, could be very possessive in what Mai considered to be an irrational way, a trait which had not been in evidence before they married. Be that as it may, this could hardly affect her decision to redeploy some of her time, for surely, reasoned Mai, no one could possibly feel threatened by a political movement.

Could they?

Chapter Seven

Augusta's ingratiation of herself with Countess Olga took a great deal longer than it might have done had she been nicer to the other in the past. Olga was not about to overlook old slights easily. And the princess, it seemed, had lots and lots of suitors. There were days when Augusta wondered if it was all worth it. Getting to know Zhenia was a consolation, on the other hand, and persuaded her that she was after all on the right track.

She noted with approval Zhenia's tiny waist and tiny feet and her carriage, which was superb. The Russian had the quality known as presence, of that there could be no doubt, and her English was improving by the day. As it did so the foreign accent softened, so that, rather than getting in the way, it imparted an attractive huskiness to the princess's discourse, unlike Olga's corncrake shout. Plus there was the admirable tendency only to speak when spoken to and then demurely. Zhenia was not one of those pushy modern girls. Augusta proceeded to tease out the details of aristocratic life in prerevolutionary Russia.

"Although I hope it will not upset you too much to talk about it," said Augusta, having no intention of desisting even if it did.

"What is gone, is gone," replied the princess with admirable fortitude. "But you must understand, Mrs. Langham, that although my parents spent a great deal of their time enjoying court life in Petrograd, we children were mostly brought up in the country."

"Where you had extensive estates, I believe."

"Yes, but no longer. It is a way of life that has gone forever. I fear for Russia."

Augusta was unwilling to get onto the amorphous subject of Russia in general.

"And you had brothers and sisters, Princess?"

"Yes. Three brothers. All were older than me and all were murdered. My father was a distant cousin of the Romanovs. . . ."

Only a distant cousin. That was a shame. But never mind, despite the fact that the royal family had met a similar fate, the name Romanov still counted for a good deal.

"And your mother?"

"My mother was a countess in her own right and a celebrated beauty at court. It is a shame that her life was so brutally cut short."

Yes, well, in those circumstances thank heaven for Olga. Though those were the only circumstances in which Augusta could ever envisage saying *Thank heaven for Olga.*

Here Olga butted in with, for once, a helpful suggestion.

"Why don't you bring Bertie with you the next time you call, Augusta? I should like the two young people to meet again properly."

"And so would I. What a very good idea. Yes, I will."

That evening Augusta reported back to Henry, newly returned from his endeavours in the country, most of which had centred around the delectable Daisy, "So far, so good! The princess is a charming girl, *very* well connected and with impeccable manners. . . ."

"Oh and don't forget those emeralds!"

Choosing to ignore this, Augusta continued, "The next time I call I have been asked to bring Bertie, so I think I can safely say we are on our way. . . ." Here a note of asperity crept in. "That is if Bertie doesn't commit one of his witless acts of social sabotage."

"*On your way.* Are you quite sure about that? To be frank, I'm amazed the countess hasn't set her sights on our own royal family. And while we're on the subject, you do realise that if you bring this match off, *if* you do, you're going to have to put up with an awful lot of Olga."

"Yes, thank you, Henry, that's a very helpful observation. May I point out that Olga can't go on forever. She's already ancient and in poor health so I don't anticipate that particular martyrdom extending for too long."

Henry flapped open his copy of *The Times*. "You're a hard woman, my dear."

"No, no. Merely practical, that is all."

A week after this conversation took place, Augusta, who knew exactly how women go to work on men watched Zhenia going to work on Bertie. As a study in well-bred seduction (though not of the physical variety, of course) it was impeccable. *I really couldn't have done it better myself*, thought Augusta. Low, melodious laughter greeted Bertie's probably unremarkable sallies and was combined with shyly flirtatious sidelong looks. Occasionally she allowed silence to fall thereby affording herself an opportunity to look charmingly pensive, even daring to be interestingly distracted, so that just for variety she presented Bertie with a profile as pale and perfect as a cameo and a neck whose length would not have disgraced a swan. This was a virtuoso display, no doubt about it, and raised the question as to whether Princess Zhenia treated all her suitors to the same. If so, Bertie had better hurry up. Sitting at the opposite end of Olga's long sitting room with her hostess so that they were there but not there, so to speak, Augusta reluctantly accepted yet another dubious Russian sweetmeat and admired the performance while Olga reminisced.

Travelling home afterwards, Augusta said to her son, "So! What did you think?"

"About the princess?"

God give me strength!

"Obviously!"

Bertie was cautious.

"She's a dazzler, no doubt about it . . ."

"No, there's no doubt about that."

". . . but she's very *foreign*, isn't she?"

Augusta gave him a long look.

Better try the patient approach. Bertie can be stubborn like Henry if pushed too hard.

"Bertie, she *is* foreign."

"Yes, I know, but you know what I mean. . . ."

"No, I don't know what you mean. What *do* you mean?"

"I mean she's not the same as us."

"The princess has two arms and two legs, what more do you want?"

It occurred to Augusta that, despite her husband's assurances to the contrary, Bertie had been got at.

"I have also ascertained that when Olga dies, Zhenia will inherit a fortune, at least the size of Mai Fielding's."

Mai Fielding. Bertie was aware of a pang. A man of instinct, he sensed that something was not quite right but was uncertain what the something was. Where Mai had been concerned there had been no such doubt. No, the fly in the ointment there had been Mother.

"Look, Bertie, Princess Zhenia is stylish, aristocratic, and shortly to be very rich. On top of all of that, she is, as you so succinctly put it, a dazzler." She gave him a shrewd look, then, employing her own instinct, proceeded to home in on the root of the problem. "Mai Binnington is no longer available. She is now Mai Fielding. You must put all thoughts of Mai out of your head and concentrate on the future. You are about to be thirty. It is your duty to marry and marry well. I suggest you get cracking! As you know, next week the countess is giving a dance for Zhenia. *That* is your chance. Make sure you don't muff it!"

Contrary to what Olga had told Augusta, the princess was not deluged with hopeful suitors. This was due to a combination of the war, which had caused a surplus of impeccable English debutantes, and the fact that the only person to have been told about Olga's intention to make Zhenia her heir was Augusta Langham, though Augusta did not know this. The emeralds notwithstanding (though all agreed that these were superb) hard cash in the shape of a considerable fortune and the income thereof was considered a preferable option and for most this eclipsed aristocratic Russian pretensions as well. In the wake of the uncertainties of World War I the English marriage market had become even more hard-headed than before where money was concerned and preferred what it knew to what it did not.

Nevertheless the dance for Zhenia was attended by most of society and there was no lack of eligible young men vying with each other to dance with the dashing newcomer. In the forefront of these was Bertie. Waltzing with the princess, who performed with elan, he caught a glimpse of the two of them in one of the floor-to-ceiling gilt mirrors as they spun across the floor and knew that they made an extraordinarily handsome couple. Also on the dance floor were Ned and Mai Fielding, who had arrived with the Berensens. Ned, he noticed, looked sulky and Mai resigned, as though they had had an argument. Bertie's arm tightened around Zhenia's waist. Her slim body felt lithe and pliable against his. As if in response she tilted her head back and smiled up at him. Tawny, narrowed eyes lent her a distinctly feline look. The sharply sophisticated smell of her scent made him light-headed. All at once Bertie had a desire to kiss the pretty rouged mouth, unthinkable, of course, and not the sort of impulse which normally beset him as he steered well-bred, innocent young girls around the dance floor. It struck him at the same time that there was a sexual allure about Princess Zhenia which Bertie associated with women of the world rather than twenty-one-year-old ingenues. The music stopped. He relinquished her small gloved hand.

"I should like to have the next dance and the next and the next," said Bertie urgently, surprising himself.

"Impossible, alas. My card is full!"

"Then may I call on you tomorrow?"

"You may!"

He escorted her back to where Countess Olga was sitting and as she turned away from him, she slanted one last lingering glance at him before accepting a glass of champagne. In that instant Bertie was lost.

The Fieldings *were* in the middle of a row. It was not their first disagreement but certainly their nastiest. The instant Mai broached the subject of a resumption of her role in the women's movement, she regretted not following her first instinct, which had been to test the water first by means of oblique reference. Depending on his response, if necessary she could have gone the route of winning her husband round to her point of view gradually rather than coming out straight out with a firm statement of intent. For Ned did not even pause to consider. Ned, once apparently so supportive, vetoed the whole idea and even attempted to forbid discussion.

Astounded, Mai pressed him.

"But why? I don't understand. . . ."

"You don't have to understand, Mai."

Her husband's face darkened in a way that was becoming all too familiar. What had happened to the man she thought she had married? It suddenly seemed to Mai that now the mating dance was over, Ned was revealing himself as a much more complicated man than she ever would have suspected and not complicated in a very nice way either. This confused her because at other times, often for weeks at a time, he was the old, relaxed Ned. But then a storm could blow up out of nothing with the result that Mai was learning to tread very carefully around her husband. They had been man and wife for six months.

Indignation, never very far below the surface, overtook her. With a tilt of the chin that Bertie would have recognised, Mai decided to make a stand.

"Ned, I may be married to you, but I should like to remind you I do not *belong* to you. So, if I wish to resume my activities in the women's suffrage movement, I shall do so!" Then softening, she added, "Oh, but darling, I would prefer to do so with your blessing. You must know that."

Unmollified, Ned ignored the last. "Oh, I see. So asking me for my opinion was merely a formality!"

Feeling misunderstood, Mai fired up all over again.

"Not at all! I had assumed that we would talk the matter over. I did not expect a flat refusal even to entertain the idea! Up to now you have given me no good reason why I should not do what I wish."

"Isn't it enough that you are my wife?"

"It *is* a wonderful thing that I am your wife..." Speaking the words Mai was conscious for the first time of no longer fully endorsing this sentiment. "... but, Ned, that should not preclude other interests. And duties. I regard helping the cause as my duty...."

"What about charitable work? Most women in your position regard *that* as their duty...."

"Horses and courses," riposted Mai smartly. "I am not by temperament a Lady Bountiful...."

"I am beginning to think that you are not by temperament a lady!"

"Oh!" Mai was seized by an almost overwhelming desire to slap her husband. Successfully resisting this caused an outpouring of hot tears instead. Humiliated and furious, she ran from the room. Upstairs in her little sitting room, she wept alone and waited for Ned to come and make his peace. He did not. It was to be a week before Ned spoke to Mai again. His days were spent behind the locked door of what she thought of as the Butterfly Room, his nights in a bedroom adjacent to his dressing room, and he did not join her for meals. Sitting by herself, served by the staff with silent sympathy, she supposed he must have ordered his food to be sent to him on trays.

And then, one morning, Ned arrived in the breakfast room at eight A.M. Mai flinched. As though nothing had happened, he sat down opposite her and began to read that day's copy of *The Times*. Still feeling too bruised to risk initiating anything herself, she waited for him to speak. Finally he folded the newspaper, put it down by the side of his plate, and went to help himself to food from the serving table.

"What can I get you, darling?" asked Ned. "Kedgeree?"

"Nothing, thank you," said Mai faintly, beginning to wonder if the last ghastly week had been a bad dream. She further wondered what was going to happen next. It turned out to be an apology. Of sorts. But not a capitulation.

"I shouldn't have spoken to you like that, Mai. I'm sorry." He put down his teacup, leant across the table and picked up her hand and kissed it. "Forgive me?"

Mai's first instinct was generosity and her second wariness.

Uncertainly, she said, "Yes, of course ..."

"And I'm sure that now you have had time to think things over ..." *Presumably he meant the week in Coventry.* "... you will have come round to my point of view."

"I'm still not sure what your point of view is, Ned."

Mai took her hand back. Her dignity was such that her husband lowered his eyes before her clear-eyed gaze.

"I would like you here, with me."

It struck Mai that this was rich coming as it did from someone who had spent the last seven days assiduously ignoring her.

Choosing her words carefully, she said, "And I would like to be here with you ..." *Though not as much as I once would have liked it.* "... but not all the time ..."

The brow clouded. With resignation she saw that she had upset him again.

"There are times, Mai, when I think that my love for you is greater than yours for me. ..."

Oh heavens, now we are competing about who loves whom more. Or at least Ned is. How has this come about? It's nothing to do with it.

"It is nothing to do with that and everything to do with individuality. But perhaps you could join me in this particular endeavour. Other women's husbands do. Mrs. Nuttall's, for instance. Then there would be no need for us to be apart. Ned, I have *no* desire to be parted from you, but I *do* wish to support the universal suffrage cause. Please try to understand."

Apparently he could not.

"Dearest, I would rather we did not speak of this matter again." Then with a further infuriating nod in the direction of good works, he said, "There surely must be something else you could do to pass your time. Other ladies seem to succeed in gainfully occupying themselves. And now I must go. Some new specimens arrived for me yesterday."

He went. Mai sat on in front of a cold cup of tea feeling mutinous. Togetherness, it seemed, meant Ned closeted in his butterfly mausoleum while she filled in her days on the other side of the door as best she could until he deigned to make himself available again.

That night in bed, Ned insisted on making love to his reluctant wife. As a consequence, for the first time Mai endured rather than enjoyed and, moreover, suspected that a man as intuitive as her husband probably knew it. It was in this spirit of disenchantment that, the following night, they attended the countess's dance for Princess Zhenia. For the first time since her marriage, as she watched Bertie waltzing his princess around the room, Mai was conscious of a treacherous pang of regret.

There was an uncomplicated kindness about Bertie and at the end of the day, once she had got him away from his managing mother he would probably have let her do whatever she wanted, including standing on soapboxes and shouting through megaphones.

Maybe, thought Mai, *I married the wrong man after all.*

PART THREE

Social Death

Chapter Eight

When the countess left Russia on the occasion of her marriage, she brought her maid, Tatiana Volkovska, with her to England. Tatiana, who had been born into a family of serfs, had been taken into the Fedorov household when a very young girl, taught to read and write and generally groomed for the position she still held. Though ignorant and, at the beginning anyway, ill educated, Tatiana was clever and learnt quickly. Very early on she realised that the key to remaining in the post she held was to become indispensable to her mistress and she had. Until Princess Zhenia arrived on the scene, that was. Like all such helpmeets, Tatiana was the curious hybrid which was both a servant and a friend. This meant that, as a confidante, especially after the countess was widowed, she was allowed to speak her mind but only up to a point. The name of this particular game was to know where plain speaking in the shape of loyalty and concern stopped and familiarity began.

Though in no sense a beauty, being big-boned and beak-nosed, Tatiana, who was some ten years younger than her mistress, had learnt to make the most of herself. Her main physical asset, namely her long, thick hair, once black, now iron grey, was drawn into a huge knot at the nape of her neck and there was an austere stylishness about her dress which lent her authority. In the household of the countess, Tatiana had made herself into the equivalent of the grand vizier and was treated with respect by the rest of the staff.

Now that the countess was almost blind, Tatiana, who apart from the odd creaking bone retained all her faculties, was protective of her employer. To date there had been two hiccups in the course of her domestic domination. The first had been the countess's marriage. The husband, unused to Russian ways, had disliked the close relationship between his wife and her maid and had said so with the result that tact decreed that Tatiana Volkovska fade into the background. But then he had died, leaving his widow bereft, and once again Tatiana had moved into the position of faithful companion. There had been discussions about whether to return to Petrograd, a course of action Tatiana, still homesick after all these years, had encouraged. In the end it had not happened and, in the light of what subsequently took place in Russia, it was probably a good thing it had not happened. Instead, unless the countess went out to some reception or other, the two of them would sit and reminisce. As the countess's eyesight began to worsen, she began to live more and more in the pictorial past.

"Those carriage drivers in the city with their blue, peasant coats! And the hats they wore with the buckles. The way they used to tuck their gloves in their belts when they weren't driving! Oh, it takes me back, Tatiana."

"Fur hats. Don't you remember? They had fur hats in winter," interjected the other, on cue.

"Yes, so they did!"

It takes some back more than others, reflected Tatiana, since although the countess may have found it all very picturesque, she had had her own transport and therefore had probably never travelled in the sort of vehicle she was describing.

"But those troika rides through the snow . . ."

Again, it was easy to remember such things with affection when the nearest you got to it was a short walk to a sleigh where the likes of Tatiana herself had wrapped you in sables to keep out the marrow-freezing cold. Never mind about troika rides, the pitiless Russian weather was not missed by Tatiana either. Before she had been selected for service, Tatiana recalled a barefoot childhood spent living mainly in one room with numerous siblings, her prematurely aged parents and the revered icon of the house which had stood in what they all called the *krasnyi ugolok*, the beautiful corner, together with its attendant votive light. Whatever happened to that? We had a wooden bathtub, remembered Tatiana. Luckily, because in summer there had been a yard strewn with manure and a plague of flies. The harsh winters had been another matter, each an icy purification, with snow as high as the walls of the house and when shoes, passed down from one to another, finally fell to pieces feet were wrapped in rags tied with string. *Which is why,* thought Tatiana Volkovska, *I would do anything to preserve life as I live it now.*

The countess was talking again and was tetchy.

"Tatiana, Tatiana, are you listening?"

Tatiana was also tetchy. "Yes, yes!"

"Do you recall the great fire of 1862? The one that ravaged Apraksine Dvor on the Fontanka Quay?"

Tatiana did. She nodded. This was a story which was endlessly repeated.

"What a blaze that was. And then Count Apraksine rebuilt the bazaar and put up the Church of the Resurrection. That was when Alexander was on the throne. He wasn't a patch on his father. Now Nicholas . . . *he* knew how to rule. Look at what he did to the Decembrists. Five hanged and over a hundred sent to Siberia. No more trouble after *that*, I can tell you. The Iron Tsar, they used to call him. Better than the last lot, though. They lost everything . . ."

Here Tatiana was silent. Living off the fat of the land (comparatively speaking) did not mean Tatiana had forgotten her own antecedents and early privations. Nor had she forgiven them but had only put them to one side in the interests of getting on with life. Endorsing the Iron Tsar and the iron heel which had ground down the likes of her own family was another matter. Mainly, though, the trips down Imperial Russia memory lane centred on palaces and balls and the Countess's heyday. The Winter Palace figured large.

"A triumph! Magnificent! Rastrelli, now he knew a thing or two. What an architect! He showed them how."

Then, blithely forgetting that although Tatiana as her maid had been on hand to help shoehorn her into her costly but uncomfortable gown and her equally uncomfortable satin slippers, she had not actually been at the ball, she said, "Didn't we have fun in those days, Tatiana? All those divine hussars . . ." On and on it went. Tatiana had heard this story so many times she almost felt she *had* been at the ball. It did seem a pity, though, that with all the divine hussars in the offing, the marital upshot had been a particularly dull Englishman. What she did remember was sitting up, night after night, intermittently dozing, until her mistress had finally come home at four A.M. at which point all the frippery had to be carefully undone and put away and hung up and so on and she, Tatiana, dropping with tiredness, had finally got to her bed at five thirty A.M. All the same, it had been infinitely preferable to the alternative.

With the husband out of the way, for quite a few years it looked as though life had finally sorted itself out. Her mistress had promised her devoted servant a generous allowance when she died and, meanwhile, Tatiana reigned over a substantial household as queen bee.

She had not, of course, bargained for the arrival of the princess. Well, who could have? For a while she hoped against hope that the mysterious newcomer was a bird of passage, or that, better still, the countess would see through her. None of this happened. Instead, after an initial probationary period during the course of which the countess quizzed the princess every day concerning their mutual relations and family history, she declared herself satisfied and the princess looked set to become a fixture in the house. This was bad enough, but on top of everything else, the newcomer treated Tatiana with disdain and was seen to do so by the rest of the staff. Worst of all, the countess was like a child with a new toy and could not have enough of her guest so that these days Tatiana found herself sitting alone in her room in the evenings instead of sharing tots of vodka laced with caviar and past memories.

Probably due in large part to her peasant roots, Tatiana relied a lot on instinct and instinct told her that despite her impeccable front, the princess was a fraud.

If she's a princess, I'm a duchess was Tatiana's view.

On the other hand, she recognised that instinct could have been contaminated by jealousy in this case. Whatever the truth of the matter, there was nothing for it but to wait and hope that the *soi-disant* princess slipped up. To date there was no sign of such a thing happening. On the contrary, the cuckoo in the nest also known as Zhenia appeared to be going from strength to strength with dances being given in her honour and heaven knew what else. Presently unaware of the countess's decision to make the cuckoo her heir, Tatiana *was* aware that there was a socially desirable suitor in the wings and hoped that marriage might at least get the interloper out of the house.

The day she overheard the countess telling Mrs. Langham about her will put an end to all that. Thunderstruck, Tatiana immediately saw the implications for herself. However much the princess promised she would, it was Tatiana's opinion that the princess would never honour the countess's undertaking to herself, not in a thousand years. Desperation overtook Tatiana. To have worked so hard for so long towards a cushioned old age and now, when the end was in sight, to face the prospect of being deprived of it was a bitter pill. So bitter that Tatiana crept away to her own room where she lay on the bed trembling with fear at the prospect of the bleak future which now lay before her and in a foreign country.

By the time morning came, the grit instilled by her hard, impoverished childhood had come to the fore. *Nobody* will take what I have striven for and *earned* away from *me. And certainly not an adventuress whom I suspect of being no better than she ought to be and, what's more, despite her airs and graces, no better than I am.*

The will was altered, the princess jubilant.

So far, so good.

Unaware that she was being spied upon by Tatiana Volkovska, with Olga's encouragement Zhenia continued getting to know Bertie Langham better. There were other suitors, but none who fitted the bill quite as well as Bertie did.

"Bertie Langham is used to being told what to do by women," shouted Olga, who was apparently getting deafer by the day. "Augusta has bossed him around all his life. If you marry him, no, *when* you marry him . . . Augusta wants it so it will happen . . . when you marry him, it will be the same for you, Zhenia. You will only have to snap your fingers. Moreover, he is the only son with money of his own and much more to come. And, of course, a country estate and a large house in London are not to be sniffed at! On the debit side, it is said that Bertie is not very clever. I see this more as a credit. You have brains enough for both of you and therefore can make your own rules."

Zhenia, who had worked out the form where Bertie was concerned almost immediately, reflected that if Olga had made this speech once, she had made it twenty times. On one level she regretted that she had so comprehensively squeezed out Tatiana Volkovska, for the old lady was insatiable where company was concerned and before Zhenia arrived presumably it had been the other who sat up with her ruminating about the Imperial Russia of yesteryear. Such was Olga's stamina that sometimes they were still in the drawing room at one A.M. All in all, the close proximity of her supposed elderly relation together with her hectoring manner was beginning to get on Zhenia's nerves. The solution to this was obvious. Never mind about Olga's hundred and one good reasons for marrying Bertie Langham, the biggest benefit would be to be in an establishment of her own and away from her benefactress.

Bertie and Augusta discussed where Bertie had got to in his courtship of the princess.

"I should get on with it, Bertie, if I was you," said Augusta.

"But what if she won't have me?"

"For heaven's sake! To coin a platitude, faint heart never won fair lady. Besides, she won't turn you down. Olga wants it, so it will happen!"

Bertie did get on with it and she did accept him.

The announcement of the engagement in *The Times* newspaper was read by Mai Fielding with more than a little ambivalence. Her own marriage seemed to have settled down for the moment, though the quarrel they had had over women's suffrage still rankled with Mai. Married life did have its ups and downs. Mai knew that and though they were devoted to each other, she had seen Jacob and Juno have the odd tiff. But what had happened with Ned she instinctively felt was different. It was as though there was a fault line in her husband's mental makeup. More than once Mai had considered defying Ned and pursuing her own ambitions without his approval. After all, what could he do to stop her, short of locking her in the bedroom? But of course it was not as simple as that, for Ned was capable of making her life at home a misery with a prolonged sulk. So unvaried day followed unvaried day and stubbornness stopped her entertaining the idea of charity work as a substitute. Although, thought Mai, if Ned had just supported me and let me do what I want, I could easily have fitted in both. As it is, he just wants me pinned to the board of this house, like one of his beastly butterflies.

Sudden diversion came in the shape of a suggestion from her mother over a family lunch.

"I'm going to London next week while Jacob's in Paris and I wondered whether you'd like to keep me company, Mai. Assuming Ned can spare you for a couple of days, that is. I'm sure you wouldn't mind, would you, Ned?"

In the light of what had gone before, Mai was sure of no such thing.

She waited for her husband to make a fuss. To her immense relief he did not, probably because her parents were there. Mai felt her heart lift at the prospect. Maybe, while she was in the capital, she would pay a visit to the WSPU office. Just to say hello to old comrades.

Juno was saying, "You see there is something special I intend to do while I'm there and I would like Mai's advice on the matter."

Jacob was immediately alerted. "Something special! What is it?"

"Aha!" said Juno, laughing. "It's a surprise! You'll see."

"Juno . . . !"

"What's the matter, darling? Don't you trust me?"

"No, not entirely," said Jacob. "Why can't you tell me what it is?"

"Because if I tell you everything, I'll become dull and predictable and you'll get bored and leave me!"

It was, of course, perfectly obvious from the indulgent look Jacob sent his wayward wife that he would never leave her.

Why can't my marriage have that sort of easy camaraderie?

Mai glanced across the table while this badinage was going on and could see that, despite his public endorsement of Juno's expedition, Ned was displeased. Intercepting her candid gaze, he sent her a loaded look together with a slight shake of the head. Mai decided to ignore this and parried it by pensively staring down at her plate. When she raised her eyes again, it was to say, "I can't wait! Ned, thank you so much for not minding!"

Ignorant at this stage of the strains inside what was, after all a young marriage, Juno said, "Why should Ned mind? We all need to get away from time to time. Jacob doesn't mind, do you, darling?"

"I don't know if I mind or not," said Jacob, "since, if you recall, I don't know what it is you're going to London for. In fact, like Ned, I'm deeply suspicious."

This last apparently jocular observation was greeted with general laughter.

Changing the subject, Juno said, "So when is the wedding of the year?"

"Oh, Bertie and the princess? Quite soon, I believe," answered Mai, without elaborating.

"No doubt ambitious Augusta will be relieved to have Bertie settled at last. Aristocracy, emeralds, Olga's money, all in the family. Plus, butter wouldn't melt! What more could she ask for?"

"*Butter wouldn't melt?* If we are talking about Princess Zhenia, I don't think so, Juno." The speaker was Jacob.

"What do you base that on?"

"My famous intuition. You wait and see!"

When the Fieldings had gone, Jacob said, "He is, you know."

"He is, you know, what?"

"Deeply suspicious. Ned is deeply suspicious. He does not want Mai to go to London with you."

"Then why didn't he say so?"

"Because," said Jacob, "there's a lot going on beneath the surface of that marriage."

"You keep saying things like that and I'm by no means certain you're right. Besides what harm could possibly come out of an innocent trip to London? I'm her mother. I'm hardly going to lead Mai astray, am I?"

Jacob laughed. "Jury's out on that one."

"All marriages take a while to settle down," resumed Juno. "In some cases it's *years* before they do. I think you're starting to rely far too much on what you call your famous intuition. According to you, nobody is what they seem."

"I will only say I followed it when I married you. If I had taken any heed of all the lurid drawing room gossip, I wouldn't even have considered it. I rest my case."

"All right. Ten out of ten for intuition, then."

"Darling Juno!"

They kissed.

"Darling Jacob!"

Tatiana Volkovska grew tired of waiting for Princess Zhenia to put a foot wrong and decided that more desperate measures were called for. Time was running out. What if the countess died tomorrow? It had to be said that the unswerving loyalty Tatiana had felt for her mistress had been sorely tried by her marginalisation after the advent of the princess. Put not your trust in countesses! By now it was early December. Squired by her fiancé, Mr. Langham, shortly to be her husband, and chaperoned by the countess, Princess Zhenia had gone to a formal dinner at Londonderry House. This was the moment.

After a safe interval, Tatiana mounted the stairs to the first floor and walked along the corridor almost to the end where Zhenia's bedroom was. Her feet made no sound on the Turkish runner. She tried the door, which opened easily and stepped inside, quietly closing it after her. She knew the room of old. Until the princess had come on the scene, it had been the principal guest bedroom (not that the countess ever had any guests) and had its own small bathroom and sitting room. It was very untidy. Shoes, scarves, dresses, even jewellery were strewn all over the bed and floor *Slut!* thought Tatiana. Presumably Zhenia's maid, currently in the kitchen having her supper, after helping her mistress into her finery, was due to come back later and tidy up. A cursory glance over the surface of the mess revealed nothing of a particularly personal nature, though since the cuckoo had turned up with nothing, this was hardly surprising. With no clear idea of what she was looking for, Tatiana decided to start her search in the sitting room secretaire. Against all the odds, this proved to be a disappointment. There was a small silver framed photograph of Bertie Langham relegated to the back of a drawer, a couple of old dance cards and that was it. The princess, it appeared, was not a sentimental person. The wardrobe, a fine walnut affair, and a chest on a chest, also walnut, both yielded nothing. Tatiana even searched under the bed, though without much hope, for it was more than the job of a maid in this house was worth not to pull out the bed for cleaning on a regular basis. In desperation she went back to the wardrobe, moving aside racks of dresses, courtesy of the countess's largesse, and still drew a blank.

Baffled, Tatiana stood in the centre of the bedroom and cast her mind back. When she had arrived on the doorstep, over the rest of her clothes, which were shabby, Zhenia had been wearing a majestic fur coat and, incongruously, together with a muff, had been carrying a fraying carpet bag.

Where was the carpet bag?

It was possible that such an item had been thrown out, but, if so, where were the contents? Most likely still in the bag and somewhere in this room. The feeling of proximity was so strong that Tatiana looked around the room yet again, but this time she raised her eyes to ceiling level. As she did so, the bedroom door quietly opened. It was Ellie, Zhenia's maid, who, once she realised that someone was in there and who the someone was, went out again and knocked timorously thereby announcing her presence.

In her absorption Tatiana had completely forgotten about Ellie.

"Come in, come in," commanded Tatiana. Then, seeing no need to explain away her presence to one as lowly in the household hierarchy as Ellie, she said, "I suppose you are here to clear up all this. . . ." She gestured at the mess left behind by the princess.

"Yes, Miss Volkovska."

Uncertain what to do next, Ellie waited.

"Well, it can wait for the moment. Come back later."

Dismissed, Ellie went.

Tatiana turned her attention back to the top of the wardrobe. This was a handsome piece of furniture, probably French, with an elaborate pediment of carved fruit and flowers. It was high enough up to be inaccessible except by means of a ladder and, from what Tatiana knew of servants, because of this probably had not been dusted for a decade. How to see if there was anything up there was the problem. She stared up at it and then remembered the laundry cupboard at the end of the passage which housed a set of steps which enabled the housemaid to reach the linen on the highest shelf. Tatiana went and got it. The ladder, which was made of wood, was heavy and it was with difficulty that she carried it then set it up and climbed it. At the top, the supervisory housekeeping habit of a lifetime asserted itself and before doing anything else she drew a finger across the polished wood. Ha! As she had expected, it was thick with dust. *We'll see about that tomorrow!*

Precariously balanced, she reached behind the pediment.

And found what she was looking for.

With difficulty she lifted the bag, which was surprisingly heavy, over the carving and got it down the steps. What to do next was the question. Tatiana decided to take the carpet bag away to examine it. This was probably less risky than it sounded since she doubted that, assuming it to be safely stowed out of sight, Zhenia hardly ever, if ever, climbed the ladder to check her property. And certainly would not do so tonight at the end of an onerous evening spent dancing and drinking champagne. Tatiana replaced the laundry room steps, made sure that everything was as she had left it, and then mounted the stairs to her own bedroom.

What she found astounded her.

The Fabergé eggs in particular were extraordinary. Tatiana knew they were because the countess possessed two of them, but neither was as impressive as this group. She burrowed further and found, among other items, including a caviar spoon, a triumvirate of cigarette cases, also clearly very valuable. To Tatiana's eye the disparate collection had more the look of swag than personal possessions. A further rummage revealed a pair of ballet shoes and a battered purse. Perplexed, she examined the shoes. They were not new, for though the pretty, trailing ribbons were in pristine condition, the soles were scuffed and the peach satin of the uppers was stained too. For the moment she put them to one side and examined the purse. It contained some French money and what looked like papers. Tatiana unfolded these and spread them out. They were printed in Cyrillic and bore the name Vera Kalanskaya. Under *Occupation* were entered the words: Dancer (Mariinskiy).

I've got her! Tatiana moistened her lips.

She picked up the little pumps again and, preparing to hold them up, attempted to slide a large square hand into each, at which point she received another surprise, for the toes appeared to be stuffed with some sort of paper, probably to stop them getting crushed. Or maybe the princess had used the ballet shoes to hide money. One by one she tapped the shoes on the surface of her dressing table so that the blocks were dislodged. What fell out was not money but something far more interesting. The paper plugs appeared to be covered in handwriting. With difficulty, she smoothed them out. Tatiana knew what Zhenia's hectic handwriting looked like. The fragments were all written in one tidy hand, which was not that of the princess. Avidly she began to piece them together and found herself reading the tattered remains of a history of the countess and her family. Names, dates, births, deaths, all were there, together with the residue of family anecdotes and eccentricities. More important, there were copious prompts and reminders, such as *Nobody but the family knows this* and *Make sure you mention this, it was the princess's pet name for her little dog,* and so on. Whoever had coached Zhenia had done a very thorough job and must, deduced Tatiana, have been part of the Dashkov household in Petrograd to know as much as she (or he) did. Which raised the question, who were they and, more interestingly, *where* were they now?

But never mind about that for the moment. She considered the treasure currently lying on the bed. It would have to be returned to the top of the walnut cupboard tonight. For if the princess did discover the removal of the carpet bag, she, Tatiana, could find herself accused of stealing. However, while the princess could make a legitimate fuss about the disappearance of Fabergé eggs and so on, Tatiana doubted she would wish to publicise the secret of the ballet shoes, or the contents of the purse. Accordingly, she put both these items aside along with the fragments and then wrapped up the eggs in the red shawl in which she had originally found them and put them back in the carpet bag, together with the other items. Then she descended the stairs to Zhenia's room. No drizzle of light seeped under the closed door, which indicated that Ellie had come, done her work, and gone. She edged it open. The bed had been turned down and the heaps of frivolous detritus all put away. Without further delay, Tatiana went back for the steps and then the bag. It was the work of a moment to put it back, after which she went back upstairs to savour the prospect of the next step.

Chapter Nine

Juno and Mai started their journey to Victoria at Lavant's half-timbered little country station. Because the London Brighton Railway stopped at numerous villages, the journey of sixty-five miles or so was a slow one and could take anything up to two and a half hours. Apart from another couple, they were the only ones standing beneath the ornate platform canopy. As they waited for the train to arrive, Juno found Mai preoccupied but, tactfully, decided not to mention it. For the moment, anyway.

Once on board, watching the frozen winter countryside pass, Mai pondered the course her life had taken. Except life hadn't taken this particular course, she had. *I was like a sleepwalker where marriage was concerned*, recognised Mai. *I did it without the slightest idea what I was getting myself into. I now see I never knew Ned at all. Why* did I do it? Realising that she had not spoken for at least twenty minutes, she became aware that Juno was looking at her quizzically. Mai collected herself.

"I'm so sorry. Am I being unsociable?"

"Yes, but it doesn't matter." Juno took a chance. "Marriages do take time to settle down, you know."

Without exactly rising to the bait, Mai said, "Yours and Father's never did settle down, though, did it?"

"We soldiered on for quite a few years."

"But even at the beginning it wasn't a union made in heaven, was it?"

Mai cast her mind back to her own wedding when she had been treated to a rare sighting of her affable but lackadaisical parent, who had been prevailed upon to turn up by Juno, more for the look of the thing than for any other reason. *I don't even call him Father,* thought Mai, *but Rollo. And Mother just treats him like a distant acquaintance, which on one level I suppose he is these days. Which goes for me as well.* She tried to remember when she had last seen him before that and decided that it must have been at a family funeral some two years earlier. Before that, when she was seventeen, eighteen, that sort of age, he had had a brief resurgence of interest and there had been an erratic spate of lunches, one notably at the Savoy. But then those had died away and regular communication the way everyone else knew it had died away as well. *Thank heaven for Jacob!*

"None of them are," Juno was saying, uncharacteristically brisk. "You show me someone who claims to have the perfect marriage and I'll show you an illusionist."

"Well, you and Jacob do."

"My dear girl, I adore your stepfather but there are still days when I could *kill* him."

Mai was silent.

"And if there wasn't a bumpy element," Juno resumed, "it would be a very soporific happening, wouldn't it? Seems to me we should be stimulating each other, not the opposite. What's the point of being bored for forty years?"

"But what if one partner is holding the other back?"

Well aware that Mai was into the personal now, Juno said, "Then the other must defend his or her position. Except as a last resort, I don't recommend doing a bolt and certainly not as an uninformed choice."

An uninformed choice. Good way of putting it. That's what I've made, thought Mai.

"Never forget I was a drawing room pariah and still would be if Jacob hadn't come along and socially rehabilitated me!"

"So you're saying settle for what you've got."

"No, I'm not saying that. I'm saying do your best with what you've got and work on it, but don't be a door mat. Be realistic. If it still doesn't work then radical action may be required."

Mai had never heard her mother talk like this before and had never, *ever* heard her use a word like *realistic*. Realism was the last thing she would have associated with Mother. Or radicalism, come to that.

"But be that as it might, Mai, you have a lot to offer and you shouldn't let anyone else stop you. And someone who really loved you wouldn't *want* to." Here Juno paused, beginning to feel fatigued by the dispensation of all this atypical sensible advice. "I think my last word on the subject is that sometimes a problem in a marriage is nothing to do with the marriage it-self but is caused by something *outside* the marriage. So bear that in mind, too. And now, let's talk about something else. Do you know you haven't asked me what I'm going to London *for?*"

Entering into the spirit of it, she asked, "All right, what are you going to London *for?*"

"To have my hair cut!"

"Well, that's not very remarkable. Couldn't you have had your hair cut in Chichester?"

"Not like this. You'll see!"

The morning after the Londonderry soirée saw Zhenia enjoying a late breakfast in her room while Ellie brushed her hair. Like a cat being stroked, she revelled in it.

Finally, she said, "That's enough, Ellie. Run my bath and when you've done that, you may take the tray away."

Ellie did as she was told then picked up the tray, after which she stood for a moment, irresolute.

Suddenly noticing she was still there, Zhenia said, "Well, what's the matter? Go along!"

"Miss, may I ask you something?" Here Ellie blushed scarlet. "Is Miss Volkovska satisfied with me? Only I shouldn't like to think that she wasn't."

Surprised, Zhenia said, "Why shouldn't she be? Besides, you work for me. It's a question of whether *I'm* satisfied with you, not Miss Volkovska."

"It's just that when I came back here last night to put everything away, I found her here and I thought she might be checking my work," stammered Ellie.

"You found her in *here!*" Zhenia's fine brows drew together and her eyes became slits. As always when excited or agitated the Russian accent, hardly there at all these days, became pronounced. Very sharply, she said, "What was she doing?"

Her mistress suddenly looked so furious that Ellie became flustered. "I'm sure I don't know, miss . . ."

With a sudden eruption of rage of which a large component was fear,

Zhenia pounced on Ellie and shook her. "Come on, you stupid girl! Think!" Pointed finger nails dug into Ellie's flesh.

Ellie, who had never seen Princess Zhenia like this before and was now in a panic, tried to marshal her thoughts and failed. "Really, miss, I *don't* know." Frantically she cast her mind back. Nothing significant came to the fore. "Like I say, she, Miss Volkovska I mean, was standing in the middle of the bedroom looking round. That's why I thought . . ."

"There is no need for you to think anything. As I say, you work for *me.* I am disappointed in you, Ellie. On no account, on *no* account, are you ever to let anyone into this room when I am not here! Do you understand?"

Filled with a burning sense of injustice and on the verge of tears, Ellie nodded without replying. Clearly she must have either said or done the wrong thing but was not quite sure what this was.

By this time the bath was close to overflowing.

"And now, Ellie, do as I request. First the bath and then the tray. After that, I shall not require you again for another hour."

"Yes, miss. I'm sorry, miss."

Red in the face and openly weeping, Ellie did as she was asked and then, clutching the tray with trembling hands so that all the crockery on it rattled, fled.

When she had gone, Zhenia, cursing, in her turn went and fetched the steps. At first glance everything on the top of the French armoire was as she had left it, including the carpet bag but then closer inspection revealed a smear which looked as if a finger had been drawn along the dusty walnut top. Not just content with burgling her room, the old bat had also used the opportunity to check the standard of the housework. Zhenia wrestled the bag down the steps and then returned these to their rightful place. Now the hiding place had been discovered, there was no longer any point in it. She would have to find another one. Or maybe there would be no need to find another one.

She undid the clasp and opened the bag.

All appeared to be in order. One by one she extracted the Fabergé eggs followed by the cigarette cases, the match case, and the caviar spoon, and then pulled out the red cashmere shawl in which they had all been wrapped as well. She looked into the dark well of the bag. There were her ballet shoes wrapped in their ribbons and there was her purse. The moment she picked the pumps up she saw that the toe blocks had gone. After that, when she checked the purse, the discovery that her papers had gone as well came as no surprise.

How I have underestimated Tatiana Volkovska!

Zhenia was in turmoil as she came to terms with this unexpected, covert raid. Which was of no use, for whatever she did next required a clear head and a plausible explanation for Olga. In an effort to gather her thoughts she walked across her small sitting room and stood, breathing deeply and staring out of the window which looked over Bruton Street. Slowly she began to calm down. It was obvious to Zhenia that Tatiana would have wasted no time in telling the countess what she had found. Explaining away *how* she had found it was another matter, though one which was likely to be eclipsed, at least for the time being, by the import of what she had to reveal. In the circumstances, an inquest on whether trusted senior servants should take it upon themselves, whatever the motive, to ransack their employers' relations' rooms was likely to take place later rather than sooner. That's if it ever took place at all. For try as she might, except by undermining Tatiana, Zhenia could think of no way of explaining away either the crib or her papers. One thing was very certain, however. If she did not come up with something and quickly, the glittering future of marriage to Bertie Langham and a passport to the top echelons of London society, combined with Olga's money, would evaporate and she, Zhenia, would be back out on the street instead. The idea of concealing one of her treasures, the caviar spoon perhaps, in Tatiana's room and proclaiming that a theft had taken place was entertained and then overtaken by events.

As Zhenia had known she would, Tatiana Volkovska *had* wasted no time. Downstairs in the countess's drawing room the interview which was about to destroy her was already taking place. The countess was sitting in an armchair which had been a favourite of her husband and now was her own preferred seat. In her old, liver-spotted hands were the incriminating evidence and the magnifying glass she used to help her failing eyesight. To Tatiana's eye her mistress looked shrunken, as though what she had just been told had diminished her both physically and mentally. In that instant it crossed Tatiana's mind that maybe, despite the seriousness of the fraud, she would have preferred not to know. As it was, an unexpected social Indian summer which had entered her life with the advent of the princess was about to revert back to social winter.

After reading them carefully for the second time, the countess put the papers on a small table which stood to the right of her chair.

"And you found these, how?"

Tatiana hesitated and then the honest habit of a lifetime asserted itself, and she said, "I am embarrassed to say I searched her room. Yesterday evening, when you were both out . . . Countess, forgive me, but I knew she was up to no good . . . I did it for you. . . ."

Her employer was not deceived by this.

No, you did it for you.

There was no need for Olga to say it. Unspoken, the words hung in the air between them. At that moment Tatiana realised that, whatever the upshot of all this was, her relationship with the countess would never be the same again. She bowed her head.

"It seems to me," the countess said finally, "that I have put my trust, as well I might, in those closest to me who, at the end of the day, will do anything to achieve their own hopes and desires. *Anything.*"

It was not, of course, as simple as that. They both knew it was not. All the same, Tatiana burned with shame as a result of her atypical action but, because she had served her mistress loyally and well for decades, also felt wrongly impugned and harshly judged.

"For now," resumed the countess, "you may go, Tatiana. We'll discuss your part in this sorry mess at a later date. Please be good enough to tell Princess Zhenia that I wish to see her immediately."

Tatiana was not above relishing passing on this command. She found Zhenia alone in her room.

"The countess would like to see you immediately in the drawing room," said Tatiana in Russian and then, unable to resist it, "Vera."

"I shall never be Vera again!" replied the other, also in Russian. "But you will always be a servant, Tatiana Volkovska!"

Russian was a very good language for invective and Tatiana did not see why she should put up with this. "And you, Vera, will always be a slut! And a whore, I have no doubt. Out on the street is where you belong and that's where you're going."

Apparently moving to pass her enemy who was standing to the left of the doorway, the princess achieved both her exit and a spiteful, stinging Russian slap on Tatiana's face as she passed.

"Take that!"

Ellie rounded the corner of the passage just in time to witness the whole thing and nearly fainted. Instinctively, like a film going into rewind, she shot backwards. Safely out of sight and unable to resist it, she peeped around the corner and was in time to see the princess, clearly in a temper, stride off down the corridor in the opposite direction, whither she was followed after a short interval and more slowly by Miss Volkovska.

Not for the first time that day Ellie wondered what on earth was going on.

Zhenia found the countess where Tatiana had left her.

"Come over here. No, *here*, where I can see you!"

Zhenia, who had decided to say nothing until she had established exactly how much the other two knew, silently complied. Eyes downcast, feet in the third ballet position, an old discipline which had proved hard to break, she stood in front of her benefactress.

"So! Zhenia . . . or is it Vera? I must say who ever coached you made a very good job of it. She, or he, must have lived in my niece's household to know so much. And been in a position of considerable trust to have had access to the emeralds and all the rest of it. Truly yours was a faultless performance. Yes, performance, that's the word! Perfect for a dancer. How the English all admired your dancing and your deportment! Well, there'll be no more dancing here!" This last was delivered with the furious energy of a steel trap snapping shut. "Here's what is going to happen. Firstly, I do not intend to inform the police. Unless I have to, that is. The scandal would be dreadful. You will break off your engagement to Bertie Langham, who must be getting used to it by now, and announce your intention to return to Petrograd. Or Paris if you prefer. Anywhere, so long as it is away from here. You will be out of this house as soon as it can be conveniently arranged and when you go you will leave behind you the jewellery, all of it. Where you go after that is of no concern to me. Lastly, I shall, in the light of all this, alter my will. I have instructed my solicitor to come here later this afternoon to do it. Now what do you have to say to that?"

Outwardly impassive, inwardly full of bile, Zhenia had nothing to say to that.

"Nothing," stated Olga. "I see. In that case I suggest you go to your room and begin to pack. On your way out, perhaps you would hand me my stick."

In order to do this, Zhenia had to pass behind her adversary. As she did so, on impulse she seized one of the many velvet cushions which were strewn about the room. After wrapping the tassels around her hands to give her leverage, with one swift movement she leant across the back of the chair and put the cushion over the old lady's face. Then she pulled it tight with all her strength.

Dancers are slender but muscular.

A combination of shock and the physical feebleness of old age made the countess a surprisingly easy victim. When the struggling ceased, Zhenia removed the cushion, plumped it up for all the world like a conscientious housewife and threw it back where she had got it from. Then she swiftly crossed the room, picked up the incriminating papers, and tossed them on the fire, which reduced them to ashes with a satisfying orange flare.

The countess sat on in the chair, slumped sideways as if asleep. The last thing Zhenia did before slipping out of the drawing room was to check the nonexistent pulse.

The death of the countess came as a shock to everyone.

"Heart failure," stated Augusta. "Poor Zhenia is too distraught even to see Bertie. How sad that Olga will not be there to see her married."

"I thought it was what you wanted!" said Henry from behind *The Times.*

"Well . . . yes and no," Augusta was forced to admit. "She was found by her maid, you know. That woman she brought with her from Petrograd. Tatiana. I expect there was much Russian wailing and gnashing of teeth."

"Do Russians wail and gnash their teeth?" enquired Henry mildly.

Ignoring what she regarded as a flippant remark and getting on to more practical matters, she said, "I suppose this means we must postpone the wedding."

Screened by the newspaper, Henry's face fell. For Henry, London was turning into his worst nightmare. No smoking room so no peace and no Daisy either. It was a time for quick thinking.

"I wonder if you're right. Rather than putting it off, maybe we should tackle the problem another way and have the wedding in the country rather than in London. You know, make it a quieter affair to show respect for

Olga's memory. I don't think Olga would have wanted to put it off, do you? As it is, getting Bertie married is turning into a life's work. Let's get it over and done with."

He held his breath and waited.

For different reasons, namely getting the countess's money and the emeralds into the family, Augusta was willing to go along with this.

"Yes, maybe you *are* right for once, Henry. And you are *quite* right about Olga. She was absolutely set on this match . . ."

Not like you, of course, thought Henry.

". . . and she *wouldn't* have wanted it put off. Now you mention it, I'm *certain* she wouldn't. Well, that's settled then. Will you tell Bertie what's going to happen, or shall I?"

"I think you should do it, my love. You usually do."

Zhenia decided to sack Tatiana Volkovska straightaway. However, courtesy of Tatiana herself, Zhenia had learnt a thing or two about servants since moving into the countess's house, the main one being that old, trusted retainers were capable of wreaking more havoc than she had previously realised. For however much she might have disapproved of Tatiana's actions, it had not, for instance, occurred to Olga to disbelieve her story. On that level she had trusted her maid more than she had trusted one she assumed to be her own relation. With this in mind and although it went against the grain, in the interests of keeping Tatiana quiet, she decided to honour Olga's promise of a pension. At first, just to get rid of her, Zhenia considered a lump sum and then discarded the idea. Once the money was paid in its entirety, Tatiana was a free agent. Where a pension was concerned Zhenia still retained leverage.

Once again the interview took place in Russian.

The offer was made and the conditions spelt out.

"You will not say one word of what happened in this house to anyone. The day you do, I will cut off the money." Inverted blackmail.

Out of pride, Tatiana, who was still grieving for her mistress, would have liked to be in a position to refuse it. Alas, this was out of the question. Anyway, rationalised Tatiana, the countess had wanted her to have it. She also guiltily felt that maybe her own behaviour had been a contributory factor to her mistress's death. When questioned about the cause of death, the doctor had simply spread his hands and said, "She was an old lady. All hearts give up eventually." Just the same, Tatiana could not rid herself of the idea that the countess's demise had been partly her fault. But only partly. The other one bore responsibility for it, too.

As she stood sullenly before the cuckoo, who had appropriated the countess's favourite armchair, it struck Tatiana that, at the end of the day, they had both got what they wanted. She had an income for life and the other would be rich as Croesus for the rest of her days.

But where shall I go?

The countess had been Tatiana's family, a conduit to her Russian origins which Tatiana missed immeasurably. *I could even bear to listen to that story about the Winter Palace ball and the hussars again without inwardly yawning.* Although she had been in London for years, without her mistress it all felt as foreign as the day she had first set foot on English soil. On every front, except, it unexpectedly transpired, the pecuniary one, Tatiana felt bereft.

"I wish you to leave this house as soon as possible," Zhenia/Vera was saying, meting out the same humiliating dismissal she had received from Olga. "Where you go is no concern of mine, though I shall, of course, need a bank address to lodge the money. Oh and *when* you go . . ." She gave the Russian blue which had just slipped into the room a look of disfavour. ". . . you can take Ivan with you."

Abruptly the princess got out of the chair and walked over to the fireplace, graveyard of the case against her. Her slight figure looked almost boyish in one of the new short-skirted, long-sleeved tunic dresses whose severity was leavened by a large diaphanous bow at the neck. High heels graced her small feet. The days of ballet shoes were gone. For the first time Tatiana noticed her tendency to stand in the third ballet position, a legacy of the Mariinskiy school, no doubt. Remarking on it caused her to remember the papers she had given the countess, evidence of the princess's perfidy. In the coruscating grief which had assailed her in the wake of the countess's death she had forgotten about them. Now she remembered and wondered what had become of them. Surely the countess would never voluntarily have given such things up to the interloper unless she had been in no position to hold on to them. Nevertheless, the fact remained that they appeared to have vanished.

Ah!

A flicker of suspicion stirred in Tatiana. And was quenched. Tatiana had great respect for doctors. The doctor had said heart failure and he should know. Just the same . . .

"If that is all you have to say to me, I shall go to my room. I have much to do," said Tatiana. She retained a sort of forlorn dignity which would have impressed anybody but the other woman.

"Yes, go and do that, Tatiana Volkovska."

Zhenia took a small case out of her bag and lit a cigarette. Tatiana had never seen her do such a thing before. She inhaled deeply. "Ironic, isn't it, that at the end of the day the one who is out on the street is you, not me?"

Tatiana flinched in the face of this gratuitous insult. *Unjust* might have been a better word than ironic but it did not alter the fact that Vera Kalanskaya was indubitably the winner.

Frightening thoughts crowded in.

As she says, out on the street . . .

Alone in a foreign country . . .

Who will take me in?

What shall I do?

Tatiana's suffering was acute. Hatred for her foe and despair compounded by a paralysing fear of the unknown struggled for ascendancy.

Where will I go?

Despite her embattlement, with a supreme effort she pulled herself together and rounded on the other with venom. "You *wait! You just wait!* Your time will come, Vera Kalanskaya. Retribution! Yes! *Certain!* If not in this world, then in the next. Evil does not go unpunished. The Holy Father sees to *that.*"

Or does He? Even to her ears it sounded like a hollow threat. For after all the Holy Father had stood by and had let it get to this. Still more unnerving, it had been Tatiana's depressing experience that, at least on this earth, evil often did appear to prosper.

A moue of distaste coupled with a dismissive shrug greeted her outburst. Evidently Zhenia/Vera had worked this out for herself. And in any case probably was of the opinion that such an interview with the Almighty was far enough off for the prospect to be discounted.

There was nothing left to say. Indeed there was nothing left. Without another word, inwardly crying but too proud to show it, Tatiana turned on her heel. Head held high, she left not just the room but life as she had known it for the last fifty years.

Chapter Ten

"*Bonjour,* Monsieur Boissonnet," cried Juno, very breezy. "*Je vondrais vous presenter à ma fille,* Madame Fielding."

"*Bonjour,* Madame Berensen." He bowed low over Juno's proffered hand and kissed it. "Madame Fielding." Another bow.

Monsieur Boissonnet snapped his fingers and an acolyte took their coats. His black hair and even blacker moustache were as shiny as the scissors in his belt. Mai hoped the whole haircut was not going to be conducted in torrents of effusive, fractured French. It was not. After the initial flurry of foreignness they settled back into English. By now Juno was installed in a large chair in front of a large mirror.

"*Eh, bien,* Madame Berensen. What can I do for you today?"

As he talked, with dextrous fingers, one by one he removed the pins in Juno's hair so that it slithered in a thick, lustrous rope down her back.

"I want you to cut it all off, Monsieur Boissonnet. I want a *garçonne!*"

Flamboyance drained out of Monsieur Boissonnet as if a balloon had been punctured. He paled.

"Does Madame's husband know about this? Forgive me, Madame Berensen, but there have been such scenes in this salon. The gentlemen do not like the new haircut."

"What *is* a *garçonne?*" asked Mai. "Is it a bob? Mother, are you sure this is a good idea?"

"You'll see," replied Juno. "And yes, I am sure. It's been far too long since I did anything outrageous." Then, turning her attention back to the nervous Monsieur Boissonnet, she said, "In that case I promise not to tell Mr. Berensen where you live. Now, can we please get on with it? If you won't do it, I'll just have to find somebody else who will."

Visibly shocked by this threat of defection, Monsieur Boissonnet flexed his scissors. Half an hour later most of Juno's hair was on the floor.

"Next we shampoo and then we finesse."

Mai was aghast.

"You're not going to cut any more off, are you?"

"Certainement!" By now Monsieur Boissonnet was no longer in a funk but in his element. Another flourish of the scissors. Snip, snip, on it went. By the end Juno looked as if she was wearing a sleek, feathery helmet. The transformation was complete. Against all her expectations, Mai was entranced.

"So, what do you think?" enquired the shorn one.

"You look wonderful! I'm going to ask Monsieur Boissonnet to cut my hair too," exclaimed impulsive Mai.

Afterwards the feeling of lightness was extraordinary and so was the feeling of independence. The symbolism of being a new woman did not escape Mai. The sleek, cropped hair balanced the shorter skirts and the two combined gave a totally modern look. *For the first time since the end of the war,* she thought, *I really feel as though I'm stepping into a new century and it's intoxicating!*

"Ravissante!" was Monsieur Boissonnet's comment.

At his insistence ("A memory of past glories for the gentlemen."), giggling and admiring their own reflections in the Bond Street shop windows, the two of them carried their redundant tresses home with them in bags. However, later that evening, as euphoria began to ebb, Mai asked, "What do you think Jacob will say?"

"What can he say? It's done now." Certain of her husband's affection and, therefore, his ultimate indulgence, Juno was complacent. "I've had this in mind for a long time! What about Ned?"

Yes, what about Ned.

The following day, while Juno paid a visit to a friend, Mai went to visit her old friend Beatrice Nuttall at the Women's Freedom League, one of the successors to the now defunct Women's Social and Political Union. As she went in she encountered a man she had never seen before, who lifted his hat as they passed.

Apart from Beatrice, the room was empty.

"Mai!" cried Beatrice, clearly delighted to see her. "I was beginning to think you had given us all up!"

"Not at all!" Mai decided not to elaborate. "It's just that marriage seems to have taken up more of my time than I had bargained for." Then, changing the subject, she went on, "By the way, who was the gentleman I passed on the way in?"

"Oh, you must mean Edward Soermus. He's a Russian and he used to be very in with Sylvia."

"A Russian!" said Mai, thinking of Princess Zhenia. "How romantic."

"Yes, he's a violinist and, my dear, if you can believe this, he's also a Russian agent!"

"A Russian agent? What's all that got to do with Sylvia?" Speaking the words, Mai thought, *I've been away for too long. I don't know what anybody's doing any more.*

"Sylvia supports the Bolsheviks. Anyway, the upshot was that Soermus advised her to open a Russian People's Information Bureau here in London and she did. So that's the connection. But never mind about him, let's go and have some lunch and I'll bring you up to date on everyone."

Sitting opposite Beatrice in the little local restaurant as she gossiped on, Mai was frankly envious. Beatrice, it seemed, had a fulfilling existence fuelled by a sense of purpose and she, Mai, no longer did. Not for the first time she tried to analyse what had happened to her since her marriage and could not. After all, she had seen off both the fearsome Augusta Langham and Bertie on the vexed subject of the suffragette movement, but when it came to Ned she felt paralysed. *It's as if he's put a pin through me,* thought Mai. She frowned down at her plate.

"Penny for them," said Beatrice. "What's the matter?"

Embattled by the inner conflict and tired of keeping it all to herself, Mai told her. The feeling of relief which came with telling Beatrice her problem was immeasurable.

The response was typically robust.

"You stick to your guns, Mai. Out of interest, what does Ned do with himself all day?"

The answer to this was very little.

"He's a butterfly fanatic. He spends hours and hours in his butterfly room sorting and pinning specimens. He's got hundreds of them. He was supposed to be writing a book about butterflies, but I never see him doing it."

Extraordinary, was Beatrice's reaction listening to this.

"What does he expect you to do all day?"

Mai shrugged. "Just be there and fit in the odd charitable work. I don't understand it. Before we married, Ned claimed to be supportive of women's suffrage. Now he isn't."

"That's one of the oldest tricks in the book. Saying one thing before marriage and another afterwards, I mean. And sulking for days on end is a form of bullying. Mai, if you let him get away with this now, a pattern will be set. You'll just have to educate Ned. Besides, we need all the helping hands we can get."

Mai was silent.

The prospect of weeks of freezing silence did not allure, but neither did the prospect of clocking around the house every day.

"He'll come round. If you think about it he'll have to. Come on, Mai, you used to be one of the militant ones. What's happened to you? Just tell Ned what you're going to do and do it!"

In response to this call to arms, the radical in Mai, crushed by a year of marriage, reasserted itself.

"I will!" said Mai.

In the event, as Monsieur Boissonnet had feared, it was the haircut which caused ructions rather than the campaign for universal women's suffrage and not just in the Fielding household either. Jacob made his displeasure plain.

"Juno, what *have* you done?"

Insouciance drained away in front of this stern enquiry and was replaced by bravado.

"Darling, it's the latest thing. I thought you'd love it!"

"You thought no such thing, otherwise you would have told me what you were going to do. And I would have said no. You didn't egg Mai on to do the same, did you?"

"Well, I . . ."

"You did! I feel like horsewhipping your coiffeur. . . ."

Outwardly contrite in the face of her husband's ire, Juno suppressed a smile. The idea of Jacob horsewhipping anyone was risible.

". . . Come on, what's his name? I'll go and see him. The man's a danger to the public. He shouldn't be allowed out with a pair of scissors! As it is he's scalped two of the prettiest women I know and, for all I'm aware, hundreds more!"

Juno, who had assumed the Monsieur Boissonnet was joking when he expressed fears for his own safety if he went ahead and did what she wanted, now perceived that he had, in fact, been in deadly earnest.

"On the other hand," Jacob resumed, "I can probably leave murdering him to Fielding and his cyanide bottle."

In a desperate attempt to bring the tirade to a halt, Juno said, "How was your trip to Paris, darling? Next time I'll come with you."

"Yes, you will. I'm certainly not leaving you on your own again. Anything might happen!"

On her arrival back from London, Mai paid off the taxi and stood in front of the house for a few moments mustering her courage before picking up her grip and going in.

"Where is Mr. Fielding, Cora?" she asked the housemaid.

"I think he's in with his insects, madam," replied Cora, who had never properly understood what it was her employer did all day.

Mai found herself reluctant to go to the Butterfly Room. She handed her coat and gloves to Cora.

"Could you please tell him that I'm back from London and that he'll find me in the drawing room."

"Yes, madam." Cora turned to go, hesitated, and then said shyly, "I hope you don't mind me saying so, madam, but your haircut's *lovely*."

Mai smiled at Cora.

"No, I don't mind at all. Thank you, Cora!"

The drawing room had an unused look about it as though Ned had hardly been in it since she left. The fire was made up but unlit and there were no flowers. Mai walked over to the window, where she stood looking out into the garden. In one corner of it was the remains of what had been a hard frost and each blade of grass was still traced in white. Probably it would freeze again tonight. Winter gardens were melancholy things, thought Mai, twisting her wedding ring round her finger. Her eye rested on a stone Artemis, goddess of the wild and the hunt, which Juno and Jacob had imported from Italy one year. Behind her voluptuous form skeletal trees massed and a fiery sun the colour of mountain ash berries was sinking, throwing long, black shadows down the lawn.

Mai turned away and, as she did so, Ned entered the room.

For one brief, uncomfortable beat they faced each other without speaking and then Mai walked towards her husband to greet him, arms outstretched. Ned did not move but stood stock still, staring at his wife with a look of fastidious disbelief. Disconcerted, Mai stopped in her tracks.

She became aware that he was addressing her in a furious voice, so low that she had difficulty in hearing what he said.

"How could you? You have made a laughingstock of yourself and of me!" Ned turned on his heel and left the drawing room. Mai stood where she was. He did not speak another word to her for four days.

If nothing else, this afforded an opportunity to take stock.

Whether he likes it or not, thought Mai, *it is imperative that I talk this out with Ned. We simply cannot go on like this. I just won't put up with it!*

This was all very fine, but it was impossible to have a constructive dialogue with someone who avoided her company to the point where, when she entered a room, he left it without a word. For Mai, the days of trying to keep the peace were well and truly over. Her husband's intransigent, no, *cruel,* behaviour had eroded her love for him to the point where she wondered if there *was* any point in trying to save her marriage. But, as Jacob had shrewdly understood, Mai was a curious combination of intelligence, defiance, and the sort of conventional upbringing which for the present anyway was successfully neutralising both the former qualities. Courtesy of the teachings of the church and her own mother's social ostracism after her bolt, Mai had grown up with the perception that marriage was a sacred thing and not lightly to be thrown away without severe reprisals.

Sitting by herself trying to make sense of what was happening to her, she suddenly remembered Juno's words. What was it Mother had said? *Sometimes, when there is a problem, you have to look outside the marriage for the cause . . .* or something like that. Mai decided to go and see Isabel Fielding at

Woodend. Of all Ned's sisters this was the one with whom she had most in common and since the days before her marriage, when she and Ned and Isabel had been in the habit of riding out together, the two of them had remained in spasmodic if not regular contact.

Isabel Fielding received her sister-in-law's unheralded visit with warmth and a degree of apprehension. At Mai's insistence, the two of them went for a walk in the garden which, like Mai's own, was glassy with frost. The cold was of the still, penetrating sort which stung the face and froze the bones and made it imperative to keep moving. Nevertheless, Mai preferred to be outside. To sit in a drawing room, albeit somebody else's, reminded her too much of the claustrophobia of her own house. The two ladies walked in silence as far as the end of the lawn, their shoes crunching on grass candied with hoarfrost and then passed through a wooden gate which led out of the garden and into the park. In front of them spread a small lake which was covered with thin shards of broken ice. In its centre was a miniature, overgrown island.

"Ned and I used to row out there when we were children," observed Isabel, more to break the silence than anything else. "What idyllic days those were."

Isabel, who was older than Ned, had never married. As with so many others, there had been a beau killed in the war. Maybe she never would marry. At one point Mai, who liked her sister-in-law, had thought this a shame but now was not so sure.

"It is about Ned that I wished to talk to you," said Mai.

Isabel, who had rather thought this might be the case, was cautious.

"There is nothing wrong, I hope?"

Mai felt disloyal and desperate in equal measure. Now was her chance to say no. She did not take it. Desperation won.

"Yes, I'm afraid there is. Isabel, if I tell you, you must give me your solemn promise that you will never speak to anybody else about this."

Isabel braced herself. "Of course."

Leaving out very little, Mai recounted the story of her marriage.

Isabel listened without comment until she got to the end, at which point she said, "And you say the first month or two was tranquil?"

"Yes. We were very happy. At least _I_ was."

There followed an awkward pause. Wondering what to do, Isabel stared into the middle distance. This was a moment she had dreaded.

I feel awful about this, she thought. *I told the family that we should have informed Mai about Ned's medical history but they all counselled against it and now it has come back to haunt us. The view taken was that she might not marry him if she knew.* Although, in this case anyway, it was true to say she had been on the side of the angels, she had not prevailed and Isabel felt as guilty as if she had been a willing participant in the conspiracy of silence. Now there was nothing for it but to tell Mai the truth.

"I'm so sorry about this, Mai. You should have been told. Perhaps they all thought Ned would tell you."

Mai stopped short and faced Isabel.

"Tell me what?"

By now they had circled both the lake and the problem and were on their way back to the house. Mai pulled her fur around her and was glad of her hat.

"When he was nineteen," said Isabel, "Ned had a bad fall from a horse and I mean a bad fall which resulted in a very serious head injury. After it he was unconscious and there was emergency surgery. The aim was to relieve pressure on the brain from bleeding. A trepan, I believe it was called. It was why he wasn't sent to the front. After it, Ned was never the same person again. How much of this was due to the accident and how much to the operation we shall never know. Of course it was all hushed up. Oh, it was generally known that my brother had taken a tumble out hunting, but then almost everyone did. What was kept very quiet was the extent of the damage. As I'm sure you are aware, mental illness carries an awful stigma. And, as I say, afterwards Ned was different. Though, that being said, I must admit that Ned was always uneven. Looking back, after Father died I suppose we all spoilt him. Anyway, the abrupt changes of mood became much worse and when crossed, he would become hostile and unpredictable, even violent. To begin with laudanum helped a little, but only a little. We took medical opinion, of course, and eventually Ned was prescribed bromide in order to calm him down when he became agitated.

"Then you came into the picture. There was a view in the family that marriage to someone as strong and *good* as you, who loved him, would be the very best thing for Ned."

But it hadn't ended there. Remembering venal family discussions about Mai's inheritance and how to secure it, Isabel burned with shame.

The very best thing for Ned! What about me? thought Mai. It raised the question of how disciplined her husband was with regard to his medication these days. The answer would seem to be not at all. Though presumably he had been in the early days of their marriage. *If I'd known I could have helped. Insisted that he took it. Why did nobody tell me?*

Mai felt betrayed.

No, *used.*

Used was a better word.

To Isabel's concerned eye all the lustre had faded from Mai. Her sister-in-law looked pinched with a pallor that rivalled the frosty landscape.

"Mai, I don't know what to say," Isabel said. "Except that I hope you can find it in your heart to forgive us." The words were inadequate but there were no others that she could think of. Uttering them, Isabel reflected bitterly that Mother should have been the one dealing with this rather than herself. By now they were at the house. She put a tentative hand on Mai's arm. Mai jumped as if she had been stung.

"I must go. What a fool you all must have thought me. Good-bye, Isabel."

When she arrived back at the East Dean house, Mai went to their, currently her, bedroom to try to compose herself before confronting her husband. She felt queasy and faint. The idea that all the Fieldings, including Ned, had lied by omission revolted her. *How could they have done it?* More to the point, *why* had they done it? Anger began to replace shock. Mai stared at herself in the dressing table looking glass. The light was beginning to go and her image in the darkened mirror had a wraithlike insubstantiality. Distractedly she ran her fingers through the new short hair. I have a life to lead, thought Mai, *and I'm going to lead it.* Regardless of what anyone else thinks about it. *This is do or die.* It was at that moment that she realised she was afraid of her husband. Notwithstanding a flutter of the heart, she mustered all her resolution and went in search of Ned.

He was in the Butterfly Room (where else?) and looked up in surprise when she entered without knocking.

"Oh." (Grimace.) "Mai. I'm afraid I'm busy at the moment. As you can see."

He was in the act of setting a large butterfly which Mai recognised as a purple emperor. While she stood there he plunged an entomological pin through the centre of its thorax. Beauty transfixed. One more for the collection. There was a dreadful sterility about the Butterfly Room which repelled her. *Everything in here is dead*, thought Mai, *and I might as well be if I let Ned go on calling all the shots.*

Ned showed no sign of desisting from his work.

"What I have to say is too important to wait," said Mai.

"Can't you talk while I go on with this?"

"No!"

"Very well." Reluctantly he put down the forceps he had just picked up.

"Moreover, I should prefer not to say what I have to in here at all."

Mai turned and left. Through the doorway, he saw her head towards the drawing room. Ned tidied up the work surface, put away the half-finished butterfly and then followed. Once they were both inside, she turned to face him.

"Yesterday I went to see Isabel," said Mai. "She told me."

Flushed out, Ned flew into a rage.

"You discussed our private affairs with my sister!"

Mai raised her voice.

"Not so private, for it transpired that what she told me was known to everyone but me. *Ned, I was desperate!*"

He turned abruptly away from her.

"I don't know what you're talking about!"

"Then let me tell you! I'm talking about the serious hunting accident after which you had brain surgery. *I'm your wife! Why didn't you tell me?*"

By now they were both shouting.

"BECAUSE IT IS HISTORY!"

"NO IT ISN'T! IT'S STILL GOING ON!"

Mai was flushed and breathing fast. She felt she might be about to faint. Better get a grip. Steadying herself with a hand on one corner of the mantelpiece, she lowered her voice.

"If you had told me, we could have worked around it. I might have helped you! As things stand, your refusal to acknowledge that you have a problem is wrecking our marriage." *Has already wrecked our marriage might have been a better way of putting it.*

"Since you raise the subject, it is my view that it is *your* attitude that is the problem and it is *that* that is wrecking our marriage!"

Mai threw up her hands. "Then there is no hope for us! Ned, you don't realise what you are like!"

"AND *YOU* DON'T REALISE WHAT *YOU* ARE LIKE!"

Ned struck Mai.

The following day came contrition and tears. Mai sat dully listening to it all and wondered how to explain away her bruised face. The memory of the butterfly he had been setting with its brown and purple sheen passed before her inner eye. Another riding fall, perhaps. She did not believe the entreaties and promises that it would never happen again. Kneeling at her feet, Ned took both her cold, inert hands in his and kissed them.

"Forgive me. *Oh darling, please forgive me!*"

Staring over his bowed head, listening to his protestations of undying love, Mai felt nothing but distaste. She wished he would leave her alone. The problem of what to do next was paramount.

Finally, expecting resistance, she said, "I need some time on my own."

To her surprise and relief, there was no resistance, only instant agreement. So long as she didn't leave him, he kept saying, she could have anything she wanted. The emotional storm was as wearing in its way as the chilly silences.

Standing up and disengaging herself as she did so, Mai said, "I'll go to London tomorrow. I'll stay in Jacob's flat. They're away at the moment. They won't mind."

She felt suddenly very, very weary.

Once in London Mai did two things. The first was to go and see Beatrice with a view to discovering what, if anything, she could do to help further the cause of universal women's suffrage.

"We could always do with another pair of hands," said Beatrice Nuttall. "But, Mai, what have you done to your face?"

"Riding fall. Horse stumbled. Stupid thing to do . . ."

"Riding's a dangerous sport."

"Yes, it is isn't it? Time I gave it up, perhaps . . ."

The second was to go and see Juno's doctor in Wimpole Street.

"I've not been feeling at all well," said Mai, prior to describing her symptoms. "It's a feeling of general malaise. I'm tired all the time."

"We'll do a test." He gave her a speculative glance. "May I ask what happened to your face, Mrs. Fielding?"

"Riding fall. Horse stumbled. Stupid thing to do . . ."

A few days later, she got the result.

Dear God! Pregnant!

Why hadn't it occurred to her?

"No more riding for the foreseeable, Mrs. Fielding," said the doctor.

"No, of course not," said Mai automatically. Panic overtook her.

Not just used now.

Trapped.

Chapter Eleven

Bertie and Zhenia married.

The wedding took place just before Christmas. Fittingly for a half Russian winter wedding, snow fell and inside the country church all froze. All except Zhenia, that was, who knew about weather. Zhenia wore a cream floor-length fitted embroidered coat whose hood was lined with mink and carried a matching muff, also lined with mink. Emeralds were eschewed in favour of Olga's diamonds artfully wound through hair which had not been cut. She had the dramatic, faintly medieval air of a refugee from the court of Ivan the Terrible and, with no member of her own family to give her away and much to Augusta's disapproval, insisted on making the journey from the church door to her fiancé's side in solitary splendour. "For after all," the princess pointed out, "there *is* no one to give me away." Those who watched her skim down the aisle were not to forget the sight. For Zhenia, formerly a humble member of the corps de ballet and never a principal and no hope of ever being one either, it was a satisfying moment.

Watching the ring, a family heirloom, being slipped onto the third finger of the princess's left hand, *Thank heavens for that,* was Henry Langham's view. *Now we can get back to normal.* Together with the London contingent, all the neighbours were in the congregation, including Harold and Daisy Mainwaring and the Fieldings and the Berensens.

"Another one storing up trouble for himself," murmured Jacob to Juno as the happy couple proceeded to the vestry to sign the register.

"Given your jaundiced view of marriage, it's a miracle the you ever made an honest woman out of me," responded his wife.

"What makes you think that made the slightest difference? It's my view that honest women are born, not made," said Jacob dryly. "For your information, Juno, my reservations are nothing to do with marriage per se and everything to do with the judgment of certain of those who choose to unite their fortunes. Bertie would have done better with Mai."

"That's what *we* all told *you* at the time," Juno pointed out, "but you wouldn't have it."

"Exactly because it just proves my point. Both of them were hell bent on marrying the wrong person, i.e., each other. Prevented by circumstance and Augusta from doing that, for all the wrong reasons I may say, they've gone ahead and succeeded in getting it maritally wrong anyway. You're not about to tell me that Mai is happy!"

Well, no . . . Juno, who was worried about her daughter, was silent. Mai had not confided in her mother but Juno intuited that there was something greatly amiss. For a start, the pregnancy. Mai should have been blooming and was not. It was almost as though she resented the child in her womb. Though, to be fair, Juno conceded to herself, *I was never very maternal either.* Ned, on the other hand, seemed delighted and could not do enough for Mai. Of course, *it's all right for men,* thought Juno. They don't have to go through the discomfort and then the pain of childbirth. After which life is never quite the same again. And an overly solicitous husband could irritate. In fact obviously did irritate. She had noticed Mai being quite terse with Ned.

In the front pew, Augusta Langham was also considering the next generation and finding it less than satisfactory. All attempts to become mistress of ceremonies and organise her son's wedding had been circumvented, though charmingly circumvented. The princess, it seemed, had her own ideas. Complaints to Bertie had fallen on deaf ears, too. In a way she could not quite define but was rendered uneasy by, Augusta felt edged out and these days was by no means sure that the dutiful one was quite what she had first appeared to be.

There was another hurdle, too. Zhenia wanted a Russian orthodox ceremony as well as the one they were currently attending. She, Augusta, had had her work cut out putting obstacles in the way of this particular whim.

Finally, "Olga would have wanted it" was the reason given. In point of fact *Olga would have wanted it* had become the key to getting through all sorts of unsuitable ideas, the barbaric wedding dress being one. It had got to the point, Augusta crossly reflected, that Olga dead was doing more interfering than Olga alive. Here she conveniently looked away from the fact that the wedding had gone ahead instead of being cancelled owing to the repetition of the very same mantra.

Within the peaceful confines of the smoking room the men talked over the tensions manifesting themselves between the women.

"Just let them fight it out, old boy," Henry counselled Bertie. "No need for you to get involved. Zhenia is perfectly capable of dealing with your mother. No doubt about that. Another cigar?"

This felt like the easy way out and, characteristically, Bertie took it.

Because Christmas followed hard on the heels of the wedding, it was decided to delay the honeymoon until afterwards. In bed with his wife for the first time on their wedding night, Bertie, who knew a thing or two about sex courtesy of copious assignations with married ladies of easy virtue, not to mention encounters with ladies of the night, was amazed by his bride's sheer voracity. Lucky, some might have said and while there was no doubt that Bertie enjoyed himself, at the same time it was hard to ignore the fact that there appeared to be very little that was virginal about Zhenia. Or modest. It was a small thing, but most women in his experience, for instance, closed their eyes while being kissed, but she did not and Bertie found it both arousing and disturbing as her strange, light eyes fluttered open and stared into his. Despite her refined pedigree and gentle upbringing, her athleticism reminded him of nothing so much as a wild creature. Bertie gave up trying to work his wife out. Maybe they did things differently in Russia.

Once the wedding was over and Zhenia was no longer the centre of attention, Augusta relaxed back into being mistress of all she surveyed and having the last word. A small house in the grounds was being prepared for the newlyweds, within the confines of which her daughter-in-law could have the last word, but that was it. Here, in her own domain, signs of an independent spirit would not be tolerated and as a result of this return to the status quo, certain markers were put down. Cognisant that this was now a waiting game, on the whole Zhenia toed the line and concentrated on getting her own establishment up to snuff as soon as she could. One day it would *all* be hers. In the event it turned out to be a shorter wait than any of them anticipated.

The honeymoon came and went. By now it was March. Wild daffodils flowered all over the park and the house in the grounds was almost ready. Bertie, who was anxious to get away from his mother's dictates, calculated that one more week should do it.

One particularly clement spring morning, knowing that Harold was in London on business, Henry Langham decided to walk over to Daisy Mainwaring's house. It was a breezy, fresh day of blue skies and blossom and as Henry made his way along, he congratulated himself on his good fortune. Bertie was safely married to the delectable Zhenia, he had Augusta, the perfect chatelaine for a house the size of his, and although the physical side of their marriage was now for all intents and purposes nonexistent and had never been all that hot from the word go, he also had Daisy, the perfect mistress. *Actually, I have it all,* thought Henry. *What more could any man want?* As he strode along with his dog, he twirled his silver knobbed cane and hummed.

The Mainwarings lived beyond West Stoke and the walk was a longish one. Daisy's house was surrounded by woods and was situated where the plain met the Downs, which rose steeply behind it. Though it was by no means as grand as The Hall it was charming, being a long, low, pebble-dashed affair with rosily tiled, mossy roof, and it harmonised with its surroundings so felicitously that it might have grown out of them. By the time he got close enough to see the sunlight glancing off the chimneys, Henry was breathless and had a stitch. It must be *anno domini* catching up on him. Perhaps he had better cut down on the whisky. Never mind, it was downhill all the way from here on. All the same, he decided to take a short break before making the last push and sat on a milestone, with his dog beside him, for fifteen minutes or so before proceeding.

On his arrival, Daisy's parlour maid, Clarice, showed him into the drawing room and before too long Daisy herself appeared. Daisy was how he liked them, which made his marriage to Augusta all the more mysterious when he thought about it, which was hardly ever these days. She was tall and generously proportioned with large breasts and long legs. The new flat-chested boyish look was not for Henry, who liked his woman to be a generous armful and lamented the passing of the Edwardian era of the hourglass figure. But best of all, Daisy made him laugh. There was none of Augusta's drive extant in Daisy but an engaging, easygoing indolence which was both relaxing and endearing. As a wife she was probably a nightmare, Henry recognised, but when the household arrangements broke down, it wasn't his problem, thank God, it was Harold's. In his own establishment the sort of crises which attended Daisy on a regular basis happened very seldom and when they did constituted a hanging offence. In this way Augusta kept her staff on their toes.

"Drink, darling?"

Henry consulted his watch. Midday.

"Yes, why not . . ."

Pouring it for him, Daisy was saying, "Darling, you'll *never* guess what happened yesterday," the usual prelude to another story of domestic chaos. As he watched her fixing herself a gin and it, still chattering as she did it, he was conscious of a surge of affection for her. When she had finished, they touched glasses.

"When does Harold get back?"

"Not till Wednesday."

Henry put down his glass and kissed her wide mouth. Daisy smelt of violets.

"Shall we go up?"

"Why don't you go ahead. I'll tell Clarice that if anyone calls I'm not to be disturbed."

Clarice received this message without surprise. There had been a lot of below stairs tittle tattle concerning the fact that Mr. Langham was a very regular visitor when Mr. Mainwaring was away.

Upstairs in Daisy's pretty bedroom, Henry had shed his tweed jacket and was removing his cufflinks. He still wasn't feeling quite himself and the whisky stood untouched on her dressing table. No doubt the arrival of Daisy would solve all that. For a while it did. His mistress swept in wearing a floor-length robe. This concealed, though not for long, an underbodice, the better to display her glorious breasts to Henry when he got that far, and a wasp-waisted corset whose severe lacing emphasised generous hips and endless tapering legs. The new cami knickers were not for Daisy and certainly would not have been endorsed by her lover. *I'm never going to be flat as a board*, reasoned Daisy, considering the matter of the new fashions and the new underpinnings, *so why even try?*

Henry slipped off the robe and kissed each rosy nipple. Then he took the pins out of his mistress's blonde hair one by one, a ritual they both enjoyed, until, like a ship going down, it slowly descended to her shoulders before tumbling in a rush to her waist. Thank heavens Daisy, unlike the unconventional Juno Berensen, hadn't gone for one of those hideous boyish short cuts. Rolling down her stockings was another particular pleasure. As he turned his attention to the corset, Daisy in her turn began to undress Henry. Once they were in the bed she pulled the curtains of the four poster and within its cloistered haven the two of them began properly to enjoy each other. Finally Henry entered Daisy.

"Mmmm!" murmured Daisy. "Bliss!"

Henry groaned and then sighed.

Without warning all activity ceased. The thrusting, ardent lover became a dead weight. Pinned beneath Henry's inert body and wondering what had happened, Daisy called his name and received no answer. Maybe he had fainted. With a heroic effort she managed to roll him sideways. Henry lay as if asleep. Frantically Daisy slapped his face and chafed his hands. No response and never likely to be. Henry, she realised with horror, was dead.

To say Daisy panicked would be an understatement. Accident-prone domestic arrangements were one thing but this catastrophe was in a different league altogether. She leapt out of bed and stood trembling and naked, wondering what to do.

What would Harold have done? A helpful inner eye vision of Harold, always on hand to pick up the pieces, presented itself.

Get dressed, Daisy! insisted the inner voice which went with it. *And when you've done that, get Henry dressed!*

Tearfully, Daisy did it, though getting Henry back in his clothes proved difficult for Henry dead was very heavy.

Now make the bed!

Make the bed? Daisy, who had never had to do such a thing or do anything very much for herself at all, looked at the bed dubiously.

The voice was patient.

Roll Henry off it first, then make the bed.

The thud as Henry's body hit the Persian carpet upset Daisy more than anything else. She drew back the curtains and made the bed. It did not look as tidy as when her maid Milly did it, but at least the suggestive quality of tumbled sheets had gone. Now what? The presence of Henry, even fully dressed Henry, on her bedroom floor remained compromising.

Now bribe Milly!

Yes! Bribe Milly. Daisy rang for her maid.

She met Milly at the door.

Voice quavering, trying in vain to sound in command of the situation, "Milly, it's Mr. Langham! He's dead!"

Milly, who was not aware that Mr. Langham was in the house, was fazed by this information and uncertain how it pertained to her.

"Oh madam, how sad. When did it happen?"

"Just now." Daisy felt on the point of collapse. "Look!"

She stepped aside. Milly stared, transfixed.

"Milly, we need to get Mr. Langham out of here. . . ."

Collecting herself, Milly rose to the occasion. Well-trained obedience triumphed over stupefaction. "Yes of course, madam. Should we put him in the drawing room?"

Another scene rose before Daisy's mind's eye, that of the two of them struggling Henry down the main staircase in full view of the servants, and was rejected.

"No. Let's put him in Mr. Mainwaring's study. I'll take the feet, you take the shoulders." Milly, a strong young country girl, complied. Together, with difficulty, they heaved Henry along the passage and into Harold's study where they sat him on a chair which was reserved for visitors. Panting, Milly waited for her employer's next instruction.

"I want you to know I shall make this worth your while, Milly. In the meantime I wish you to speak to no one about this matter. No one! Do you understand? Where we first found Mr. Langham must remain our secret!"

New in her job and still under probation, Milly nodded.

"And, Milly, you have done *very* well. So well, that I should like to confirm you in your post as from today and there will be a substantial increase in your wages. I think we understand each other, don't we, Milly?"

"Yes, madam. Thank you, madam."

"Now you may go."

Alone again, Daisy sat down in Harold's chair on the other side of the desk, buried her head in her arms and wept for Henry. Eventually, when she had recovered her composure, she lifted the telephone receiver off its hook and telephoned the doctor.

"This is Mrs. Mainwaring speaking. I'm afraid there has been an accident. . . ."

Next, she rang The Hall.

With much clearing of the throat an old retainery voice took the call. Stiggins, probably.

"Mrs. Mainwaring speaking. I should like to speak to Mrs. Langham, please. Not in? Then perhaps you could fetch Mr. Bertie Langham instead . . ."

The third call was to her husband at his London club.

"Daisy speaking, Harold. Harold, you'll never guess . . ." Here Harold rolled his eyes. ". . . Something *awful* has happened . . ."

"Good Lord," said Jacob Berensen, folding his newspaper to get a closer look at the obituaries. "Henry Langham's gone!"

"Gone?" said Juno blankly, helping herself to another cup of tea. "Gone where?"

"Nowhere on this earth, darling. He's dead!"

Juno was visibly shaken. "But he's no age at all!" Uncomfortable intimations of mortality surfaced. "What was it?"

"Heart failure, according to this."

Instinctively generous, Juno said, "Poor Augusta and *poor* Bertie! I must write."

"This will be a terrible blow for Augusta."

"Yes, of course it will. How long have they been married?"

"I wasn't really thinking of that. I was thinking of the house. Augusta married a house. With Henry's demise, the house goes, too."

"Well, yes, but I'm sure Bertie will give her time to get over her bereavement before insisting on his inheritance."

"Maybe Bertie will, but I doubt Princess Zhenia will display any such scruples when it comes to Bertie's inheritance. You watch."

PART FOUR

Trouble and Strife
in the Country

Chapter Twelve

Augusta felt badly let down by Henry. As a result of his premature promotion to a higher plane, for once in her life she felt both vulnerable and at a loss. Vulnerable because she found herself at the mercy of a young woman who was not at all what she had first supposed. At a loss because after a decent interval she would now be expected to vacate The Hall and remove herself to the little house in the grounds formerly designated for Bertie and his uncooperative bride. Because in such circumstances that was what always happened, whereas she might succeed in putting things off, ultimately there could be no appeal. Where Zhenia was concerned, Augusta found herself in the position of those who, having learnt nothing from history, had carried on trying to conquer Russia. To put it mildly, it was galling to have made the same mistake twice and in the same connection.

Augusta's realistic assessment of her future proved prescient. Almost before the funeral was over, Zhenia began to pressure Bertie. *Actually,* thought Bertie, nag *would have been a better description.* Hitherto he never would have used such a word in connection with a princess. In Bertie's head the two simply did not go together. Working class women nagged, ladies (unless they were Mother) voiced their displeasure once and then subsided. Now he knew better.

Finally he attempted to put his foot down.

"Of course Mother will move out in the fullness of time," said Bertie. "She knows she has to. That is how houses the size of this work."

Zhenia was relentless. "When?"

"When I say so," smartly replied Bertie, sounding testy and surprising himself. "And I don't want to hear another word on the subject, Zhenia, for at least twenty-four hours."

For his own part Bertie missed the companionable smoking and drinking sessions shared with his father. There had been the pleasurable and informative country hikes too, used by Henry as an irreproachable method of getting away from his managing wife for a few hours. A favourite of the two of them had been the climb up Kingley Vale, through the viridian gloss of the yew forest to the mysterious tumuli, the culmination of which was a spectacular view across the Lavant valley. During such treks, Henry had passed on his own appreciation and knowledge of the countryside to the point where there was very little Bertie did not know about the flora and fauna which surrounded him. The wild orchids were a particular passion. Early spider, bee, lizard, fragrant, musk, man and lady, right down to the tiny, elusive frog, he was able to recognise them all. Brought up to understand bucolic pursuits together with their timeless rhythms and their seasons, Bertie relished the rural way of life and, unlike the restless Zhenia, could take or leave the more sophisticated delights of the city. Because of the sheer size of the acreage and despite the diligent endeavours of an efficient land agent who had been there during his father's incumbency and knew the drill, there was still a great deal to do. Unlike some in his position, Bertie saw this as his *raison d'être*. For him the work of running his huge estate and overseeing its farms was also his hobby and, as such, was a pleasure, not a chore.

Now, after the death of his father, there was nothing to come between him and two sparring women and, as had been the case with Henry, walking became both Bertie's refuge and his solace. It did not escape him that, having been forced to take a back seat while Zhenia was centre of attention as the Bride, Mother was now back in the saddle as the Widow. Attempts to speak to her about the future were met with reproachful looks and martyred silence. Eyes were dabbed with the sort of minuscule lace handkerchiefs he had never seen her use before. But then she had never been widowed before. Old friends, in so far as Mother had old friends, neighbours, and acquaintances all came to pay their respects and were mournfully entertained to tea and biscuits. For many of these visitors, the death of genial, clubbable Henry Langham in the prime of his pampered life had come as a salutary shock. Among these were the Berensens and the Mainwarings. The situation in which Augusta found herself would never happen to Juno because there was no son to inherit and anyway on that level, though it was a grand house it was not a one-family house of the sort which is handed down from generation to generation.

By the time May came, Zhenia decided enough was enough and *faute de* Bertie doing anything about the situation, tackled Augusta herself. On this occasion Augusta dispensed with the little lace handkerchiefs (useful with Bertie but a waste of time where her daughter-in-law was concerned) and prepared to stand her ground.

After an initial skirmish, the princess remarked, "You'll have to go in the end, Augusta."

"I am well aware of that but do not see why I should be hounded out of the house I have lived in for thirty-five years just because you happen to be in a hurry, Zhenia."

"Bertie should have his inheritance."

"You mean *you* should have Bertie's inheritance!"

"Let us put it this way," said Zhenia, "when Bertie's son is born, I should like it to be in this house with me as mistress of it. But before then I should like to arrange things to my own convenience."

"*Are* you *inceinte?*"

A half nod and a modest, downcast smile of the misleading sort her mother-in-law should by now have recognised were the answers to this.

Taking in the fact that Zhenia still looked as thin as a pin, Augusta was suspicious. "Does Bertie know that you are expecting? If so, he has said nothing to me!"

"It is my intention to tell him tonight," said Zhenia. "I think it will concentrate his thoughts on the future...."

Augusta thought it would too. Trumped! Though in the best possible way, it had to be said. In the light of this news, competitiveness ebbed. Making way for an heir was much more palatable than making way for her daughter-in-law.

"I should, however, prefer it if you did not refer to the matter until I have had a chance to tell Bertie...."

"Of course." Augusta was gracious, for what alternative did she have? In the light of what she had just been told it also made sense to leave gracefully rather than waiting to be pushed. She decided to broach the subject of her departure to the little house in the park that evening over dinner.

That night, when Bertie and Zhenia were in bed, Bertie said, "I was amazed when Mother said she proposed to leave this house of her own accord. I was frankly dreading having to dislodge her. Do you have any idea what changed her mind?"

"No, no idea at all," answered Zhenia.

Bertie pursued it. "But that wasn't all. I couldn't get away from the idea that she was *waiting* for something. There was a sort of air of *expectancy* if you know what I mean . . ."

It was an unconsciously apposite phrase.

"No, I can't say I did notice that," replied his wife, laughing to herself as she closed her book. "What could it have been, I wonder?" She gave her husband a chaste kiss and then turned off her bedside light. "Well, we shall probably never know. And now, my love, I am tired. Good night, Bertie."

As Zhenia would have done well to remember after her dealings with Tatiana Volkovska, when one thinks one is dictating terms life has a way of redressing the balance. So it was that, having feigned pregnancy to get her hands on The Hall and Augusta out of it, she discovered that she actually was pregnant. While the timing was not exactly what she would have wished, Zhenia recognised that sooner or later she was going to have to produce an heir and it might as well be sooner as later. Afterwards, whatever might come to light (and there was no reason why anything should), at that point her position would be virtually unassailable.

There are those who enjoy pregnancy and those who do not. Zhenia, an active young woman who resented her expanding waistline and the restrictions placed on her normal lifestyle by an anxious and solicitous Bertie, was firmly in the latter camp. *Holy Father, make sure it's a boy*, was the latest self-seeking prayer, *otherwise I will have to go through this again. And again. And maybe again until I produce one.* It did not bear thinking about.

By now in the smaller but still substantial Dower House, Augusta enjoyed observing the corralling of her daughter-in-law. All in all, given Zhenia's filthy mood, it was probably as well to be at one remove although custom dictated that she always had Sunday lunch at the Hall with her son and daughter-in-law. At this point it was possible to employ the afternoon which followed this regular event spreading alarm and despondency before withdrawing to her own camp.

In the early months, Zhenia was sick.

"It is probably a girl," said Augusta, very authoritative. "That is what happens with girls. *I* know!"

"*How* do you know?" enquired Zhenia of her tormentor. "You only had Bertie!"

"Ah, yes, but I had a friend, Laetitia Tattershall . . . do you know Laetitia? No? Well, never mind. *Poor* Laetitia had *four* daughters. Four! All this before she produced the desired heir. And she was *crucified* with morning sickness, *crucified!* But there was nothing for it but to go on . . ."

And on and on and on and on . . . thought Zhenia sourly, listening to this recurring nightmare.

"But when she was pregnant for the fifth time, with a son as it turned out, she wasn't sick *but*, to make sure she didn't lose it, she had to lie on a sofa for nine months."

At this point Bertie came to life.

"Oh yes, I remember Laetitia Tattershall. And all those horsy girls. I went to school with the son. Mrs. Tattershall was an absolute brick. What happened to her?"

"Her husband left her and took the children with him!"

Appalled silence fell in the face of this announcement.

"But why? After all she'd done for him, too," said Bertie.

"That's as may be, but he said she was no fun any more," stated Augusta.

No, I shouldn't think she was at the end of six years of pregnancy, was Zhenia's curdled reaction to this.

"Anyway that was that. And then I had another friend, Violet Makepeace. She kept losing babies and was castigated as Very Careless Violet by her husband. Eventually she did succeed in holding on to one and luckily it was a boy. Needless to say, he wanted her to go on trying for a spare but it never happened."

Listening to this, she thought, *A spare? Not if I have anything to do with it!* Aloud, Zhenia said, "I can't see the necessity. After all, you only had Bertie."

"Yes, but let us suppose Bertie had been killed in the war. What then?"

"Well, he wasn't." Zhenia was snappy and inclined to blame her husband for her current discomfort.

Bertie, whose forte had never been timing, picked this moment to say,

"I should like to have a large brood. At least six. What do you think, my love?"

"I think I'm feeling faint," said Zhenia, getting to her feet and preparing to leave the room. "Will you excuse me?"

In the Fielding household things were not much better. Ahead of Zhenia in terms of her pregnancy, Mai looked like a ship in full sail. The burgeoning wastline did not bother Mai but what happened after the birth occupied her thoughts all the time. Her relationship with Ned had settled into polite distance. Or, rather, armed truce. *I'm armed with the fact that I'm about to bear his children and he's armed with the fact that, whether I like it or not, he's my husband.* By now she knew she was carrying twins. In the wake of their last disastrous row, Mai had indicated to Ned that she did not want him in her bed and he appeared to have accepted this, at least for the time being. Which was a relief though not a state of affairs which could be expected to go on forever.

Depression engulfed Mai on a daily basis and more than once she considered cutting her losses and simply going home to her parents. But even Juno had not done that. Juno had struck out on her own. Mai was a proud and stubborn woman and, at the end of the day, pride vetoed this craven course of action and stubbornness dictated that to give up on her marriage at this comparatively early stage did not do either. So the days passed, each one exactly like the one before it to the point where Mai thought she might go mad with boredom. It also irked that Ned, on the other hand, simply went on with his life much as he had before, spending large amounts of time sequestered in the Butterfly Room happily pursuing his passion with an oblivious singlemindedness that Mai found infuriating. *It's all right for Ned,* thought Mai resentfully, *he does exactly what he likes each and every day and meanwhile he's got me exactly where he always wanted me. At home and at his beck and call.*

Though *at home* proved to have its advantages. The day Princess Zhenia, Mrs. Bertie Langham, paid her an unexpected visit marked a change. Zhenia, it transpired, was almost as fed up as Mai, but for different reasons. Once she got over her surprise at the unheralded visit, against expectations Mai began to enjoy herself. It was quite simply bliss to talk to someone who was in the same boat, more or less, as herself, besides which Zhenia was indiscreet. Very indiscreet.

"Bertie wants six children!" confided the princess, rolling her eyes to heaven. "Can you believe it? I hope," here she indicated a small, enviably compact bump, "that this is a boy. Because if it is, afterwards I stop!"

"Doesn't Bertie have a say in the matter?" Despite a certain wariness concerning Zhenia whom she felt she hardly knew and did not entirely trust, Mai couldn't resist joining in.

"Why should Bertie have a say in the matter?" Zhenia was tart. "Bertie doesn't suffer from the morning sickness and he doesn't have to listen to his mother on the subject of maternal duty either!"

No. Mai saw that this could prove very trying.

Without appearing to do so, the two women appraised each other. It was Zhenia's view that although Mai Fielding was one of those wholesome English girls, contrary to expectations, or Zhenia's expectations anyway, pregnancy did not suit her. Mai's vivid colour had faded and along with it her whole vivacious persona, as though her pregnancy was sucking the life out of her. The cropped hair did not help her either these days because, instead of enhancing as it used to, now it only added to an aura of spiritual famine. Short hair and a tall, whippy figure such as Mai Fielding sported when not eight months pregnant sent out a message of independence and action. These days the fashionable cut combined with bulky unhappiness looked incongruous.

For her part, Mai was conscious of envying Zhenia. Despite her self-confessed dislike of her condition, there was an unquenchable vitality and *toughness* about the other which signalled that she intended to live life on her terms. Had Bertie noticed this? More to the point, had Augusta? Yes was the answer to the last because after Henry's death Zhenia had got her mother-in-law out of The Hall and into the Dower House with commendable speed and efficiency. Not for the first time, Mai wondered how she herself had come to move so far from the person she used to be. Her eye ran over the princess's chic ensemble. There was an odd suggestion of physical detachment. The bulge that was (possibly) the heir in a curious way did not look part of Zhenia or her outfit but as though it had sneaked on board for the ride, however long that might be, rather as a cat might have climbed onto her lap whence it could be summarily brushed off if it became tiresome. But there was no denying that she looked good. In her presence Mai realised that a combination of sadness and despair had caused her to neglect herself, for who was there to dress up for these days?

Collecting herself, she rose to her feet and rang for tea. Despite her companion's unwieldiness, Zhenia noticed that the elongating movement of standing restored some of the old Mai.

"It will soon be over for you," remarked Zhenia. "Alas, I have longer to wait."

There was a moment's reflective silence while they waited for the tea to arrive and each wondered how much it was safe to say to the other. Starting from the opposite direction, rather than confiding any more in Mai, Zhenia decided to try to flush her hostess out.

"Forgive me for saying so, but you do not seem very content to me, Mai."

This was so unexpected that Mai's composure, already precarious, collapsed. For months she had been conscious of Juno and Jacob and the whole of her household, come to that, carefully refraining from referring to her decline, presumably attributing it to her pregnancy, and now a comparative stranger had come right out and said it.

Mai wept.

At this inconvenient moment Cora arrived with the tea and knocked. Zhenia rose to her feet, went to the drawing room door and opened it.

"Your mistress does not want to be disturbed at present. You may give that to me," said Zhenia. "What is your name?"

"Cora, madam."

Taking the tray, she said, "Very well, I have it. Thank you, Cora."

The princess crossed the room and set it down on a sofa table where it was destined to remain untouched. Clearly all was not well in the Fielding household. Tunnel vision of the sort which sliced through mountains of other people's dreams and aspirations and bored a straight line through to her own wants and ambitions did not make Zhenia a very willing or interested confidante. In this case, though, she and Mai Fielding had in common the temporary disadvantages of being both grounded and bored by their circumstances. Instinct told her that all knowledge is potentially useful, be it tomorrow or in ten years' time. One never knew. In this less than charitable spirit, Zhenia decided to winkle as much as she could out of Mai.

By now Mai had recovered herself.

"I'm so, so sorry," said Mai. "I don't know what came over me."

"I am sorry too that you are so bereft," replied the other. "I am not at one with myself and my situation either so although we do not know each other very well, at least we have that much in common. . . ."

The oldest lure in the world.

"So if it would help you to talk to me, I should be delighted to listen. But only if you wish it . . . who knows? Maybe you can help me, too."

Lonely, embattled Mai fell for it.

With exhortations that what she was about to tell her must never go beyond the room they were in, she told Zhenia almost everything. At the end of it, purged, she fell silent.

"But, Mai, why don't you leave him? You have money of your own. And if you don't want the children, you could leave them with Ned."

Under normal, more thoughtful circumstances the way this heartless advice tripped off the tongue would have been assessed and found wanting and Mai would have been alerted to the moral gap between the two of them. As it was, not until she and Zhenia had parted with sisterly kisses and the uninvited visitor had gone home did it strike Mai that only she had confided. The other had proffered nothing.

September became October and during the onset of an Indian summer Mai's twins, Sophie and Jerome, were born two weeks early. At the end of the pain and the blood transfusion which followed a difficult birth, the first time she was able to hold the two children in her arms, Mai felt a rush of tenderness and, for almost the first time since her marriage, uncomplicated love. Maybe, after all, everything would be all right.

"Mai seems much better," Juno said to Jacob. "*Much* better. I think the arrival of the children will stabilise that marriage."

"Do you!" Jacob's response was a statement rather than a question.

"Why, don't you?"

"No," said Jacob, "I don't. If a marriage needs children to stabilise it there's fundamentally something wrong with it in the first place."

"Ned is besotted with the babies and seems to be spending less time with his butterflies. . . ."

"He probably thinks of them as promising larvae. Woe betide them if they metamorphose into cabbage whites!"

"It's really no laughing matter," scolded Juno, smiling in spite of herself.

"I'm not laughing. Quite the reverse. I fear for Mai."

Zhenia's child was born two and a half months after the Fielding twins and, to her chagrin, was a girl. Unaware of his wife's unmaternal instincts, Bertie had no such reservations and doted on his daughter, who at birth looked rather like a leveret with a pointed face and a mass of hair the same shade as Zhenia's. The scatter gun approach to pregnancy as epitomised by Laetitia Tattershall ought to ensure that eventually the all-important heir would make an appearance.

Augusta was pulled in two directions by the sex of her grandchild. The gratifying opportunity to say *I told you so* was not to be passed up, but the fact remained that a boy was what was required. It was irritating, therefore, that Mai Fielding had produced one first time around, thereby activating the competitive spirit in Augusta and, hopefully, her daughter-in-law.

"There, what did I tell you?"

Lying sulkily back on the pillows, Zhenia said, "I don't know what you mean, Augusta. *What* did you tell me?"

"That you were carrying a girl."

Listlessly, she said, "Oh, that . . ."

"And now we must think of a name!"

The supine figure on the bed was suddenly on the alert. "We?"

"Yes, it must, of course, be a family name. What do you think, Bertie? I had Dorothy in mind. Or maybe Winifred. Henry's favourite sister was called Winifred."

Over my dead body.

Zhenia sent her organising mother-in-law a sulphurous look.

"Bertie and I have already chosen a name. Haven't we, Bertie?"

He was startled. "Have we?"

"I thought we talked about it. Don't you remember? No? Oh, well, maybe we didn't. I certainly meant to."

"So what *is* the name you have in mind?" Scenting insubordination, Augusta did not like the way the conversation was going.

"Not just in mind," corrected Zhenia, "it is *the name.*"

"Well?"

"Saskia."

"Saskia? *Saskia?* How do you spell that? There has *never* been a Saskia in the family!"

"Well there is now! S-A-S-K-I-A. Saskia!"

"Bertie?" Outraged, Augusta turned to her son.

Being trapped between the hammer and the anvil was becoming a familiar position for Bertie. How he missed Father's wise counsel. On the other hand with Mother safely stowed away in the Dower House he was well aware that it was Zhenia who was in position to make his life heavy going these days rather than his difficult parent.

Accordingly, he replied, "Saskia. I rather like it. Saskia Langham..."

"What about Saskia *Dorothy Winifred* Langham?" Augusta was disinclined to concede victory and eyed her son with disfavour, daring him to let her down on this distinctly unsatisfactory compromise.

Zhenia was undiplomatically definite.

"No to Winifred and no to Dorothy. Saskia may not be one of your family names, Augusta, but it is one of mine. As is Zinaide."

"How do you spell *that*?"

"Z-I-N-A-I-D-E. And..." Zhenia was unable to resist it. "...so is Nadejda. N-A-D-E-J-D-A. So: Saskia Zinaide Nadejda Langham."

"In this welter of ethnicity we seem to have forgotten your benefactress, Olga." Augusta was acid.

The princess was unabashed. "Oh, yes, Olga! In that case: Saskia Zinaide Nadejda *Olga* Langham! Very distinguished. There, that's that out of the way. And now I am tired and should like to sleep."

Outside the door Augusta turned on Bertie.

"You are a fool, Bertie, an absolute *fool*! She is running rings round you and you don't seem to notice. Saskia Whatnot Whatnot Olga Langham, fiddlesticks! How do you think the vicar is going to get his tongue around that little lot at the christening?"

What you don't like is that she's running rings round you, and there's nothing you can do to stop it, was Bertie's mental reaction to this withering pronouncement.

"I'll write it down for him. While we're on the subject, Zhenia would like to have a Russian christening ceremony, too. She says Olga would have wanted it."

Jacob Berensen's prediction that children were not a solution to marital discord proved to be percipient. As the novelty of fatherhood began to wear off, Ned reverted to his previous autocratic behaviour. Not pregnant any more, Mai was no longer treated like a particularly precious piece of Meissen and was frequently left on her own as he disappeared behind the door of the Butterfly Room, sometimes for whole days. The announcement that he intended to make a trip to Germany without her in the near future therefore came as no surprise. Given the current state of their marriage Mai was disposed to welcome this news rather than the opposite. On the other hand, though the twins were, of course, divine, they were hardly a substitute for intelligent adult company. Eighteen months after the birth, along with the return of her waistline, Mai was conscious of a surge of the sort of energy and resolution which appeared to have deserted her after her marriage. She was also determined not to become pregnant again.

"You need some new clothes, Mai," said Juno. "Why don't I get my dressmaker to pay you a visit?"

"No need, Mother," was the answer to this. "I have Zhenia Langham's woman coming over to see me tomorrow when she has finished at The Hall."

Juno was intrigued. "Really? I hadn't realised that you and the princess were close."

"We aren't particularly. But we were both in the same pregnancy boat and that brought us together. She paid me an unexpected visit and as a result of that we began to get to know each other better. An occasional lunch, that sort of thing."

Curiosity prompted the question, "What on earth do you talk about?"

With a faint smile, she said, "Well, we have Bertie in common, don't forget."

"Apart from him."

"She's had a fascinating life, you know . . ." *Which is more than can be said of mine to date.* ". . . and she's very interesting when she talks about Tsarist Russia and the court . . . It's a completely different world."

Mindful of Jacob's view of the princess, Juno asked, "And what does she get from *you?* I wouldn't have thought Zhenia was one to bother very much with other women."

It was a good question. Mai thought for a minute and then said, "In an odd sort of way, respectability. No, *endorsement,* that's a better word. Oh, I know she's married to Bertie and that should be enough but on certain levels it doesn't appear to be. A lot of people, women mainly I have to say, don't like her. Maude, for instance, can't stand her."

"Jealous, perhaps," commented Juno. "Zhenia does have very good taste."

"Yes, she does. Her advice is invaluable when it comes to choosing clothes."

"You'll know, *do* tell me, what was the Langham reaction to a daughter?"

"Well," said Mai carefully, "Zhenia was very disappointed. Obviously she wanted to get the whole business of providing an heir out of the way. . . ."

"Yes, I should think she does. Do you remember poor Laetitia Tattershall? That woman was worn out. Girl after girl after girl before, finally, a son. After which her odious husband upped and left her!"

I wish Ned would leave me, Mai caught herself treacherously thinking.

"Oh, I don't think that will happen in this case. Bertie adores both Saskia and Zhenia."

The bohemian surfaced. "Saskia! What a pretty name!"

"Augusta doesn't think so! Augusta wanted Winifred and, failing that, Dorothy."

"Oh no, no, no! The poor child would have got Winnie. Or worse, Dotty! Dotty Winnie. I think Zhenia was wise to see that one off. How's Bertie coping between two determined women? Now poor Henry's no longer there to act as a buffer it must be very fraught for Bertie."

"Less so now Augusta's in the Dower House and consequently neutralised most of the time. Though it does seem to be Bertie's fate to be surrounded by warring females. Dear Bertie."

Detecting a reflective note, Juno gave her daughter a long look.

"Have you ever regretted breaking off your engagement to Bertie?"

All at once there seemed no point in going on with the pretence.

"Yes, I have."

Juno would have liked to hear Mai elucidate but at this inconvenient moment the drawing room door opened and Ned entered. For a fleeting moment he looked put out to find Juno there and then collected himself. There was a palpable heightening of tension. After some very perfunctory pleasantries, abruptly he said to Mai, "Where are Sophie and Jerome?"

Evenly she replied, "They are asleep at the moment, watched over by Cora."

"It is my view that they should be watched over by *you*, their mother, rather than Cora."

Mai looked levelly at Ned. "That may be your view but it is not necessarily mine. Cora is a sensible girl who is perfectly competent to look after

Jerome and Sophie while I devote a little time to my mother, whom, as you know, I have not seen for a while."

Listening to this exchange, it occurred to Juno that muted rows were by far the most menacing sort. In a paradoxical way shouting and ornament hurling dissipated energy, whereas exchanges like the one she was listening to were resonant with the sort of repressed aggression which had the potential to erupt into murder.

As if he had not registered Mai's last sentence and apparently undeterred by his mother-in-law's presence, Ned said, "I will go and tell Cora that you will be coming up to the nursery in five minutes. There is something else I need her to do for me in any case."

After this speech, he took his leave of Juno and pointedly left the room without addressing his wife again. Plainly seething, Mai flushed and her chin went up.

An alerted Juno followed her daughter up to the nursery floor.

Very perturbed by what she had witnessed, as she sat opposite Jacob at dinner that evening Juno wondered whether to tell him and decided against it. The marriage was obviously going through a rough patch (another one!) and for all concerned it would probably be better if a protective Jacob did not interfere. All the same she decided to try and catch Mai on her own. She had a dim recollection of Mai saying that Ned was going to the Continent for a fortnight at the end of the month. That would be the time to do it.

What made Ned tick was a puzzle to Jacob, and now it was a puzzle to Juno, too. What about that delicate fiddling about with butterflies, by their very nature fragility personified and all the time the man was a heavy-handed, domestic tyrant? It seemed Jacob had been right about Ned Fielding. But, oh, the pity of it! Juno's heart bled for her daughter who, she knew, had gone into her new life with such high hopes. Thinking about Mai's dilemma caused her to review her own unsatisfactory marriage, something she hardly ever did these days.

But it wasn't a battleground such as this one appears to be, she remembered, *it just ground to a halt. And after we parted and when the dust has settled, Rollo, who might have been the least electrifying man in the world but was still a gentleman, wished me luck. I can't see that happening here. Now when we very infrequently meet, it's like meeting a stranger. I can't believe we shared the same bed ever. There's just nothing there. Probably never was. Only suitability, whatever that is. Rollo was deemed suitable, Jacob unsuitable. Jacob's right. The English view of what constitutes an acceptable marriage is flawed and the latest victim of this is Mai. Of course the other helpful thing about it was that, although for all those years I brought Mai up on my own and Rollo took no more than an avuncular interest in his daughter, if that, it left the way clear for Jacob, with no children of his own to be a real father to Mai, on whom he dotes. Which is why I have to be very careful what I say to Jacob because if he thinks Mai is being ill treated he is quite capable of punching Ned. Which would not be helpful.*

Juno rang up her daughter and suggested lunch.

"After Ned has left for Germany, why don't you come here with the babies? Stay for a few days if you would like to. Bring Cora to help you."

"I'd love to." Mai's acceptance was fervent. "I'm having a final dress fitting this week so I'll bring my new wardrobe as well and you can tell me what you think of it."

"I'll send the car for you."

To Mai's surprise Zhenia arrived together with her dressmaker.

"I simply had to come," explained the princess. "I *adore* clothes almost as much as I adore jewellery."

On that level she would probably be very useful. In common with a lot of Englishwomen, Mai liked clothes but was far more passionate about other things. It was 1923. *Force majeur*, pregnancy had put a great many of the dashing new fashions out of court. And they *were* new. Unlike Zhenia, who was of medium height, Mai was tall and rangy. On order were two suits, two day dresses, but only one evening dress. For after all, reasoned Mai, we never seem to go anywhere these days. She commenced by trying on one of the suits. The severe, tailored look suited Mai, noted Zhenia, because she had the height to carry it off.

"What sort of hat should I wear with this?" enquired Mai. "A cloche, I suppose."

The princess, who had retained the Russian habit of bringing all present into the conversation, said, "Not the cloche. *Never* the cloche. The cloche hat is a hideous invention. Don't you agree, Paula?"

Paula, who was on her knees sorting out the hem with a collection of pins in her mouth, was in no position to comment.

"Paula agrees with me," confidently asserted Zhenia. "No, Mai, with your height you should wear a plain, dramatic shape with a large brim. Very dashing. And no ankle strap shoes, they are not becoming. Now let us look at the day dresses."

She held up a knee-length chocolate brown creation which had long, bell sleeves and, although one garment, produced the effect of a tunic over a pencil-slim skirt. Hems and cuffs were each trimmed with a broad stripe of russet and a similar stripe ran down one side of the dress.

"Ah, this is exquisite. Paula has excelled herself. Try this on. Now, with *this*, Mai, no hats! You need to wind a scarf around your head. Paula, where are the scarves? Fetch the scarves!"

Paula got them.

Zhenia selected one in burnt orange.

"Orange as a colour is usually disastrous," pronounced Zhenia, "but *burnt* orange is good but only, *only*, as a detail. This is what you do." Deftly, she wound the *devore* scarf twice around Mai's sleek blonde head and then tied it in a sumptuous knot on one side. As she stared at her reflection in the peer glass, Mai was surprised at the transformation. The princess was still talking.

"Paula, this needs taking in here and here. Mrs. Fielding is very slim."

Paula retrieved her pin box from the floor and set about it.

"Now, what is missing? Jewellery! How could I forget? Pearls! You need a long string of pearls, by which I mean waist length . . . tie them in a knot, echo the scarf . . . and one pearl stud earring . . ."

"One? I usually wear two."

"Yes, yes, as does everyone. So predictable and boring. Here you need only one on the other side as a witty counterpoint to the drama of the *devore* velvet knot. Next we must set about the evening gown. . . . Paula, fetch it please!"

The princess, it seemed, was indefatigable where clothes were concerned whereas she, Mai, felt as if she could have enough of them.

"By the way, let me show you what I have bought. Where is Cora?"

When she came, she said, very imperious: "Cora, bring me my little case!"

Cora complied, reappearing with a small lizard skin valise.

Zhenia opened it and extracted a beetle black, shiny record which she held aloft. "This, Mai, is the new music! Where is your gramophone?

Here!" She pounced on it and tossed the current occupant of the machine to one side. "Now, listen to this!"

The gramophone had a brass horn and a dog on the front and was mainly used by Ned to listen to Chopin. What happened to it next must have come as a severe shock to the system. The princess put the record (which also had a dog on the label in the middle) on the turntable, wound the machine up, turned over the large silver-coloured head at the end of the arm, and slotted the needle into the groove. There was a short, crackling pause and then the music burst out into a normally sedate drawing room.

"Ladies! The Charleston! Now watch this!"

Zhenia began to dance. Short, flirty skirts swirled above slender silk stockinged legs displaying opaline knees pale and polished as semiprecious stones. Her rhythm and exuberance were mesmerising. Such was her expertise, she almost might have been a professional, thought Mai, entranced and tapping her feet. Eventually, to her regret the record ended. Flushed and laughing, the princess threw herself into an armchair.

The raw energy was catching and the applause spontaneous. Mai clapped her hands, "Brava! Play it again."

"Wait, I have another! Mai, get ready! Paula, spit out those pins! We all dance!" She launched into it. "BLACK BOTTOM, THE NEW RHYTHM!" sang Zhenia at the top of her lungs, her Russian accent becoming more pronounced with excitement. "...A NEW BOTTOM TO GO WITH 'EM, DO THAT BLACK, BLACK BOTTOM ALL THE DAY LONG..." Caught up in the razzmatazz and sheer frivolity Mai felt light-headed, almost giddy, and almost as buoyant as Zhenia, who could probably have danced on glass without breaking it.

The music came to an end. The dancing was over. Zhenia looked at her watch. Midday. Augusta was expected for lunch. Paula picked up all her pins, reverted to being a dressmaker, and began to gather together clothes. Exhilarated, Mai thought, *After this morning I shall never be quite the same again. I had forgotten what it is like to have fun.* Seeing the two of them out, she asked, "What does Augusta think of the new dance?"

"I'm not certain she knows there is one!"

"Just wait till she finds out! What about Bertie?"

"Bertie does not know it yet, but I am about to turn Bertie into the dancing partner of the decade."

She probably will, too, reflected Mai, closing the door after them.

After dinner that evening, when the two little children were in bed, Ned, who had been in London all day, sat with Mai in the drawing room. The weather was warm for the beginning of September and, as a result, the doors to the terrace were open. In the tranquil garden where Mai had walked that afternoon mulling over the contradictions which bedevilled her life, heavy-headed late roses and fragrant white nicotiana were still in flower. Silence. Not for the first time, Mai conjectured why she found the atmosphere in the house oppressive. It had not been oppressive this morning. It must be because her husband was here, or maybe because the two of them were here together. Maybe with someone else Ned would have been more at one with himself. As it was, the Fielding hope that she would be his saviour had proved to be misguided. Tomorrow was Wednesday. On Wednesday nights Ned came into her bed. There was a terrible ritualistic quality about the regularity of this that caused Mai to dread this particular day of the week. Even more, she dreaded becoming pregnant again.

Finding it impossible to concentrate, she put down the novel she was reading. Restlessly she got up and switched on the lamps. As she passed the sofa table, she was assailed by the sweet scent of old-fashioned garden flowers all clustered together in a blue and white Chinese bowl. She sat down again and picked up her book. Again, after fifteen minutes or so, she laid it aside. As she did so, a dreadful, insidious sadness invaded Mai.

Ned shut his own book with a bang. Chopin was what he needed. Music drove out demons and soothed the mind. Catlike he moved across the room, velvet embroidered slippers making no sound on the thick pile of the carpet. As he went, he shut the French doors. On reaching the gramophone where a record already reposed, presumably the last one he had listened to, he wound it up, swung over the head prior to placing the needle in its groove and then lingered, anticipating the first bars.

"They call it BLACK BOTTOM, the new TWISTER!" roared the gramophone and then, very raucous, proceeded to compound the insult, *"It's sure got 'em! OH, SISTER!!!"* Mai froze. The princess, who had departed in something of a hurry, must have inadvertently left it behind. Ned also froze (*"... They clap their hands and do a raggety trot! IT'S HOT!!!"*) and then swooped on the needle, threw it to one side and, in a rage, seized the record.

"Is this your idea of a joke, Mai?" Inside his head a rhythmic vibration, like the relentless beat of a metronome, intensified. "Is it? IS IT?"

In order to protect herself should he become violent, Mai leapt to her feet and moved out of range of her husband.

"Of course it isn't! It belongs to Zhenia Langham. She was here this morning. She must have forgotten to take it with her when she went! For heaven's sake, Ned, why would I want to do a thing like that?"

Head pounding, he said, "You would! It's just the sort of thing you would do!" To Mai's appalled eye, her husband appeared demented. "Well, here's what I think of you and your taste in music!" Before she could stop him, he broke the record in half across his knee. "Now explain *that* to your friend Zhenia!"

Mai struck across the room so that he and she had a sofa between them and then made a dash for the garden doors, which she flung open. Once safely outside, sobbing wildly, she ran across the lawn, past the Artemis and on until she reached a wooden seat which reposed under a tree out of sight of the house and was reserved for those who wanted to get away from their croquet partners. Mai knew that Ned would not come after her. There she sat, very still, for a long time. Eventually, cold and extremely distressed, she rose and slipped like a ghost across the grass to where she could see the back of the house. The drawing room was in darkness. He must have gone to bed. Heavy hearted, she retraced her steps and, once inside, relit the lamps.

The pieces of the record were lying where her husband had tossed them. No dancing now. Mai knelt down and picked them up. Silent tears coursing down her face, she fitted the fragments together and, still holding them, made her way up to bed. On her way, as was her habit, she checked her children. They lay in adjacent cots, both peacefully asleep.

"Whatever happens," said Mai, "I will never betray you."

Chapter Thirteen

Because Ned was not speaking to her, Mai was let off the Wednesday ordeal. On Friday, still not speaking to her, he set off on his Continental trip.

The same evening, Mai summoned Cora.

"Cora, I have something to say to you which I should be grateful if you would not discuss with anyone else. Not even Michael." (He was Cora's young man). "Tomorrow I intend to leave this house with Jerome and Sophie. I shall not come back. If you are willing to come with me, I should like to take you, Cora. But, if not, I shall perfectly understand."

None of this came as a great surprise to Cora. Gossip had been rife for months among the servants and there were those who took the view that Mr. Fielding, notoriously unpredictable, was certifiable. There was also a great deal of lurid speculation about what went on in what was popularly known as the Insect Room which no one else was allowed to enter. It looked as though she never would know what went on in there now.

"If you come with me, Cora," continued Mai, "I shall, of course, guarantee you a post."

Cora was very tempted. The idea of being left behind at East Dean with an incandescent Mr. Fielding after all this took place did not appeal, especially since Lavant Park was substantially closer to Chichester, which was where her own family lived. But what about Michael? Michael worked in the garden. Diffidently she voiced her request.

"I am certain that a post could be found for Michael also. With Mr. Berensen's staff, probably. But, of course, I should have to ask him first."

The following morning Mai rang Jacob.

"I have a young man here, very reliable, who needs a job. He is a gardener."

"We always need more gardeners, but don't you have need of him, Mai?"

"Yes, but not in the way you think. And not here."

"Then the answer is yes. What time are you arriving tomorrow?"

"There is a lot of packing to do. I would think early evening . . ."

"There's something going on," said Jacob to Juno after this call. "She says there is a lot of packing to do. *And* she's giving away gardeners!"

Disregarding gardeners, she said, "Well, of course there is a lot of packing to do, Jacob." Juno thought, *How little men know*. "Moving around the countryside with two babies is like organising a travelling circus. One baby was bad enough. You men have no idea."

Sitting with her parents before dinner with her children at her feet, Mai said, "I have left Ned."

"I thought you had a lot of packing for a two-day stay," said Jacob, throwing a pointed look at Juno.

"Have you told him?"

"Of course not and anyway he isn't here to tell. I have left a letter. Ned would have stopped me taking the children. Also Ned has a tendency to be violent. . . ."

"*Violent?*"

They both stared at her.

This was a dimension neither of her parents had expected. Jacob's eyebrows drew together.

With something of a sigh, Juno spread her hands. "It will not be easy for you, Mai."

"Stuff and nonsense, Juno, we'll *make* it easy for her," said Jacob.

Juno, who had long ago given up trying to explain the absurd prejudices of the English to her husband, was silent.

"Whatever happens it will be easier than living with a man who frightens me and whom I no longer love."

This was true.

"All the same, you had better prepare yourself for a fight. He won't give up easily," warned Jacob.

"Perhaps Cora should put the twins to bed. We will talk about what happens next over dinner," said Juno.

Later that night, when Mai, who was plainly exhausted, had gone to her room, Jacob said over a brandy, "This could get very unpleasant, you know. By which I mean we could end up going to law."

"Well, obviously if it comes to a divorce . . ."

"That's not what I had in mind. I'm talking about custody of Sophie and Jerome."

Juno was shocked. "Surely Ned would not want to take two such young children away from their mother!"

"Want to bet?"

Ned arrived back from his lepidopterous trip to a house which looked the way it always had. Presumably he would find Mai, whom he had not deigned to contact while away, suitably chastened and he looked forward to seeing his offspring. It came as a surprise, therefore, when there was no one to take his hat and gloves. Ned went into the drawing room and rang the bell. A flustered-looking young girl whom he had never seen before arrived.

"Where is Cora?" said Ned. "And who are *you?*"

"My name is Hetty."

"Yes, but where is Cora?" said Ned again. "Is she ill?"

"I'm sure I don't know, sir."

"All right, where is Mrs. Fielding?"

"I don't know that either, sir."

Getting nowhere, he decided to move on to someone who would, or certainly should, know. "Go and fetch Mrs. Styles, would you please, er, Hetty."

"Yes, sir."

Fielding looked around the drawing room. It had a curiously neglected look. There were no fresh flowers and, although it was six o'clock in the evening, the fire had not been lit. Or (he checked) even laid. The servants, it seemed, were getting slack, which meant Mai was getting slack.

He would have to speak to her about it. Waiting for Mrs. Styles, he noticed that there was an unlived-in look about the room in which he stood and that it smelt stuffy, as though the windows had not been opened for days. The second thing he noticed was that the pieces of the record he had snapped in half, which according to Mai belonged to Zhenia Langham, had been replaced on the gramophone turntable. Very odd. He went across to have a closer look and found himself inspecting the shattered remains of Chopin.

A discreet cough informed him that Mrs. Styles had entered the room.

"You wanted me, sir?"

"Yes, Mrs. Styles. I have only been gone two weeks and already nothing in the house is quite as it should be. For a start Cora is not here and Mrs. Fielding is not here either. Perhaps you could shed some light on where everyone is."

He waited.

Here it was. The moment Mrs. Styles, who did not much like her employer, had been both anticipating and viewing with trepidation.

"Well?"

Inscrutable and not about to be intimidated, Mrs. Styles said, "I believe Mrs. Fielding and the children to be staying with Mr. and Mrs. Berensen and Cora has gone with them. And Michael has left us, too."

Michael? Oh, yes, the gardener.

Disregarding the inconvenient defection of Michael for the moment, he said, "Did my wife say when she expected to be back?"

"No, sir." There was a pause. By now Ned was growing impatient. This was like drawing teeth.

"I presume, since she was aware of the date of my return, she will arrive back this evening."

"I don't know, sir." At this point Mrs. Styles decided to disgorge the one item of information relevant to Fielding's interrogation. "But before she left, Mrs. Fielding did say that she had left a letter for you on the table in your dressing room."

Why on earth hadn't the stupid woman said so in the first place!

All the same, Ned did not like the sound of it.

"I see. Thank you, Mrs. Styles, that will be all for the moment."

When she had gone, he took the stairs two at a time up to the first floor.

There *was* an envelope, addressed to him in the familiar sloping hand. Fielding slit it open with a paper knife and extracted the contents.

Dear Ned, said the letter,
By the time you read this I will have gone and taken the children with me. I can no longer live in a house where I am required to be little more than an ornament, nor can I cope with your erratic behaviour. The upshot of this is that I'm afraid our marriage was the most dreadful mistake. Better that it comes to an end now while each of us is young enough to start again. Cora, who loves Jerome and Sophie, has elected to stay with me. There will be a great deal of disentangling to be done which I hope may be left to the lawyers. Please do not try to make me change my mind. I am quite set upon this course of action. The good times were wonderful but, alas not enough to compensate for the rest. Should you wish to make contact with me, I shall be staying with my parents until I find somewhere else to live.
Mai

Fielding screwed up the letter and threw it in the nearest wastebasket. He was conscious that another frightening headache of the sort which had been plaguing him more and more lately was gathering. Viselike, it felt as if it was constricting his temples. He put his head in his hands and moaned. The pain rendered deciding what to do next impossible. Tomorrow he would make an appointment to see his doctor and attempt to get back on an even physical keel.

To the amazement of all in the Berensen household, there had been no word from Ned. With her own lackadaisical husband, Rollo, in mind, Juno said to Jacob, "Maybe he's going to let it go at that."

Jacob was dismissive. "Not a hope!"

When asked about the eerie silence, Mai simply said, "This is how Ned plays it every time. He shows his displeasure by sulking sometimes for as long as a week. Then, suddenly, he's speaking again as if nothing has happened although not really because he is still hell bent on whatever it was he wanted in the first place . . . it's uneven war of attrition."

"How very confusing," observed Juno. "And wearing, too."

I don't know about confusing and wearing, was Jacob's reaction, listening to this. *Fielding sounds mad as a hatter to me.*

Mai, along with her stepfather, did not share Juno's optimism. The feeling of foreboding was hard to shift. Though currently dormant, Mai knew that her husband, like a volcano, could erupt at any moment. The thought that all this ire was unpredictably smouldering only a few miles away was not a comfortable one.

"I have a request to make," said Mai. "I wondered if you would mind me using the London flat for a month or two."

Jacob and Juno spoke as one. "No, of course not."

"But what are you going to do?" asked her mother.

"Firstly I need to find somewhere to live. A little house to rent, that sort of thing, until I find what I really want. Secondly I need to find something to do apart from looking after the children all day."

"In that case, I suggest you leave the twins, oh and Cora, I definitely can't survive without Cora, so that you can concentrate on getting yourself sorted out. But why London, Mai? Why not here?"

"Because Ned is here and too close for peace of mind. Besides, I need to keep my mind active. That's mainly what all this has been about."

Once back in London, Mai lost no time in visiting Beatrice Nuttall at home.

After some desultory conversation about mutual friends and acquaintances and where the push for universal women's suffrage had got to now that the Pankhursts were no longer so heavily involved, in a rush she came out with what was really on her mind.

"Oh, Beatrice, I don't know who else to turn to. I need some good advice, but mainly I need an ally . . . support from someone who won't judge me . . . whom I trust . . ."

"Steady on, Mai, what on earth has happened?"

Mai hesitated and then said, "I've left my husband. . . ."

Beatrice, who had been undeceived by the story of the riding fall, made no comment but just let her go on. It all came out.

"Beatrice, it has not been easy. There are times when I think that I have given up without trying hard enough. And then, when I look back . . . But then again, what about the children? Ned adores the children and they need their father . . ."

On and on it went. It was clear that guilt and confusion were waging war within Mai. Support was one thing, giving advice another. Beatrice, who had only had the briefest of encounters with Ned Fielding at the wedding, did not feel she knew him well enough to pontificate. On the other hand, although she did not know him, she did know Mai.

"For what it's worth, Mai," said Beatrice, "I've known you for a long time and it is my opinion that it is not in your nature to give up easily. So I shouldn't breast-beat too much about that. Where Ned is concerned, I couldn't say, but the fact that you have left him will either bring him up short and, if he cares about you, cause him to review his own behaviour..." Here the memory of her friend's bruised face presented itself. "...and mend some fences, or he will entrench himself in the conviction that he is the one who has been wronged and act accordingly. Either way you are about to discover the true nature of the beast. Meanwhile, you need something to do to take your mind off it all. As I've already said, it really doesn't matter that the Pankhursts have fallen away for the present because there are plenty of others, among whom I include myself, and *you* if you're up for it, to carry the banner."

"I *am* up for it, Beatrice!" Mai dabbed her eyes, in which hot tears had been welling. "And you're quite right. I do need something to do."

"Then *courage*, Mai. What about starting tomorrow?"

In the Langham family certain situations were equally unsatisfactory. It was slowly becoming apparent to Bertie, for instance, that Zhenia did not seem very interested in her daughter. Nor, these days, did she seem very interested in *him*, come to that. He hoped marital history was not about to repeat itself. By now Saskia was two, almost the same age as Mai Fielding's children. *Saskia is adorable*, thought Bertie, throwing his little girl up in the air so that she shouted with laughter, *absolutely adorable, but that doesn't preclude the need for an heir. Really we should be cracking on with it.* Augusta, wary these days of tangling with her daughter-in-law, intimated as much to Bertie who, in his turn, intimated the same to Zhenia.

Zhenia's response to this observation was elliptical. Zhenia said, "I think I need a change, Bertie...." Here she could have added but did not, *because I am bored stiff in the country*, but added instead, "I think we should go to London. It would do us both good. We could leave Saskia behind with Matty and your mother." Bertie was not too sure about this. Firstly he was not keen on going to the capital at all and especially not in the shooting season, and secondly Mother was not very maternal either. On the other hand there were higher things at stake here and if what Zhenia was saying was that this was what it would take to kick-start a currently static marriage, then it made sense to humour his wife and go along with it. Reluctantly, he assented.

The day Bertie and Zhenia were due to leave for London, Augusta rang up.

Without beating about the bush, Augusta said, "I learn on good authority that Mai Fielding has left her husband. It is said that she has bolted with the children and is currently staying with the Berensens."

At the other end of the line there was the sort of stupefied Bertie silence that Augusta knew all too well.

"Are you still there, Bertie?"

"Yes. Are you sure about this, Mother?"

"*Quite* sure! I heard it from one of the servants who heard it from one of their servants, so it must be right."

"It doesn't sound like Mai to me."

"Like mother, like daughter! I am not at *all* surprised."

"Poor Mai!" ejaculated warm-hearted Bertie. "Things must have got very rough for her to do that. . . ."

"As I don't have to tell you, at least I *hope* I don't have to tell you, things *never* get rough enough to do that! And now I should like to talk to Zhenia."

All the way to London, though it would probably have been more than his life was worth to admit it, Bertie thought of his childhood sweetheart. The old yearning resurfaced and refused to go away. Despite the years of proximity, since their marriage Bertie still felt as though he was in a foreign country in dealings with his wife. The way he perceived it, this was not so much to do with nationality as such but more to do with attitude. Look at his mother, for instance. For all her faults, Augusta had opened fêtes, hosted local events in the grounds of the Hall and generally been an active protagonist in local society. Too active, some might have said. At the other end of this spectrum, the idea of noblesse oblige seemed to have passed Zhenia by altogether, which was odd for a princess. Unlike Mai (to take another example) self-gratification seemed an end in itself for her, and staff were not always treated with the consideration they deserved either. Mild remonstrance on this front got him nowhere. As Zhenia did not hesitate to point out, Augusta herself was more than exacting in this regard. Be that as it may, was Bertie's private reaction, Mother was born into the Victorian era. These days it was quite different. The war had changed everything and on all sorts of subtle levels had eroded the status quo and, by extension, the old class system. As more and more men had departed for the front, women had begun to move into areas hitherto regarded as a male preserve. They worked in munitions factories and on buses, for instance, for much improved wages, and on the land where, to his mother's outrage, many of them wore trousers. An altogether more egalitarian spirit prevailed and at the end of it, unsurprisingly, nothing went back to where it had been before. As Bertie could not have failed to notice running an estate the size of his, an increased variety of other, more lucrative, options made getting hold of reliable staff difficult and meant that those who did opt to go into service were not prepared to put up with high-handed treatment. If Zhenia wasn't careful, she might find herself with nobody to order about.

The Langham London house had always fallen short for Zhenia. It was central, which was good, but despite a promising interior, though this had not been redecorated for at least thirty years, was gloomy. Now she had finally dislodged Bertie from the country where he much preferred to be, Zhenia decided the time had come to do something about this. *For if I have my way, as I fully intend to, we shall be spending more and more time here. Or I shall anyway.* Unsatisfactory habitat aside, there remained the vexed question of an heir. This was something Zhenia knew she could not sidestep. If only to consolidate her own position, she had to do it. The prospect caused the spectre of the luckless Laetitia Tattershall to rise before her inner eye. At times like these, Zhenia caught herself envying Mai Fielding, who not only had produced the required heir but had managed to get shot of her husband as well. Zhenia wondered what Mai would do next and, more to the point, what Ned Fielding would do next. She had always considered him attractive. There was a subtlety about him which appealed to her own serpentine disposition and was sadly lacking in the straightforward Bertie. On the lookout for diversion, it was Zhenia's view that this did not necessarily have to be restricted to her husband.

That night Bertie made love to his wife with vigour and desire and for the first time in months felt that this was reciprocated. Watching her afterwards as she lay for once quiescent and almost asleep, with her hair spread over the pillows, he felt a return of the old optimism. Maybe she was right and a change of scene would redress the balance of their marriage.

PART FIVE

Sorting the Succession

Chapter Fourteen

Ned Fielding sulked in his tent for a month. Just when Juno Berensen was beginning to relax into the idea that he was not, after all, going to make a fight of it, one day when Jacob was away, to her consternation, he paid her a visit. It was lucky that Mai was away as well, in London with her children and Cora. Juno was too late to intercept his entry for by the time she had been informed who the visitor was, Fielding was in the house.

This being the case, there was nothing else for it. Juno braced herself.

"Very well. Show Mr. Fielding in, would you please, Sally!"

The uncomfortable idea that a homicidal Ned might be about to erupt into her drawing room in hot pursuit of his recalcitrant wife presented itself. On the whole Juno did not like confrontation unless it was orchestrated by herself, which was practically never. The contrast then between this alarming vision and what actually happened next was almost as alerting in its way. Ned strolled in for all the world as if nothing was amiss. Far from being haggard and dishevelled with grief or incandescent with rage, he looked immaculately sleek and totally at ease. Urbane, even. *Anyone for tennis?* might have been his opening line.

Conducting a conversation was the next hurdle.

"How are you, Ned?" essayed Juno, an innocuous enquiry which she immediately regretted. He might tell her.

Mildly he batted it back.

"Very well, thank you, Juno . . ." Pause. ". . . all things considered! And how are you?"

"I'm very well, too."

She eyed him.

All things considered. An oblique statement of the purpose of today's visit.

"Yes, I can quite see it is very difficult . . . Mai, I mean . . ."

Ned stared at her. "Difficult? It's not difficult at all!" This was delivered in an impatient *you silly woman* tone of voice. There was the feeling of a man keeping himself in check. Just.

Despite her annoyance, this time it was Juno's turn to stare.

"Isn't it?"

"Of course not. Mai has made her point, whatever *that* is. It is now time for her to do her duty and to come home bringing my children with her, after which she can resume her rightful place in society as *my wife* . . ."

"They are her children, too," ventured Juno.

Disregarding this last and waving it away as he did so, he said, "I should like to see her. Is she here?"

It was satisfying as well as an enormous relief to be able to inform him that her daughter was not there.

"May I ask when you are expecting her back?"

"You may ask, but I am afraid I am not at liberty to tell you the answer."

Ned frowned. Juno waited for the explosion. It did not come.

Instead, politely and appearing to subside: "I quite understand."

Did he? Juno was beginning to feel confused. For the moment anyway the undercurrent of menace appeared to have subsided. All the same, the whole exchange had been very uneven.

Carefully preparing her ground, she said, "I should, of course, like to help you all I can. . . ."

He was onto it in a flash. "Would you? Would you really, Juno? I knew you would see it my way. Mai is a married woman and, as such, her place is at home with me. Tell her that if she returns to me we will never speak of this aberration again. . . ."

Listening to this it crossed Juno's mind that promises not to rake up old aberrations ever again were seldom honoured. But never mind about that now. Now, and dreading the prospect, she found herself hastily obliged to spell out an unpopular message for her son-in-law. "Oh no, Ned, you misunderstand! I was going to continue and say that I see no prospect of Mai changing her mind. As I have heard it you have been *very* cruel to Mai to the point where I believe you struck her! Not just my daughter but *any* woman would be hard put to forgive that."

Anticipating shame and contrition, once again the reaction was the last thing she expected.

Fielding flatly denied it.

"I have *never* laid a finger on Mai! Never! I cannot believe she said that! There are times when I think my wife must be mentally ill. Maybe the place for my wife is in an institution."

In an . . . ? Juno gaped. Surely she could not have heard aright? With an effort she collected herself.

By now furious, she said, "Mai says you struck her. You say you did not. One of you is lying." She sent Ned a very long, very haughty look. "Like all of us, among her many virtues my daughter has her faults. She can be headstrong and impetuous, for instance, *but* she does *not* lie! If anybody is mentally ill, I assure you it is not Mai!"

The inference of this was so clear that Juno flinched in anticipation of an extreme reaction. To her amazement Ned was impervious, smug even.

"Perhaps, my dear Juno, you do not know your daughter as well as you thought you did. Indeed I will go further and say that here you are not alone and perhaps I do not know my own wife as well as I thought I did!"

Infuriated, Juno rang the bell.

"Sally, Mr. Fielding is just leaving. Please fetch his coat and see him out."

Ned rose to his feet. "I suppose it should come as no surprise to me that I can expect no support from this particular quarter. However, before I leave, her address would be appreciated so that I can get in touch with my wife directly."

"As I have already said, I cannot undertake to do that but I will tell Mai that you would like to speak to her. Then, if she wishes, she can get in touch with you."

At the door he paused.

"I will get what I want, you know. I am fully resolved to have what is rightfully mine."

"Good afternoon, Ned."

When the door had finally closed behind him Juno discovered that she was trembling. What you saw was not what you got with Ned Fielding.

Jacob had been right. Reviewing the whole conversation and charting it from an apparently conciliatory beginning to a frankly acrimonious end, she saw that initial false smiles had been only the shallows and that there had been only one agenda all the time, duplicitously hidden in the deep until a misunderstanding had brought it to the surface. The question was, now that he had finally activated, what would Ned do next?

Once again Juno rang the bell.

"Sally, should Mr. Fielding call again at any time, in future you are to say that I am not at home!"

The next step was to ring Mai.

There was a silence at the other end after she related what had happened.

Finally Mai said, "This is only the beginning. I'm glad you didn't tell him where to find us. Though no doubt he will make it his business to discover it for himself."

"He wants you to return to him."

"Yes, I dare say he does, but there can be no question of it. Was he angry?"

"No, not angry . . ." Juno groped for the words ". . . reasonable, no, silky in a understated threatening kind of way. Righteous menace is the only way I can describe it. By the end there was a feeling of imminent explosion. It was all quite unnerving. Thank heavens Jacob doesn't behave like that. When are you coming back?"

"At the weekend. *My* news is that I've found a house. Or, rather, Beatrice found me a house. I'm going to rent it from friends of hers who are going abroad for a year which will give me a chance to find a property of my own. The handover takes place next week, so I'd be grateful if the children and Cora could come and stay with you for a few days while I get myself sorted out."

"Yes, of course!" said Juno, reflecting that Mai sounded vibrant and happier than she had been for ages. "But what are you going to do if Ned lands on your doorstep?"

"Now I am no longer living under the same roof as him, I am confident that I can deal with Ned!"

"Good for you!"

Following this exchange, Juno next rang Jacob.

Jacob said, "I've been waiting for this. Once he discovers that Mai has no intention of going back to him and, moreover, intends to keep the children, the gloves will be off. Next stop the law courts and a massive scandal. Fielding v. Fielding."

There was a sharp intake of breath at the other end.

"Don't worry about it, darling. We can afford it, certainly better than he can. No, what really concerns me is that the man's like a chameleon and as such perfectly capable of pulling the wool over the eyes of a senile, judicial misogynist. Which means that if it does come down to that we shall need a brilliant barrister who can needle Fielding into displaying his true colours."

Amid jubilation, though not her own, Zhenia became pregnant again. When she miscarried it was revealed that she had been carrying another girl. It was beginning to feel as if she was going to be pregnant for the rest of her childbearing life like the luckless Laetitia. Despite the status, for the first time she began to wonder if the game was worth the candle. Spinning out the recuperation process as long as she could while at the same time working out new colour schemes for the London flat, it did not escape Zhenia that it took two to create a child and that what was happening was just as likely to be Bertie's fault as hers. Ned Fielding, on the other hand, had sired a male heir in one go. Ergo, her chances of getting off this treadmill might lie in the direction of Ned rather than her husband.

Accordingly, "Darling Bertie," said Zhenia to her husband one morning, "I should like to give a dinner party."

"At The Hall?" hoped Bertie, who couldn't wait to get back to the country. The visits to London were becoming more and more frequent.

"No, not The Hall. Here. To cheer myself up, you know. Among others, I should like to invite Ned Fielding. He is on his own I believe since Mai left him . . ."

This put Bertie in something of a quandary. First, it was a long time since his wife, who appeared to think he should shoulder the blame for a second daughter, had called him *darling*. On the other hand he did not feel like fraternising with Fielding who, if rumour was to be believed, had treated Mai badly. By now, knowing Zhenia as he did, he understood that if she cheered up, as she put it, then he stood a fair chance of being allowed back into her bed and, for whatever reason, the quid pro quo in this arrangement was the inclusion of Ned Fielding in her proposed entertaining. The fact remained that Zhenia in a bate was one thing, Zhenia vivacious and accommodating was quite another, and after a certain amount of grumbling, more to make a point than anything else, Bertie gave in.

A month after this discussion took place, Ned was surprised to receive the invitation to Zhenia's soirée, the moreso since he had assumed the princess to be a friend of his estranged wife and, because of the history, Bertie Langham was bound to be firmly in the enemy camp, too. The card, he noticed, was addressed to both of them. Perhaps the Langhams did not know what had happened. So far he had had no luck in tracking down Mai who, he learnt, had either rented or bought herself a house in London but without apparently divulging the address to anyone. Except, perhaps, to certain intimates of which the princess might well be one. Ha! On the off chance, he wrote and accepted on his own behalf, indicating as he did so that Mai would be unable to come as she had a prior engagement that evening.

With the help of Cora, Mai settled quickly into life in London. The little house, which had a little garden to go with it, was charmingly furnished. By now it was the summer of 1923 and the twins were two years old and very active. Thank heavens for Cora. Mai frankly dreaded the day her helpmeet finally had enough money saved to marry her young man.

"For what will I do then?" she asked Juno.

"Find somebody else!" said an airy Juno, whose lack of practicality where such matters were concerned was notorious.

Mai sent her parent a narrow look.

"Easier said than done. Just anybody won't do."

"I should cross that bridge when you come to it."

After his visit to the Berensen house, there was no further communication from Ned. All knew that this was not the end of the matter and none could guess what the next move would be. The only certain bet was that there would be one. In the interim there was nothing to do but get on with life and work and Mai did.

It was through her work with Beatrice that she first met Nicolai Zourov.

"Where has he come from?" Mai wanted to know.

"Oh, he's just another dispossessed Russian courtesy of the revolution. He's either a relation or a friend of Edward Soermus. I forget which. Anyway, initially he was one of Sylvia's stray dogs. Now she's gone, he's attached himself to me."

The talk turned to other things and Mai forgot about Nicolai. Nicolai, who was not cast in the Tartar-eyed mould of the princess, but was a
tall, blond-headed individual, did not forget his first brief encounter with
Mai Fielding.

"She is very beautiful, your friend," he said to Beatrice.

"Mai is not for you, Nicolai. Don't even think about it."

Nicolai was intrigued. "Why not?"

Why not?

"Because Mai is not a free woman."

"But she lives alone. She told me so."

"In a manner of speaking she does." Beatrice felt uncomfortable talking about Mai's affairs with the young Russian. He was very persistent.

"In a manner of speaking? What does that mean?"

With a sigh Beatrice pushed aside the speech she was trying to write.

"It means that Mai, who has two young children by the way, has run
away from her husband. In the fullness of time, I imagine there will be a divorce and, no doubt, a custody battle. Given the morally hypocritical times
in which we live, if Mai is to have any chance at all of keeping her son and
daughter, her reputation, like that of Caesar's wife, has to be above suspicion. The same does not, of course, apply to her unsatisfactory husband.
Liaisons with handsome Russians are therefore quite out of the question."

"For now!"

"Yes, if you like. And now may I get on with my writing?"

Watching Princess Zhenia at her own dinner party, Ned Fielding was
struck both by her vivacity and her chic. This evening she shimmered in
a subtle shade of purplish blue and a long rope of flawless pearls. The
dress she wore was knee length at the front and was cunningly cut so that
at the back it descended into two gauzy floor-length streamers which floated
in her wake. Her hair, which, unlike his own headstrong wife, Zhenia
had never had bobbed, was pulled severely back from her pointed face and
swirled in a dramatic chignon on top of her head where it was embellished
by two antenna-like peacock's feathers. Moving gracefully from group to
group, she reminded Ned of nothing so much as one of his most prized
specimens, the long-tailed blue butterfly, moving from flower to flower. It
was clear to Ned that in that particular marriage the princess was mentally

miles ahead of Bertie, who had a faintly put-upon air these days, which in Fielding's view was what happened when a man let the women get out of control in his own house. Though in Bertie's case it had to be admitted that his problems were compounded by his very autocratic mother.

The gathering was a large one with all the men in evening dress. Remembering Augusta Langham caused him to think in turn of the late Henry who had so signally failed to rein in his domineering wife, after which Ned's eye naturally progressed to the Mainwarings, who were also there. The whole county had known about Henry's affair with Daisy and after Henry's unexpected demise in the Mainwaring house, prurient speculation about what had really happened had been rife. Fielding wondered who was bedding Daisy now. Not Harold, that was certain. Statuesque in garnet red, she was a head taller than her husband and sported a bosom (no other word for it) that would have done credit to a figurehead on the stem of a ship. Good for Henry!

As he looked around, Ned estimated that, not including his host and hostess, there must have been twenty people present, one of whom was a rather dull girl who must have been invited for his benefit and to even up the numbers. Some of the other guests, which included Lady Londonderry and her husband, he knew, but there were quite a few others whom he had never seen before.

When he took his place at dinner, it was an agreeable surprise to find himself sitting on Zhenia's right. At the other end Edith Londonderry was on Bertie's right. As the first course was served, Zhenia immediately turned to Ned. Under cover of the buzz of conversation round the rest of the table, she said, "You must allow me to express my disappointment that your wife was unable to be here this evening."

Fielding hesitated for a moment and then said, "It's not as simple as that. In fact, she has left me!"

Zhenia contrived to look both amazed and prettily contrite. "Mr. Fielding, I am so sorry. I should not have brought the subject up if I had known."

"I don't mind talking about it. Sooner or later everyone will know."

"I suppose she has gone back to her mother and stepfather?"

"No, I believe she has come to London and brought the children with her. I don't know where to."

"Then how can you sort this rift out?"

"It may not be possible. Whether Mai returns to me or not, I intend to make sure my son and daughter do. There can be no question of the children remaining with their mother if she is determined on a separation."

Zhenia studied Fielding for a moment. Since she last saw him he had grown a moustache, which gave him a faintly rakish air and was what Zhenia thought of as made for evening dress. His hair was romantically long on his collar, she noticed, and the fluid movements of his tapering hands as he gestured and talked reminded her of certain of the young male dancers she had known at the Mariinskiy. There was an element of the bohemian about his appearance which appealed to Zhenia but which she doubted extended to his real life. Noting the petulant mouth, it occurred to her that exacting standards might be expected of a wife which would not extend to a mistress and probably meant that Ned was a better bet as a lover than as a husband. *Which is fine,* thought Zhenia, *since that is what I want him for.*

"I could probably find out where Mai is living for you," she said, getting back to the means to this end. "If you would like me to, that is. I have no wish to interfere but I should very much like to be of help in bringing the two of you back together again."

"On the contrary, I should be very grateful." Was it his imagination or, as she turned away to the guest on her left, did she send him a look of frank flirtation? If so, who could blame her? Ned eyed Edith Londonderry at the other end, gamely slogging on with Bertie, who was probably talking about partridge shooting.

Reluctantly, he proceeded to engage the young woman on his right in an inconsequential conversation.

The following day Zhenia was as good as her word and was lucky enough to catch Juno Berensen at home.

"I'm so sorry to trouble you, Mrs. Berensen, but I heard on the grapevine that Mai has moved to London and since Bertie and I are here for a week, I should like to call on her and wondered if you could let me have her address. . . ."

"Yes, of course. It would be simply lovely for Mai to have a visit from a friend. Would you mind waiting while I find it?" Sounds of riffling. "Ah, here it is." She dictated it, together with a telephone number. "And how is Bertie?"

"Bertie is just the same as ever," replied Zhenia, with something of a sigh.

"And your little daughter? Saskia, isn't it? Such an unusual name."

"Saskia is well, I believe. She is currently in the country with her nursemaid."

"You and Bertie must come to dinner with us. It's time I did some entertaining."

"Thank you, Mrs. Berensen, we should like that very much."

When Juno replaced the receiver, Jacob, who had just entered the room, said, "Who was that?"

"Zhenia Langham. She wanted Mai's address."

"You didn't give it to her, did you?"

Juno was defensive. "Yes I did. Why wouldn't I? She and Bertie are in London for a week and she wants to visit Mai. . . ."

"I wouldn't have done that. And if I had been here I would have stopped you doing it."

"Jacob, why ever not? It will be very nice for Mai to see a friend. . . ."

"Juno, you are too trusting. The princess does not strike me as the sort of woman who does anything without a very good reason. She is the archetypal cat who walks alone and nobody's friend but her own. When does she ever spend time with that child of hers, for instance?"

"I think she's just one of those women who isn't very maternal, Jacob," offered Juno, guiltily remembering a similar shortfall in the same department and wishing he would drop the subject.

"I'll bet she is!"

Zhenia did not telephone Ned, who was back in Sussex, on immediate receipt of Mai's address for if she did and passed it on verbally, that would be that. Better to see him face to face and be in a position to inch the wished-for intimacy forward. So she waited and the week following her return to the Hall, on a day when Bertie had another engagement, she commandeered Stiggins and the car and called on him.

The Fielding house had a bereft air and a quiet deadness about its interior which was positively depressing.

"Mr. Fielding is in the Insect Room," said Hetty, showing her into the drawing room. "I'll tell him you are here."

The Insect Room?

Peeling off her gloves, Zhenia wandered across the room as she did so.

Unlike the last time she had been there, it had a bachelor impersonality about it with none of the paraphernalia of joint living. There were no flowers either. Outside, a mature garden underlined the sad sterility within. It was all a far cry from the day Mai had tried on frocks and the three of them had giddily danced. Zhenia wondered what had happened to the record she had inadvertently left behind.

The door opened and Ned entered.

"Princess! What a pleasure!"

"Well, I was passing and decided to visit. Besides, I have that which you seek . . ."

"The address?"

"Yes, and telephone number . . ."

"Do you, by Jove!" Ned was avid. He held out his hand eagerly. "May I have it?"

"You can if I can find it," parried the princess, searching through her bag. "Where can it be? I thought I'd brought it. Maybe I left it in the car with Stiggins. In which case I can give it to you when you show me out."

"But you're not going yet?"

"Not if you want me to stay." The coquettish look she sent him was unmistakable. Fielding was reminded of the sight of her at her own dinner party and how she had put him in mind of one of his butterflies. Since Mai had left, there had been no one. In the wake of her defection Fielding felt he had had enough of intractable women and had spent long hours in the Butterfly Room poring over and redesigning his collection. This was his passion and on that level it was all very well, but it did not solve sexual deprivation. Today, despite his disenchantment concerning the female sex in general, he was aware of a resurgence of desire. For Zhenia *was* very desirable and, if he read the signs aright, available.

"Tell me why did you really go to so much trouble on my behalf?"

"No trouble at all! I simply rang up Mrs. Berensen and asked her."

"I went and *saw* Mrs. Berensen and asked her and was not granted the same privilege."

"Well, you would know the reason for that better than I. . . ."

With a shrug and a dismissive half smile, as if to say *all that is beside the point,* she turned away from him. Fielding caught her hand and pulled her round, moving a step closer as he did so. He was wary of making a fool of himself. It was imperative that he did not make a move only to discover that what he thought was happening was not happening at all, but was only a figment of an overheated imagination. Though she left her hand in his, he noticed.

"All right, why did you bring the information? It is, after all, a longish journey from the Hall to here and you could have telephoned."

"I came here to see *you* and I very much hoped that you wanted to see *me*."

Without a trace of embarrassment, Zhenia had come right out with it. It seemed that she had more courage than he did. Time to stop fencing. Ned caught her to him, bent his head and kissed her. Just before he did so she smiled, revealing white teeth, small and pointed as those of a cat. There was a greedy rapacity in her response which he found both surprising and gratifying.

Nevertheless she stepped back, disengaging herself as she did so.

"I must go. Stiggins is waiting for me. . . ."

"Let Stiggins wait!"

"No, I must get back. Augusta is coming for lunch and Bertie will wonder where I am."

It was the first time Bertie had got a look in during the course of their tête à tête. Ned had all but forgotten about Bertie. By now the princess was running a comb through her hair.

"We can't leave it there," urged Ned. "When shall I see you again?"

"No, we can't leave it there. Very soon is the answer. Next time I *shall* telephone . . ." She gave him a mischievous look. ". . . to let you know when I come."

Her Russian accent had charmingly intensified.

"Before you go, Zhenia, that is if you *must* go . . ."

"I *must* go!"

"The address! Let me quickly have another look." She opened her bag and once again turned over the contents.

"Ah! It is here. I found it! I had it all along!" Prior to kissing him lightly on the cheek, she handed it to him. "*À bientôt*, dear Ned."

With that he had to be content.

Fielding handed her into the car and then watched it until it was out of sight. The precipitate manner of her departure just when he had thought they were both getting somewhere ensured that for the rest of the day and most of the following night he could think of nothing but the princess, and even his beloved butterflies, with the exception of the evocative, elegant long-tailed blue, failed to distract and console.

Over lunch, for which Zhenia was late, Augusta observed her daughter-in-law closely. Honed social antennae told her that something was different. Maybe it was her air of ... of what?" Thinking about it, Augusta finally came up with *triumph*. Not that triumph was anything new and anyway it was too overt for what she was witnessing. No. The more she analysed it, the more *secret satisfaction* seemed to be a better way of putting it. The suspicion that the princess was up to something refused to go away. She looked across the table at Bertie, who, as usual, appeared to be oblivious. There was, as yet, no sign of a third conception either. In Augusta's view it was all very lackadaisical. Bertie should take a firmer stance with his wife. Thinking of *taking a firmer stance* put her in mind of Mai Fielding. For look where sacking Bertie had got Mai. On the other hand, look where marrying the princess had got Bertie. It never used to be like this. Marriage, especially dynastic marriage, had always been a straightforward affair. The war, it seemed, had changed everything, including the expectations of women and the perception of where their duty lay. Eyeing Zhenia with disfavour, Augusta gave up on it. When the meal was over and the servants dismissed, she cleared her throat and broke the silence.

"What is the latest news concerning the Fielding scandal?"

"Hardly a scandal, Mother," protested Bertie. "Mai has left Ned, that is all."

"That is all?"

Bertie was stubborn. "Yes, that is all. I assume in the fullness of time there will be a divorce." Speaking the words he remembered his father with affection. Father had had the knack of the inflammatory remark uttered in the mildest of tones.

She was satisfyingly outraged. *"Divorce!"*

Zhenia smothered a smile.

Augusta recovered herself and addressed the practical. "And what about the children?"

"They are currently living in London with their mother. Rumour has it that there will be a custody battle. Lawyers, that kind of thing ..."

"You had a very lucky escape there!"

With his wife sitting at the same table it was not politic for Bertie to dispute this so he said instead, "It is my intention to visit Mai in London, just to show support."

"Why should Mai need support? What about the deserted husband?"

"We had the deserted husband to dinner," said Zhenia.

Bertie grimaced. "It's said that Fielding treated Mai very badly . . ."

Although she had heard it too, since it did not help her argument, Augusta decided to ignore this statement. "Visiting women in the throes of divorce is a perilous pastime, Bertie. You will end up as co-respondent if you are not careful!"

Bertie did not quake in the face of this awful warning but merely said, "Mai is not yet in the throes of divorce. And I shall take Zhenia with me. You are fond of Mai, aren't you, my love?"

"Oh, very," answered Zhenia with alacrity. "Yes, I should like to see Mai very much."

After this exchange the three of them sat on in silence for a while, though not companionable silence. Finally, Augusta, who had evidently been smouldering prior to regrouping, remarked, "Although her behaviour subsequently may have been lamentable, at least Mai Fielding produced a son in short order."

The inference was not lost on either Zhenia or Bertie.

Zhenia was entertaining murderous thoughts. "I am not a brood mare, you know, Augusta," said the princess. "Besides, why attack me? Maybe you should be looking to Bertie for the solution to your problem rather than myself."

"Oh, I say, Zhenia," protested Bertie, wounded by the deflection of his mother's attack on to himself.

"I'm afraid, my dear, that when you marry into a family such as this your first duty is a dynastic one. I should have thought that as an aristocrat you of all people would have understood that."

"I *do* understand that!"

If that old trout mentions Laetitia Tattershall again I'll kill her!

"Well then, better get on with it! Remember . . ."

"Mother, that's enough!" One day, Bertie thought, he would have to sit his tactless parent down and explain that pointed suggestions such as that put Zhenia in such a phenomenally bad temper that procreation was set back at least six months as a result. He looked at his watch, dropped his napkin on the table and stood up.

"Ladies, you will have to excuse me. I have an appointment elsewhere on the estate."

As Augusta had been well aware, in Henry's day *an appointment on the estate* had been a euphemism for an assignation with Daisy Mainwaring.

"How *are* the Mainwarings?" she enquired, apparently apropos of nothing in particular but, in fact, still in competition. "Is Daisy still as large?"

Preparing to exit, Bertie was nonplussed by this barbed enquiry.

"Large? Daisy? I really don't know. They came to dinner recently, too. What did you think, Zhenia?"

Zhenia was crisp. "Junoesque and handsome with it! Small wonder the men find her so attractive. Before you go, Augusta, would you like to spend some time with Saskia? I'm sure she would like to see her grandmama."

Although she had a lot to say on the subject of an heir, Augusta was less than keen on being dubbed Grandmama. As a word it had a distinct aura of being on the way out about it. It was redolent of dower houses and waning power, both factors she did not like being reminded of.

Nevertheless, she said, "Of course I should love to see darling little Saskia."

As they walked upstairs towards the nursery wing, Zhenia made one of her few mistakes.

"She is such a pretty little girl and reminds me so much of my sister, Katya."

"Sister?"

Augusta stopped and turned to stare at her daughter-in-law.

"I thought you told me all your siblings were brothers!"

"Did I say sister? I meant cousin, of course." Even to herself, Zhenia sounded lame. "Ah, here we are!" She opened the door. "Saskia, come and say hello to Grandmama."

Starched to within an inch of her life, Saskia *was* a pretty little girl. A miniature version of Zhenia, in fact. Precocious, too. *She must get it from me,* thought Augusta complacently, enchanted in spite of herself. All the same, Saskia needed a brother. Or two. *Though, when one thought about it, I am the best man this family ever had.*

"Saskia come and give Grandmama a kiss!"

That night, lying in bed beside a lightly snoring Bertie, for the first time for years Zhenia thought about Katya. And not just Katya either, but also her brothers and her parents. Until her mother had taken her to Petrograd, together with her younger brother, for the Mariinskiy audition, Zhenia spent her life in surroundings very like those remembered by Tatiana Volkovska. The difference between them had been looks and the polish conferred on Zhenia by her ballet training and those she mixed with during the course of it. Her brother, Alexei, had been turned down by the school.

Zhenia wondered where they all were now. Probably still in the mire. It was unlikely that the revolution had made much impact on the sort of far-flung country outpost that had been her home until she was twelve. As a rule of thumb, she recalled, it was when the rooks, the last birds to leave, set off for the south that the weather significantly worsened. In autumn and spring the roads, never much good at the best of times, used to be impassable but, sandwiched in between these seasons, the winters, while enhancing the landscape with their pristine frozen beauty, had been truly ferocious. *If it hadn't been for the huge old stove* (which had taken up half the house) *I really believe we would all have died of cold.* Packs of famished, marauding wolves roaming the countryside had not been uncommon either. Worst of all had been the food, which tended to be devoid of variety. Cabbage soup with lumps of gristly meat in it, for instance, had more often than not been the staple diet for weeks. Just remembering it made Zhenia's stomach heave.

I was lucky with the priest, though. Comparatively literate, which many of the clergy were not, this kindly old man had taken it upon himself (with varying degrees of success) to teach the children in the village how to read and write. *Without which I wouldn't have got anywhere,* recognised Zhenia. *And if I hadn't been accepted by the Mariinskiy I'd have ended up working in the fields, just like my brothers and Katya and still sewing my own clothes. And constructing my own shoes, come to that. Lapti. We made them out of birch bark.*

It hadn't been all bad, though. In particular Easter week, which brought to an end the dismal interlude of Lent, had been a memorable festival with its dyed eggs and sonorous services culminating in the midnight procession which was followed by feasting and copious quantities of vodka. But it still hadn't made up for the rest.

I never want to go back. Never, ever!

She put out the light.

In the Dower House, also lying in her bed, Augusta thought of Katya, too. She knew an inadvertent revelation when she heard one and was aware that although it was hairline, nevertheless a fissure had opened up in the princess's story. All the original reservations and question marks over who the princess really was and where she had come from, eclipsed by both the emeralds and Olga's endorsement, resurfaced. Whatever the truth of the matter, even supposing Zhenia was a fraud, there could be no question of doing anything about it. *For we should become the laughingstock of both London and the county*, recognised Augusta. Rationalisation notwithstanding, the uneasy sense that something might be seriously amiss persisted and it was a long time before she finally drifted into uneasy unconsciousness.

Chapter Fifteen

The fact that Mrs. Nuttall had warned Nicolai Zourov off Mai Fielding only served to increase his interest in her. Nicolai had something of a history of pursuing what he should not have. For a young buck in Petrograd, married women had had the attraction of experience allied with apparent unavailability. *Of course*, he recalled, *some had been more special than others.* In particular there had been Natalia, married to an army officer, who had been quite exquisite but silly. Cards and dancing and gossip, that had been Natalia. Still, it had to be said perfection of form went a long way, especially when one knew there was no prospect of enduring his pretty mistress's idle chatter for the rest of his life. In those days it was Nicolai's view that romantic free-booting had much to recommend it, providing all the fun (and for a while Natalia, though vacuous, *had* been fun) and none of the responsibility.

There was nothing silly about Mrs. Fielding.

Watching her in the tiny office she shared with Beatrice as they both composed their speeches and wrote hundreds of lobbying letters, and knowing about her troubles as he did, he could only admire her professionalism. The threatening marital situation was never talked about, or not when he was present anyway. Soermus had gone back to Paris where there was a large contingent of Russian émigrées and Nicolai, who was lonely in London, was considering whether to do the same. Meanwhile he kicked his heels in the office and ran errands.

His chance with Mai came on a day when Beatrice was out at a rally, and he took it.

Mai was poring over a notepad and having a fourth go at reshaping a difficult sentence when, noticing the time, Nicolai said, "Mrs. Fielding, it is one o'clock. Perhaps you would join me for lunch?"

"Is it really?" Mai looked at a small gold watch. "Heavens!" She appeared to consider for a moment and then raised her head. She put down her pen. He braced himself for a refusal. Her smile was luminously unexpected and directed straight at him.

"Thank you. I should like that very much."

"I know a small restaurant near here. It is Russian. Run by a friend. We could have caviar, if you like."

"Caviar?" Her eyes opened very wide.

"It is only for the privileged few. This is my friend, don't forget."

He helped her on with her coat. Outside, the weather was clement and the London trees in bright green bud. After a particularly drab winter, the high, light blue sky and buttery sun were invigorating. A brisk walker, Mai in her high-heeled shoes tapped smartly on the London flags and she inhaled the fresh air with pleasure.

The restaurant was tiny, with red-and-white-checked tablecloths and a dark interior. Well-dripped candles in defunct wine bottles were the only light and the walls were covered in framed sepia photographs which mainly appeared to be of prerevolutionary Petrograd. Painted Russian dolls stood everywhere. Apart from one other couple huddled in a corner it was empty.

"It's charming," exclaimed Mai.

"Nicolai!"

"Vladimir!"

The two men embraced.

"This, Vladimir, is Mrs. Fielding who works with Mrs. Nuttall."

Vladimir clicked his heels and bowed, then seized a bottle of vodka from another table and put it on the centre of theirs.

Mai was startled. "Vodka? Oh, I don't think so in the middle of the day . . ."

"Here we are in Russia! No caviar without good vodka," announced Nicolai. He inspected the bottle. "Sinopskaya. Excellent!"

Two shot glasses materialised and were filled.

"I go now," said Vladimir. "The kitchen needs me."

As she sat opposite him, Mai looked at Nicolai properly for the first time. No concessions had been made to tidiness, in Mai's view an overvalued attribute anyway. Nicolai's suit was rumpled and the quaintly old-fashioned high shirt collar, which had rounds rather than points, was rigidly starched. This raised the question: *Who starched Nicolai's collars?* What an absurd thing to wonder, she chided herself. Most surprising of all, as they walked to the restaurant she had noticed that he wore boots rather than shoes. It struck Mai that Nicolai was probably more at home on the Russian steppes than in the confines of an office.

He raised his glass to her.

"Here's to fortune," said Nicolai. He drained it in one swallow.

Mai raised hers (*Oh, why not?*) and also drained it in one swallow.

They smiled at one another.

"Now tell me all about yourself," said Mai.

"Then you tell me all about *you*. We have a deal, yes?"

Mai laughed. "We have a deal, yes!"

"But first we order! You have eaten Russian food before?"

Mai shook her head. She had a sudden wild desire to laugh.

"Then I order for you!" Nicolai signalled to a tactful Vladimir who was hovering beside an impressive samovar. "Vladimir, I shall have *zakuski* but that might be too much for Mrs Fielding. . . . For her the borscht and we both have caviar. Then stroganov . . ."

"No stroganov today. *Kulebiaka.*"

"*Kulebiaka!* Even better. Ladies like fish. And more vodka."

Thank heavens Beatrice isn't coming back into the office today was Mai's view of more vodka.

Sipping this time, Mai said, "Okay, tell me about your family."

"Family," gently mocked Nicolai. "This is very English!"

"Not at all. We've all got one. It's very English *and* very Russian."

He subsided.

"Very well. My father was a furrier, by which I mean he ran his own establishment in Nevsky Prospekt and my mother ran the house. I have two sisters, both of whom are married. So, what you in this country would call a very middle-class family. But scattered by the revolution."

"And what is your view of what happened in 1917?"

Unselfconsciously he called her by her Christian name. "I believe in it, Mai. It had to happen. The excesses and deprivations were too great. The tsars did themselves no favours. We all expected the revolution, the question was when. There was a lot of talk. Bets were taken. Ironically, the timing still took most by surprise but once it began its impetus and speed made it unstoppable. Dreadful things happened. Blood and bullets. As I say, it is my belief that it was inevitable but all the same it will be a long time before a new equilibrium is established. It may not happen in my lifetime. . . ."

The first course arrived together with another shot of vodka. Mai was beginning to feel light-headed. It was also a relief to have been let off the *zakuski* which looked very vinegary and which Nicolai ate with relish. The caviar was fit for gods though, and not as salty as she had been anticipating.

"No," said Nicolai in response to a query about this. "Alas, it is not beluga. Beluga has a larger grain. That is beyond even Vladimir. By the look of it, it is probably osetra. See that golden glaze?" He tasted some. "It *is* osetra. Here . . ." He used a bone spoon to put sour cream and a spoonful of caviar on a blini which he rolled up and handed to Mai. The casual intimacy of the gesture made her blush but she took it all the same.

"What part, if any, did you play in the uprising?"

A sombre shrug. "I was nobody. Simply one of the crowd. Like all seismic events it was both extraordinary and terrible to behold. Better to be an extra rather than a principal."

Mai leant forward. "Tell me about it."

"The first I knew things had started to move was when I learnt there had been shooting on Nevsky Prospekt. Apparently they fired on the crowd, most of whom were on their way to the Mariinskiy. There was panic followed by a rush for safety and many casualties, women and children included, were left wounded or dying in the snow. Some fell and were crushed to death underfoot, others were run over by sledges pulled by stampeding, terrified horses, and still the firing went on. That was the Saturday. Prior to this, on the Friday, there were Cossacks everywhere, even riding two abreast along the Nevsky pavements. I remember the sun shining on spurs and gold braid, turning their long lances into needles of light. After the shooting on Saturday evening I noticed there were none to be seen. A tactical withdrawal, perhaps. Rumours proliferated. Nobody knew what to expect next. It was odd because, for some, life appeared to go on as usual, the mundane teetering on the brink of chaos. Significantly, though, food, bread especially, was beginning to run short. Sunday, a fine day I remember, brought it to a head. All over Petrograd thousands congregated outside and *nobody stopped them.* None of the bridges and thoroughfares were closed.

Belated warnings not to take to the streets were disregarded. Ironically, it was another fine day."

Nicolai paused, clearly deeply affected by the memory of it all and drank deeply before resuming.

"Anyway, having let it go as far as it had, orders were given at last to clear the streets and a volley of shots was fired near the Anichkov palace. This time I was there and saw it. There must have been a hundred dead. At least. The bloody snow was strewn with bodies. Spent cartridges lay where they had been dropped. By then everything was breaking down. There were no trams and no cabs either and a lot of anger against the Romanovs. I heard them called the 'German gang' and there were shouts of *Doloi Sache!* Do you know what that means? Do you, Mai? It means down with Alexandra! They hated her. The very same day there was another shooting in Znamenskaya Square where a huge crowd had gathered. Police machine-gunned the people from the tops of buildings. I was there, too. We all saw the puffs of smoke. Carnage and panic! After that there was no holding it and, so far as I could see, nobody really leading it. And, in the middle of all of this, the Radziwills gave a dance!" Nicolai threw up his hands in despair. "*That's* how it was!"

Their *kulebiaka* arrived.

"I don't understand. Why couldn't the tsar have commanded the army to put the insurrection down?"

"The tsar?" Nicolai spread his hands. "The tsar was a weak, indecisive man and by then it was all too late. Troops who arrived in Petrograd with orders to put down the insurgents defected. I myself had a friend in the Pavlovsky Guards. After the Anichkov palace shootings, virtually the whole company went over to the side of the revolutionaries."

"What happened to your family?"

"My father was shot by accident through the window of his own house."

"By *accident?*"

"Yes. You see, Mai, you have to understand what it was like then. The mob opened up the prisons and let out not just political dissidents but hardened criminals. Guns were freely available everywhere. Children were handling them . . . *children!* . . . and there was a lot of random firing by those who did not know what they were doing. . . . There was anarchy. It was hard to watch. This was my *country* and these were my countrymen."

Now, if truth be told, I no longer have a country, thought Nicolai.

He fell silent. The pain of dispossession predominated.

Gently Mai said, "Go on."

"As soon as she could, my mother left the city for Minsk, where her brother lives, accompanied by my elder sister, Anna, with whatever they could both carry. I and my younger sister, Irina, remained behind. Irina because her husband, who was a lawyer by training, had political ambitions and saw his chance with the forming of the Kerensky government and I because, as a young man, I did not want to be incarcerated miles away. I wanted to be at the heart of the action."

Listening to this, it struck Mai that, unlike the man she had nearly married and the man she finally did marry, Nicolai had an uncomplicated energetic zest for life akin to her own.

"But you left!"

"Yes, I left."

Her question brought him face to face with life as he lived it now. Confronting it, Nicolai's face darkened. His mood became suddenly bleak. *Yes, I left,* thought Nicolai, *and now I have nothing. I am a refugee, without property or status and a family I may never see again. Regret is a destructive thing. It poisons the present by sucking the life out of joy. For the time being, the only solution is to look away from it. One day, though, I will go back . . .*

He became aware that she was watching him with concern.

"*Why* did you leave?" Mai was asking.

Nicolai collected himself. "Why? Well, new allegiances were being formed. Political ones, I mean. By dint of keeping his head down, my brother-in-law, as a lawyer and something of a chameleon, survived by successfully bridging the divide between the old and the new. Whereas *I,* a dissolute young man about town in those days, I was too firmly identified with the old way of life. Informants were rife. People disappeared. These were volatile, dangerous times and, until things settled down, I decided to take my chances elsewhere. . . ."

But things haven't settled down and maybe they never will, thought Nicolai, *and sometimes I feel it is quite possible that I shall end my days in exile, separated from my roots and all that makes me what I am . . .*

Rising above it (for what else was there to do?), he continued, ". . . Still, that is another story. Now, you promised, Mai. Tell me about you."

That is another story. Tantalising. By now it was two-thirty P.M. and lunch should have been over half an hour ago. Besides, he was quite right. She had promised.

"Where do you want me to begin?"

"With family, of course!" This was said with only the lightest touch of irony.

"Very well. My parents separated when I was little. Theirs was a marriage which was neither happy nor unhappy, just mediocre. Whatever else she is, my mother is not one for mediocrity so she ran away and went to live in an artists' colony in the East End of London, where she posed in the nude for whoever wanted to paint her...." *This can't be me speaking,* thought Mai. *It must be the vodka. I've never talked to a comparative stranger like this about my family before.* "... And plenty did. Anyway, my stepfather fell in love with a painting of her, found her and married her, thereby plucking her out of Bohemia and reinstating her in the bosom of the upper classes which was where she came from. By then, as Mother confessed to me, she had had enough of romantic poverty and was glad to be rehabilitated. Theirs has been a very happy marriage, which is more than can be said for mine."

Tears came into Mai's eyes.

For God's sake, don't start crying.

"Have you ever been married, Nicolai?"

"No."

"I don't recommend it. I married a man with a secret. After an idyllic honeymoon, I slowly and painfully came to realise that the person I thought I knew and loved did not exist. What did exist was a cold, occasionally violent, domestic tyrant."

"Violent?"

"Yes. By the time I finally decided to emulate my scandalous mother and bolt, I discovered that I was pregnant and it was too late. So I stayed. I thought when the children were born things might improve but they didn't. Finally, when Ned went abroad on a butterfly trip..."

"Butterfly trip?"

"Butterflies are my husband's passion...."

Nicolai bit back the words, *If you were mine, you would be my passion,* and waited for her to go on.

"I packed my bags and left, so here I am in a rented house in London with two small children, a nursemaid, and no idea what is going to happen next. Except that one way or another there will be no respite because that is how Ned works."

Blue eyes looked into blue eyes for a moment, before Mai lowered her gaze.

"I must take you back," said Nicolai, wishing he could take her to bed instead. As they walked back to the office, he recalled Beatrice Nuttall's words. *Liaisons with handsome Russians are quite out of the question,* and his own reply, *For now!* Well, he could afford to wait.

That evening, not relishing the prospect of his own sparse room, he went back to the restaurant to share a companionable vodka with Vladimir.

"She is lovely, your Mrs. Fielding," observed Vladimir slyly.

"But unavailable."

"That never stopped you before!"

"This one is different!"

During the next few weeks Mai and Nicolai began to get to know each other better and Zhenia and Ned Fielding got to know each other much better. Oblivious to what was happening under his very nose, Bertie congratulated himself that his marriage seemed finally to be settling down and ascribed this to the fact that his wife was gradually becoming anglicised. As a result of a newly discovered interest in charity work, it was true that she was out a lot these days, but then so was he. An estate the size of the Langham property required a great deal of time and attention to detail. Bertie did not enquire too closely into what charity work but the fact that she was doing it at all was pleasing. It seemed that Zhenia was getting the idea at last.

Doing what she shouldn't have been doing with a lover improved the princess's mood wonderfully and, although he did not know the reason, her husband was the beneficiary. Still claiming to be in a delicate state of health after the miscarriage, Zhenia managed to keep her husband out of her bed. Bertie basked in the warmth of her smiles but was less happy about the sexual side. However, rather than upset what was happening, he decided to let it take its course. No doubt when she felt well enough, normal marital relations would be resumed.

Ned, a man who probably always should have had a mistress rather than a wife, found Zhenia delectable and, as she had rightly surmised, celebrated behaviour in a lover which he would never have condoned in a wife.

"Aren't you worried about becoming pregnant, my love?" asked Ned one day as they lay in bed after a particularly abandoned session of lovemaking.

"No," replied Zhenia, telling the truth for once. "I'm not."

This puzzled Fielding. Maybe she was unable to have any more children. Whatever the reason, it worked for himself so he did not pursue the matter but turned his attention to pleasuring her (and himself) all over again.

By unspoken mutual consent they did not mention either Mai or Bertie. Unlike the one he was currently in bed with, Ned knew his wife to be a virtuous woman. Which raised the question of custody of his son and daughter. There was, of course, the intransigent suffragette past (and present, come to that) but all that had become respectable and hardly made Mai an unfit mother. Possession, it was said, was nine tenths of the law. The best of all possible worlds would be for Mai to come back home of her own volition bringing the children with her.

How to achieve this, after all that had gone before, was another matter.

By contrast, the growing friendship between Nicolai and Mai was a chaste and, on her part anyway, tentative affair. Normally an impetuous man, especially where affairs of the heart were concerned, Nicolai nevertheless found himself conceding that a slow start had its rewards. During the course of their regular lunches he watched with fascination the lights and shadows passing across Mai's mobile face as she talked and he admired her gallantry and grace in the face of the difficult circumstances in which she found herself. When he began to have sleepless nights worrying that she might return to her husband, he knew that he had fallen in love with her. The intensity of the experience was such that he realised he never had been in love before. Infatuated, yes; in love, never. It was, Nicolai discovered, an inconvenient emotion, a state of being which inhibited both independent thought and independent action. *I am no longer my own man.*

"You must be mad to think such a thing, Nicolai," said Mai when he pressed her on the subject. "I will *never* go back to my husband."

In Nicolai's experience, although people believed themselves when they made such statements, the world was littered with those who subsequently changed their minds. He could but hope that Mai wasn't destined to be one. Meanwhile he could only adore her at one remove while being her friend and, should it ever become necessary, her protector. All of this raised the question of what she thought of him. Obviously she liked him very much.

By now he knew her well enough to know that Mai would never have spent so much of her time with anybody unless this was the case. But did it go any deeper than that? Sometimes he thought it did, other times he thought he was imagining that it did. It was certainly true to say that there was a flirtatious component to their meetings, but, as Nicolai well knew, flirtation came as naturally to some women as breathing and often signified nothing more than that. Whether this mutual attraction contained the potential for sexual charge was currently unclear.

Beatrice, who did not miss much, saw what was happening and said as much to Nicolai.

"I warned you not to get involved, Nicolai."

"I know."

"Now you have, what you must not do is to compromise Mai."

"I know that too."

He looked so unhappy that Beatrice felt sorry for him.

"You see, never mind about burnt fingers over the marriage causing inhibition, Mai can't afford to even *think* about falling for anybody else until it's all sorted."

"Beatrice, do *you* think she will return to him?"

"Ned Fielding's such an unpleasant piece of work that I wouldn't think she would contemplate such a thing for one minute. But that's not her only consideration. There are the children. And I've told you what the position is there. It's a shame. Mai deserves to be happy."

"He hasn't made a move. Maybe he won't."

"Don't you believe it. The silence is not reassuring in my opinion. Quite the opposite, in fact. The feeling I have is of thunder in the air. What happens next and when is the question. I fear there might be some shocks in store."

Chapter Sixteen

The man standing on Tatiana Volkovska's doorstep was no one she had ever seen before. Accustomed to assessing after many years of dealing with staff on the countess's behalf, she ran her eye over him. The newcomer, hat in hand, was tall and balding with a moustache and a small, pointed beard. His frame, encased in a shiny black suit which had certainly seen better days, was cadaverous with a slight stoop.

"What can I do for you?" said Tatiana, who had very few callers of any sort and was astonished when the visitor replied in Russian.

"My name is Sergei Litvinoff. May I come in, Miss Volkovska?"

Tatiana was a lonely woman these days and did not even entertain the idea of turning away a stranger who spoke her native language. These days she only heard it in church, which was both her solace and her sad reminder of what had been.

She stepped aside, allowing him to pass by her and into the hall.

"May I ask how you know who I am?"

He balanced his hat on the bentwood coat stand. "I heard about you from someone within the Russian community." He gestured towards the small sitting room. "May I?"

"Yes, of course."

The sitting room was filled with pre-1917 memorabilia, rescued from a pile of Olga's most cherished belongings, most of which had been thrown out by the cuckoo. In one corner there was the samovar and, in one of the armchairs, Ivan, also deemed superfluous after his mistress's death.

"Sit!" commanded Tatiana. "I will make some tea."

"If you wish, but I have something you may prefer."

Litvinoff drew a flask from his pocket. Vodka.

"I will get the glasses," said Tatiana.

When she returned with them, the cat was sitting on his lap. She filled the glasses and then sat down opposite the two of them. The only sound in the room was Ivan's loud, throaty purring.

"Put him down, if you would prefer."

"No, I like them," said Litvinoff. He raised his glass. "Your good health."

"And yours," concurred Tatiana. They both drank.

She waited.

Not a Russian agent for nothing, without appearing to do so, he sized up the woman before him. Tatiana Volkovska was of the sort of peasant stock he recognised, but, at the same time, courtesy of her old post with the countess, retained an air of authority. Litvinoff divined her to be a proud woman and probably an intelligent one, too.

"You must be wondering why I am here."

Tatiana Volkovska did not speak but waited.

"I am here because I am looking for a certain Vera Kalanskaya."

He looked at the other closely. Not by a flicker did Tatiana indicate that she had ever heard the name before. All the same, the heightened awareness of the spy registered a wariness in the atmosphere that had not been there before. He would have to tease her out.

"Why do you want this . . . Vera Kalanskaya?"

"It is my belief that she is a thief." He could have added *murderess*, but for the time being chose not to.

This time he did get a reaction. Guard dropped for a fleeting moment, Tatiana looked distinctly rattled before collecting herself and swiftly resuming the mask. She remembered her misgivings about her mistress's death. On the other hand there was her stipend to consider. It had been made very plain to her by the cuckoo that if she breathed a word of what she knew this would cease forthwith. *And with everything else gone*, thought Tatiana, *I couldn't bear to lose that as well. For how would I live? I could starve for all she cares. And I probably would.*

Litvinoff considered the woman opposite him with shrewd, hooded eyes and intuited that reassurance was the name of this particular game.

"Ah, well, there was just a chance that you might have known something . . ." He tickled Ivan under the chin, just as Olga used to do. "Of course, I don't have to tell you that any information I might receive would be treated in the strictest confidence. Before I say anything further I must have your assurance, Miss Volkovska, that you will treat what I am about to say in the same spirit."

Not trusting herself to speak, Tatiana nodded.

"You see I am here on behalf of Soviet Russia. I have every reason to believe that Vera Kalanskaya made off with the Dashkov emeralds, since 1917 regarded as the property of the state. In the process of doing so she left the former custodian (also an illegal possessor of the gems, I may say) to die. At least that's what it looked like. She was last heard of in Paris and then the trail went cold, as they say."

This left Tatiana in something of a dilemma. There could be said to be safety in shared confidences. Maybe one revelation deserved another and the temptation to wreak a belated revenge on her enemy was almost overwhelming. She wondered how much Sergei Litvinoff already knew. More than he was telling her, averred cunning peasant roots, but not so much that he did not need help from her in the shape of supplementary information.

Foxily, Litvinoff decided to leave her with it for a while and to reminisce about home. Tatiana, it transpired, was famished for news of her native country. As he talked, her severe mien was replaced by an almost girlish wonderment. It sounded as if she would not have recognised Petrograd. It had been hard enough to get used to the name when she had been accustomed to St. Petersburg. It wasn't even the capital these days, Moscow was. The more he described the cataclysmic change that had taken place, the more her aim of eventually going back there one day was revealed as a pipe dream. *For it sounds as though I should be as much of a foreigner there as here.*

Sensitive to the fact that he had probably got as far as he was going to today, Litvinoff picked up the flask and found it to be empty. He put it in his pocket. Then he lifted up a reluctant Ivan, put him on the floor, and stood up, indicating that the visit was at an end. For Tatiana it had been the most exciting day she had had for years, certainly since the fracas with the so-called princess had culminated in tragedy together with her own downfall and she would have liked to prevent him leaving and instead to go on chewing the cud all afternoon.

As they stood once more on the doorstep, she said, timidly, "Do you have an address that I could have. Then, if something does come back to me, I could let you know...."

PART SIX

Russian Connections

Chapter Seventeen

In March of 1926, Zhenia found she was pregnant. Remembering the last time with disfavour, she did not need a doctor to tell her. She knew. The upshot of this was that after a longish spell in the sexual wilderness, Bertie found himself welcomed back into the marital bed. Patience and tolerance appeared to have paid off. Everything, it seemed, was back to where it should be. Now, for Zhenia and for Bertie and his managing mother, come to that, though the other two of course did not yet know of the pregnancy, everything depended on the child being a boy. After a suitable interval of Bertie in the bed, Zhenia went to see her doctor and the happy event was confirmed. Since there was no way anyone could tell her what the sex of the baby was, there was nothing left to do but get on with it for the next eight months. *But if it proves to be another girl,* Zhenia promised herself, *whatever happens, I am not going through this again.*

The announcement of her condition also meant the end, for the time being, of delectable charitable afternoons with Ned Fielding. Zhenia felt she dared not risk it.

"How can you be sure it's Bertie's?" enquired Ned, giving his inamorata a long look when she told him.

"Because the dates are right," blithely lied Zhenia. "Do you recall when you went abroad for two weeks? Well, that's when it happened. Let's hope it's a boy and then I don't have to go through this again."

"I shouldn't bank on it. They'll want another just to be sure. Anyway, never mind about that now. What about once more, for old time's sake?"

"That would be divine."

She slanted a smile up at him. Though it was only the mouth that smiled, he noticed. The strange, amber eyes were devoid of expression. Fielding had always known that the princess was unscrupulous but in that instant the word dangerous entered the equation. He looked at her intently for a minute, before slipping her fur coat off her shoulders and beginning to kiss her.

Mai revelled in Sophie and Jerome. By now they were becoming interesting. It occurred to her that it might be a good idea for them to begin meeting other children and that Saskia Langham should be one of these.

Apart from the brooding absence of Ned, the only cloud on the horizon was the anticipated but dreaded departure of Cora for marriage and a family of her own. At Juno's suggestion, Mai spent a weekend with her parents in order to choose another country girl in the same mould. The result was Lizzie who, although not as bright as Cora, seemed to have a sensible kindness about her, which reassured Mai.

April was mild that year, a watercolour month of drizzling skies and the palest of suns. One day, while Mai and Nicolai were lunching together, a man whom she had never seen before greeted Nicolai. When he had gone, Mai, who had not found the newcomer very prepossessing, asked who he was.

"Sergei Litvinoff," replied Nicolai. "I first met him in Paris. Rumour has it he's a Soviet agent."

Mai was surprised. "Really? But what on earth is he doing here?"

Nicolai shrugged. "He wouldn't be here without reason, but whatever it is, he has not told me."

What a curious experience it must be, reflected Mai, *living in the aftermath of revolution when the whole world as one knew it has been turned upside down. Whether one had become a wanderer like Nicolai or an agent of the new regime like Litvinoff, with all the old absolutes gone the sense of disorientation must be total.* Though now she came to think about it, exile did not seem to have fazed Princess Zhenia very much if at all. Zhenia appeared to have taken to her new life like a duck to water. Smiling across the table at her companion, as they went on to talk of other things she wondered what it must be like to live in Russia now.

Three weeks later, after Mai had departed for the office one morning, the telephone rang. Lizzie put down the child (Sophie) whom she was carrying around on one hip and, as she had been instructed to, unhooked the receiver and answered it. At the other end, a man's voice asked for Mrs. Fielding.

"Mrs. Fielding is not here," enunciated Lizzie and was preparing to offer to take a message when the caller continued speaking.

"Could you possibly tell me when she will be back?"

"Not until six o'clock," said Lizzie helpfully. "Would you like me to . . ."

Click. He'd gone.

She went back to her work.

That afternoon there was a knock at the door. She stopped what she was doing and went and answered it. A delivery. Thirty minutes later there was another knock at the door. It was clearly going to be one of those days. Once again Lizzie put down her cloth and went to get it. This time it was not a delivery. A well-dressed gentleman stood before her.

"Good afternoon. I am Mrs. Fielding's husband, here to pick up the children as arranged."

As arranged? Lizzie was confused. This was a complete departure from the normal routine. Nobody had said anything to her about any arrangement. Taking advantage of her uncertainty, Mr. Fielding walked round her and into the house, saying as he did so, "What's happened to Cora?" This was reassuring. Presumably if he knew all about Cora, he was who he said he was. The two children seemed to know who he was as well. Better to be on the safe side, though. On the pretext of fetching something, Lizzie went into the hall and made a telephone call to Mrs. Fielding at her office. There was no answer. She and Mrs. Nuttall must be out.

"I thought I would take them to the park," said Mr. Fielding when she went back into the sitting room. "Little children like parks. Perhaps you would like to get them ready . . . ?"

"Lizzie," said Lizzie.

". . . Lizzie. I promise to have them back by six o'clock."

This was delivered with the sort of genial authority which was hard for a mere employee to gainsay. After all, he was the other parent. Instinct told Lizzie that what was happening was not quite right but she was at a loss as to how to stop it. Making one last attempt, she said haltingly, "Mrs. Fielding never mentioned anything about it to me, Mr. Fielding, and I don't feel very happy letting Sophie and Jerome go without her permission . . ."

The friendly façade vanished and was replaced by something much brusquer.

"As an employee, Lizzie, it is not for you to feel happy or unhappy but to do as you are told. Now get the children ready, straightaway!"

At the sound of a raised voice, Sophie began to cry.

Miserably and very slowly, Lizzie did as she was told. If only Mrs. Fielding would suddenly return, but there was no hope of that until at least five thirty. The last she saw of her charges was Mr. Fielding putting them in his large shiny car prior to driving away.

Mai and Beatrice arrived back in the office from a rally they had been attending at approximately four fifteen. Immediately the telephone rang. Mai answered it and Beatrice heard her say in surprise, "Why, Lizzie. There's nothing wrong, I hope?" There followed silence while Mai listened to whatever was being said at the other end. Humming, Beatrice hung up her jacket and returned to her desk to get on with her work. As she did so, she caught sight of Mai. Mai was trembling.

"Lizzie, what time did all this take place?" asked Mai in a shaky voice little above a whisper. Another loaded silence, at the end of which Mai said, "Six? He said six? I'll come back straightaway!" She hung up the receiver and turned to face Beatrice.

Shocked by her pallor, Beatrice said, "Mai, what is it?"

Mai looked dazed.

"He's taken the children."

"He?"

"Ned. He's taken them away. He called at the house and lied to Lizzie. He said it had all been arranged. He told her he would bring them back by six, but he won't . . . Oh, Beatrice, what am I going to do?" Distraught and sobbing, she fell into the arms of her friend. "I may never see them again!"

Staring over Mai's bowed head, Beatrice stroked her hair and let her weep. Better to get it out of the system now. Tomorrow would require cogent thought followed by a plan of action, although for the life of her Beatrice could not think what that could be. For wasn't it said that possession was nine tenths of the law? And, just like Mai herself, she couldn't see Ned Fielding compromising on that one. Worst of all, the reality was that in this sort of messy situation with the law structured as it was, the man had the upper hand. It was at this moment that Nicolai entered the room.

He stared at the two of them.

"What's happening?"

"I'll tell you later," replied Beatrice. "The first thing to do is to get Mai home as quickly as possible, just in case that bastard keeps his word!"

Nicolai, who had never heard her use such a word before, was startled. "What bastard? No, never mind. I'll take Mai home. It will be a pleasure for me."

"Then you'd better know that her unspeakable husband has kidnapped the children. There will be pandemonium now!" As she said this, she suddenly thought of Jacob Berensen. Berensen should be told about this as quickly as possible. Mai was in no shape to do it so she, Beatrice, should. "But if you could do that, Nicolai, it would be very helpful and meanwhile I shall do some telephoning."

Once the two of them had gone, she tried the Berensen number. When it was answered, she said, "Could I please speak to Mr. Berensen?" Then, in response to the query, "Beatrice Nuttall."

He must be there. Thank heaven! Beatrice had dreaded being told that the Berensens were abroad. When he came on the line, he sounded anxious.

"Mrs. Nuttall? I remember we met briefly at Mai's wedding. What can I do for you?"

"Look, I'm so sorry to ring you with bad news, but I'm afraid we have a crisis on our hands."

She told him the whole story.

There was a profound silence and then he said, "I feared that something like this would happen. Where is Mai now?"

"I have sent her home by cab with Nicolai."

"Nicolai?"

"Don't worry. She is in good hands. Nicolai Zourov is a mutual friend and very supportive of your daughter. He will look after her until I can get there. The question is what happens next."

"What happens next is all-out war." Jacob Berensen sounded grim. "But whereas before the odds were marginally in our favour, now they are not."

Tears gathered in Beatrice's eyes. "It pains me to think of those two little children without their mother."

"It should pain Fielding to think of them without their mother but it won't. The man is a lunatic. Unfortunately, he is also plausible which makes him doubly threatening."

"Couldn't he be persuaded to see reason?"

"Before anybody can be persuaded to see reason in extreme circumstances there has to be an element of humility. Bertie Langham, for instance, had humility thrust upon him by his appalling mother so there's a human dimension to him which is notably lacking in Fielding. Fielding, I suspect, has been indulged by the women in that family all his life and now takes the view that the female sex is there solely to service him. Will you be able to stay with Mai tonight?"

"Yes, of course."

"Very well, in the morning, when Mai has regrouped, I'll speak to her and we will make some decisions. Meanwhile, Beatrice, you have been, *are* being, a true friend and my gratitude knows no bounds."

Replacing the receiver on the hook, Beatrice reflected briefly on the vicissitudes of life and marriage in particular. Her own had been unexciting but durable. *I married Tom because he asked me,* recognised Beatrice. *I am not a beauty and it seemed to me that it was better to be married than unmarried. But most of all I wanted children.* Tom, who was a solicitor by profession, had been steadfast and there for her when she needed him. *Solid* was the word most often used to describe her husband. At the end of the day theirs had been a successful marriage. More successful than most, anyway. With Tom, what you saw was what you got and, in the light of what she was currently witnessing, let it not be underestimated. *And I* have *underestimated him from time to time,* Beatrice thought. *I have been impatient. I have wished that Tom could be more exciting, less predictable.* Seeing Mai caught in the emotional quicksands of a completely different set of values was a sobering and informative experience.

She looked at the clock. Five thirty. She put on her jacket, locked up the office, and went down into the street to look for a cab.

As he sat in Mai's sitting room between two lamenting women, Nicolai found himself having to come to terms with watching Mai's cool, English demeanour fragment. He would not have suspected that below a calm surface lay so much raw emotion. Lizzie, the nursemaid, blamed herself for letting Mr. Fielding take the twins, Mai blamed herself for not having foreseen that this might happen. Now it was too late. Nicolai wondered what sort of a man could do this to his wife and family. On the other hand Fielding had been separated from his children, whom presumably in his own way he loved as much as Mai did. Nicolai gave up on it and anyway there was no point in worrying about the other man's finer feelings. *For I owe my allegiance to Mai.*

To his relief the hysteria abated as six o'clock approached and was replaced by the silent nail-biting tension of waiting to see if Fielding's self-imposed curfew was observed. For the first time for years, Nicolai found himself sending up a prayer to the Holy Father. With Lizzie quietly sobbing in the background, Mai sat like a statue, silent and pale.

All watched as the hands of the clock edged towards the hour. When it struck, Mai jumped to her feet and ran to the front door. She flung it wide and ran out onto the pavement, where she stood, tears running down her face, frantically searching in vain for the return of the car. It was where Beatrice found her when her cab finally reached its destination. She paid the driver off and then put an arm round her exhausted friend's shoulders and turned and led her back inside.

At eight o'clock, feeling that there was nothing more he could do that night, Nicolai left. In need of the company, he went to Vladimir's restaurant, where he recounted his problems to his comrade.

"Married women are trouble," opined Vladimir. "You know that from days in Petrograd. English married women even more trouble." Then, unwittingly echoing Henry Langham, "Find a nice, pretty Russian girl who understands you. Much better."

"Much better. But it's too late for that."

Chapter Eighteen

Tatiana Volkovska spent a week agonising about whether to contact Sergei Litvinoff or not. For Tatiana there was a lot at stake. On Sunday morning she went to the Russian church and prayed for guidance. As is so often the case with prayer, there was no immediate answer. Maybe the Holy Father took the view that she knew the answer to her question already.

Thief, Litvinoff had said.

Thief and possibly murderess by default.

There really was not much of a moral grey area about *that*. On the threshold of extreme old age, Tatiana was frightened of the consequences in the hereafter if she did not do the right thing, but was equally afraid of the consequences in the here and now if she did. On the other hand, if she told Litvinoff all she knew in confidence, what was there in it for him if he divulged the source of his knowledge? The answer to that was probably nothing. If it got about that an agent went about divulging his sources there wouldn't be much more useful information coming his way in the future. On top of the moral dimension, Tatiana's heart still bled when she thought of her mistress. *She was both my employer and my friend,* recognised Tatiana, *and at the end she felt I let her down. I should not let her down again.*

Still mulling it over, she lit a candle and set it in front of her preferred icon, one of the Blessed Virgin. As she did so, she became aware of an angular figure by her side, standing silent as a ghost in the candlelit interior.

It was Sergei Litvinoff.

Tatiana, who would not have thought of her compatriot as a religious

man, was taken by surprise. Then it struck her that maybe his sudden ma-
terialisation at her elbow was not a coincidence but *the answer to the prayer.*
Russian fatalism set in. She would take it as such. No more agonising.

"Well, well, Tatiana Volkovska!" said Litvinoff. He accorded her a half
bow.

Tatiana beckoned him closer.

"As I thought I might, I have remembered certain things that could be
of interest to you," whispered Tatiana, looking around her as she spoke, for
who knew who might be listening. "But I should prefer it if we did not
talk here."

"No doubt the priests would also prefer it if we did not talk here,"
replied Litvinoff. "Where would you like to go?"

"There is a small tea shop that I know."

"Very well." Courteously he stood to one side. "Perhaps you would
like to lead the way?"

There was something comforting and very fortifying about tea,
thought Tatiana, especially after an unheated hour in church. She cradled
the cup in her hands in order to warm them. Litvinoff did not hurry her,
but sipped his own and waited.

Finally Tatiana began to speak.

"Mr. Litvinoff, before I tell you anything, anything at all, I must have
your assurance that no one will ever know that I was the source of your information. You see, she said if I told anybody what I knew about her she
would cut off the pension she pays me."

"She?"

"Vera Kalanskaya . . ."

Ah.

"Since my mistress died, it's all I have. . . ." She looked at him almost
pleadingly. "It is for her that I do this."

Yes, and revenge is sweet.

Softly, seductively even, Litvinoff said, "No one will ever know. You
have my word, Tatiana." His use of her Christian name almost had the feel
of a caress to lonely, bereft Tatiana.

Haltingly at first and then, as the story went on, with gathering confidence, she told him all she knew. How the cuckoo had appeared out of the
blue one day and what had happened subsequently, concluding with her
sudden intimation that the countess's death had not been as straightforward

as it had appeared. Litvinoff, who in the course of a long career had learnt that very little was as straightforward as it appeared, listened impassively.

"What did the doctor say?"

"He said she was an old lady and it was only to be expected. Her heart had given up. I accepted it. He was a doctor, after all. . . ." Apparently still far from reassured, Tatiana spread her hands with resignation.

"And the papers and documents that you gave the countess, what happened to them?"

"I never saw them again. I can only suppose that she, Vera that is, destroyed them. . . . After that there was no proof."

"But the countess knew of the deception. You are sure of that?"

Tatiana hung her head, remembering with shame her last interview with Olga. "Oh, yes. I told her myself. She was going to throw Vera out. All the same, I think she would rather not have known. By telling her I felt I may have contributed to her death."

Litvinoff studied the smattering of tea leaves at the bottom of his cup.

"Not you, Tatiana, not you. Circumstances maybe, but not you. So where is Vera Kalanskaya now?"

"I don't know," was the disappointing answer to this. "The money just appears at the bank every month. I don't know where it comes from. She married a wealthy man, though, the son of a friend of the countess."

"Whose name is . . . ?" prompted Litvinoff.

"Mr. Langham."

Retelling the story had reactivated the pain and the sorrow. Tatiana dabbed her eyes.

Litvinoff leant back in his chair. It had been a very good morning's work. The wealthy Mr. Langham shouldn't be too hard to find.

"And she's still posing as Princess Zhenia Dashkova?"

"Yes, as far as I know. After all, why wouldn't she?"

Why wouldn't she indeed?

Litvinoff appeared sunk in thought.

Shyly, Tatiana asked, "Do you know what happened to the real Princess Zhenia Dashkova?"

Rousing himself, "No," said Litvinoff laconically. "But she must be dead. The rest of them were executed, I know that. Probably she was, too. Thousands died or just disappeared. But be that as it may, the hunt isn't for her or, except as a means to an end, Vera Kalanskaya. The hunt is for the emeralds."

"She's certainly got those. My mistress recognised them as family jewels straightaway. May I have another cup of tea?"

"Of course!" He summoned the waitress.

"Vera said she was in Paris before coming to England," said Tatiana.

"Yes, that was the truth for once," answered Litvinoff, without elaborating. She hoped the other was going to tell her the rest of Vera Kalanskaya's chequered history. How she had come by the Dashkov knowledge and the emeralds in the first place, for instance. To her chagrin, he showed no signs of doing so, but seemed content to let the subject drop and to let the talk turn to other topics.

Half an hour later they were both out in the street. An unseasonably cold wind caused both to put their coat collars up.

"Allow me to escort you back to your house," offered Litvinoff.

"It is too far to walk. I shall get a bus."

"Then let us take a cab."

When they were both ensconced in the back of one, Litvinoff said, "As you know, you have my assurance of confidentiality. In return I should like yours. What we have shared today must remain between the two of us."

This declaration of mutual dependency caused Tatiana to feel less vulnerable in the wake of the risky course of action she had just committed herself to. On the doorstep, he reached into the deep pocket of his coat and pulled out a small, flat, round tin which he gave to Tatiana.

"In memory of Mother Russia," said Litvinoff.

Caviar.

Her face lit up.

Brushing aside thanks, he lifted his hat and then turned on his heel and left her. Watching his tall figure tacking along the pavement, coat flapping, Tatiana wondered if she would see him again and whether she would ever hear the end of the story.

PART SEVEN

Fielding vs. Fielding

Chapter Nineteen

In advance of Mai's arrival at Lavant Park, Jacob Berensen consulted first of all his family solicitor, whose practice was located in the Pallants in Chichester. The discussion was not encouraging. Michael Hanson had been the lawyer used by Juno to untangle her own untidy matrimonial affairs.

"But, as I don't have to tell you, both Mrs. Berensen and her husband wanted a divorce so it was an amicable arrangement. From what you tell me this is a completely different kettle of fish."

"It is. Fielding's a cruel bastard and, in my view anyway, a crackpot. But he's cunning and perfectly capable of presenting himself as the soul of sweet reason in front of a judge."

"And he has the children."

"And he has the children."

Hanson sighed. "Jacob, as you know, the divorce law as it is presently constituted is orientated to the rich, the poor don't get a look in . . ."

"Money is no object," interrupted Jacob.

Hanson held up his hand.

"I know that. I was going on to say that it is also heavily weighted in favour of the man in this patriarchal society of ours. And the only ground on which a divorce can be granted is that of adultery. So however unpleasant Fielding is, it is not going to help your stepdaughter."

"Daughter," said Jacob automatically. "I regard Mai as my daughter."

"Do you realise how few divorces have been granted since the war? Under five thousand, I would guess. Obviously the whole process is made much easier if the parties involved collude. Which brings me to my next question, does Fielding want a divorce?"

"Mai does. My supposition would be that he does not. The very fact that Mai left him has caused Fielding to lose face as well as his children. If only for that reason he would probably take her back, even though the marriage remained a sham. I'll know more tomorrow. I'm going to see him in advance of my daughter's arrival here."

Jacob, who was not looking forward to this particular interview, grimaced.

"Mai is distraught at the loss of Jerome and Sophie. Surely even the most hard-hearted judge would not separate a mother from her children?"

Hanson forbore to observe that there were quite a few chauvinistic stony hearts currently occupying the benches of the legal profession and, after a moment's dickering, said instead, "Possession is . . ."

"Nine tenths of the law, I know, I know!" Jacob was impatient. "But these are small children we are dealing with, not property."

"What do you know about the life your son-in-law has been leading since Mrs. Fielding left the matrimonial home?"

"Nothing, and please don't call him my son-in-law, Michael. The very sound of it offends me." Berensen frowned and then resumed, "As far as I know his butterfly collection is his only grand passion."

"His butterfly collection?"

"Yes. He's besotted with them. Dead ones!"

"I ask because it seems to me that this could all get extremely unpleasant." Hanson hesitated, wondering how to phrase his next question. "And what about Mrs. Fielding?"

"What *about* her?"

"She has nobody else in her life?" *Although,* thought Hanson, *in the light of some of the things I've been told, who could blame her if she did?* "I'm sorry to have to ask you this. . . ."

"Not at all. I can see that every eventuality has to be covered. The answer to your question is, not as far as I know. My daughter is a very choosy young woman, dedicated both to the work she does and to her children."

Hanson, who met a lot of rich young women who did nothing at all, was interested. "What work does she do?"

"Mai is campaigning for universal women's suffrage. Before her marriage she was a very active member of the Votes for Women movement."

Ah! Hanson felt his collar. This was not something likely to go down well before certain reactionary, crusty old judges he could think of. Cautiously he said, "It sounds to me as if you are going to need a very astute, not to say persuasive, barrister. In which case, because of the acrimony and the wrangle around the children, you could end up in the high court. As I don't need to tell you, the ensuing publicity would be horrendous."

"I don't care about any of that," said Jacob, "I only care about the outcome."

"However, be that as it may, as things stand, if there is no evidence of adultery on either side, there are no grounds for divorce. Neither desertion nor cruelty can be taken into consideration, although in my view they should be. That is the law as it stands."

"Then the law's an ass!" Jacob was terse.

"There are some of us who agree with that," concurred Hanson. "But many more who don't. I'm fairly certain that eventually change will take place, but not in time for us, alas."

"So what are we talking about? Judicial separation, presumably, and who retains custody of the children." Berensen got to his feet. "Oh, the hell with it! I'll tell you what, Michael, let's wait until I've seen Fielding tomorrow. It may change everything!"

In the event it did not.

Jacob arrived at the Fielding house at ten A.M. as he said he would and was shown into the drawing room where a particularly smug Ned awaited him. Although since his abduction of the two children everything had not gone swimmingly for Ned. Emotionally disconnected himself, he had been surprised at the extent to which the two of them had missed their mother. Jerome in particular had been very bereft. Treats and surprises had made little difference to this state of affairs. In the light of this unlooked-for complication, Ned decided that the only solution was for his wife to return to the family home where she belonged.

If she wants to see the children, then she'll have to play it my way. Otherwise, no dice. It was in this spirit that he waited to see what Jacob had to say.

Jacob, who could hardly stomach being in the same room with the other man, decided not to beat about the bush.

"Let's start by saying I think we are both in agreement that the marriage has broken down."

"Wrong. It is not my view that the marriage has broken down."

"That is not how Mai sees it!"

"Mai, it seems to me, is shirking her duty . . ."

"Oh, don't be so pompous, man!" Jacob was infuriated.

". . . She has deserted me and her children . . ."

"She may have left you, but no one could ever accuse her of deserting her children. *You* abducted them!"

"Nevertheless, the fact remains that my son and daughter are here and where is Mai?" Fielding shrugged. "Refusing to come to them, I fear."

Thinking, *This is getting us nowhere.* "Do you want a divorce?"

"Of course not. Anyway, as I'm sure you have found out for yourself, unless my dear wife has been misbehaving herself, there are no grounds."

Jacob did not see why he should have to listen to this. "What about *you*? You might have been misbehaving yourself!"

Was it Jacob's imagination or did Fielding's denial almost imperceptibly miss a beat?

"Well, I haven't." Because he had no knowledge of the dalliance with the princess, Berensen was in no position to dispute this. All the same, the more he thought about it, the more convinced he became that there had been the faintest of hesitations as though the other had been wrong-footed. Since there was nothing to be done about that now, he filed it away for future reference.

"Are you proposing that, although you know that it is the very last thing Mai wants . . ." *That Mai loathes you* would have been a more accurate summing up, but was rejected in the interests of keeping antagonism to a minimum. ". . . you would be prepared to try to force her to come back and live in this house . . ." Here he gestured at the four walls of the room in which they sat. ". . . using the children as a lever?"

Fielding appeared surprised at the vehemence with which this speech was delivered.

"Yes. Why not? Lots of people who don't like each other much go on living together. You know that. Why shouldn't we? There is, after all, a greater good at stake here."

"You mean your status in society, perhaps," said Jacob with disgust. Then, controlling his temper with an effort, he said, "Look, why not go for a separation. Let Mai have the children. Small children need their mother *and* their father. I'm certain unlimited access could be agreed and no need to go to law with all the resulting brouhaha."

"Thank you for the promise of unlimited access, though I fail to see how that can be in your gift since I already have it. This being the case, I don't feel like being quite so generous and would go so far as saying that, unless my wife agrees to come home, I shall do my damnedest to make sure she sees as little of them as possible."

"I'll see myself out!" said Jacob.

The same morning that Berensen's interview with Fielding took place, Nicolai put Mai, together with Lizzie, currently redundant and therefore going home to her family, on the train to Sussex. At that time of day Victoria was very busy, the human hubbub compounded by the hissing and cranking of trains. The high roof was wreathed in steam. Latecomers, many of them mothers with small children, ran along the platform followed by peak-capped porters wheeling the luggage. Others, presumably seeing off friends or family or maybe lovers, crowded around open carriage doors and windows saying their farewells. Concentrating his hopes and his dreams on Mai, Nicolai was oblivious to it all. He had no way of knowing how long she would be away or even if he would ever see her again. Despite the fact that it was etched with strain, her face still enthralled him. Nicolai helped both women onto the train, found them seats, and then got off. There was a dreadful finality about the slamming shut of the heavy door. Mai pushed down the window and leant out.

"How long will you be gone?"

"I don't know. It depends how long it takes to sort things. I'll keep in touch, though. Through Beatrice." Her eyes filled with tears. "Pray for me, Nicolai."

On impulse, he seized her gloved hand and kissed it.

The whistle blew. Stragglers jumped aboard. Slow and sedate, the train began to move.

"I love you, Mai," shouted Nicolai. Amid the noise she probably never heard him. His last sight of her was of a waving hand and then she was gone.

That night he was unable to face dinner at Vladimir's but went home to his dingy lodgings and moped. The feeling of powerlessness was hard to bear and so was the knowledge that she had gone probably without hearing the declaration of his feelings for her.

But it doesn't *have to be like this,* Nicolai suddenly saw. The solution was so obvious he wondered why he had not thought of it before. *I will write to Mai and tell her. Beatrice will know the address.*

Writing to Mai and telling her proved easier said than done. How would an English suitor have written to an English lady? Nicolai had no idea. On the other hand, he did not want to look a fool. In the end, after several stilted goes at it, he decided to stop trying to second-guess the mores of another nation and to write like a Russian in love. This presented him with language difficulties of its own and the ensuing result was heartfelt rather than fluent.

Mai,

wrote Nicolai in a black, sloping hand,

> *I can no longer keep silent. I love you. Watching the train taking you away from me I thought my heart would break. Now I am here alone and all I think of is you . . . I do not eat and I do not sleep.*

Here Nicolai paused and looked around his tiny room.

He would have liked to have given her a present. Something worthy of her and therefore precious. But what? Nicolai had left Russia with very little. In the end he settled on one of his most treasured possessions, a small early travelling icon which depicted an angel whose beautiful, pensive face reminded him of another more famous one, the Angel with the Golden Hair far away in Petrograd.

> *Come back to me soon, my love. I send this angel for your protection and for that of your children. Keep it with you always. Darling Mai, I send you a thousand kisses and I count the days until your return.*
>
> *Nicolai*

The next day, with Beatrice's help, he sent it.

Mai listened in silence as Jacob outlined the interview he had had with Ned. Also listening, although she had heard it before, Juno's heart ached for her daughter. The happy, blooming Mai as last seen had been replaced by a haunted young woman, reminiscent of the worst days of her ill-fated marriage. Hardest of all was the thought that she might have been responsible for what had happened. *Although surely Zhenia wouldn't have passed on Mai's address to Ned. After all, why would she? On the other hand, maybe he had just asked her for it and then, why wouldn't she? No matter what had happened, as Jacob had pointed out it was done now. Better look forward not backward. All the same . . .*

This uncomfortable, not to say guilty, reverie was interrupted by Mai breaking down completely. Juno rushed to comfort her daughter. Jacob was uncharacteristically stern.

"Mai, you've got to hold up. If you don't we won't get anywhere."

"Jacob!" Juno was reproachful.

"No. No, he's right." Mai straightened her back and began to dry her tears.

"That's my girl!" said Jacob.

"As things stand, I can't see any way out of this unless I give up my children." Mai was sombre. "The way I read it, what Ned is doing is blackmailing me into going back to him. He knows that I could not bear to be separated from them. I may *have* to do it."

"Oh, Mai, no!" Juno was shocked

"I agree with your mother that that's unthinkable. However, there just might be another way. . . ."

They both stared at him.

"Which is?"

"For you to apply to the courts for a judicial separation and custody of the twins. Of course the whole thing would be much easier if we could prove that Fielding has committed adultery."

"What makes you think he has?" asked Mai.

"When I put the question to him, he wasn't evasive, quite the contrary, but there was the faintest hesitation before he answered and then, when he did answer, he was just a little too definite. Put it this way, it didn't feel right."

"Even if he has been unfaithful, it would be very hard to prove it," said Juno. "I mean, people don't exactly rush forward with confessions of adultery, do they? Even these days. But, of course, you're quite right, that would be the key to it."

"I'll try anything," said Mai.

"Good, because I have made an appointment in London with a barrister who specialises in matrimonial law."

That night, alone in the bed she had occupied as a girl, she reviewed her life to date and found her own conduct wanting. It must be, otherwise how had things come to this pass? And what about Jerome and Sophie? What must they make of her absence? These painful thoughts caused another upsurge of grief. Mai had little confidence in a judicial separation either, even supposing such a thing existed. A mutual desire to separate was one thing, but Ned did not want it and would fight it every step of the way, no doubt presenting himself as an upright husband whose selfless wish it was to keep his family together. *Virtue would be seen to be his and I,* thought Mai, *will be vilified as an absentee mother and a flighty wife, at which point no court in the land will give me custody.*

A few hours of fitful sleep followed and, in the end, Mai gave up on it and read until the morning light began to filter in, at which point, exhausted, she finally fell into a deep slumber. When she awoke, she was pale, composed, and ready for battle.

Two days later a small parcel arrived for Mai and was handed to her at breakfast time. Perplexed, she turned it over.

"Well, come on, why don't you open it?" Juno was equally curious.

"Juno," reproved Jacob, "it isn't your parcel!"

"I'm so intrigued by it, I feel as if it is. By employing your instinct, I *know* that is a very special parcel."

Jacob subsided. There wasn't very much more to be said about the efficacy of instinct and Juno knew it. To everyone's surprise Mai rose from the table.

"I'm not very hungry this morning."

She went, taking the parcel with her. In the privacy of her room, she opened it. The icon made its presence felt before the letter. Wonderingly, she turned it over. A miniature diptych, it opened. One panel was simply undecorated wood, but the facing one was painted with the image of an angel with gilded, braided hair. For a brief moment, as she held it, the little icon almost seemed to glow and Mai was conscious of a charge of energy from it. She turned to the letter. Mai had never received anything like it. Hot tears gushed, this time happy tears.

"I am no longer alone," said Mai to an empty room.

The next day she announced her intention of returning to London within the week.

"But first," said Mai to Juno, "I'm going to see my children."

"Are you going to telephone him first?"

"No. He'll try to stop me."

"All right. I'll come with you."

"Thank you, it's a kind offer, but I would prefer to go by myself."

Mai drove herself there along the old familiar roads. By now it was early May and the hedgerows were bedizened with white blossom. She turned into the short drive. The house which had once been hers, still *was* hers in fact, looked exactly as the day she left it.

Conscious of a feeling of trepidation, Mai got out of the car and made her way up the steps. With resolution, she knocked on the front door.

Hetty answered it.

"Oh, madam!" Her dismay was palpable.

"Hetty. Is Mr. Fielding at home?"

Hetty looked embarrassed.

"Yes, madam."

"May I see him?"

"I'm afraid Mr. Fielding has given orders that you are not to be admitted. Madam, I'm so sorry . . ."

"Hetty, *please*. I'm here to see my children. I *must* see my children."

From the far reaches of the house Mai could hear them playing. The sensation was extraordinary. It was like being on the other side of an invisible barrier.

"I can't let you in. It's more than my job's worth. . . ."

"Hetty, I can *hear* them." Unable to bear it any longer, tears streaming down her face, Mai stepped forward.

From behind the maid, a man's voice said, "Close the door, Hetty!"

By now Hetty was distressed and weeping, too.

"Oh, madam . . ."

"CLOSE THE DOOR, HETTY!"

The door closed.

A tragic figure, Mai was left standing on the step.

From an upstairs window, Ned watched his wife slowly make her way across the gravel and then get into the car, where she sat for a while, before driving away.

That evening, sitting in her room before dinner and with the little icon beside her, Mai wrote to Nicolai.

> *Darling Nicolai,*
> *How badly I have needed an angel during this desperately fraught period of my life and now I have two. I shall be travelling home on Wednesday, taking the train which gets in at 11:36 A.M. Will you be waiting for me on the platform? Will you? I hope so!*
>
> > *With all my love,*
> > *Mai*

The train was fifteen minutes late. Pacing up and down the platform, Nicolai began to wonder if he had imagined both it and the imminent arrival of his beloved. To reassure himself, every so often he took her letter out of his pocket and reread it. At long last, there the train was, swaying over the crossed shining rails before slotting in alongside platform six where it finally drew to a halt in a cloud of steam and a scream of brakes.

And there *she* was! Walking down the platform towards him, a case in each hand and, in order to avoid taking up a whole third case with it, wearing a fur coat as fine as anything his father had ever supplied for the aristocracy of Petrograd. To Nicolai his beloved looked like a Russian princess. At the same time Mai saw him and stood still. She let her luggage fall. Nicolai ran towards her, picked her up in his arms and swung her round and kissed her. The combination of her scent and the soft, shining fur pelt against his face intoxicated him. Arm in arm they walked to the barrier, pausing only to kiss once more before passing through it.

As they did so, they were seen by an employee of Fielding's called Paget, who was waiting with his wife, Margaret, to take the same train back to Sussex and who recognised his former mistress immediately, though not her handsome companion. The change in the household arrangements arising from the marital separation had resulted in the defection of some who had never liked Fielding and the promotion of others whose interests had been served by staying put. Mr. and Mrs. Paget, elevated to head gardener and housekeeper respectively, were in no doubt as to where their loyalty and future preferment lay. Just the same, despite the temptation to do so, Paget realised it was not his place to inform on Mrs. Fielding to his master, for this could be seen as impertinent familiarity and, as such, backfire. Nevertheless it was a pity not to capitalise on such potentially important knowledge. On the train he said as much to Margaret.

Margaret, who had also been thinking along the same lines and was sharper than her husband, had already reached a conclusion.

"We should make sure that servants in certain other households know what we saw and that we didn't want to cause trouble by telling Mr. Fielding. Then, when it finally gets back to him, *he'll* ask *us*," opined Margaret.

In this way the news of the sighting was allowed to become scurrilous, common gossip and as such did the rounds until, in the fullness of time as Mrs. Paget predicted, it finally reached Fielding's ears via a well-meaning friend and, also as predicted, he did summon the pair of them to learn exactly what it was they had witnessed.

Chapter Twenty

As Zhenia's waistline grew, her temper shortened. Rightly, Bertie put this down to her condition. The sexual flowering was brief and withered and died away almost as soon as it began but in the light of the longed-for pregnancy, on his side anyway, it seemed churlish to complain. Better to get the next seven months over with and then have a straight talk with his currently unenthusiastic wife about marital rights. *I've been very forbearing,* thought Bertie, *but it can't go on like this. I'm simply not putting up with it.*

It also seemed to Bertie that the bickering between his mother and his wife had got worse lately. What had always been an uneasy truce now verged on open warfare. Beside all of this, never mind a huge estate to run, Mai Fielding and her troubles occupied Bertie's thoughts. The story of Fielding's abduction of the children had become common knowledge by now and his heart bled for Mai. On the other hand, *could* a man be accused of abducting his own children?

Augusta, of course, had plenty to say on the subject and reserved the right to both deplore the scandal and enjoy it.

"There is a great deal of gossip," announced Augusta with satisfaction during the course of a visit to the Dower House. "Mai is being censured in *all* the drawing rooms and *rightly* so."

"Why rightly so, Mother?" Bertie was uncharacteristically snappy.

"Children are the property of the estate," stated Augusta, probably inadvertently revealing more about herself than was altogether wise, "not the mother. One can't have dissatisfied spouses running off with them every five minutes!"

"I certainly wouldn't!" said Zhenia, whose double entendre was lost on the other two. "But besides that, may I point out that Ned Fielding doesn't have an estate as such so I can't see that that argument applies here at all!"

"No, but the precedent does," pointed out Augusta smartly. "Precedent is a dangerous thing. Once a selfish action is condoned, heaven knows where it might lead."

Reflecting that where selfish actions were concerned, Mother ought to be an expert, Bertie said robustly, "I have every sympathy with Mai. I think she deserved better. In the drawing rooms *I* frequent, clearly different from the ones *you* frequent, rumour has it that Fielding is a brute."

Refusing to concede the point, Augusta said, "What does that matter? Personal peccadilloes should never be allowed to get in the way! It will be divorce next!"

"*Personal peccadilloes!*" Bertie could hardly believe what he was hearing. "Mother, the man's violent!"

"A lepidopterist violent? Oh, no, no, no! You must have got that wrong, Bertie!" Augusta stabbed her petit point.

As she recalled certain aspects of their lovemaking, Zhenia was not so sure about this. And if Ned was as rough as that when allegedly being tender, what was he like in a rage? Mindful of this, she said mildly, "Maybe he uses up all his finer feelings on the butterflies with none left over for his wife." She lowered her eyes demurely.

"And maybe it's all poppycock! What could you know about such things, Zhenia?"

"Society is changing, mark my words," said Bertie. "Divorce may have been unthinkable in your heyday, Mother, but that is not the case today. The war changed all that. Women are no longer prepared to put up with dire marriages."

She wasn't having it. "There is no such thing as a *dire* marriage, only a marriage. *None* are perfect!"

"I wasn't thinking of the odd imperfection," said Bertie, "I was thinking of hell on earth."

"I look upon mine as perfect!" said Zhenia, setting out to annoy and compliment in equal measure.

Another jab with the needle. "Do you! Well, aren't you the lucky one!" Augusta was sarcastic, perversely put out by this butter-wouldn't-melt endorsement of the wedded state.

"I should have thought it was what you wanted to hear," said her daughter-in-law.

"Do you, my love?" Bertie was gratified. "Do you really?"

He leant across and took his wife's hand.

If he believes that, he'll believe anything. Augusta felt like shaking her son.

She remembered Zhenia's slip of the tongue concerning her own siblings. The conviction that there was more afoot here than either of them realised resurfaced and this time refused to go away. But then again, maybe that's just what it was. A slip of the tongue. Nothing more, nothing less.

Nevertheless, Augusta promised herself, *insofar as I can, I shall watch her like a hawk from now on.*

Although he stayed with her that night, Nicolai did not make love to Mai the day he brought her home from the station, nor were they destined to consummate their love affair for a long time to come. For Mai, he recognised, could not have enjoyed the physical act against the background of her acute grief and pain at the loss of her children. So they slept together like brother and sister and, in the morning, for all the world as if they were de facto lovers, over breakfast they looked into one another's eyes, held hands, and talked about their future together. All the same, Nicolai was not confident. He had a strong presentiment of dark forces gathering. On that level Vladimir had been right. What he did not know was that by meeting her off the train that day at her own request, he had unwittingly and comprehensively compromised Mai and that such a single mundane act would affect their lives for years to come.

"I should like you to meet my parents," said Mai.

Nicolai was by no means sure about this. From what she had told him, Mai's family were extremely wealthy and he, Nicolai, was an impoverished Russian exile. It seemed to him that something rare and very precious to both of them might be misunderstood and, worse, denigrated. Catching Mai's openness he said as much.

"Trust me!" was her response. "Jacob and my mother are coming to London next week. We have an appointment with a barrister to discuss the strategy of what to do next. Afterwards perhaps we could all have dinner together."

Several days later and before this appointment took place, Mai received a letter from Ned. Nicolai watched her read it and instinctively knew that it contained bad news. Mai read it twice and then, without a word, handed it to him.

Dear Mai,

it ran,

> *I am writing this letter in the light of certain information which has been brought to my attention. Namely that you were seen on Victoria Station platform embracing an unknown man in such a way that there could be no doubt as to the relationship between the two of you. I need hardly tell you how disappointed I am by your behaviour . . .*

Disappointed? Nicolai read on.

> *. . . but let us put this to one side for the moment. The question for you to ask yourself is how would it be viewed in a court of law. It is my view that I would be within my rights to sue for divorce on the grounds of your adultery with person (or persons) . . .*

Nicolai clenched his fist.

> *. . . unknown. As I do not have to tell you, no court in the land will give you custody of the children under such circumstances and in the face of such loose behaviour I should be forced to curtail any future contact you might envisage enjoying with Sophie and Jerome. Having said all that, there is another way of approaching this . . .*

Here it came.

> *. . . The twins, who, of course, know nothing of this sordid side show, miss you. Never mind about being my wife, for better or for worse you are their mother. On that level, if on no other, I should be prepared to take you back. There then would*

be no need to go to court with all the undesirable attendant publicity (remember
your mother?) and, at least in public, we should be seen to resume our marriage.
And you, my dear Mai, would have your children back. I assure you that under
no other circumstances will such a thing happen. Perhaps you would like to think
about it. But not for too long or I might feel tempted to withdraw the offer.
I look forward to receiving a reply at your earliest convenience.

Your loving husband,
Ned

Nicolai had never read anything like it. The mixture of threat and reward, culminating in frank blackmail, and all finished off with the sort of
affectionate language any normal husband might write to any normal wife
was repellent not to say sinister.

Nevertheless, he felt Mai slipping away from him.

Swaying slightly, she stood up and went over to the mantelpiece where
she picked up the travelling icon. Holding it to her breast, she went into
the bedroom and quietly shut the door. Minutes later, he heard her sobbing as if her heart would break.

In the light of what had happened, Jacob and Juno travelled to London
earlier than they had intended and there was a council of war. The three of
them met at the Berensen flat. To Juno's concerned maternal eye, Mai
looked like a somnambulist. *Stunned* was the word. It raised the question of
how much more of this her beleaguered daughter could cope with.

Aghast, she and Jacob looked at the letter together.

"He's right," said Jacob, "it does not look good."

"It is *not* as it looks," said Mai with spirit.

"No, I'm sure it isn't but that doesn't matter in a case like this. It's *how*
it looks that matters."

"Who is the man, Mai? And how could he compromise you like this?"
The speaker was Juno.

"His name is Nicolai Zourov. And he didn't compromise me. I compromised myself. I asked him to come and meet me. He loves me. I need
that."

"Are you in love with him?"

"Yes. But we are not lovers. Not in the physical sense, anyway. I want you to meet him. It may be the only chance you have. It is becoming obvious to me that, for the sake of my children, I shall have to go back to my husband. Not to see them again would be unthinkable." Her voice trembled.

"Mai, if you do go back . . ."

Juno was startled. Until today she had never heard Jacob talk like that.

". . . *if* you do, you will be in a position to dictate certain terms. In his warped way, I'm willing to believe him when he says he wants a reconciliation for the children's sake, but it's mainly, I suspect, for his own *amour propre* and the look of the thing. This line here, 'at least in public, we should be seen to resume our marriage,' tells me everything. So: under the same roof, separate beds and separate lives. Mai, I know it isn't your style but plenty do it like that. Given that he is determined to use the children as a bargaining chip, it may be your only option."

Juno knew this was Jacob's way of saying it *is* your only option.

"I should like to meet Nicolai very much," said Juno, wanting for a moment to dwell on the positive.

"I've already organised it," said Mai. "There is a Russian restaurant that we go to. . . ."

As he knotted his tie that evening, prior to dinner at Vladimir's, Jacob said, "I have to say, I'm rather dreading this."

"Why?" queried Juno, the eternal optimist. "I'm anticipating that it will be quite the nicest thing to happen all day."

"Because Mai's record where choosing men is concerned has been less than distinguished. Besides, where has this Nicolai come from? According to Mai he trekked out of post-revolutionary Russia, found his way to Paris, and ultimately landed up over here. Who is he and what are his prospects? What does he do with himself all day? That's what I'd like to know."

"Jacob, you sound more English than the English! Quite pompous, in fact." In spite of all her anxieties concerning her daughter and her grandchildren, Juno was amused. "*You* were no one when you first arrived here. Now look at you."

Not keen on the *pompous* shaft but privately conceding that he deserved it, Jacob decided to try a different tack. "Do you think he'll look like a Tartar?"

"What, covered in animal skins and on one of those plucky little ponies? How romantic! I hope so! Why don't you finish getting dressed and we'll go and find out."

Mai had deliberately chosen Russian territory for this meeting and had privately decided that whether she went back to Ned or not, she was not prepared to give Nicolai up. Whether he would be prepared to settle for such an arrangement remained to be seen. In fact, unbeknown to her, Nicolai had already taken his own decision. For him, living through the turbulence of revolution had honed his appreciation of the value of what he had and, and more importantly, the need to hold on to it. Even if Mai went back to her odious husband, it would still be possible for him to go on loving Mai. If it was what she wanted, she would make it possible, *and I will be there for her*, vowed Nicolai to himself. *In the fullness of time we will be together. And one day I will take her to Russia and I will show her Petrograd.* Meanwhile he would have to carve out a career for himself. The idea of living off his wife, should she ever become his wife, was out of the question.

Against this background of uncertainty and resolve they all sat down to eat in Vladimir's little restaurant though Vladimir himself was not on duty that evening. Nicolai was not what either Jacob or Juno had expected. Listening to the young man talk about the colossal upheaval of 1917, Jacob, who had arrived in England following political upheavals of his own, was interested.

"One day," said Nicolai, "I should like to go back. I should like to take Mai with me."

Mai blushed.

"But what would you do?" Juno could not envisage going back to a country in chaos.

Nicolai shrugged. "My father was a furrier. He wanted me to follow in his footsteps and eventually take on the family business. To that end he taught me a lot about it. Eventually certain constants return even after revolutions such as that of 1917 and maybe one day it will be possible to go back and start again."

"Why go back?" asked Jacob. "Why not start a business here?"

"Because," replied Nicolai, "I left Russia with nothing, along with friends who have nothing. What would I start a business with?"

"You would need backing. I, myself, left my own country with nothing. . . ."

"Except a very good business brain!" pointed out Mai.

"Exactly! You've made my point for me. Nicolai's talent is different, but it's there. Nicolai knows about fur and he knows about the business, he says. You ladies like the luxury of fur. Maybe with the aid of his father's old contacts, he would be in a position to supply it for you and other young women. Also, perhaps, for not so well-heeled young women. Maybe some of them would like to wear fur and maybe Nicolai could make it possible for them to do so. Success is all to do with determination, hard work, and supplying a demand in the market."

Listening to this, Nicolai remembered the evocative sensation of Mai's own magnificent, shining fur against his cheek, together with the sharp, expensive smell of her scent as he kissed her. He looked at Jacob with respect. Neither of Mai's parents was what Nicolai had been expecting either. Nicolai had been expecting social grandees in the mould of the old Russian aristocracy with no idea about how to make a living because they had never had to do it.

Jacob eyed Nicolai for a minute and then smoothly changed the subject. The one topic that, by unspoken mutual consent, was not raised was that of Mai and her future and, by extension, the future of Mai and Nicolai. One step at a time. The purpose of this evening was simply to meet and assess each other so all knew where they stood before the inevitable complications set in.

Taking her home afterwards, Nicolai said, "Mai, despite what you always said, I know what you are going to do and I understand why you are going to do it."

"You mean going back for the sake of the children?" Mai was relieved that he had got there first and that she did not have to break it to him, which she had been dreading. Her eyes glimmered with tears. "If I stay with you, I lose them. If I go to them, I lose you. It's very hard."

"Of course you must put your children first. You will not lose me. Provided we can still meet, I will wait for you."

In the face of his devotion, Mai felt humbled. Tremulously, she said, "Nicolai, it could be years."

"Mai, if I offer it, you can accept it. I only ask that we continue to meet."

"Oh, darling, we will continue to meet. I intend to make it plain to Ned that this is the price of my return and that, behind the façade of living under the same roof, we have separate lives."

"Will you allow me to make love to you tonight?"

She smiled up at him.

"Of course not!" She smiled up at him. "I shall insist on it!"

Also going home, but in the opposite direction, Juno said to Jacob, "Well, what did you think?"

"I liked him."

Wonders would never cease!

Juno was jubilant. "I liked him too. So attractive. All that blond hair and those blue eyes. Best of all, he obviously adores Mai . . ."

"I would say best of all he's from good solid stock. Not like the effete toffs Mai has seemed determined to saddle herself with up to now. Butterflies! I ask you!"

"Of course, he hasn't any money. . . ." Juno decided to tackle that one straightaway.

"Very few of those who leave a country in the wake of that sort of revolution come out with any money. . . ."

"Except Princess Zhenia."

"Very few who are honest!"

Juno blinked and decided not to pursue this for the moment.

"Answer to that is, he'll just have to do what I did and make some."

"You could help him!" suggested Juno.

"If I think he's got what it takes I'll help him. If I don't, I won't. I'm a businessman, not a charity."

"How are you going to find out?"

"Man to man. I'll take Nicolai out to lunch."

The following morning, Mai rose from the bed she had shared with her lover and prepared for martyrdom. Her first act was to telephone her husband.

When he answered, Mai said, "I suggest we meet, in order to thrash this out."

"Are you going to come back?"

"That is what I want to talk about, Ned. Shall we say the Ritz, Thursday, one P.M.?" She turned to Nicolai. "The die is about to be cast. It's a dismal prospect, but with your support and my children, I can face anything."

When the day came, Ned was there ahead of her. Seeing him from the doorway, Mai was surprised by her own detachment. This was a man by whom she had had two children, *and he means nothing to me*, thought Mai. *Nothing. It's like approaching a stranger.*

The waiter led her to the table, pulled out her chair for her and, with a flourish, draped a starched napkin across her knees.

Her husband started to rise to his feet.

"Mai."

"Ned. Please don't get up."

Still hovering, the waiter enquired whether they would like a drink. Ned declined.

Mai said, "Yes. I would like a bloody Mary, please."

Ned raised his eyebrows. "Vodka? In the middle of the day. Are you sure?"

"Yes!" said Mai.

They appraised each other. Fresh from the arms of another man, Mai wondered what she had ever found attractive about Ned. These days the studied languorous hand movements seemed effeminate and the dandified dress an affectation, too. His tie, she noticed, was patterned with butterflies. Ned, on the other hand, was put out to note that in his absence his wife appeared to be thriving. Mai was calm and svelte. There was no discernible hint of contrition on the part of a married woman caught embracing a man not her husband on Victoria Station. Rather the opposite. Her level look verged on the judgmental.

The menus arrived and were studied. When they had ordered, both sat back.

"How are the children?"

"Sophie and Jerome are well. They look forward to the return of their mother. Which will be when?"

"When we have sorted one or two things between us, which is the purpose of this lunch."

Ned narrowed his eyes. "Such as?"

"The bedroom arrangements, for instance."

Their hors d'oeuvres arrived. Caviar for her, to his surprise (he had not known she liked it), and lobster for him. All in all it was turning into a very expensive way of ironing out the rags of their marriage.

To the waiter, she said, "I should like a neat vodka with this, please."

"Mai!"

"Yes?"

On second thought, he decided not to pursue it. Retraining Mai in the habits of obedience and moderation could come later.

"The sleeping arrangements." With forensic precision he delicately began to extract the flesh from the claw with a long silver fork. "Go on."

"Things cannot go back to where they were. I shall require my own bedroom. From now on I shall be your wife in name and outward appearance only."

"Is that all?"

The caviar tasted nutty and very good. Maybe the Ritz had succeeded in obtaining beluga where even Vladimir had failed.

"It is not. Whilst, as I say, I will maintain the public façade, otherwise I expect to lead my life as I wish with no interference from you. If you cannot see your way to agreeing to this then I cannot come back. That is all I have come here to say."

Bluff.

Mai held her breath.

What am I going to do if he refuses?

What Mai could not have known was that the heartrending scenes in the nursery every night because she was not there had worsened rather than improved with the passage of time. A flawed, complex man, with a sadistic streak, in his own way Fielding nevertheless loved his children and though he would not have, *had not*, thought twice about depriving them of their mother, the inescapable reality was that her absence was now proving destructive. In the face of the emotional damage, it seemed to him that he had no choice.

"You have become hard, Mai."

"No, not hard. Merely unwilling to live my life as you perceive it should be lived. If I return it will be purely and simply for the sake of my children and on jointly agreed terms. That way there can be no misunderstanding."

Fielding picked up the wine list. Though he could not claim to be pleased with the turn things had taken, he still appeared to be about to achieve what he mainly wanted. He ran his eye down it.

"What is your next course?"

Mai reminded him. Ned ordered a claret. When the wine waiter had gone to get it, he said, "Very well. Am I to assume that you intend to continue the liaison with your fancy man?"

"What an awful expression! That is nobody's business but mine. Though since you no doubt intend to continue the liaison with your mistress, disapproval of anything I might do could be construed as rankest hypocrisy," riposted Mai sharply, remembering Jacob's suspicion.

It was another shot in the dark. She was amazed at her own daring. Once again she had unwittingly hit the mark. With no idea what, if anything, she knew, Fielding was brought up with a jolt. Adultery on both sides could open up the possibility of a cross-petitioning legal battle in which a decision on custody would be on the cards. Time to relax back into the comparatively civilised, perhaps.

He said as much.

"If we are to try to coexist, we must keep hostilities to the minimum."

"Yes, we must!"

At last some sort of accord, though ironically it was still all to do with discord.

"So when *will* you return?"

"I shall return on Monday in time for dinner. Perhaps you would ask Hetty to make up the main guest bedroom for me? Now let's talk of other things. I am told that Princess Zhenia is expecting another child. Let's hope it is a boy this time."

Zhenia.

From Ned's point of view, things were less than satisfactory in that direction. Because of the forthcoming happy event (happy for Bertie at least, even if others were more ambivalent), the princess was currently firmly out of bounds. He briefly allowed himself to entertain the memory of her lean, supple body and the voracity of their unaffectionate coupling. There was, he had long since recognised, nothing soft about Zhenia. On the other hand, there was nothing soft about Mai either these days.

Fielding raised his glass.

"Yes. Here's to Zhenia. Let's hope she pulls it off this time!"

PART EIGHT

The Litvinoff Papers

Chapter Twenty-One

Other unexpected business took Sergei Litvinoff back to Russia, where he went first to Moscow and then to Leningrad. Notoriously secretive, he told no one about these travels, but simply disappeared from London one night and just as mysteriously reappeared five months later, at which point he resumed his search for the Dashkov emeralds.

During this period, Tatiana Volkovska regularly attended the same Russian Orthodox church where they had last encountered each other and was disappointed not to see Litvinoff again. Though intuition told her she *would* see him again. Certain wheels were always destined to come full circle and this, Tatiana instinctively felt, was one of them. Until this happened, there was nothing to do but wait.

Finding the *soi-disant* Princess Zhenia proved more of a task than Litvinoff had anticipated. She appeared to have swooped into English society trailing no personal streamers of any kind, married her well-heeled Englishman and then disappeared again, taking the emeralds with her. In the end, he hit upon the idea of visiting Countess Olga's house, long since sold, which was where he had his first stroke of luck. On the off chance that some of the original staff might still be there, he rang the servants' doorbell. It was answered by Ellie, who had found herself redundant when the princess married and went to the country and had transferred herself to the new owners of the countess's mansion. In the light of all that had gone before, Ellie was not unhappy about the course events had taken. The previous set-up had been altogether too Russian for Ellie's taste.

Now she found herself confronted by another one. The bearded gentleman on the doorstep was dressed in a beetle black suit which had seen better days, and claimed to be in search of either Princess Zhenia Dashkova or Countess Olga Fedorovna. Glad of any excuse to stop work for five or ten minutes, Ellie prepared to chat.

Mr. Litvinoff, who advertised himself as an old friend of the Dashkov family, did not, it transpired, know that the countess was dead.

"Oh, yes," said Ellie, ignoring this odd fact and only too pleased to be able to pass on the details. "It must be, let's think, at least three years since she died. I used to be Princess Zhenia's maid before she married. Miss Volkovska . . . she was the countess's housekeeper, and what a Tartar! . . . She could probably tell you more than I can. It was all very sudden. Afterwards the princess couldn't wait to get out . . . She and Miss Volkovska, they didn't get on, not like the countess and Miss Volkovska, they were thick as thieves . . . Anyway, when the princess married Mr. Langham, it was in the country . . . quiet, you know, to show respect for the old lady . . . Around that time Miss Volkovska left too, practically overnight . . ." Here Ellie cast her mind back, frowning. There had been gossip. "Oh, and she took that cat with her. . . ."

In an effort to stop this disjointed account and to get back to where he wanted to be, namely finding out the fate of Princess Zhenia, Litvinoff said, "I don't suppose you would know where in the country the wedding took place, would you?"

"No," said Ellie. "She didn't take me with her, you see. It was almost as if she wanted to put everything to do with this house behind her. . . ."

You bet she did, was Litvinoff's reaction, listening to this.

"It was in the paper, though," augmented Ellie, "and there was a picture. It looked like a lovely wedding. Cold, though. I never saw a dress like hers before. It had a hood with fur. . . ."

Interrupting a threatened stream of sartorial reminiscence, Litvinoff said, "Which newspaper?"

It was a question only a foreigner would have asked.

"*The Times,* of course," said Ellie, surprised. "Just before Christmas it was."

"So! December, 1920."

Inside the house a bad-tempered voice could be heard shouting, "Ellie! ELLIE! Where is that girl?"

Ellie jumped. "I'd better go!"

Litvinoff pressed a note into her hand.

"Thank you, you've been very helpful."

"Thank *you*, sir! But, I'm sure I don't deserve this!"

"You'd be surprised. Keep it."

Dazzled, she looked at it before carefully folding it, prior to putting it in her apron pocket and turning back into the house.

The following day, Litvinoff took himself off to the offices of *The Times* newspaper, where, with their permission, he painstakingly went through the back copies for December 1920 and finally found what he was looking for.

There she was. It was the first time he had seen Vera Kalanskaya. With looks like those and the Dashkov emeralds in her dressing table drawer, no wonder her upward trajectory had been so dramatic. There was an aura of triumph about her, as well there might be. Standing by her side and smiling confidently, not to say obliviously, into the camera, her very English husband clearly had not the slightest clue what he was getting into. Beneath the photograph there was a report, detailing who had attended and where the ceremony had taken place. Litvinoff religiously wrote it all down.

Chapter Twenty-Two

The day she was informed by Stiggins that there was a Mr. Markov to see her, Zhenia instinctively knew that this did not bode well. For one thing, since her arrival in London, she had made a conscious decision to draw her skirts aside from the Russian émigré community and was consequently alerted that, despite a pointed lack of encouragement, here was one of them on her doorstep and requesting an interview. Furthermore, the use of the indefinite article, as in *a* Mr. Markov, accompanied by a sniff, indicated that Stiggins did not consider the newcomer to be a gentleman. All the same, instinct also told her that it would be politic to meet him, whoever he was.

Her first reaction was that Markov, whom she had never seen before, looked like a tall, skeletal bank clerk. The ancient suit and starched collar took her back to her penurious days in Paris. There had been quite a few of his ilk in there. Shabby, dispossessed refugees from a life which would never be the same again.

"Mr. Markov, I believe."

She was very pregnant, he noticed, and extended her hand without getting up.

Litvinoff bowed low over a huge diamond. The assumed name had seemed a wise precaution.

"Princess!"

Was it her imagination or was there just a hint of irony in the depth of the bow and the respectful reverence of the address?

"Would you like some tea?" She rang the bell.

Each waited for the other to begin. In Petrograd, Litvinoff had garnered something of a sinister reputation for himself owing to his watchful ability to sit an interview out in virtual silence until the resulting jitteriness of the other translated itself into some verbal indiscretion. He did not, however, deceive himself that the woman opposite was likely to be one of these. Just the same, until he was able to gauge her attitude and the way she was likely to jump, proven methods were perhaps the best.

Finally, she said, "Well, Mr. Markov, what can I do for you?" Her Russian accent appeared almost nonexistent. In ways like that, she had all the hallmarks of the born chameleon.

"It may be that there is nothing you can do for me!"

Neither of them believed it.

He did not elaborate.

As had many before her, Zhenia found herself having to make the conversational running.

"It is a long way to come without a clear idea of what you might expect to get out of it."

The smile, insofar as there had ever been one, had gone. There was a stillness about the princess which indicated to him that, like a wild animal, she was by now very much on the alert. It was at this juncture that Litvinoff decided to throw his stone into the pool and see what happened.

Without preamble, he said, "On the contrary, I have a very clear idea of what I might get out of it. I am looking for a certain Vera Kalanskaya."

He waited.

The stone appeared to sink without trace. Her expression did not alter one iota. The eyes were opaque.

She shrugged. "What is that to me?"

"That is what I am here to find out."

Round and round in circles. Cat and mouse.

At this interesting point the tea arrived.

"Milk and sugar?"

"Neither. Black."

He fell silent again.

"What do you want with this . . . this Vera Kalanskaya anyway?"

"I don't want her. I want something that she has. Perhaps, *Princess,*" Here there was no mistaking the inflexion. ". . . it would be better to speak in Russian. Walls, as they say, have ears. . . ."

Outwardly unperturbed, inwardly at bay and furious, she decided to play him at his own game.

"As you wish."

She waited.

Reflecting that it made a stimulating change to deal with this sort of opponent, Litvinoff put his hands together, finger to finger almost as if he was praying, and then appeared to meditate for two minutes. The princess, who was beginning to wonder why he didn't get on with her execution since they both knew that was what he was here for, quelled a rush of fear and tried to collect her wits. Maybe instead of this sadistic game of hide and seek, it would be better if they both put their cards on the table and then did some hard bargaining.

But did she hold any cards?

More to the point, did he?

Hold the nerve.

The baby turned over and kicked and then rotated again.

All the trouble I've gone to and now this happens.

Like a poisoned dart, the name *Tatiana Volkovska* lodged in Zhenia's brain.

If she's betrayed me, she'll never get another penny. I'll leave her destitute!

At this precise moment, Litvinoff said, "You must be wondering how I found you."

Helping herself to a cigarette and fitting it into a tortoiseshell holder before lighting it, Zhenia said, "Yes, I was actually." With all the turmoil going on inside her head, her own voice sounded very far away as if the exchange between the two of them was going on in another room.

"Your maid. Your former maid, I should say."

"*Ellie?* Not Tatiana?"

Now it was Litvinoff's turn to present a poker face. At the same time he was too old a hand at this sort of thing to deny he had ever met the old countess's housekeeper. It was better not to lie more than you had to.

"Tatiana? Ah, yes, Miss Volkovska. Miss Volkovska declined to speak to me. I tried to persuade her but she was adamant. So I was forced to look elsewhere."

"Really? But I can't think that Ellie was able to tell you very much. She knows hardly anything about me."

"That is correct. Ellie was merely the geographical connection."

"So where has all this about Vera Kalanskaya come from?"

"Paris," said Litvinoff. "Last heard of in Paris. She made off with the Dashkov emeralds among other things."

"No, she didn't," asserted Zhenia. Given all the publicity they had received there was no point in denying it. Seeing no alternative, she decided to brazen it out. "There is no mystery about the whereabouts of the emeralds. *I* have the emeralds. In the bank. They are Daskov property and, since I am the sole family survivor of the revolution, they now belong to me."

"Quite so. And so they would if you were. The sole Dashkov survivor, I mean. But you are not."

Playing for time, she asked, "Are you saying there is another?"

"No." He did not directly answer it. "I'm not saying that."

Zhenia could hardly contain herself. "Well?"

"I refer you to Mathilde Ivanova. Governess to the Daskov family. What about her?"

Litvinoff did not raise his voice and no doubt felt he did not have to. There was an inexorable muted bullying in the way in which the information he commanded was beginning to seep out.

Ah! Zhenia felt her heart begin to pound like that of a cornered fox. The temptation to put an end to the agony, throw herself on Markov's mercy, even give up the emeralds, was entertained for the first time so long as he would leave her alone.

"Mathilde Ivanova died alone in her squalid lodging. The stroke incapacitated her but did not finish her off. By the time she was found, she had starved to death. Or perhaps she froze to death first. Who knows? No matter, it's all the same in the end. Somebody, Vera..." The name was slipped in so softly and so naturally, like the thinnest of stilettos, that the princess scarcely noticed it and insofar as she did, did not feel predisposed to make a fuss about it. "... *somebody* sifted through Mathilde Ivanova's belongings and plundered everything of value, even the sables that Princess Katarina Dashkova used to wear on her way to the opera...."

Zhenia shivered. It couldn't have done, of course, but the room they were sitting in felt as if it had suddenly grown cold. Even after all this time, the memory of the immobile woman on the bed whose burning eyes had followed her all around the room while she ransacked it remained potent. Did the dead come back to seek revenge? Sometimes, in her dreams at night, Zhenia thought they did. Sometimes, perhaps, they sent emissaries of the living instead, such as the man who sat opposite her.

"Mathilde," Litvinoff was continuing, "had lived with the Dashkovs for years, almost but not quite family. Governess and general factotum, she knew all their foibles and their intimate secrets. She knew the names of their dogs and the pet names they used to one another. She knew all their scandals and as an impoverished member of the nobility must have hated her lowly status. Maybe she hated them, too. Anyway, came the revolution and it was every man, or should I say in this case, every woman for herself and after the family was disposed of, shall we say, Mathilde had no compunction about flying the coop with a great deal of booty. No doubt she told herself she had earned it. All those years of being patronised and taken for granted when, but for a profligate father, she would have been up there with the best of them."

The two of them digested what he had just said.

"And then, in Paris, she met you."

A long silence ensued.

Litvinoff helped himself to a biscuit.

"Why don't you tell me all about it? You might as well."

Vera shrugged and lit another cigarette. She inhaled deeply.

"As you wish. I arrived in Paris via Odessa and Marseilles. It took almost all my savings, though God knows they didn't amount to much. Anyway, I arrived knowing no one and with only the clothes I stood up in. The first thing I did was to go to the Nevsky church in the Rue Daru. I needed to find somewhere to live and it seemed to be a good place to start asking around."

"And of course it was. The best." Litvinoff knew it well.

"Yes. Through someone I met there I heard of Mademoiselle Mesureux's boarding house. Seedy but respectable, they said . . ."

"Quite so. Was that in the Rue Vaugirard? Maybe not . . . I forget. Go on."

"Luckily, there was a room available and I took it. After that I had to find work in order to pay the rent. It was hand to mouth. I strung beads, I did embroidery, I worked as a cloakroom girl in restaurants, and all for a pittance. At Christmas I inscribed Christmas cards and was paid the munificent sum of ten francs for every thousand. Can you imagine that?"

Litvinoff, who had seen it all at firsthand, could.

"When you think, a *coffee* cost six sous. I used to sit over the same cup for hours in La Closerie des Lilas or sometimes Le Dome (remember

Le Dome?) just whiling away the hours. A lot of the time I was very hungry and very cold."

It hadn't stopped her leaving the stricken Mathilde Ivanova to starve to death in a freezing room, though. He let her go on. He had a strong presentiment that she needed to reminisce like this. Maybe she felt that by doing so she was forging a common bond with him which would help her case when it came to talking terms.

"You could have worked at the Renault automobile plant. A lot of them did. How did you learn English, by the way?"

Vera crushed the lipstick-stained remains of her cigarette into an ashtray, saying as she did so, "I had an English lover for a month or two. Or was it three?" She smiled faintly. "Useful, as it turned out."

Vera got up and walked across the room to the fireplace, where she leant against the mantelpiece. Despite her pregnancy she still moved gracefully. The current fashion suited her, though in Litvinoff's view there were many it did not. It had to be said, too, that the no doubt rigorous training of the Mariinskiy corps de ballet had served her well. There was a fluid melding together of hand and body movement together with a classical disdain which perfectly underpinned the aristocratic pretensions. On top of all of that Vera Kalanskaya appeared to be a consummate actress. It was possible that another of her compatriots might have worked her out (although the countess, it seemed, had not) but never an Englishman of the type she appeared to have married, for whom Russian social nuance and all its pitfalls would have been impenetrable.

Listening to her talk, it struck Litvinoff that, like Tatiana Volkovska, this one also found herself cut off from her roots and, despite the hard brittleness, missed them too. Living a lie day in, day out could not have been easy either.

"Tell me how you came to join the Mariinskiy Ballet School?"

"My mother travelled from Georgia to Petrograd with my brother and myself for the auditions. He was turned down and I was accepted. It was as simple as that."

"Did you enjoy the life you led there?"

"I infinitely preferred it to the mud and the flies of Georgia, if that's what you mean. The training was very rigorous but, as time went on and I became a member of the corps de ballet, a completely different life began to be revealed to me. For instance, one evening a group of us were asked to dance at the Yusupov palace where there is, or there used to be, a small family theatre."

Remembering it, Vera was silent for a moment. It was in the palace that she had first seen and marvelled at a collection of Fabergé eggs at least as intricately magnificent as the clutch she now regarded as her own.

"Let's get on to Mathilde...."

"Ah, yes, Mathilde. She sought me out. It was Mathilde's view that we could be good for one another."

"A fatal miscalculation, if I may say so."

Disregarding this thrust, with a toss of the head, Vera said, "It was Mathilde's idea that I should be groomed to impersonate Princess Zhenia Dashkova. She coached me in all aspects of the family's life. We spent months perfecting it all. At that point I knew nothing about the emeralds."

Vera decided to leave it at the emerald set. There had been no mention of the rest of the loot. Maybe he didn't know about it. If that was the case, there was no point in telling him. Now that the initial shock of Markov's sudden appearance had worn off, a resolve to hang on to the lot was crystallising, whatever it took to do it.

"What was the end game to be?"

"The end game," replied Vera, "was to be more or less what happened, though without Mathilde. It was to get out of Paris and penury and to launch ourselves on English society through the medium of the countess."

"But why, if Mathilde had the Dashkov jewels, would she need you? The emeralds alone would have set her up for life."

Noting the word *alone*, which indicated that he probably did know of the existence of the rest, Vera said, "With the countess still alive, there was no way Mathilde Ivanova could sell the emeralds as her own. They were famous. Whereas Princess Zhenia Dashkova would have faced no such difficulty. I suppose the idea was that we were to work together. And split the proceeds, maybe. I don't know. I only found out about them by accident. You'd have to ask her that."

Since he knew the remains of Mathilde Ivanova were now incarcerated in the Sainte-Genevieve-des-Bois Russian cemetery thirty kilometres outside Paris, Litvinoff forbore to respond to this heartless suggestion. 'The princess,' it seemed, had a compassionate cog missing, always a help where criminal activity was concerned.

Mildly he said, "Be that as it may, it is the emeralds I am here to reclaim for the state. Justice is not my concern. Much as I may deplore the fact that you left Ivanova to die and whatever else you might have done, all that is between you and the Almighty. But now, let's get away from God and concentrate on Mammon. To commence, I know who you are not. You do not want anybody else to know who you are not. You have the Dashkov emeralds. I want the Dashkov emeralds. Ergo, I will swap you the secret for the jewels. Nothing could be simpler."

In the face of her sceptical silence, he asked, "Well, could it?"

"It's not as simple as that. Firstly, as I say, they are in the bank. . . ."

"Get them out. They're your property, after all."

"Secondly, how do I explain their disappearance?"

"That," said Litvinoff, "is your problem, *Princess*. Get copies made."

Inwardly enraged, after some cogent thought, Vera said, "I know how to do it without causing speculation. The shooting season is about to begin. When it does my husband likes to give a ball, here in the country. This will be the perfect reason to take the emeralds out of the bank. I suggest you come and stay here for the duration and we will do our exchange then. What do you say?"

"I say yes."

All the same, Litvinoff was bemused. It felt too easy. On the other hand, what could go wrong? And it was not every day that in the course of his work a weekend at an English country house was on offer.

Before he left, like any conscientious hostess she insisted on taking him on a tour of the house and garden.

Chapter Twenty-Three

Explaining away her Russian guest, who turned up with one black suit for her well-heeled shooting party, was not easy. In the end, Zhenia decided to promote him as an aristocrat dispossessed by the revolution. Only a real Russian aristocrat would have known by dint of voice and manner that this was unlikely and with her own secrets to keep, never mind about those of Sergei Markov, Zhenia had made a habit of steering well clear of persons of that ilk.

"What an unprepossessing man. Such a terrible suit. *And* he has arrived early, which is as unpunctual as arriving late. Where did he come from?" Augusta wanted to know, looking down her long nose.

Uncharacteristically taking the charitable high ground, Zhenia said, "I won't hear a word of criticism. Poor Count Sergei lost all his family in the uprising and came out with nothing."

Not to be deflected, Augusta went on, "A *count*? Surely he must have had a better suit than that to escape in."

"It seems not. But Zhenia's quite right, Mother. We must all be nice to the count," said Bertie. "How did you meet him, my love?"

"Oh, he was a friend of the family in the old days," answered his wife vaguely, thinking as she said it that she must remember to mention his social elevation to Markov. More pressing, though, was putting into operation the plan she had formulated. The more she had thought about it, the more Zhenia had decided that she had come too far to lose the Dashkov emeralds now. Or anything else, for that matter.

"We shall have to find the count something to wear for the ball," she added, "otherwise, like Cinderella, he won't be able to go. But what I really want to talk about are the shooting arrangements on Monday and Tuesday. Such a pity I won't be able to join the men this year."

Just as well. Augusta folded her lips. Her disapproval of her daughter-in-law's eccentric insistence on participation in the sport and Bertie's ridiculous indulgence of this particular foible irritated beyond measure. Even more trying was the fact that, aided by a gimlet eye, Zhenia had become a good shot.

Bertie said, "You can always just follow the guns. It's the usual set-up. The first day, Monday, it's a drive to get there, and a lunch at the Lodge. On Tuesday it's a drive to the other side of the lake and lunch at the Folly."

"I'd certainly like to do that on either Monday or Tuesday," said Zhenia. "Tuesday, probably."

Unable to resist it, Augusta intervened. "Are you sure it's wise in your condition?"

"Quite sure." Zhenia was terse. "The exercise will do me good. Besides, the child isn't due for another month."

"Second babies are often early. . . ."

"Well, of course, Augusta, you would know all about that, having only had one. . . ."

"Actually, I had Laetitia Tattershall in mind. Laetitia had a nasty experience on the grouse moor with her second."

"Since that was a daughter anyway, presumably nobody got too worked up about it. Except her, of course."

Zhenia wondered if Laetitia was dead yet. If not, she certainly deserved to be. Although no doubt the awful legend would live on. Augusta would make sure of that.

She changed the subject. "Good heavens, is that the time? The train contingent will be arriving in a couple of hours, closely followed by the motor brigade."

"I'm sure you'll find Stiggins has it all under control," said Bertie.

"Your faith in Stiggins is touching," observed Augusta, without elaborating. "Have you asked the Fieldings this year?"

"Yes." Bertie was terse.

"I gather Mai has gone back to her husband and about time, too!"

"From what I hear Mai has gone back to her children rather than her husband. But to answer your question, no, I haven't. If you really want to know, I can't stand the fellow."

Bertie's brow clouded.

Determined to pursue it, Augusta said with relish, "I am reliably informed that Mai had a lover in London whom her husband found out about. They were seen embracing on Victoria railway station by one of the staff. *On the platform.* Really! Whatever next? It is my opinion that Mai is fast. Her morals are deplorable, just like those of her ridiculous, unreliable mother!"

Self-righteous old bat. Zhenia stole a look at Bertie and noted with interest that his expression was thunderous.

Oblivious and warming to her theme, Augusta changed tack. Prurient gloating gave way to piety.

"All I can say is that, in the wake of this sordid behaviour, I hope Mai does not present herself at church for matins tomorrow morning. I fear I shall be forced to cut her if she does."

Zhenia was thinking, *Fat lot Mai will care about that,* when Bertie lost his temper. Like a dormant volcano he exploded without warning. Instinctively Zhenia ducked.

"MOTHER! DON'T YOU *DARE* SPEAK OF MAI LIKE THAT! I WILL NOT HAVE IT! DO YOU HEAR?"

It would have been hard not to. In that instant it became obvious to Zhenia that Bertie was still in love with Mai. She awaited her mother-in-law's response with interest.

Years of ruling the roost and regarding having the very last word as a God-given right ensured that Augusta did not lose *her* temper. She did, however, straighten her back, lean back slightly, and raise her eyebrows.

In glacial tones, accompanied by the notorious lorgnette look: "And may I point out that I have every right to say whatever I like in my own house! And, while we are on the subject, may I also say that your manner leaves a great deal to be desired! I am your mother, don't forget."

This reproof, rather than halting the lava flow, exacerbated it.

"THIS IS NO LONGER *YOUR* HOUSE, IT IS *MY* HOUSE AND, I REPEAT, I WILL NOT HAVE IT!"

As with many placid people with no experience of managing rampaging emotions because they practically never had to, Bertie found stopping once he had started very difficult. Without the usual checks and balances he consequently went on to add, "BESIDES, SINCE YOU BROUGHT THE SUBJECT UP, WHAT ABOUT *YOUR* LOVERS? WHAT ABOUT *THEM*?

There followed a deathly hush. For once Augusta, who had turned an alarming shade of puce, could find nothing to say. Stealing a look at her before bending her head over her teacup to hide a gleeful grin, Zhenia thought her mother-in-law might be about to have a seizure. Years of so-cial terrorism enabled Augusta to regroup more quickly than most. Side-stepping the question for to have answered it would have been unthinkable (though in fact it had been more of a statement with its own inbuilt an-swer) she stared at her son for a very long time in sulphurous silence, haughtily driving home the principle of *lèse-majesté*, before finally saying, "Bertie, you are clearly unwell. I would go further. I think you have gone mad." She stood up and stalked to the door where she paused. "When you are yourself again, I shall expect an apology!"

After her departure, wracked with guilt, Bertie said to Zhenia, *"What* made me do it? She's an old lady. . . ."

Zhenia did not see why Augusta should get away with this.

"Bertie, she's a *lethal* old lady and you will find she was a lethal lissom young thing, too."

"All the same . . ."

"She's a battle axe. You'll find the house much more relaxing with-out her."

This was hard to deny.

"How many lovers is she supposed to have had? You never told me about it before."

"No. I thought it wouldn't be seemly."

"Well?"

"Oh, I don't know. A few down the years. They came and went," an-swered Bertie vaguely. "Mother isn't really an easy ride. She's keener on en-slavement than partnership."

"Yes, I have noticed. Are *you* going to church tomorrow morning?" Zhenia had used her pregnancy to get her out of this chore some time ago.

"I don't think I could stomach watching Mother cutting Mai."

Zhenia was scornful.

"For God's sake, Mai won't care. Why should she? She probably won't even notice. I have to tell you, Bertie, that Augusta has a much higher estimation of her own social potency than almost everyone else."

Bertie was relieved to hear it.

"What are you going to do with your count?"

"No idea, though he seems to be a great walker."

"He says he wants to follow the guns on Monday, and on Tuesday he's either going to do the same or simply pass the time exploring the estate. Or maybe we could sit him on a horse," Bertie suggested.

Zhenia shrugged. "I don't think he wants it. You could always ask him. But what would he wear? He can't hack out in that threadbare suit."

"We'll rustle him up something from somewhere," said Bertie. "When's he going?"

"Thursday."

"I say, there's the first of the cars. I'd better get cracking."

"So you are going to brave your mother's wrath?"

"Well, she's hardly going to attack me in church, in front of everyone, is she?"

"No. Much more likely to cut you dead as well. In front of everybody. Maybe you and Mai Fielding should sit together. Two for the price of one."

"She's right. I *will* have to apologise."

"Yes, I suppose you will."

The following morning, after a prowl around the house, Litvinoff finally ran his hostess to ground in the library. There was nobody about. The house party had divided into the slugs who were still asleep after the excesses of the formal dinner of the night before and the more energetic, or maybe the more abstemious, who had got up early in order to go to church.

Zhenia was not pleased to see her compatriot.

"Ah, here you are," said Litvinoff.

"Yes. Here I am."

"We need to talk. May I say, incidentally, that you looked magnificent last night. I look forward to the Dashkov emeralds on Tuesday night."

Zhenia thought this was rich since Markov was about to try and take them off her but decided not to comment.

"I'll look a lot better once I get rid of this." She indicated her stomach with distaste.

"Oh, come now. It's your passport!"

"Only if it's a son."

"Quite so. But, if you think about it, there is an element of uncertainty in almost everything we do," observed her foe.

Given that there was more of an element of uncertainty in his dealings with her than Markov knew about, Zhenia could only agree. As she sat facing him, the half formulated plan fell into place.

Litvinoff crossed one long bony leg over the other. The sole of one of his shoes had a hole in it, she noticed.

"I wonder if there is any point in postponing the hand-over until Thursday. After all, the jewels will have had their outing by Wednesday morning. . . ."

Zhenia thought quickly.

"It would excite comment if you left early, *Count*." Passing his own ironic inflexion back to him gave her a certain satisfaction.

"Ah, yes," said Litvinoff with the wintriest of smiles, "thank you for my ennoblement, *Princess*. You would seem to have a rare talent for organising elevation. All the same I beg to differ. It is my opinion that any discussion generated by my early departure would be minimal and soon over."

"Well, maybe. Nevertheless, I still suggest we keep to the original plan and that you enjoy what remains of your stay. You may, after all, never get the chance to stay in a house as grand as this one again. Not too many of them left in Russia these days, I wouldn't have thought."

She was right there. Not that Litvinoff had ever been invited to such a place when they were there. It had to be conceded that being waited on hand and foot had its novelty and what was two more days in the great scheme of things?

"Believe me, an opportunity to go out with the guns is not to be missed and you like walking, I believe? Then, maybe a walk around the estate tomorrow afternoon could be followed by an excursion further afield on Tuesday?"

Mindful of his unlovely, poky lodging in London, Litvinoff hesitated and then, in spite of himself, assented.

Why not?

The shooting party left very early. Grey dawn slowly metamorphosised into a day of wind and sun. High white cloud, reminiscent of the Prince of Wales's feathers, streamed and frothed. There had been a shower of rain the night before and the air smelt tangy and fresh. Standing back from the action, a lonely figure crowlike among the tweeds, Litvinoff stood looking up, watching the birds go over and the guns as they swung round to pick them off. Ritual slaughter. There were times when he felt he had seen too much death. This was sport, of course, and not to be compared with the river of blood which had sprung out of the revolution of 1917 whence no doubt there was more to come. Despite being worth a tsar's ransom, even the Dashkov emeralds were merely a frivolous sideshow compared with the sheer scale of what was happening in Russia, he recognised. Sometimes it seemed to Litvinoff that, like a damaged leviathan, his country was lurching towards disaster rather than a brave new world and that idealism and patriotism, or what there had been of them, were largely things of the past. The revolution had become a monster and, as such, had acquired an unstoppable impetus of its own. These days a different, brutal breed was jockeying for position and fighting for power, men like the sinister Joseph Stalin, for instance, currently general secretary of the Party. It raised the question of what would happen when Lenin either was deposed or, and maybe more likely the way things were going, died. Then again it was worth remembering that Lenin had ruthlessly quelled all opposition following the Kronstadt mutiny. Sometimes Litvinoff felt himself better off away from his homeland. There was safety in comparative anonymity and another country. Better to be out of it when the next inevitable blood-letting took place. Though, on the other hand, being out of it meant missing opportunities for preferment when, *force majeur,* certain job vacancies were created in the ensuing turmoil.

The dry whirring of beating wings heralded another wave of birds. The sky was black with them as the flight soared over accompanied by a flurry of shots and the soft repetitive thud of the casualties falling to earth. Orderly and efficient, the dogs retrieved the dead and carried them tenderly back before laying them down.

Lunch, when it finally took place, was a lavish picnic at a house called the Lodge where three or four of the ladies, including the princess, had foregathered. The guns all appeared to know one another and it fell to

Bertie to engage the count in conversation since his wife showed no sign of doing so. Zhenia, in fact, was feeling far from well. It was probably the strain of the past week and there was more to come. *No good buckling now.* She swallowed a little champagne and picked at some chicken.

At the other side of the room, Bertie was having difficulty drawing out the count.

"So you don't shoot?" Bertie, who had never met a member of the aristocracy anywhere who didn't, found this curious. But then, as he had frequently told himself with regard to his volatile wife, maybe they did things differently in Russia, now to be known as the Soviet Union. Litvinoff, who had shot dead at least two men in the dangerous days when the revolution first broke out, said no, he did not.

Undeterred by the other's taciturnity, he said, "My wife tells me that you are an old friend of the Dashkov family. . . ."

"Yes, that is so."

Another silence. Not an unfriendly one, Bertie sensed, just a silence. But then who could be surprised when, like Zhenia, the man had lost his entire family in 1917. Although Zhenia, now Bertie came to think of it, appeared to have risen above her own family tragedy with remarkable resilience. In the circumstances better not to mention the demise of the Dashkovs, though. So it was, in his anxiety to steer clear of personal disaster, that Bertie raised the subject of the dire fate of the emperor of all the Russias instead. The moment the words were out he regretted them. A vision of his mother giving him one of her *What a FOOL you are, Bertie,* looks presented itself before his inner eye. Thank God she was still sulking and therefore not here today. Too late now, he had said it. To his surprise, the count's reaction was robust. Animation became the order of the day.

"The tsar," pronounced Sergei Markov, "brought most of his troubles upon himself. Although it was an accumulator, I suppose, and he could be said to have been the one who reaped what the ones who went before had sown. Nevertheless he was a weak man, seen as a pawn of his wife. We all knew the revolution had to come. It was just a question of when. Nicholas was so far from his people, he had no idea." There was a pause. Then, with a dismissive shrug: "He was a good family man, I'll grant him that. But there are plenty of those about. Good tsars? Not so many, I think."

Bertie noticed two things about this unexpected speech. The first was that the count had been self-evidently less than enamoured of his late sovereign and the second was the use of the word *we* thereby identifying himself with the mass rather than the elite. However, it was also true that Bertie himself was not overfond of his own royal family, secretly regarding them as Hanoverians and not English at all. Though he acknowledged to himself that if either King George or Queen Mary had been at all *likeable*, this probably wouldn't have mattered. As it was, one was a martinet and the other a haughty and difficult houseguest, graspingly prone to carrying off with her whatever took her fancy, be it a choice piece of porcelain or a set of six Hepplewhite chairs. Bertie knew of at least one panicky family who had put away almost everything in anticipation of a regal descent and had still been forced to watch a cherished clock which they had overlooked being loaded into the back of the royal Daimler at the end of it. Furthermore, it was not until later, when a venerable ivy cladding the back of the house turned brown and expired, that they realised the queenly visitor, who disapproved of this particular plant, had sliced through the stem with the royal scissors. If that was the way the Romanovs behaved, it probably explained a lot.

To his relief, Zhenia came and joined them, thereby affording him an opportunity to move on.

"You must let me design your walk tomorrow for you," she said to Markov. "There is some particularly fine scenery in the direction of the lake, for instance."

"I should be honoured," said Litvinoff, this time without a trace of sarcasm. It occurred to him that, under other circumstances, he and she might have had a good deal in common.

"And now," said his hostess, "comb your hair, Count. It is time for the obligatory photograph."

This took place outside and, insofar as anything was at the Hall, was very egalitarian in that it featured everyone, including the servants who had laid out the lunch, an idea of Bertie's deeply deplored by his mother. Luckily the weather had held up. In the middle were the gentry, the back row of which, including Litvinoff, balanced precariously on a form. To right and left stood beaters *et alia* and flanking them the female servants in black dresses and white starched aprons and caps, accompanied by Stiggins. In front sat the dogs, bright eyed, ears cocked, eager to get on with it and in the foreground, on the grass, the point of it all, a heap of slaughtered pheasants, their ruffled, bloody plumage bright in the fitful sun.

The next morning showed none of the promise of its predecessor. The day was ochrous and dark. Bulbous clouds leaned over the grounds, heralding rain. As before, the shooting party had set off at dawn and, since it was customary for the ladies to dine off trays in their rooms at that hour, Litvinoff enjoyed a solitary breakfast. Sumptuous, though. Scrambled eggs with smoked salmon, kedgeree, bacon, sausages, kidneys, kippers, and more reposed on fine china serving dishes. For the ascetic a huge dish was laden with fruit, the downy sheen of perfect peaches complementing the polished gloss of apples and the plump purple velvet of grapes. Crystal, crisp linen, silver, flowers, all were immaculate, and servants so discreet that tea and *The Times* almost appeared to materialise by themselves. The princess had been right. For Litvinoff such cosseted magnificence was a revelation and one not to have been missed. This was how the very rich lived, insulated from the traumas of the world outside and no need to lift a finger. From the very beginning of every day until they made their way to bed at night there was nothing to offend the eye or jar the sensibilities. Except each other, of course. Unless one became a hermit, there was no getting away from the human condition. No doubt it was how the Romanovs had lived, too. Though ironically that very insulation, designed to soothe and calm, had had the reverse effect in that it had been partly instrumental in bringing about their downfall and brutal end. Despite his commitment to the new regime, even Litvinoff found the thought of the Yekaterinburg murders in the cellar of the House of Special Purpose hard to stomach. It was not the German woman and her weak dolt of a husband that disturbed him but the children, those tall vivacious girls and the young tsarevich. *Massacre of the innocents.* Mentally he veered away from it.

Instead, for a few silent moments he surveyed the serving table, committing its opulence to memory before beginning to help himself. There was no sign of the princess, nor had he expected any. As promised, she had written him an afternoon itinerary and, scanning it as he ate, Litvinoff saw no reason to deviate from this.

As I said, the best walking is in the direction of the lake, wrote Zhenia, in a sprawling hand. *Should you need one, Stiggins will find you a redingote. This is a long hike but a rewarding one . . . I may see you before you leave and I may not. If I do not, bonne chance!* There followed a simple map. In point of fact it didn't look like a particularly long hike to Litvinoff, who had been used to covering much greater distances in his youth in his native Russia where country transport had been sparse to nonexistent and the roads atrocious. All the same he decided to take up the offer of a coat.

The morning was spent updating his report. Rather than leaving this in his room when he had finished doing it, Litvinoff put the document in an envelope which he sealed and addressed and asked a servant to send to his London address. One could not be too careful. As he finally set off after a light lunch there was a low rumble of thunder and a sudden broad illumination of the lowering sky above the trees in the park. Wild fire. The stillness as he strode out was oppressive with a curious air off ... what? Litvinoff finally called it expectancy and put this down to the coming storm. Inured to rough weather, he was not daunted by the prospect, but rather relished it.

From an upstairs window Zhenia watched his progress for just long enough to ascertain that he was about to take the route she had recommended before turning away. The moment had come.

When Bertie had suggested that she learn to drive a car, mused Zhenia, she had initially resisted the idea.

'But, Bertie, why should I learn when there is Stiggins to drive me about?'

Very patient: 'Freedom, my love. There might be times when Stiggins is unavailable for some reason.'

The unwitting wisdom of this was borne out during the affair with Ned Fielding. It was not that Stiggins was unavailable during these assignations but just undesirable. As it was, she simply commandeered the car and nobody knew where she went. Freedom! Good for Bertie. Finally he had bought her her own. In her current condition it would have been impossible to carry out her plan without it.

The thunder was closer. It felt to Litvinoff as if the storm was circling around prior to exploding overhead. There was no rain as yet but the clouds had the violet lividity of a bruise. It would not be long in coming, he thought. He had been walking for an hour and a half. In the distance he could hear the guns though the shooting party was nowhere in sight. He consulted the map. Not far from the lake now.

Back at the house, Zhenia looked at her watch.

Time to go.

On her way out she informed Stiggins that she was taking her car but that she would not be requiring his services to drive her. Before she left she checked that the mother-of-pearl–handled gun, one of a pair (a present from Bertie, as it happened) was still on the back seat where she had left it the night before, wrapped up in one of her jackets. Letting out the clutch, she sighed softly. Sighed with anticipation and relish. One way or another the end of her torment was in sight.

Litvinoff breasted the top of a small hill, emerging through a clump of trees as he did so, and there below him, just as she said it would be, was the lake. At its centre was a massive stone Triton holding aloft a mossy conch. Probably it had been a fountain once. Under the threatening sky, the expanse of water surrounding it was matt as a stone. Litvinoff loped down the incline towards it.

Behind him Zhenia stepped through the same clump of trees. Coolly, she put up the gun. Without hurrying, squinting down the shining barrel, she got Litvinoff's retreating back in her sights. Against her cheek the rifle felt silky smooth, intimate as the body of a lover. She licked her lips and waited. By now her target was at the water's edge. Large heavy drops of rain were beginning to fall. She was conscious of a gathering series of muted reverberations as they struck the leaves of the trees.

Now!

Under cover of a flurry of shots from the invisible shooting party, Zhenia pulled the trigger.

What happened next could not have been foreseen. Something must have caught his attention for Litvinoff swooped unexpectedly to the right. All the same, she thought she must have winged him because the impact of the bullet (presumably) caused him to stagger and then spin round. As in a dream, she noticed that the expression on his face was one of intense astonishment. He appeared to be looking straight up at her though in the confusion it was impossible to say if he saw her or not. Then, to her horror, he lurched towards her. *Hold the nerve.* Thoroughly rattled and trembling violently, Zhenia took aim and shot him again. As she did it, there was a violent crack of thunder overhead and the rain sluiced down in a silver sheet. This time Litvinoff fell and lay still, half in the pitted shallows and half out of them, surrounded by the delicate creeping tendrils of a seeping carmine stain.

Was he dead or wasn't he?

Zhenia dared not wait to find out. Still shaking, she turned on her heel and left him to his fate.

The ball (popularly known as the Shooting Ball) was a lavish affair to which were asked friends from London as well as those who lived in the county. Since it was a fixture on the social calendar and had taken the same form for years, all the staff knew what was expected. Consequently, all the pivotal decisions having been taken decades earlier, it was one of those events which practically organised itself. Striding around checking that all was in place, Bertie was conscious of a surge of gratification. Events of this nature were what grand houses like his were all about. The form was a champagne reception followed by an elegant candlelit buffet dinner which was served in the dining room together with more champagne. In the ballroom, counterpointed by tall, graceful palms, floor vases filled with seasonal flowers massed in shades of topaz, peach, chartreuse, and cream. The storm, a spectacular one, had passed over, leaving in its wake a sultry closeness so that Bertie had given instructions for the doors to the terrace to be thrown open, causing the glistering lustres of the chandeliers to make a faint music of their own as they moved and touched.

Elsewhere, Zhenia, who, unsurprisingly, was feeling far from well, was lying down. As if party to her inner turmoil, the baby heaved and kicked and rotated. Of course it was not every day one shot somebody, she reminded herself with an invigorating flash of black humour and a hysterical desire to laugh. It was either that or cry. All the same, for once in her life she would have given anything not to have been starring in her own jamboree that evening but there was no getting out of it. And nor should there be, Zhenia recognised. All must appear to go on as usual. With an effort, she got off the daybed and summoned her maid to help her dress.

At eight the first guests began to arrive. Among them were the Fieldings. For different reasons both looked at Zhenia with admiration as, together with Bertie, she greeted her guests. The princess was wearing the Dashkov emeralds. Pregnancy had enhanced her breasts, Ned noticed, which swelled creamily over the deep décolletage of a glossy holly green dress. It brought back the memory of the sort of abandoned lovemaking that he got all too little of these days. Bending to kiss her gloved hand, he said *sotto voce* and urgently, "When?"

Understanding him perfectly, but affecting not to, she replied, "In three weeks, but the doctors say that second children often arrive early.... Well, we shall see...." She turned away from him to greet Mai. From the front Zhenia did not look pregnant at all to Mai. Ingot shaped, the bump was all in front. Old wives' tales held that this indicated a boy. Mai hoped so, for Zhenia's sake.

As he appraised his former love, Bertie felt the old treacherous pang of regret. There was still something about her which touched his heart in a way that his wife never had. These days Mai was thinner and in danger of becoming handsome. The bloom of girlish prettiness had been superseded by something altogether steelier. Bertie knew that he and she were cast from the same ethical mould, just as he now knew he and Zhenia were not. The days of ascribing this particular fault line to Russianness were long since gone. Not for the first time Bertie found himself wondering what would have happened if the pair of them had married, despite the machinations of his interfering mother. Well, it was all water under the bridge now. Rumour, corroborated by Mother so it must be right, said that Mai had a lover. Good for Mai. Another Russian. Russians seemed to be everywhere. His eye strayed across the room to where Augusta stood, unamused in plum red, talking to Harold Mainwaring. Probably wisely, Daisy was nowhere to be seen. The Fieldings also moved in different directions the moment the formalities were over, he observed.

Bertie consulted his pocket watch. By now the guests were arriving thick and fast and Zhenia, who looked exhausted, was sitting on a small gilt chair to perform her receiving duties.

"Are you all right, my love?" solicitously enquired her husband.

"*Quite ... all ... right!*" She sounded snappy.

It suddenly struck Bertie that so far there had been no sighting of the count, who, since he was staying on the premises, might have been expected to be one of the first to arrive. In between shaking hands, he said as much to Zhenia, who shrugged.

"The nearest are usually the last. You should know that. Besides, am I the count's keeper? No doubt he will appear in his own good time."

Augusta was also keen to talk to the count. It was her opinion that all did not socially add up in that direction and an inquisition might have elucidated why not. For the time being she was forced to give up on it.

The stream of arrivals began to dry up and finally, with Zhenia on his arm, Bertie felt able to go and circulate among his guests in the dining room where food was about to be served. It was in the course of doing this that he found himself once again opposite Mai. Actually, if Bertie was honest with himself, he had engineered his perambulation so that he now stood opposite Mai. On the other side of the room coincidentally he spied Zhenia talking to Fielding.

Bertie opened with, "I'm so sorry your parents weren't able to be here, Mai."

"Yes, so am I," said Mai. "But Mother isn't well, and Jacob won't go anywhere without her. He says he can't leave her on her own because she might go off and have her hair cut again." None of this made sense to Bertie, who was not up to speed on the disruptive saga of hair in the Berensen and Fielding households.

Never mind. She smiled at him, an uncomplicated open smile which was like a breath of fresh air after the Byzantine intricacies of his wife.

Dazzled and at the same time envious, observed Bertie, "Theirs seems to be a very happy marriage."

"Very," said Mai, sipping her champagne. "Although they have their ups and downs too, you know."

"Don't we all!" Bertie spoke with feeling. Mai gave him a narrow look.

"Are *you* happy, Bertie?"

He had forgotten how direct she could be. *Was he happy?*

Aware that the fact that he had to think about the answer *was* the answer, "Oh, yes, very," said Bertie. He wondered if he sounded as unconvincing to her as he did to his own ears. "What about you, Mai?"

"I'm as happy as I *can* be." Mai stared down into her glass, which was almost empty. "I have some of what I want. Maybe, in the fullness of time, I'll have everything I want. . . ."

"I wonder what would have happened if we'd married."

"We'll never know."

He regarded her bowed head for a moment in silence.

"No, we never will." Gently he took her empty champagne glass. "Allow me . . ."

Though all were currently eating and none were dancing as yet, from the ballroom came faint strains of music, the prelude to the long night ahead. It brought to mind other parties and other days. *I never appreciated what I had when I had it*, thought Bertie. The age-old lament.

Elsewhere there were no regrets, only forward planning.

"When are you going to come to me again?" pressed Fielding in an undertone, having first checked that no one was close enough to hear them.

"Not for a while, Ned," said the princess dryly, indicating her stomach. "And anyway it would be hard for you to get close to me the way things are, I think. Besides, where would we meet? With Mai under your roof again, or rather *her* roof, as I believe it to be, things are not as straightforward as they were."

He decided to disregard the roof jibe. "Where we meet is the least of our problems. One can always find somewhere. I get nothing from Mai these days. Nothing. She is my wife in name only." Self-pity escalated. "No man should be forced to live as I am being forced to live."

"No man *is* forced to," said Zhenia tartly, who, what with the hated pregnancy and the predatory intentions of the count vis à vis what she looked upon as her own jewellery, was not in the mood to listen to complaints concerning the male lot. Although it did occur to her that standing down Ned as a lover looked as though it might prove as difficult as standing him down as a husband. There was an obsessive quality about Fielding which did not augur well on that front. All the same she felt she must get rid of him somehow for it suddenly seemed to Zhenia that she had been sailing close to the wind for far too long and unless she wanted to lose everything, the time had come to pull back. *Otherwise, sooner or later, my luck will run out. . . .* No need to do anything about it right now though, thank heavens. *But no need to alienate Ned either*, prompted the voice of self-preservation.

"Forgive me, dear Ned. I did not mean to sound unsympathetic. It must be very difficult for you. After all it is difficult for me too, you know. But what can I do with things as they are?"

Misunderstanding this ambiguous statement to mean that she missed his body as much as he missed hers, Fielding, who had been prepared to be offended, was mollified. Though unsatisfactory in the short term, the inference that in the fullness of time all would be as it had been was probably the most he could expect for the moment. He was saying as much when Zhenia caught sight of her mother-in-law staring across the room at the two of them. Time to call a halt to this tête à tête. Zhenia stood up.

"I will let you know when the time is right. Now I must attend to my other guests."

Aware that he really did not have much choice, Fielding acquiesced and watched her move across the room in the direction of the Londonderrys, after which he went to help himself to more lobster and champagne.

It was at this point in the proceedings that Litvinoff made his entrance through the terrace doors. Augusta saw him first. Her jaw dropped. There was no time to snap open, let alone raise, her lorgnette. The contrast between the gentlemen and ladies in evening dress and the dishevelled figure before her was extreme. Previous carping about the suit faded into insignificance before this dripping apparition. The count was covered in mud and what looked as if it might be (though it couldn't be, of course) dried blood. Slimy water dribbled on to the Aubusson. As others turned to see what she was staring at, there was a collective intake of breath.

Amid waves of pain, Litvinoff felt consciousness coming and going. The chandeliers above his head appeared to explode in prisms of light. He caught hold of one of the serving tables to steady himself and then he saw his quarry. Zhenia also thought she might be about to faint. The count raised a skinny arm and pointed at her. This was the finish, Zhenia saw with devastating clarity. At the end of the day she had gambled and lost.

Murderess!

Litvinoff tried to speak and could not.

Murderess!!

He tried again and still could not. His last vision was of her petrified face cut off at the neck by the superlative, unlucky Daskov emeralds. It was to be his first and last sight of them. As the lights went out, one hand convulsed gripping and gathering up the tablecloth. Litvinoff crashed to the floor in a welter of Crown Derby, lobster and champagne where he lay, shrouded in damask.

From the ballroom filtered the strains of a waltz.

No dancing now.

"Mother? Have you heard?" The speaker was Mai Fielding. Then, without waiting for an answer, she said, "There has been a shooting at The Hall!"

The line was crackly.

"I can't hear you, Mai. What?"

"A SHOOTING! AT THE HALL!"

"*What!* Who?"

She was shouting over the interference. "Nobody you know. Although, on second thoughts, maybe you do. A shooting party guest of Zhenia's, a Russian called Count Sergei Markov, has been shot dead. It's being treated as a tragic accident. Apparently he went for a walk, took a wrong turning and wandered into the thick of the action. At least that's what they think. I've never heard of him, but maybe Nicolai has. I'll ask him. But the more I think about it, the more it doesn't make sense. How could it possibly happen? The birds are overhead, not running along the ground."

Juno was unsurprised. "Oh, you always get one or two at a jamboree like that who haven't a clue and couldn't hit a barn door at ten paces."

"Worst of all, he wasn't killed outright. Apparently a couple of men out rabbit shooting, for which read poaching I imagine, found him lying badly injured by the lake and brought him up to the house where they left him and then made themselves scarce. In the end they think a combination of shock and loss of blood killed him."

"What a dreadful thing!"

"Wait. There's more to come. Probably as a result of the shock, Zhenia went into premature labour. . . ."

"*And?*"

"It's a boy!"

Chapter Twenty-Four

Because she was a parsimonious housekeeper (for who knew what tomorrow held?), Tatiana Volkovska did not at first realise that her regular stipend from the cuckoo had ceased. The day she found it out via a letter from the bank, she thought she might have a heart attack. Trepidation engulfed her. Where a more sophisticated person might have asked her bank to find out why this was, Tatiana, who regarded these guardians of her money with much the same sort of awe she accorded doctors, did not. What she did do, after a week of sleepless nights, was to write to Sergei Litvinoff. *I shouldn't have trusted him. Whatever he promised me, I never should have told him,* agonised Tatiana, who also felt let down by the Holy Father because He had not intervened and stopped her doing it. Quite the reverse. Active encouragement had appeared to be the order of the day.

As it is, that cup of tea was my undoing!

Litvinoff did not reply but somebody else did. It got worse. The letter informed her that he had simply vanished one day, leaving the rent in arrears to the tune of two months and abandoning his few possessions, most of which had since been sold in an attempt to cover the debt. In the midst of her mounting distress, nevertheless this still struck Tatiana as odd. *Why* would he abandon his belongings? She could think of no satisfactory answer and was forced to acknowledge to herself that even if she had been able to, it would not have altered the fact that Litvinoff had gone, leaving her in the lurch.

"*Are you a relation?*" enquired the writer. "*Because, if so, there are some private papers here which you might like to have. Perhaps I could send them to you?*"

"*Yes, I am a relation . . .*" fibbed Tatiana by return, "*. . . and I should be grateful if you would do that.*"

Afterwards, lying fearfully on her bed in a darkened room with an oblivious Ivan peacefully purring beside her, just like Litvinoff before her, Tatiana suddenly saw what she must do.

It felt odd to be standing on the doorstep of a house she had lived in and run for so many years. Tatiana rang the servants' bell, noting as she did so that the cleaning of the front door brass left a lot to be desired. Once again, Ellie materialised and, since Miss Volkovska was the last person she expected to see, took a minute or two to recognise the visitor. To Ellie's eye, Miss Volkovska appeared to have physically shrunk although, as their dialogue advanced, this impression diminished. Ellie found the habit of obedience hard to shake off, even after all this time. The other also found the habits of a lifetime hard to shake off, and summarily dealt with the unsatisfactory state of the brass before proceeding to elucidate what she was actually there for.

"I wish you to discover the whereabouts of Mrs. Henry Langham for me," stated Miss Volkovska. She tucked in her chin, straightened her back, and waited. Faced with this authoritative request backed up by an implacable stare, Ellie had to remind herself that the terrifying Miss Volkovska was no longer her superior. It was therefore a relief that, in the wake of the Russian gentleman's call on a similar matter, Ellie knew the answer. She knew it because in case he ever turned up again (though so far he never had) she had made it her business to find out from the other servants. She did not deceive herself that a large, grateful sum of money would be forthcoming this time around. On the other hand, getting rid of Miss Volkovska was probably reward enough. Without more ado, Ellie passed on the information and the other wrote it down.

"Thank you, Ellie," said Tatiana. "I hope you are maintaining the high standards of domestic excellence expected in my day . . ." (Long, insinuating look at the offending brass.)

"Yes, Miss Volkovska."

"We are agreed, I think, that standards, like principles, must never be allowed to slip!"

"No, Miss Volkovska."

After watching the spare, old woman make her dignified way carefully down the steps, Ellie was intimidated enough to wait a decent interval before shutting the door. Safely on the other side of it, "Bossy old boot!" said Ellie.

The contrast between Tatiana's stern, composed exterior and her inner persona would have astonished the few who knew her. Inside, Tatiana felt like a frightened little girl adrift in uncharted waters and was well aware that, such was the pecking order of things, whilst she had terrorised Ellie, should she get to meet her, she would be terrorised in her turn by Augusta Langham. It was not an enticing prospect.

Since, in common with most, Tatiana had no telephone and anyway regarded this instrument with the same circumspection accorded to doctors and bankers, she decided to send a letter to the Langham London address. Two days of indeterminate pencil chewing finally produced the following:

> *Dear Mrs. Langham,*
> *I wonder whether you remember me? I was Countess Olga's housekeeper from the time she lived in Russia until the day she died. I hope you will forgive the intrusion but there is something you should know which concerns your family as well as myself. Since this is a matter requiring the utmost discretion, perhaps it would be better if we could meet face to face. I await your reply.*
> *Yours sincerely,*
> *Tatiana Volkovska*

Sending this missive gave her a feeling of relief mixed with apprehension. Afterwards there was nothing to do but wait.

Because Augusta was seldom in the capital these days, the letter took some time to reach her. The day it did, instinct told Augusta, even before she opened the envelope, that this was the prelude to something momentous and she sat for a few seconds considering the orderly, unknown hand writing before slitting it open. What she found was not very informative but definitely tantalising.

Olga's housekeeper. Well, well! This just might be the moment she had been waiting for. In fact Augusta, who did not notice other people's housekeepers, could not remember what Tatiana Volkovska looked like. This did not matter. The woman could come here, that way there would be no problem concerning recognition. There was no telephone number, only an address. After consulting her diary, Augusta went and sat down at the little escritoire and wrote a note which she then sealed and gave to the maid to post.

Four days later they met.

As soon as she set eyes on her, Augusta did recognise Tatiana Volkovska. Years of dealing with what she thought of as the servant problem had given her the ability to sum such people up briskly and almost immediately Tatiana was docketed as grim but trustworthy. She also appeared to be wearing clothes which looked as though they dated from 1917 although by now the year was 1924, Augusta noted, putting this down to a combination of social isolation and thrift.

It was a long time since Tatiana had been inside such a grand flat. The last one had been Countess Olga's, which had been grand, too, but depressingly so, and cluttered. Here the gloomy drapes of generations of equally artistically impervious Langhams had been swept away, by the cuckoo presumably, and the effect these days was one of airy elegance. The hawk-visaged Mrs. Langham was very much a part of all of this in knee-skimming tweeds so fine that they looked almost silky.

"Won't you sit down, Miss Volkovska?" said Augusta.

"Thank you."

"And now perhaps you can tell me what I can do for you. . . ."

With dignity, Tatiana said, "It is more what we could do for each other. But first, may I ask after Princess Zhenia?" Then, hoping no such thing, she added, "She is well, I hope."

"*Very* well!" The delivery of this short phrase left Tatiana in no doubt as to the relationship between Augusta Langham and her daughter-in-law. Though not uttered aloud, the word *unfortunately* might as well have been.

"It is concerning her that I am here."

Augusta did not respond to this but waited.

"She is not all she claims to be."

Remembering the slip of the tongue vis à vis the sister Katya who had suddenly been transformed into a cousin, this statement did not surprise Augusta as much as it might have done. What followed was more than she had bargained for though.

"A *dancer*?" Mrs. Langham was visibly upset. "A *ballet* dancer?" More upset about the cuckoo being a dancer and not a Dashkov than a thief, apparently. The values that still were extant from Tatiana's God-fearing peasant upbringing appeared to bear no relation to the way the rich viewed these things.

"Yes, I fear so."

In the wake of the social shock she had just received it took Augusta a few minutes to regroup and then to address certain omissions.

"May I ask why it has taken so long for you to come forward, Miss Volkovska?"

Tatiana recounted the story of the pension and how the cuckoo had agreed to honour the countess's pledge provided she kept her mouth shut. Telling the story, she felt ashamed.

Augusta did not mince her words. "So you were bribed!"

Stung by this, Tatiana simply said, "I need to eat to live. For that I need money. It was what was promised for years of faithful service, no more and no less. After Countess Olga died it was my right. I earned it."

Speaking the words, she was aware that *earn* probably meant nothing to Mrs. Langham, for whom it was a foreign concept. Even more foreign than a Russian. Or the bread line.

Prior to continuing, Augusta found herself in a dilemma as to what to call her daughter-in-law. Should it be Zhenia or Vera? In the end she decided to go for the status quo.

"But, as I understand it, you are in receipt of this income. Zhenia has done what she said she would do. So why are you here?"

"After Mr. Litvinoff's visit, the money stopped. I lead a very frugal life so I did not realise at once."

Augusta raised her eyebrows.

Mr. Litvinoff? This was a new component. Suddenly England seemed to be populated with Russians. Why couldn't they all stay at home with Mr. Stalin?

"Who is Mr. Litvinoff?"

Tatiana explained.

Sergei Litvinoff, it transpired. A Soviet agent in search of the Dashkov emeralds on behalf of his government. Augusta cast her mind back. There had been that other Russian, too. The spectre at the shooting party feast, the one who was a count. Russians, it seemed, were everywhere. He had been a Sergei as well. *I go all my life without meeting a single Sergei and suddenly here are two,* thought Augusta, *and the common denominator is Zhenia*. The names chimed together. All at once she saw it.

"Describe Mr. Litvinoff to me!"

Tatiana did so. There was no room for doubt.

We have entertained a Soviet agent at The Hall!

Augusta was aghast all over again.

Pulling herself together, she said, "I assume you have proof of all this, Miss Volkovska? For without it, I could not face Zhenia with what you have said. It would only be your word against hers."

"I have no proof as such. I gave what I had to the countess. In the confusion following her sudden death, it disappeared."

"Then I fear there is nothing I can do. . . ."

"Without the income, I shall be destitute . . . perhaps you could intercede for me with Princess Zhenia . . . or even see your way to paying it yourself in return for the information I have given you . . ." Too late, Tatiana saw that she should have secured an agreement first and revealed what she knew second.

"It is out of the question, Miss Volkovska. Any arrangement you might have had with the late countess is not my affair. Perhaps you should take the matter up with Zhenia herself."

"Since she is the one who cut me off, I do not think there is any point in doing that."

"Possibly you are right. All the same . . ."

Augusta Langham stood up. The meeting was at an end.

Desperation engulfed Tatiana.

I have done my best all my life, thought Tatiana, *and this is what it has brought me to.* Outside, the weather was worthy of her homeland. As the door closed behind her, she stood on the step for a moment breathing in the dank smell of snow. Large flakes were slipping down, though of the wet variety which probably would not settle. A distended sky was heavy with the threat of more and because there was no wind, a curious stillness pervaded everything. *Though I have always associated silence with snow*, reflected Tatiana, picking her way carefully along the slippery pavement. As she walked, she remembered the long, dark Russian winters with the sort of nostalgic longing which had never beset her while she endured them. A shifting kaleidoscope of events in her past life presented itself, including the image of the only young man she had ever had, who had wanted to marry her. On Olga's advice, she had turned him down. *You can do better than that, Tatiana,* Olga said. It was an unworthy thought, but she had since wondered how much this flattering assessment of her own potential was due to her mistress's selfish reluctance to lose a satisfactory maid, thereby having to train another. She had never been asked again. The first chance had turned out to be the last and the choice Tatiana had made had consigned her to a life of general ministering and lacing the countess (no sylph!) into ball gowns and the like. *Really, I lived through Olga. I had no life of my own. Her life was my life.* It raised the question as to whether, given it to live again, she would have made the same choice. Knowing what she knew now, probably not, was Tatiana's response to this.

By now the snow was spiralling down more densely. Large flakes lighted on her coat and on her hair, garlanding the loose grey knot at the nape of her neck like a bridal wreath. Tatiana turned into a small shop at the end of the road in which she lived and purchased a bottle of vodka, which she put in her bag. Then she completed the short remainder of her journey home.

After Tatiana Volkovska's departure, Augusta Langham sat mulling over what she had been told. She saw no reason to doubt any of it. It was her opinion that Tatiana was an honest woman, which was a lot more than could be said for the miscreant Zhenia. What to do next was the question. For her daughter-in-law, having produced an heir (though no spare and never likely to be now) had secured herself a position that was virtually unassailable. Augusta did not deceive herself into imagining that Bertie was in love with his wife these days, rather he tolerated her. According to Augusta's expectations of marriage this state of affairs was neither here nor there. Lots of other couples were in exactly the same boat and did not allow this fact to stop them enjoying themselves. What it did mean was that if there was a way of seeing Zhenia off without a dreadful scandal, *if* there was, Bertie was not likely to object too much. Considering the idea of people enjoying themselves brought her to the vexed subject of Bertie's heir. For Alexander did not look like Bertie at all, but did resemble Ned Fielding to a marked degree. Very marked. This fact had never been raised at The Hall, though no doubt it had been elsewhere in the county. Better to be pragmatic about it. An heir was an heir. The Hall needed an heir. Unless Bertie got his skates on, divorced Zhenia, and cracked on with another marriage with very un-Bertie-like dispatch, Alexander was all there was on offer. Moreover, because of Saskia, on whom he doted, there was unlikely to be a public pillorying of her mother.

She got up and walked across the room. Through the window she could see snow falling steadily on the streets of London, just as it had probably fallen on those of Petrograd seven years ago, the day Vera Kalanskaya left it for the last time. Fate had brought her and the Langham family together. It remained to be seen whether fate would be instrumental in dividing them again. It was unnerving, though, to have to recognise that although all her social aspirations and machinations might have been founded on sand, the consequences were, to all intents and purposes, written in stone.

Her thoughts turned to the Fieldings. Mai, it was rumoured, had a lover in London and had only stayed with her husband for the sake of her children. What Ned, who had become something of a recluse in the last few years, thought about this arrangement had never been made clear. Augusta, who saw a certain amount of the young Fieldings because they were friendly with her own grandchildren, had to admit that they were charming. Despite her lamentable insistence on votes for women, Mai, it appeared, had been a good mother. Whereas Zhenia, in Augusta's view, had not. Zhenia spoilt her son and virtually ignored Saskia, who had been allowed to run wild, steadied only by her father as and when he had the time. The predictable result of this lack of maternal discipline, not to say interest, was an attention-seeking little show-off whose manners were not what they should have been. Worse, her granddaughter was sly and, when caught out, lied. As when Augusta had caught her spitefully tormenting her little brother and an unabashed Saskia had persisted in denying what Augusta had seen with her own eyes. It was all very unsatisfactory.

Getting back to the matter in hand, on balance Augusta thought she *would* fire a warning shot over Zhenia's head vis à vis Miss Volkovska's revelations, if only to try and keep her daughter-in-law in line. She would not tell Bertie. Where Zhenia was concerned, no proof as such was needed. Zhenia knew what she had done. Where Bertie was concerned, he would require it. Better to say nothing to her son for the moment.

On her arrival home, Tatiana found a package propped against her front door. Inside the flat she was greeted by an ecstatic Ivan. The light in her sitting room seemed to have dimmed, thickened almost and taken on the yellow tinge of the outside atmosphere. She lit the lamps, turned on the gas fire, and fed the cat. Then she poured herself a shot of vodka. The glass was one of a set which had belonged to the countess. Before drinking, she held it up to the light. The limpidity of the liquid interacted with the crystal causing dozens of tiny points of light to refract. Tatiana tossed it back in one swallow, then she put down the glass and proceeded to open the parcel. It proved to contain documents written in longhand in Russian and sundry other odds and ends including a sepia photograph mounted on a card of a stout bustled woman. Litvinoff's mother, perhaps. It had been so long since the arrangement to forward his remaining belongings had been made that Tatiana had virtually given up on ever receiving them. For the second time in her life she sat down and began to read somebody else's private papers. They were headed CONFIDENTIAL. FOR THE ATTENTION OF BORIS MOROZOV.

My dear Boris,
commenced Litvinoff,
I take it my last report reached you safely. To pick up where we left off, Tatiana Volkovska is a sad old woman whose loyalty to her former mistress appears to have been absolute.
Here a tear trickled down Tatiana's withered cheek.
Still is, although the countess is dead and has been for three years. Because of this, I believe she will eventually give me the information I seek concerning Kalanskaya. To date, after two hours of teasing her along, I have to confess I am no further forward. Nevertheless, instinct tells me that it can only be a matter of time. Tomorrow, Sunday, it is my intention to attend the Russian church where I am reliably informed I shall (accidentally, of course) run into her.

Resuming:
I did go to church, something I have not done for twenty years and there Tatiana Volkovska was. Afterwards, at her suggestion, (a good sign) we repaired to a local tea room. The revelations which can take place over a humble cup of tea never cease to amaze me. Volkovska was still very cautious, however, and it transpired that Kalanskaya, whom she refers to as the cuckoo, had bought her silence in return for a generous stipend, which no doubt would have been hers anyway, had the countess lived. Not unnaturally she is terrified of being left destitute in what, for

her, even after all those years, is still a foreign country. As you know, there is a great deal at stake here and it occurred to me to offer an equivalent amount in return for the information, but, until I could obtain your permission, this had to wait. In the end, there was no need. . . .

You will be pleased to hear that what I subsequently learnt told me that I am finally on the right track at last. Unfortunately, Volkovska does not know exactly where Vera Kalanskaya is, only that she has married and the name of the man she is married to. However, after this significant advance clues are beginning to gather . . .

Resuming:
I am triumphant. I will not bore you with how I have accomplished it, but I have found her! Not content with purloining the Dashkov emeralds, she has stolen the family name as well. Vera Kalanskaya now styles herself Princess Zhenia Dashkova, also known as Mrs. Bertie Langham. Like a snake's skin, her past has been shed. As soon as possible I intend to confront her. . . .

September, 1923

Dear Boris,
It is done. I am writing this on the train going back to London having just left The Hall as the Langham country pile is called. The high and mighty lady I met is a far cry from Vera Kalanskaya, dancer in the Mariinskiy corps de ballet. . . . She is also very pregnant for the second time and, no doubt, hoping for a son. There is already a daughter, Saskia. So: well dug in and not about to divulge anything unless terrorised into doing so. All in all, I had a stimulating hour with her which, at my suggestion, was conducted in Russian. I also took the precaution of introducing myself under an assumed name. One cannot be too careful. With me it has become a habit. To get back to the object of our search, Vera is a haughty, glacial beauty with an agile brain. I enjoyed our verbal duel, though, alas for her, it was one she was never going to win.

At first, of course, she denied everything. Wouldn't you? In fact, she did not bat an eyelid to begin with. Only when the name Mathilde Ivanova was brought up was there a flicker, but only that. Even when she lit a cigarette, her hands did not tremble. I allowed the extent of the intelligence at my disposal to emerge little by little. By the end of it she was in no doubt where she stood and did not demur when I called her Vera. . . . Though I say it myself, it has all gone very smoothly so far. Some might say too smoothly. No matter. She has agreed to cooperate. I don't trust Vera Kalanskaya, but, given the threat of exposure, what choice did she have? To facilitate the hand-over I have been invited to a shooting party due to take place in two weeks' time. Having unwisely suggested that she had copies made of the Dashkov emeralds in order to stave off awkward questions on her own account, it now behoves me to make sure she doesn't palm these off on me. She's certainly capable of doing it!

October 1923
My dear Boris,
On Saturday I travel to Sussex. On the following Tuesday they are holding a ball for half the county. Kalanskaya promises to wear the Dashkov emeralds. It will be my first sight of them and despite her advanced pregnancy I anticipate that she and they will look wonderful together. It almost seems a shame to take them off her. Why is it that hard-hearted beauties set off spectacular jewellery so much better than Madonnas? When the first shoot takes place, though not participating, I intend to follow the guns. On Wednesday the deal is to be struck. As soon as the gems are in the bag (so to speak) be sure I shall let you know.
Sergei Litvinoff

Report ends

It was not just the derogatory term *sad old woman* (though she knew she was) that upset Tatiana. It was the cynicism of it all. Divine intervention had played no part in any of it. She had been betrayed by her own naiveté not once but twice, used as a pawn and then discarded. There had been two opportunities to release information in exchange for a resumption of her pension and twice she had given it away for nothing. Even the prospect of the cuckoo's comeuppance could not lift Tatiana's spirits.

Wearily she went in search of the cat. Ivan had eaten his food and was preparing to settle into his favourite chair where Sergei Litvinoff had found him the day of their first meeting. Tatiana lifted him off and put him down outside the front door of the flat. Hopefully someone would find him and take him in.

Having done this, she collected the empty glass and the bottle of vodka and went into the bedroom, where she opened the drawer of the bedside table and extracted a box of sleeping pills. These had belonged to Olga and as the years passed and her mistress's memory was not what it once had been, it had become Tatiana's job to dole them out in the correct quantities. Feeling all at once very tired, propped up by pillows, she lay down on the bed. Then she took two of the tablets and washed them down with vodka, followed by two more and another gulp of vodka (whose fiery purity tasted like nectar) and two more and so on, alternating the one with the other until consciousness began to come and go and finally began to fade altogether. Just before the end, Tatiana thought herself in a sunny meadow bordered with birch and fir and starred with wild flowers in the midst of which stood her sister, arms outstretched.

Suffused with joy and no longer old but young and fleet again, Tatiana ran towards her.

"I'm home, Anastasia, I'm home!"

On her return to the country, Augusta waited until Bertie had gone to London on a business trip before tackling Zhenia. There was no point in getting Bertie in on the act at this stage and quite possibly never would be. That remained to be seen.

On her arrival unannounced at The Hall, she found her daughter-in-law in the drawing room.

"How can I help you, Augusta?" enquired Zhenia, employing an unwelcoming opening salvo which made the one sound like a tradesperson and the other feel like a particularly tiresome customer.

Augusta, who had walked across the park and was chilled, stretched out her hands towards the shooting flames of a log fire. Outside it was darkening and the snow had intensified.

"Well, Zhenia, like you, I won't beat about the bush. A fortnight ago, while I was at the London house, I had a visit from Tatiana Volkovska. Remember her?"

There was the minutest of wary pauses, before Zhenia said, "Yes, of course I do." Then, with a studied, casual air, "What about it?"

"What about it? Here's what about it. She claims that you are not who you purport to be. She says you are a dancer called Vera Kalanskaya and not a member of the Dashkov family at all. In short, she says you are a fraud." Then, sugaring the pill in order to indicate at least a semblance of support, "Of course, dear, I am sure it is all nonsense, but I thought you should know."

Without directly denying this, Augusta noticed, Zhenia replied, "Then why has she waited until now to come forward?"

A log fell with a crash into the heart of the fire, sending up a shower of yellow sparks.

"She says she was driven to it. She says that for reasons best known to yourself you have cut off the pension you were paying her in return for her silence, which, in the circumstances, if what she says is true, *if* it is (which I don't believe for a minute, of course) would seem to have been a rash thing to do."

"What!"

Apart from rage, Zhenia's response to this charge was one of genuine astonishment. Witnessing this unusual manifestation of innocence caused Augusta to be aware of how very dishonest her daughter-in-law usually was in her day-to-day dealings. Getting a straight answer out of Zhenia was akin to getting blood out of a stone.

"Are you saying you didn't?"

"Of course I didn't. The woman is being ridiculous. Either her bank or mine has made a mistake."

"But you were paying her money."

Attempting to limit the damage, it seemed necessary to give something away. "Yes, but here I should clarify and say the pension was nothing to do with buying Tatiana Volkovska's discretion over nonexistent misdemeanours and everything to do with honouring a promise the countess made to her before she died."

Like Tatiana before her, Augusta was sceptical. Zhenia did not have a history of philanthropy or of honouring anything not in her own interests unless forced into it.

She leant down and placed another log upon the fire and then turned and looked the other squarely in the face.

"And the rest?"

The princess was belligerent. The foreign accent, all but ironed out these days, became suddenly more pronounced. "It's a complete fabrication. That woman is crazy. What proof does she have of all these absurd allegations, I'd like to know?"

Ignoring this since, according to Tatiana Volkovska, any that there might have been had been destroyed, Augusta altered tack. "And who was Sergei Markov? Because, take it from me, whatever else he was, he wasn't a count."

This was unexpected. Zhenia decided to brazen it out.

"Of course he was! I told you, an old friend of the family."

Augusta was caustic. "Which one? Everybody's an old friend of somebody's family! Markov's name was not Markov at all but Litvinoff. *He* was not what he seemed to be." The temptation to add *either* was overcome. "Perhaps that is why, after the shooting accident by the lake, no personal papers of any kind were discovered either on the body or in his room. Doubtless you will remember we speculated about it. Very few people travel with no means of identification of any sort. But there was nothing."

It was gratifying to see from Zhenia's expression that once again she had succeeded in wrong-footing her daughter-in-law.

"No. Because, according to Tatiana Volkovska, the man was a Soviet agent."

Tatiana Volkovska. The sound of the hated name caused Zhenia's lips to become a thin, bloodless line. *Never mind that now, I'll deal with her later.* Regrouping, she said, "I have no idea where this Sergei Litvinoff has come from. As I say, Volkovska's mad and, since poor Count Markov is in his grave, her wild accusations can never be proved either way."

This was probably true. The only satisfaction to be had for the moment was that of rattling Zhenia's cage.

Augusta stood up.

The two women faced each other.

With a syrupy smile: "Well, I just thought you should know, dear."

Through gritted teeth: "Yes, of course you did. Would you like someone to drive you back?"

Chapter Twenty-Five

"Mai is bereft at the prospect. She is afraid Nicolai will not come back."
The speaker was Juno Berensen.

Jacob was impatient. "Look, Nicolai wants to see his family again. I can
understand that and Mai, of all people, should be able to. He also wants to
see what business opportunities might be on offer. Very few is my view, incidentally, and I've told him so. But Nicolai is his own man and must find out
for himself. I respect that. There's no reason why he shouldn't come back. It's
seventeen years since the revolution. Things have settled down. Diplomatic
relations between them and us have been established since 1929. It's all on
the up again."

"Yes, you're right, of course . . ." Juno still felt uncertain but decided
not to provoke her husband by pushing the matter further. In any case,
there was nothing she could do about it.

The day before he was due to leave for Leningrad, Mai travelled to London
to spend the night with her lover. They had dinner at Vladimir's. These
days, partly due to his own efforts and partly due to a lucrative business
partnership with Jacob Berensen, Nicolai's circumstances had changed for
the better. All that was needed now was the permanent presence of Mai in
his house. Ardently he watched her across the table.

"Darling, I have to do this."

He took her hand.

"I know."

She looked down. The candle between them guttered and went out, casting her face into shadow. Nicolai rose to his feet and replaced it with another from an empty table.

"You understand, don't you?"

"Yes, of course." She raised her head and smiled at him. "How could I not?"

Just as he had done the first time they had lunch together, using a small horn spoon he placed sour cream and then caviar on a blini, rolled it up and handed it to her. They raised their glasses and drank.

Later, watching Mai undress, Nicolai reflected that in the days before the revolution when he had been a young man about town in Petrograd as it was then, if anybody had told him that he would fall in love with an Englishwoman he would have laughed at them. When, finally, she was naked he watched her move towards him with a complicated mix of love and desire and humility. *For, I do not deserve this woman*, thought Nicolai, taking her in his arms.

The following morning he went.

PART NINE

Love Letters
1934

Chapter Twenty-Six

Leningrad, November 6, 1934
My darling Mai,
Well, after an exhausting journey, I am here. It remains to be seen whether Jacob is right when he says that it is still too early for the sort of business liaison between your country and mine that I have in mind. Much has changed, but, as always, certain constants remain. The weather, for instance. When I arrived freezing, driving rain was falling. Leningrad was a quagmire of mud. Two days later the temperature dropped and last night a blizzard swept in. This morning all is white. There is nothing so romantic as a great city under snow, shining in the early morning sun. One day, my love, I will wrap you in sables and you and I will take a droshki and speed along these glittering streets and across Palace Square to the foot of the Winter Palace steps. I will show you marvels. I will show you the golden domed churches and the great houses designed by Rinaldi and Rastrelli. We will go to the ballet and the opera. All the glories of Leningrad shall be revealed to you. Darling, I long for the day when you and I can live together openly and I shall no longer be forced to make journeys such as this one on my own . . .

With all my love, your devoted
Nicolai

Leningrad, November 13, 1934
My darling Mai,
This time I write with a heavy heart to tell you that it is just as well you are not here with me. For this city is not safe. True, in certain mundane ways life

apparently goes on as normal and, superficially anyway, everything looks the same, but the prevailing climate, I have discovered, is one of secrecy and fear. Can you believe that I am advised not to make public my presence here? In this, the city of my birth. And Jacob was quite right about the business side of it all. There are no business opportunities of the sort to interest me. No doubt it will all happen eventually, but when? After all, it is seventeen years since the start of the revolution. For the moment this feels like a closed, even alien, society. On a different and personal subject, it remains to be seen whether I should try to establish contact with my brother-in-law, Igor, and, by doing so, with my sister Irina, whom I long to see again. Igor works for the party and is close to Kirov, who is party secretary here in Leningrad. Kirov, I am told, is a friend of one Joseph Stalin so Igor should be safe. All the same, something holds me back. . . .

Leningrad, November 20, 1934

Mai dearest,

The exciting news is that, last night, I had dinner with Igor and Irina. In the interests of discretion, I went under cover of darkness. Considering the fact that he is a man of some importance in the party, Igor's house is nothing special. But never mind about that, they welcomed me with open arms and my sister wept at the sight of me. It was wonderful to see her again. We talked and talked. I told them all about you, sweetheart. At one point I said to my brother-in-law that I was experiencing great difficulty tracing certain old friends, to which, with a shrug, he replied that, 'it was not uncommon for people deemed enemies of the state to disappear overnight, never to be seen again. Be very careful what you say,' said Igor, 'and who you say it to.' According to him, the word is that Stalin brooks neither opposition nor competition. Only Kirov, colleague and friend, powerful and popular satrap in Leningrad, is untouchable. By extension, thinks Igor, so is he. Maybe. Irina told me that they spent several years in Moscow where their first child was born before returning to Leningrad. I don't like the sound of any of it. As you know, I was an apostle of the revolution and felt that it had to happen but this smells like the beginning of another tyranny. I asked about my mother and was told that she and my other sister are well but still living in much reduced circumstances in the country. In a week or so I intend to travel home but before I do so, I will go and see them.

As I close, I must tell you another thing that will amuse you. I met a fellow *whose name is Dashkov. It turned out that he was a bird of passage because he is currently based in Moscow where he is part of Stalin's entourage. Anyway, in the course of conversation, he told me that he was the black sheep of the aristocratic Dashkov family, the rest of whom were wiped out in the revolution. To which I replied that this was not so and I told him about your friend Princess Zhenia and the famous emeralds. He listened intently but did not say much. This puzzled me. I should have thought he would have been more excited to discover that at the end of all the bloodshed he still had one living relation. Apparently he was here to see Kirov and goes back to the capital tomorrow so I do not expect to meet him again.*

Soon I will be back in England. Mai, I long to hold you in my arms again. Darling, there will never be another love story like ours. Kiss the angel icon for me and consider this. Your boys are about to go away to school. Now is the moment. Leave your husband and come away with me. Darling, I have been patient but suddenly have a strong sense of time passing and youth with it. My stay in this melancholy city whose glory days are gone convinces me that we must take our pleasures while we can . . . I cover you with kisses,

Nicolai

Leningrad, December 2, 1934
My darling Mai,
Something has happened here which changes everything. Kirov was assassinated earlier today, shot in a corridor outside his office, in what used in the old days to be the Smolny Institute. It's now the party headquarters and where Igor works. The city is in turmoil and rumour is rife. Word has it that Stalin was responsible. Other rumours suggest that an anti-Stalinist cell was responsible. All, including me, are waiting to see what happens next . . . instinct tells me that Igor is in danger and should get out while he can. I intend to stop writing now and walk over to their house and tell him.

Resuming the same evening.
I did so. Too late. A distraught Irina told me that Igor has been arrested and taken away. She does not know where to. Others have also been rounded up. As you know, it had been my intention to leave but now I feel it is my duty to protect my sister and her children and to try to discover what has happened to her husband. Darling, I know you will understand why I do this. And I will tell

you what I have not the heart to tell her, which is that I fear we shall never see him again. For that is how things are in this city now. There is much to do. I must break off now . . .

Two days later.
After the initial shock, a dreadful stillness has settled over Leningrad. It reminds me of nothing so much as the days before the revolution ignited. It is sinister that I have been able to find out nothing vis à vis the fate of Igor. Kirov's body has been moved to the Tauride Palace where it lies in state. Thousands, myself among them, have filed past the bier to pay their last respects. I joined the crowd, not because of Kirov but in the hope, vain as it turned out, of learning something concerning the fate of those detained in the wake of the assassination. Stalin himself has travelled down by train to be one of the guards of honour. . . .

Monday.
Retribution has been swift and savage. There has been a second wave of mass arrests, culminating in many executions. It is no exaggeration to say that terror stalks these streets and it is hard to escape the idea that the former Petrograd is being punished for an unacceptable independence of spirit and a refusal to bend the knee. Fearing for her safety, for women are not immune from all of this, I have tried to persuade Irina to leave with her children and offered to take her to the country to join Anna and our mother, but she will not go. . . .

Darling, I am going to send this now. I will write again as soon as I know when I shall be returning. I meant to say a letter from you arrived today. It had been opened and resealed. Never mind. The main thing is that I have it. I send you all my love,

Nicolai

It was the last letter.

Chapter Twenty-Seven

As the years passed, Mai's children grew up and married and became preoccupied with *their* children, and she found herself with less to do. Possibly as a result of an emptier present, the past reasserted itself and Mai began to look up erstwhile friends and acquaintances, some of whom had drifted away down the years. One who remained elusive was Zhenia Langham. Whatever happened to Zhenia? Mai hadn't heard anything about her for years. Since she was one of the few still alive who would remember the princess in her prime and, more important, might know where she was, Mai decided to pay her cousin Maude Binnington a visit.

The mention of Mrs. Bertie Langham over lapsang suchong produced an immediate and prickly reaction.

"Do I remember her, Mai? She of the famous Dashkov emeralds? Oh, I should think I do, dear. She's at the Willows. Queening it in a suite, I believe. Been sequestered there for years. It's my view she should have been put away long before she was. As I don't have to tell you, she caused a lot of trouble and that's putting it mildly. Saw off most of the Langhams *and* the Russian revolution if you think about it. Cucumber sandwich?"

Taking one, she said, "Ah! Still alive! Is she *compos mentis?*"

Cousin Maude, who was older than Mai, was starchy. "I don't see why not, Mai. She's only three years younger than I am and I think we're both agreed there's nothing the matter with my brain! Or yours."

"No, there isn't but not everyone's as lucky as we are," said Mai hastily.

Then, getting off the thorny subject of age, she said, "I wonder whether she receives visitors these days."

Maude sniffed. "Zhenia always did like a lot of attention. I should think if you asked for it she would deign to give you an audience. She probably wouldn't be able to resist it. Though why you should want one, I can't imagine." Then, giving her cousin a sharp look, she said, "Why *do* you? You quarrelled, didn't you?"

Why did she?

Mai was frank. "Let's put it down to curiosity! And yes, we did quarrel. I couldn't stomach the fact that she set her cap at the husband of a friend of mine. She caused a lot of trouble. It's all a long time ago now, though...."

"Well, watch your step. Remember that cat!"

The day she received a letter from Mai Fielding proposing that they should meet again after forty years was an exciting one for Zhenia Langham. Estranged from her family and ostracised by almost everyone, her existence had lately been conducted mostly in the past since the present had little to recommend it. The past, on the other hand, could be accused of having almost too much to offer. *Memento mori.* Zhenia, who had barely given the Holy Father a thought for four decades was now forced to contemplate the possibility of a meeting with the deity sooner rather than later and did not relish the prospect. The advent of Mai promised to be a welcome diversion.

With alacrity, therefore, she wrote a note of acceptance suggesting that Mai contact Mrs. Pelling (variously regarded as companion, nurse, dogsbody, or jailer depending on the mood of the day) to arrange a date and time.

The Willows had once been a fairly grand country house. The housing estates adjacent to the town had not been allowed to encroach on it and it was still surrounded by lush, extensive park land. In front was an apron of gravel where cars were parked, probably a combination of staff and relations visiting other inmates. Once inside, Mai presented herself at the desk.

"Mrs. Langham is expecting you, I assume."

"Yes, I fixed it up with Mrs. Pelling."

"Oh yes, poor Mrs. Pelling. Second floor, there's a lift."

Poor Mrs. Pelling?

When she opened the door Mrs. Pelling had a martyred look, Mai thought. She nodded and stood to one side while Mai passed into a small hall which was dominated by one good flower painting, possibly Dutch, and then led the way into a largish drawing room which overlooked the garden.

The princess was sitting in a button-backed chair and was so frail she looked as though a draught might blow her away. The two women shook hands but did not kiss. A cluster of clawed rings dug into Mai's hand.

"Won't you sit down." Zhenia indicated a chair opposite her own with a regal gesture.

"Shall I make a cup of tea?" The speaker was Mrs. Pelling, sounding eager.

The princess did not trouble to acknowledge this helpful request but waved a dismissive hand.

"Leave us, Pelling!"

Crestfallen, Mrs. Pelling, who had possibly entertained the hope that an otherwise dull existence would be enlivened by the forthcoming interview, trailed away into the nether regions of the flat.

Left alone together, the two old ladies appraised one another.

Zhenia, whose papery fragility put Mai in mind of a moth, was dressed in pearl grey. Tiny sparrowlike wrists were decked with bracelets and tiny feet encased in little grey satin slippers. Her hair was also silver grey and cut into a clubbed bob. What Mai was not prepared for was the aura of will which wreathed her. Isolated and dependent as she now was, the diminutive princess was still a study in steel and there remained vestigial traces of a former beauty in the little wizened face now scored all over with a myriad fine lines.

It was Zhenia's view that Mai Fielding had not aged well. Or rather, perhaps, had aged in a very English countrywoman sort of way. Tall, angular, and tweeded with sensible shoes and formidable presence, *that* was Mai these days. A far cry from the dashing beauty of yesteryear. Though the right clothes could have enhanced a certain spare elegance. It put Zhenia in mind of the day they all danced. *I had to show her how to make the most of herself then as well,* remembered Zhenia. Well, no matter. Of what use were looks now? The answer was very little. No doubt Mai had reached the same conclusion.

An appraising pause was in danger of becoming awkward. The princess decided to open the proceedings. "Tell me, Mai, how did you discover I was here?"

"My cousin, Maude Binnington, told me."

"Oh yes! Dear Maude. I remember her." Zhenia fizzed with malice. "What a sour puss and plain with it. She didn't like me, of course. None of them did. The women, I mean. They were all jealous . . . all except for you, Mai. You didn't have an envious bone in your body. There was a sort of nobility about you. *Such* a handicap. I remember it well. It was my view that it made you vulnerable. No, scrupulous, that's a better word. You were too scrupulous. I never allowed that sort of thing to stop *me*. . . ."

No, thought Mai, who had sized up the self-appointed doyenne of disgraceful behaviour a long time ago, *I'll bet nothing ever stopped you.*

By now she was well into her stride. "The men were a completely different kettle of fish, of course," continued Zhenia blithely. "They liked me all right. And the emeralds! Regardless of sex, they all coveted those."

"Oh, yes. The emeralds. What happened to the emeralds?"

Here came the first surprise. "I've got them here."

Bemused, the other stared at her. *"What?"*

"Would you like to see them?"

"Don't you keep them in the bank?" asked Mai, faintly.

"Not anymore. I keep them with me! And why not?" Then retelling the lie, more out of habit than anything else, "Never forget I escaped from Russia with them sewn into the bodice of my dress. Next to my heart."

Never mind about her heart, these days it transpired that she kept her jewellery in a velvet bag in her bureau. Apart from herself, a small ornamental key appeared to be its only guardian. Undoing the flimsy lock, Mai wondered how many other people knew they were there.

The look on the face of the princess as she slid the necklace out of the velvet was instructive. It was a mixture of greed and extreme reverence, love even. The stones did not so much sparkle as smoulder. Green fire. Lighthearted brashness was left to the diamonds, which counterpointed the sullen, spectacular barbarism of the emeralds, underlining brooding authority with glitter.

"Do you want to hold it?" said Zhenia.

Warily, she asked, "May I?"

"Yes!" Zhenia was impatient. "Go on!"

Mai took the proffered necklace which was heavy and whose spectacular stones felt freezing cold to the touch. As she did so, she had the impression that the temperature in the room dropped, almost as if the jewels were malign. And, of course, when one thought about it they had not done the Dashkov family much good. It was odd, she reflected, that though it was years since she and Zhenia had last met, when they had parted acrimoniously, now it was as though this had never happened. The princess, it seemed, had the gift of social amnesia. With no moral dimension and therefore unhampered by shame over past misdemeanours, for her all was once again as it had been in the early days of their friendship.

Desire to know more won the day over disapproval. Mai straightened out the collar by trailing it over one arm and briefly held it aloft so that the light caught it for the last time before, together with the earrings, it was deposited back in the soft darkness of its velvet bed.

She locked the bureau and handed the key back to its owner.

"And now, call Pelling, please," ordered the princess, very imperious. "We will take tea. Then we will reminisce."

When she had delivered the tray, the luckless Pelling was once again banished to the suite equivalent of Siberia. It transpired that Zhenia was agog for news and that, while she knew most of the family facts broadly speaking, she knew none of the detail.

"What about Saskia? Doesn't she visit you here?"

"No. We do not speak. Maybe we are too alike, Saskia and I." With relish, she added, "How we *fought!* Alexander comes from time to time . . ." It sounded as though Zhenia's children had inherited Zhenia's selfishness. "But tell me about Ned. He was killed in a riding accident, I was told."

"Yes. He was thirty-nine." Mai studied her fingernails with an expression of distaste. "Against the advice of his doctors, Ned still rode and usually, when he did so, alone. Anyway, there had been a lot of rain and on this day the rivers and streams were very swollen. It was assumed horse and rider tried to ford the river in the usual place. After that nobody quite knows what happened. There was a view that the horse slipped and fell on him. Or maybe Ned lost his concentration. It came to the same thing in the end. Both were swept away and drowned. The bodies were found downstream later the same day. . . ."

"Which would have left you free to marry the man you loved!" Ever practical, the princess did not waste any sorrow on Ned.

"Yes it would have done, but Nicolai had gone to Leningrad. . . ."

"Why did he do *that*?" Zhenia was amazed.

"He said he wanted to explore business opportunities, although Jacob was adamant that there wouldn't be any, it was too soon after the revolution. Most of all, though, he wanted to see his family and I think too he wanted to understand what had happened, to make sense of it all, if you like . . ."

What an idiot, was the princess's scornful reaction to this. *That was one mistake I never made.*

"He didn't come back." Mai's voice was flat. "We think he was caught up in the purges after the assassination of Kirov. Whatever, he disappeared without trace. My stepfather spent a small fortune trying to find him, but to no avail."

So Russia did for him.

Zhenia was not surprised. Some of the stories which had filtered out of Stalinist Russia post the revolution had been truly horrific.

Getting off the subject, "As for the Langhams," said Zhenia, "I never saw either Bertie or Augusta again after they sent me away . . ."

"Forgive me asking but *why* did they send you away?" probed Mai, who had often wondered. There had been the fact but no explanation that she had ever heard. "Bertie always seemed so devoted."

"Bertie *was* devoted, up to a point." Zhenia fell silent and did not elucidate further.

As if it had taken place yesterday, through the medium of her mind's eye she relived the endgame as it had been played out in Augusta's stuffy drawing room while heavy rain beat on the windows and a rogue wind rattled the sashes. Regal in purple and radiating acidic triumph, Augusta did all the talking (followed by the haggling) while in the background a pained but stern Bertie stared out across the clouded, dripping park studiously refusing to look at his wife. Sitting listening to her fate being spelled out (for, as the one in the dock, what else could she do?), Zhenia had been reminded of a not dissimilar confrontation with Olga. Though her current situation was bleak, it was gratifying nevertheless that despite their outrage at the way she had duped them, Bertie and Augusta still did not know the half of it. At the end of the interview there was a short, profound silence, broken only by the even tick of Augusta's French clock. Finally, without another word being said, Zhenia rose to her feet and was escorted to her room to pack.

Observing the princess's sudden introspection, Mai's attention was caught by the words *up to a point*. Clearly that point had been passed. She doubted it could have been the affair with her own husband which, by the end, had been widely known about and anyway was a fairly commonplace happening in that sort of society where many blind eyes were turned. So something else must have happened. But what?

It seemed the princess was not going to tell her. Zhenia had not been at Augusta Langham's funeral either, which had excited more speculation, Mai recalled.

"Before we stopped speaking, Saskia told me that Augusta collapsed and died while ticking off a housemaid. Which must have liberated Bertie," continued Zhenia. "And Saskia, come to that. After they got rid of me, Augusta kept Saskia on a tight rein. And Bertie had a mistress, as you probably know. Millicent Mainwaring, daughter of his father Henry's mistress, Daisy. Nothing like keeping it in the family. Then along came 1942 and, without his mother putting her oar in all the time, he went on to have a good war. And being Bertie he was a good father to Alexander even though he must have known that Alexander wasn't his son and he *doted* on Saskia. Whatever Saskia wanted she got. He let her get away with everything. Gambling debts, dress bills, lovers . . . Saskia never missed a trick, I can tell you. Better to be careful when dealing with *her*. Though even Bertie balked when she jilted your son and ran off with a duke. I should say here it wasn't the duke that bothered Bertie (although that didn't last either) it was the casual cruelty of it all. Saskia told me all about it. Saskia laughed!"

Mai, who had been profoundly relieved not to have to cope with Saskia as a daughter-in-law, decided to make no comment. Nor did she tell Zhenia that in their early twenties Sophie and Alexander had fallen for one another, a fact Mai had discovered by accident when she had come across them embracing in the garden. After which alerting sighting, there had been a summary exhumation of family skeletons in order to put an end once and for all to an incestuous infatuation.

Thank heavens they had caught it in time. . . .

Nevertheless, it underlined what a force for mayhem the princess had been, even twenty years later.

Mrs. Pelling knocked and entered.

"Mrs. Fielding, your taxi is here."

"Thank you, Mrs. Pelling."

Zhenia sent Mai a sly, calculating look.

"Come again. I'll tell you more. There are things you don't know, Mai, and maybe you should." Then, tantalising, "Things I've never told anyone."

Mai could believe it.

Remembering Maude's cat and against her better judgment, she said, "Very well, I will. I'll come sometime next week. I'll arrange it with Mrs. Pelling, shall I?"

Feeling energised, exhilarated even, when her visitor had gone, Zhenia sat on in the fading light of an amethyst evening. These days, rather than the dull hour to hour existence, it was the past which obsessed her and which unreeled before her inner eye with brilliant clarity. *In effect my past has become my present*, thought Zhenia. As though it was yesterday, she saw herself (Vera then, of course, and late as usual) crossing the Trinity Bridge and subsequently threading her way along the treacherous quays by the frozen river on her way to that night's ballet at the Mariinskiy. It behoved one to be careful. Dancers suffered enough injuries in performance. It had been a Saturday evening, two days before what came to be called Red Monday and the silence in the streets was eerie and loaded. Eerie because despite the crowds moving in the same direction as she was, the only sound had been the rhythmic thudding reverberation of boots muffled by hard-packed snow. Loaded because there was an unnerving sensation that any-thing might happen. And then, shockingly, it had. Just as she turned into Mikhail Street, by which time the streaming flakes had rendered visibility practically nil, there had been a loud clattering noise which, until some-body had shouted it out, she had not immediately recognised as gunfire. The rhythmic reverberation of feet escalated into drumming as a rush for cover and safety turned into a stampede. Reliving it, Zhenia experienced the same stomach-churning fear as she had felt running for her life all those years before.

I actually saw a child tossed up into the air onto the bonnet of a car. And then, before my eyes, it slowly slid off into the snow and was run over by another. Horrible!

In the confusion, others had been trampled under foot in the gory snow and abandoned. Frightened to death and for once in her life praying, she had thrown herself against the wall in a desperate attempt to avoid having her feet sliced off by a careering sledge, when salvation had stepped in and she had tumbled backwards through an unlatched door. The Holy Father had been looking out for her that night all right.

I must have lain there for at least an hour.

Finally, quaking, she had mustered the courage to look outside. The pulsating, unnatural silence was back. Apart from the bodies of the dead, the street was deserted. Within the circles of lamplight the blood on the snow was red, outside them it looked black. There had seemed no point in going to the Mariinskiy Theatre now. Presumably this was only the beginning.

And that's when I took the decision which was to change my life. I went back to my lodging in Petrogradskaya. I packed the carpet bag with my few possessions and my paltry savings and then I trudged to Finland Station where I took a train out . . .

It had all taken place a very long time ago and yet it felt like yesterday. These days Zhenia thought more and more about Russia. Rather like Olga. No, *very* like Olga, in fact. Paradoxically old age, it seemed, returned one to one's childhood and in that way certain circles were squared.

With memories came the subversive, creeping need for absolution.

I need to tell someone.

To confess.

For I cannot take such secrets with me to my grave.

On the occasion of Mai's second visit to the Willows, there was no sign of Mrs. Pelling. Zhenia greeted her, walking with the aid of two ivory-knobbed canes.

"What an old crock I am," remarked Zhenia. "I'm afraid I'm not up to doing tea but what about a shot of vodka?" Without waiting for an answer, she went on, "Would you mind organising it? The glasses are in the walnut cabinet and the bottle is on the butler's tray." While it was being done, she said, "I knew you'd be back. Nobody can resist tying up loose ends. All of a sudden Saskia wants to come and see me, too. That is if I will let her. And maybe I will and maybe I won't." The princess was complacent. "Last week she wrote again saying she would like a *rapprochement.* Well, that's her tale, anyway. She must think I'm stupid if she believes I'll fall for that. Saskia never does anything unless there's something in it for her. The emeralds, for instance. Still, never mind. That, as they say, is another story." She accepted the proffered glass. "Is there anything else I can get you?"

"Thank you, no," replied Mai. She savoured the first fiery sip. Like Proust's cake, the taste of the vodka sharply evoked another time and another place as nothing else could.

"Very well," said Zhenia, "then hear this."

She began with her days at the Mariinskiy. Listening to it, Mai was astounded. Zhenia was not and never had been a princess or even a Dashkov, come to that. Mai wondered if that was what the Langhams had discovered. Certainly it explained banishment and secrecy. Augusta would have been the laughingstock of society if this little lot had come out. It begged another question, too. *Where had the emeralds come from?*

Fearful of stopping the flow of revelation, eyes fixed on the *soi-disant* princess's small, vulpine face, Mai sat silently transfixed as the tale unfolded and found herself listening aghast to the woman opposite her serenely admitting to three murders (although in Zhenia's view the death of Mathilde Ivanova was a sin of omission rather than deliberate intent).

"That's one way of looking at it," said Mai, unable to contain herself, "but the fact of the matter is that you left her to die."

Zhenia was unrepentant. "What else could I do? I did not cause her to have a stroke. It was plain to me Mathilde was going to die anyway. What would have been the point of passing up the emeralds? What good would that have done Mathilde?"

"And what about Countess Olga? She took you in! She was your benefactress!"

"Again, what could I do?" This was becoming a familiar refrain. "If Tatiana Volkovska had minded her own business, none of it need have happened...."

"Oh, so not your doing at all!" Mai was tart.

"The same applied to the count."

The count?

Not the count as well!

Good God!

Hardly daring to ask, "What do you mean?"

"I had to see him off," blandly explained Zhenia. "The count alias Mr. Markov alias Mr. Litvinoff was a Soviet agent sent by his government to recover the emeralds and I felt I'd sacrificed too much to let them go." She must be talking about blood sacrifice, thought Mai, since the selfless sort did not seem to be part of her vocabulary. "I shot him under cover of

Bertie's pheasants. But only winged him, as it turned out. When he infelic-itously appeared at the ball I thought I was done for. In fact it was him who was done for. Well, you were there, you saw it. . . ."

I may have been there and I may have seen it, but what I thought I saw and what was actually happening in fact bore no resemblance to each other. Mai was aghast.

"It was all the exertion and trauma that brought on the premature birth of Ned's son and Bertie's heir," brazenly added the princess. "I was quite ill afterwards, you know."

Not as ill as the unfortunate Litvinoff, though.

"Are you still angry?"

Mai was dismissive. "About you and Ned? Heavens, no. On that level, so long as he left me alone, I didn't care what Ned did. What *you* did, Zhe-nia, is between you and your conscience. That's assuming you have one."

The feral light eyes glinted with amusement.

"I asked you here because I needed to tell someone, for absolution, not a lecture," observed Zhenia without a trace of contrition. "You've be-come judgmental, Mai."

Theft? Betrayal? Murder, not once but three times? Hard not to be, was Mai's reaction to this complaint, which quite took her breath away.

She was uncompromising. "There is nothing I can do for you on that score. Absolution is not in my gift. You're going to need a higher power for that. Much higher, though a priest might get you started, I suppose." It suddenly struck Mai that what had just been happening, self-justification and all, was a rehearsal for just such an interview.

Unabashed but deciding to let it go for the moment, "Shall we change the subject for now?" suggested Zhenia. "What about some more vodka? There is a postscript concerning the emeralds I must tell you. After Litvi-noff, someone else turned up on my doorstep. Wait for this! *Another* Dashkov. A real one this time, would you believe it." Mirthless cackle. "Just as I thought I was home and dry. Naturally *he* wanted the emeralds as well, though how he knew I had them. . . ."

Mai said, "*I* know how he knew. Nicolai told him. They met by chance in Leningrad. . . ."

Disregarding this, Zhenia paused for effect and then smugly said, ". . . so I gave them to him."

Amazed, Mai stared at her.

"Only one other knows this."

Enjoying her stupefaction, the other leant forward.

"The copies, of course. You remember. I had them made to give to Markov, but they weren't ready in time. Which was why I had to take other, more desperate measures . . ."

"Why are the emeralds still so important to you?" Despite her revulsion, Mai was intrigued.

"To me they are like a talisman," stated Zhenia. "While I possess them I feel powerful. Once they belonged to the rich and influential Dashkovs. Now they belong to me, who was born into peasant stock. Without them I would still be no one. As to selling them, before Vassili Dashkov came on the scene I did consider it. The fakes, not the real thing. There was a Russian in Paris, a man called Stavisky, who dealt in emeralds. This was in 1928. The jeweller who made the copies told me about him. It struck me if I played my cards right I could have ended up with both the genuine article *and* the money. I could have passed off the imitations with the authentication certificate which belonged to the real jewellery. Anyway, as it turned out, just as well I didn't. It transpired that Mr. Stavisky, who moved in the most exalted of Parisian circles I may say, had been doing just that. In 1933 or thereabouts he was revealed as a confidence trickster and the ensuing scandal and uproar rocked French high society bringing down the Chautemps government in the process. . . ."

What a pair you and he would have made, was Mai's curdled mental reaction to this revelation.

"What happened to him?"

"I later heard he either committed suicide or was murdered. Nothing to do with me, by the way," answered Zhenia, apparently feeling the need to clarify the matter, as well she might. Her voice trailed away. "Anyway, getting back to what we were originally talking about, the Langhams were terrified that the whole story would come out. It would have been in all the newspapers and made them look ridiculous. Vassili Dashkov, who had come over with a Russian delegation, went home. Nothing to keep him now. Or so he thought. It was at that point that I threatened to make public the whole story. For after all, what did I have to lose? There followed protracted negotiations at the end of which I was handsomely paid off and sent to live elsewhere. Bertie wasn't sorry to see me go and my mother-in-law certainly wasn't. Like Tatiana Volkovska, I was informed that the day I revealed what had really happened was the day the money dried up. There you have it."

The princess sighed.

All at once she looked like a tiny husk, as though the secrets she had just passed on had been a physical part of her.

"Are you shocked?"

Mai did not immediately respond to this. *In shock* might have been a more accurate description.

Zhenia tapped her glass with one long metallic fingernail.

"More vodka, I think, don't you!"

She looked suddenly drained. A life of criminal activity appeared to have taken its toll.

Mai poured it for her and then looked at her watch. "I must go."

"Will you come again?"

Curiosity killed the cat.

"No, I shall never come again."

That was a shame, but probably to have been expected. Mai Fielding had always had a strong puritanical streak.

Retelling the Stavisky story took Zhenia back to the fateful day in Paris when she and Mathilde Ivanova had talked business for the first time. Vera, as she then was, remembered narrowly assessing the woman opposite her over the chipped rim of a teacup and deciding that something was not quite right. Putting her finger on that something had proved less simple. The duchess, who was stout, had a patrician air and a cultured accent. Her dress had obviously seen better days but the same could be said of many of the aristocratic émigrées in Paris, most of whom had had to move quickly in order to effect their escape from inimical post-revolutionary Russia and most of whom had consequently arrived abroad in a hurry with little more than the clothes they stood up in. Maybe it was the hair. No lady, and certainly not a duchess, would have dyed her hair, whereas here Vera's sharp eye thought she detected a hint (though only the *merest* hint) of henna. It was hard to tell. No doubt in the interests of economy, the gas light was low.

She put down her cup just as the duchess raised hers to her lips amid a rattle of rings. Ah! That was it! The rings. Too many and too large. Vulgar, even. *If she's a duchess, I'm a princess.*

On the other hand the cross which hung around her neck was magnif-icent. The duchess leant sideways to pick up the sugar, whereupon Vera recalled seizing the moment to take a longer look. Its simple, flat shape appeared to be decorated with rosy guilloche enamel and, unless she was much mistaken (here it should be said that Vera did not make many mistakes where jewellery was concerned), there was one peerless pearl at its centre.

At the end of the day it doesn't matter who or what she is, had been her decision. *I think the putative duchess and I could go far together . . .*

So, as it turned out, did Mathilde Ivanova and that was where it had all begun. Now, with the unavoidable approach of death possibly accompanied by a final interview with the Holy Father during the course of which broken promises and much worse would have to be accounted for, the memory of the stricken woman lying on the bed and the accusatory, darkening eyes which had followed her round the room as she ransacked it refused to be dislodged.

Tatiana Volkovska had been right.

Retribution, it seemed, cast a long shadow.

Zhenia shuddered.

The upshot of this extraordinary encounter was that Mai finally took the decision to go to St. Petersburg and, in doing so, to confront her ghosts. Hitherto the past, together with its memories, had been an inhospitable land which she shied away from visiting.

But however unhappy I may have been, I am *still fortunate,* she chided herself severely. *I am cushioned in a way most aren't. I have wealth and position. I must never forget that.*

As far as it went, this was true, but the other side of privilege had been sacrifice and, still raw after all this time, loss. Bereavement was bereavement however one viewed it. It did not matter if one was rich or poor, the tragic impact was the same. Of course, down the years there had been rewards and satisfactions, too, mainly in the shape of her children and her work. Throughout what remained of her marriage Mai had continued to battle for the betterment of women's lot in general. This had been doubly satisfactory since her high profile activities in this direction had enraged her husband. During the war she had worked in the War Office and afterwards, having briefly flirted with the idea of politics, had concentrated her considerable energies to great effect on charity work. Which, since Ned had wanted it, would have been unthinkable when he was alive.

No one could say mine has been a wasted life exactly, thought Mai.

No. Not wasted, but not properly fulfilled either.

For what about love?

Love, she felt, no *knew*, had largely eluded her. The pain of this significant gap was extant to this day. These days the idea that it was better to
have loved and lost than never to have loved did not wash with Mai. The
ecstasy had been all too brief and the agony had lasted a lifetime.

Despite Sophie's offer to accompany her, Mai went to Russia alone.
She took with her the letters and the little diptych, the angel with the
golden hair. Her first sight of St. Petersburg thrilled her. The Neva was a
broad, frozen highway, just as when Nicolai had last seen it, and the city on
its banks a glacial paradise. To her enraptured eye, it seemed that the virginal effect of a heavy fall of fresh snow possessed the quality of redemp-
tion thereby, for the moment anyway, consigning past horrors to history.
Restored after the ravages of the war, golden domed churches and extrava-
gant palaces, lustrous with gilt and marble and mirrors, once again recalled
the heyday of Rinaldi and Rastrelli. Mai spent her days walking the city.
During the course of one of these, she strolled down Nevsky Prospekt,
where Nicolai's father had once made a comfortable living selling sumptuous coats to the rich and titled, and past the Stroganov Palace to the bazaar
of Gostinyy Dvor. On impulse and also, in an odd sort of way, in memory,
Mai bought a dramatic fur hat. *My love, I will wrap you in sables . . .*

She went to see *Swan Lake* at the Mariinskiy. Watching the Kirov corps
de ballet, ethereal and timeless, she imagined the young Vera Kalanskaya
travelling from Georgia to the capital for her audition and the sequence of
events which had led to her incarnation as Princess Zhenia Dashkova.
Odette/Odile . . .

Most of all, though, Mai remembered *her* Prince Siegfried, Nicolai
Zourov. And she remembered other things, too. She remembered dances
and picnics and girls in white dresses and croquet and the heady smell of
garden roses and cut grass and she remembered herself in her suffragette
days, billowing along in a pin-tucked, belted long summer dress and
broad-brimmed hat and carrying a banner. But, most poignant of all, she
remembered a spoonful of osetra wrapped in a blini received from the
hand of a lover. . . .

In her hotel room that night she took the letters out of her suitcase.
Probably because they had lain in the dark all these years, the purple ribbon

had not faded, though what it bound together had not fared so well. The paper had a blotched, crinkled appearance and looked as though the bundle might have been left out in the rain. Mai knew better. Not rain but salt tears that had fallen like rain. She loosed the bow until it slipped apart thereby releasing what it held.

Riven with regret and sorrow, even after all these years, Mai reread her lover's letters.

"Darling, I have been patient but suddenly have a strong sense of time passing and youth with it. My stay in this melancholy city whose glory days are gone convinces me that we must take our pleasures while we can . . ."

But I didn't do it. Heavyhearted, even after all these years, she stared into the middle distance. *For the best of motives, I prevaricated too long and, in doing so, lost the love of my life.* The real prospect of eventual happiness had proved at the end of the day to be nothing more than a mirage.

On the morning of her last day in St. Petersburg, standing on the Anichkov bridge in the falling snow, Mai took the little travelling icon Nicolai had given her out of her handbag and opened it. Holding it in her hands, she was aware of a marvellous lightening of spirit as if she had received a benediction. Resentment and deprivation fell away. Despite its legacy of sorrow Mai now saw with great clarity that theirs had been a love affair whose brief intensity had never dimmed but had burned brightly, lighting her way down the years like a star.

And was not over.

For sometime soon, my darling, we shall be together again.

Mai kissed the angel with the golden hair.

This I know.